12 STORIES HIGH: THE IMAGINATIVE TRIP THRU A BLACK MIND

BY

JUSTIN THOMAS

978-0-9725548-7-9

Published by Twin Griffin Books

Cover art by The Writing Moor

www.TwinGriffinBooks.com

To the Eboni of it all...

Griffin
Twin
Books
PRESENTS

The Stories

And Once, Just Walked Us ... 1

Still Remains ... 6

Vicariously Alive ... 42

Tales of the Djedhi ... 68

Headless ... 100

Ah, Moor ... 137

I Wish, Servitude ... 179

3 Cigs United ... 227

The Monk & The Moor ... 231

Freezing Reign In Summer ... 260

Waiting For What ... 280

The Curse of Cain-An ... 286

And Once, Just Walked Us

It was fall. Autumn. October 8th. The trees were beginning to shed their leaves, color fading from them. Spring delivered its rain, and summer passionately turned up the heat. Now fall was ushering in winter's cold with an early, frosty chill that already transformed the leaves to red, yellow, and brittle brown.

The leaves descended, laid out like a royal carpet for the coming snow. The once dark green and purple leaves were now withered and delicate. Without their original color and state, and without support from their firmly, rooted tree, they fell and died easily. The leaves fell, sprawled out onto the various lawns ready to be raked. The fallen leaves were vulnerable, violently gathered by claws and spikes, and stuffed into tight bags to be hauled away to a foreign place.

The snow would then colonize the land.

The Dead Season would be here.

In the distance was the city. Its buildings standing like giants, windows acting like an assortment of blank eyes staring forward. At the present moment, the giants regurgitated the people they ingested just four hours earlier. It was a lunch break. The giants would consume the people again in an hour, acting like Cronus to his children.

There stood a giant in the heart of the city that was fed historical relics. This giant was called 'Museum'. In its belly was a nine-years old black boy who was overwhelmed by a moment in time, digested by history. The black boy's name was Desmond. He was on a field trip with his fourth grade class, but he was distracted by history, and his class left him behind.

Desmond was not lost. He followed his class through the museum while watching years, decades, centuries, and millennia pass him by. Rich cultures from around the world stood tall. There were cultural artifacts displayed in glass cases with mannequins wearing both authentic and reproduced clothing of past ages.

None of these cultures represented Desmond, except one.

Desmond caught a glimpse of mannequins that looked like him as his class passed a corridor dedicated to African and African-American History. But his class continued on, his teacher not stopping to turn into the hallway. The man escorting Desmond's class did not make the turn either. His history was skipped.

Desmond stopped. His class continued without him. The black boy decided to stand still, let kids from his class walk by him one-by-one, and then purposefully get caught up in another bubble of the Museum's traffic. The new crowd of people disguised him, flowing around him like a running mudslide. When Desmond was satisfied that he was on his own, he turned into the hallway of African and African-American History.

It was in this hallway where he now stood, terrified, for what seemed like decades.

Desmond could not move, and God knows he tried.

His first attempt at movement was screaming, but his voice was choked. Desmond's second attempt at moving was pivoting his body to turn around and run from the hall to find his class, and forget the imagery in front of him.

But History had him locked down, in place.

Desmond was chained to the floor by an invisible shackle clamped around his ankle. If the shackle had a physical form, it would look much like the shackles displayed and mounted on the wall. Rusted, and made of iron. The mannequins in front of him wore the same shackles. Desmond's chains, however, were engraved in an invisible language, spelling an invisible phrase: *Your History*.

One scene featured half-dressed African mannequins chained together and being led by a white mannequin armed with a musket. Their destination was a model slave ship, constructed small to make it look like it was in the distance. To the right of the display was a drawing showing the events prior to the Africans being chained. Armed white men raked, pulled, and violently gathered the Africans. The picture was etched to give it authenticity as an old drawing of its time. To the left of the display was another mounted drawing exhibiting the slave ship's interior. A top view of the ship's interior revealed that it was stacked with black bodies, packed tightly from one end to the other. An opened view of the ship's side showed the packed scene was repeated for all three interior levels of the boat.

The display jumped in time and location. The African mannequins were in America, working the fields and being whipped. More drawings depicted enslaved African women being overwhelmed, groped by white men. Desmond shared the same look of terror etched in the women's eyes and facial features. He jumped every time a white stranger bumped him, their smiles on him distorted, looking sinister or condescending. He felt the Museum's white patrons were wondering why he was not chained and at work with the rest of his wooden people.

Desmond saw the surrounding white people peer down at him angrily. His eyes went from their angry stares to several authentic posters that screamed in large black letters: *SLAVES FOR SALE!* and *WANTED, FUGITIVE SLAVES! ESCAPED SLAVES!* Desmond believed the white people gathering around him were armed with nets and guns, ready to capture him, creeping toward him like crawling spiders. Desmond did not look back at them. He continued to look forward, concentrating on the word 'slave'. The word dissolved into *Negro* and *Colored*. There were black and white photos of black men hanging from trees. There were photos of hanging black women and black children. In some photos there were men with white robes around them. In other pictures there was a festive picnic around the bodies, with young white children smiling and playing. The children looked like kids Desmond went to school with.

The violent imagery overlapped with other authentic photographs showing black resistance. Pictures froze the time of marches, protests, and cities and communities in rage. Water hoses were sprayed violently on blacks, while attack dogs, stationed in mid-air, bared fangs. There were large photos of Martin Luther King, Jr. Among them was a single panel with etchings of Malcolm X, Marcus Garvey, Nelson Mandela, and The Honorable Elijah Mohammed. Desmond only recognized Malcolm and Martin. Above them was the phrase, *I Had A Dream.*

The Museum melted away into a nightmare.

In its place was every scene reproduced in front of Desmond's eyes. These immobile, blended scenes started to move, becoming animated. Snarls, whip cracks, gunshots, and screams echoed and mingled together in a violent flurry of sound. Desmond's heart pumped just as loud. The boy could feel an invisible hand around his neck. The grip tightened, squeezing harder. Desmond started to breath rapidly. His breath was quick, matching his heartbeat. The scene flooded his senses, swirling around him like ghosts, screaming loud like banshees.

But every howl and sound was silenced with just a single, cynical, snicker. The loud, violent sounds ceased. The images froze. The scene around Desmond transformed back into the Museum's hallway like a tornado delivering him from a nightmarish Oz.

Desmond moved his eyes to the right, focusing on the area where the cynical snicker originated. Four black men stood next to Desmond. They were Elders to him. In reality, the young men were in their early twenties, and they were dressed for the 'hood.

The one who snickered did so again, shaking his head. "Is this the African History section niggas protested to get put in," he laughed. "This shit is sad, sun." Desmond looked at the young man, and then to the display. The showcase did not intimidate the young men. Desmond moved closer to them. The same young man continued to shake his head and address his friends. "And I heard they even had this, like, big-ass dinner to celebrate this hallway of smoke and mirrors. It shouldn't be called the African and African-American History Hall, it should be called the House of Horrors. Look at this travesty. And niggas are proud?"

A second spoke. "I wonder what kind of dumb Negroes showed up for that dinner," he said. "What the hell were the conversations like? Did they have no shame lookin' at this shit? This ain't our only history, sun. White folks just went, *'Here, nigger. Now, shut up!'"*

"Meanwhile," a third jumped in, "They got white-Arab Moors in Spain two sections over. And they got white Egyptians down the hall from that comedy of errors."

"Yeah, sun," the fourth interjected. "It ain't even Arabic lookin' Egyptians—wrong as that would be. And only mention Nubia or Abyssinia when referring to where the so-called white Egyptians got their slaves. There was no slavery in Egypt, sun."

"They even got the Mayans lookin' white," the second jumped back in. "Them niggas was mixed Asiatic and African. They ain't even lookin' like Jennifer Lopez or Marc Anthony. *What the fuck?*"

The first young man shook his head. "They shittin' on our Latino brothas and sistas, man. But, you know white folks can't really tell that history. Them Latinos and Hispanics are mixed like Arabs. White people gonna have them choose they white side. Lot of them Latinos is straight up niggas. *Black,* coiled-haired niggas. They think just because they slave master taught them Spanish, they on some ol' next shit."

The fourth young man added, "And most of they culture straight from Africa. They dances and all that. They niggas too." He then concluded, "Some of them Latino muhfuckas know they nigga heritage. For poilitical reasons, them White-European Spanish-speakin' bitches got them all fucked up."

"And you notice they ain't even fuckin' with the Olmec Civilization?" the first asked the others in his small entourage.

The third young man argued, "The Olmecs is blatantly niggas. They can't get with that."

Desmond did his best to remember each of the foreign names the young men flashed in their vocabulary. They stood out even among the slang and curses. *Abyssinia. Moors. Olmecs. Nubia.* Each name sounded like a magical word.

The young men were loud. The white patrons looked nervous, even guilty. They clenched up. The sound and banter coming from the four young men made their bodies tighten uncomfortably. Their stiffened bodies impeded on their ability to escape. They were clearly trying to get away as fast as they could. The look on their faces showed their discomfort and pain. They could not hide it if they tried. There were at least twenty in the hallway.

Desmond recalled how comfortable and at ease the white passersby had been before the arrival of these four young men. There was neither a sad nor horrified look on their faces. They watched the imagery displayed in front of them with indifference.

All that changed with just four black men.

Chaos turned to K-oS, Knowledge of Self, and these four black men had it. These were the real Fantastic Four. Instantly becoming heroes in Desmond's eyes. They rescued him from the atrocities put on display. More importantly, they gave him the ability to become his own hero. Desmond shoved his hands into his pockets, leaned his body to the right, and stared at the display with a disgusted expression, blatantly imitating the young men next to him. He was catching their frequency, their redemption song. He did not understand all the lyrics coming from the broadcast, but he liked the beat.

The first one sighed. "Black folks got ninety-thousand years of civilized history under our belt," he said. "But they constantly snapping a photograph of this period in our history. And dumb niggas don't even know."

"And don't wanna know," said the second young man. "And can't complain. After all, we got Obama in the White House."

The four men started to laugh. "Not to disrespect what we've been through and accomplished within the hardships of America, but we know why we're always shown this image. It's to keep us struggling, and to keep us in one place and time. Obama ain't the first black ruler in America. He's the first Pharaoh this world has seen in ages. And that sentiment was said by a white dude."

"There have been millions of Barack and Michelle Obamas throughout our history. Why can't we get to know them?"

They stood in silence.

The first young man turned to exit the hall. "I thought they was gonna kick some real history," he groaned. "Shoulda known. Let's break."

The other three followed.

They were gone.

Desmond stood alone. He looked over the scenes that were, according to the young, frustrated black men, only a brief moment in his people's long history. *I ain't gonna be a dumb nigga,* Desmond decided. He left the hall and toured the museum in search of his class. He slipped back among his fellow students unnoticed. Desmond looked at his watch. Twenty minutes had passed. No one noticed he was gone, not even his fellow students. When the day was over, he returned to the school, and then to home.

Desmond began to read.

He went to the Encyclopedias, reading of 'black skinned' white people in ancient Africa, notably Egypt. White Northern Africans called Berbers teamed with 'tawny' Arabs to take Spain. Black people appeared in World History as slaves, and as a people who 'struggled'. Desmond closed the Encyclopedia. He was convinced someone was lying to him. He was nine years old. He had enough time in his life to find out who was lying to him and why.

It started snowing outside, early in the fall.

However, spring was inevitable.

Still Remains
How To Resurrect A Black Woman (Part One)

There were few clouds in the sky, and those that were there seemed to compliment the sun rather than threaten it. Below the sky was Fulton Park, a quaint area flourishing with the brilliance of trees swaying in a light and relaxing breeze and the activity of people enjoying its environment. There were children playing merrily, elders conversing, lovers embracing, young men playing chess, tourists on the move, and teenagers engaging in a variety of sports.

The only thing stationary was a twenty-four year old black man sitting on a wooden bench. His name was Steven Serge. He had brown skin that glowed with a red hue. His face was smooth, only scathed by the rough goatee etched around his chin and upper lip. He had an average build, with locks dangling just above his shoulders. Steven wore a tan shirt that was reminiscent of a Moorish tunic. The shirt was long-sleeved, elegantly creeping past Steven's wrists, but not at the moment. The sleeves were slipped back because of the angle of Steven's hands holding a book in front of him. The rest of his outfit was made up of baggy, blue jeans and brown Timberland boots.

Steven's backpack rested next to him. This was his partner, carrying and protecting his life possessions. Inside, scribbled between the pages of notebooks, were his thoughts. Just as well, there were books of social commentary, underground magazines, comic books, and books on Black History. A fantasy or science fiction novel was tucked inside the pack at times, but not today.

The scenery surrounding Steven dissipated. He was lost in the book in front of him, *Survival Strategies for Africans In America* by Anthony Browder. It was an old book, and it was not the first time Steven engaged in it. Steven read the book several times over the past two years. Each time there were new notes to take; something he had not caught before in the lessons organized between the pages. This time, however, he was continuing research for an article due for a Brooklyn paper he freelanced for.

The words dissolved into new scenery, fading the activities around him. Steven prided himself on his ability to focus, to not allow his mind to become distracted.

Footsteps.

Approaching.

Steven did not even see the woman, and he was not meant to. She quietly crept up to him, sneaking. The woman needed no advance stealth training, considering Steven's attention to his book. She approached closer, still careful not to stir the grass. She leaned over from behind Steven's bench and said, "Don't you think it's time for a new book?"

Steven did not jump with the sudden entrance of the woman's voice. His eyes stayed on the book, his concentration now deliberate. "I was just thinking about you," he said through a smile. "I was wondering when you would show up."

The woman stepped over the enclosing, moved Steven's backpack, and took a seat next to him on his right. The woman countered Steven's comment with a sardonic smile. Steven knew the woman had something to say. "You don't need to tell me," she said leaning closer to him, lips to his ear. "I know when you're thinking about me."

Steven's concentration wavered, finally looking up at the woman.

There she was. Her name was Prechet. She was tall and beautiful, with brown skin that resonated a darker hue compared to Steven's. She reminded Steven of the maidens and goddesses found in Egyptian hieroglyphs.

Prechet was thirty-three years old. Her locks, thick and beautiful, writhed far beyond her shoulders, and glittered with the sun's reflection making Prechet's hair look as if gold strands had been woven within them. Her eyes were wide, brown and hypnotic. She captured the attention of many men with those eyes, but only few were allowed to capture her heart. Prechet was more than what many saw. She was a spirit. Any man who approached her needed to possess as much knowledge as she had, if not more. She was an intellectual without the arrogance. In fact, she was very humble. But she loved to build on thoughts. To her, that was harmonious and loving. Only few men could match her.

Steven was her student. His knowledge was gaining ground, something he was striving for in order to transform into the ideal man Prechet sought. Steven remembered this thought every time Prechet appeared. Their relationship had a firm grounding, however, taking real estate in the brotherly-sisterly realm.

Steven asked in a serious tone, "And *what* did you come here for?" His smile never faded. He loved Prechet's presence. She was warm and comfortable.

Prechet cocked her head at Steven, her smile persisting. "Dunno," she said lightly lifting her shoulders. "You tell me."

Steven turned his body to completely face Prechet. "Well," he started, his tone sarcastic as ever. "You're probably here to see my lessons progress," he spoke, mocking Prechet playfully. This was the game the two of them played, flirtatious as always.

Prechet pointed at the book and said, "Correct. And I'm telling you to make progress with new books, too. You've learned all you can from that particular piece. What is this, the fiftieth time you've read it? Don't get stuck in one thing, bruh. Black folks got a whole lot of learnin' to do. You can't just be a Black Nationalist or Afro-centrist. We about to get deep."

Steven defended himself saying, "Hey, I'm just takin' notes for an article."

Prechet kept her stern tone as she asked, "You still putting notes together for your article?"

"Yes, yes," Steven declared, trying to calm her down. "It's been in the back of my mind for a week."

"I know," Prechet said sharply. "My brother is gonna kill you if you don't meet your deadline. He's particularly hard on you. He likes you."

Steven rolled his eyes, turning his head away from Prechet. "Yeah," he huffed. "You two have a lot in common." He faced Prechet again, his cool having returned. "It's not like I'm ever late. You know me. I can whip up an article quick-like. I got the rest of the notes together. I just need a few more. Aight? And I still got three days to finish the thing."

"Three days, Steven?" Prechet questioned. "You've *had* a month. Plus as copy editor you have to check the rest of the paper's articles, and help with the layout. You got a job—a real job. Don't get lazy."

Steven waved her comments away as he flapped his lips. "C'mon, Prechet. This is me. I may throw it together at the last minute, but it'll look like I slaved over it for a month. And I'll still have time for the other articles and help your brother with the layout. That's why your brother likes me. I'm efficient."

Prechet was about to reply when Steven became distracted, losing focus on her. Steven's distraction strolled through the park, coming from the Chauncey Street and Stuyvesant corner entrance. His head, body, and eyes rotated. It was another female, and this was not the first time Steven noticed her. Steven had seen the woman on several other occasions. He wondered if she recently moved into the Stuyvesant Heights, Brooklyn area.

Steven checked his watch, trying his best to be nonchalant. Prechet noticed, however. He timed the other woman's arrival, a ritual that had been going on for some time. Steven never worked up enough courage to speak to her. At the paper he worked for, Steven was a tough, investigative journalist with profound skills in research, interviewing, and social and political commentary that sometimes bordered on the conspiratorial.

In the presence of this woman, he was as mild-mannered as Clark Kent.

Steven's fixation had dark skin, and wore a green dress that hugged her body so well Steven became jealous of the garment, longing to have the same perfect fit on her. She wore a light, denim jacket with a small, leather backpack slung around her. The woman's hair was jet black, straight, and worn short, outlining her head like a 1920s Harlem flapper.

Prechet watched closely, holding back laughter as she spied Steven fawning over the woman's presence. Men always amused her. Prechet was kind enough to let the moment pass without comment. The woman crossed the park, walked passed the subway entrance, and took a right down Fulton Street.

Prechet could not maintain her silence. She asked, "You've been waiting for her to pass, haven't you?" There was a teasing tone to her query, using the inflection in her voice to bury the sting in her heart.

Steven checked his watch again, conspicuously this time, and then grinned. "Regular as clockwork," he said in a devious voice.

Prechet nudged Steven. "Go kick some game to her, playa," she urged.

Steven looked at Prechet and addressed her suggestion, "If I was in the mindset I had two years ago, I would." He sighed and concluded, "Now, the only game I got for her, and any other woman, is on Playstation."

Prechet snickered. Her eyes then followed the woman as she disappeared further down Fulton Street. Steven took a peak at the woman. He knew where she was heading. There was a neighborhood bookstore on Kingston Avenue, near Atlantic. This was the woman's destination at this time for the past five days. Steven admired this woman for walking, rather than taking the C train one stop to the Kingston and Throop station.

Steven decided to no longer dedicate time to his fixation, especially as she walked further from his sight. But Prechet gave him an idea, fanning the flames of his interest and mark. "You need a book," the woman reminded Steven, ever the teacher. Prechet leaned close to Steven, beaming. "You know where she's going. That's an excuse to hop up into that store. Continue to stalk her."

"Stalk her?" Steven's face contorted into an exaggerated, sarcastic, disgusted look.

Prechet raised an eyebrow. "How many times have you watched her," she asked. "How many days have you strategically sat here?"

Steven replied to the question with one of his own, "What's wrong with using someone for inspiration?"

"Nothing, according to you and John Hinckley," Prechet quipped.

"Nice," Steven said as he rolled his eyes. "Come on." He stood up. "I'll take you up on your plan, sista." He lifted a finger and began shaking it, a smile on his face. "I knew there was a reason I kept you around." He gathered his belongings, throwing his book into his bag, and then headed in the other woman's direction.

Prechet stayed behind for a moment, watching Steven's departure closely. "Are you sure that's the only reason you keep me around," she asked in a low voice. Then she stood up from the bench and followed Steven down the street. She quickly caught up to him, and they made their way toward Kingston Avenue.

Steven peered through the light traffic. His gaze cut through various passersby and other forward moving pedestrians to spy the woman he trailed. He smiled and said to Prechet, "Stalker or dedicated Investigative Journalist?"

Prechet answered Steven quickly, "A dedicated Investigative Journalist taking advantage of his skills—using them for evil."

Steven contemplated Prechet's jibe. "That's fair. I can agree to that."

The woman disappeared. Steven considered that she turned the corner, making her way down Kingston Avenue, and ultimately coming to the Hour Heritage Bookstore. Steven and Prechet continued forward, joking about being Investigators following a suspect. Steven expressed his gratitude for Prechet supporting him on becoming a stalker.

They turned the corner, walked passed a restaurant, a small grocery, and then crossed Atlantic Avenue to come to the Hour Heritage Bookstore. Steven and Prechet walked inside and were immediately greeted by the smell of incense and the decorative images of African and African-American art.

West African masks, statues, carvings, and Moorish swords were coupled with ancient Egyptian crafts and idols. Occult jewelry rested on swiveling displays, and replicated, ancient ornaments rested on shelves. Spaced between bookshelves were paintings of African-American Civil Rights figures, Black Jesus, and the most ancient of Kings and Queens. At the far end of the store was the register. In front of the register counter was an area made up of four tables. One occupied table caught Steven's eye, for obvious reasons.

There she was.

However...there *he* was too.

"Oh, great," Steven huffed, his eyes locked onto the man sitting next to the young woman he followed to the store. "She's talking to Lando Calrissian."

Prechet's eyes moved to see whom Steven was referring to. The gentleman sitting with the young woman was not named Lando Calrissian. His name was Carter. Steven was being sarcastic, considering Carter a smooth, out-of-this-world-brother-from-another-planet. Women melted when Carter spoke. His voice was sensuous, always poetic, and as deep as the Grand Canyon, making bass seem like treble. Carter was also dangerous because he had intellect to boot, which he used just as effectively for the purpose of show-and-catch, Carter's game.

Prechet seemed immune to Carter's surface appeal. He was, after all, his own number one fan. She was not at all interested in his physical appeal: smooth Jamaican-brown skin, low haircut, and a well toned, exercised body that was at the moment fit with a nice business suit, the tie undone, and the shirt a little unbuttoned.

Prechet scoped that the woman Steven pursued was bothered by Carter's presence rather than seduced.

Steven yielded early to defeat. "Looks like I lost this one," he sighed.

Prechet believed Steven had more studying to do anyway. And as Steven pointed out earlier, she was here to continue his study, or at least make sure it continued. There was a difference, according to both Prechet and Steven.

"Well, put your attention on the books," Prechet instructed as she walked over to one of the shelves showcasing diverse aspects of African History and African-American literature.

Steven moved closer to the books, his eyes remaining on the woman and Carter. He saw the woman look up, trying to escape Carter's banter. Her eyes caught Steven's. He almost looked away. He was happy he resisted, because if he had he would have missed her smile.

Did she smile? Steven wondered.

"This is good," Prechet's voice captured his attention, breaking into his thoughts suddenly. "*Black Man of the Nile and His Family.*"

Steven took the book as Prechet handed it to him. He inspected the book for a second, and then put it right back on the shelf. "Have that one," he told Prechet.

Prechet responded, "Well, anything by Dr. Ben is good. They seem to have his entire collection."

Steven kept looking back at the other woman, losing Prechet's voice and image. But he saw the woman was now engaged in conversation with Carter, so he turned back to Prechet, giving the woman's image his full attention.

"What else?" he asked.

Prechet continued to peruse the books.

"Well, I know you've read the *Isis Papers*," she said, her eyes looking over the title. "That's basic, beginners read."

"I read your copy," Steven reminded. "I could still get one of my own."

Prechet disagreed, shaking her head. "Get something you haven't read first," she instructed. "When you've completely built up a library, go back and purchase those books other people let you borrow." Her eyes stopped. They became wide.

The excited look on Prechet's face held Steven's attention. He just looked at her and thought to himself, *Her eyes are always beautiful when bright and alive.*

"Oh," Prechet exclaimed loudly, but did not seem to disturb the store's patrons. "They got Barashango's books, a lot of them. His stuff is hard to find. I think we have your prize, Steven."

Steven was entranced by Prechet's energy. He walked closer to her. "Really? What are his books like?"

Prechet handed him a book.

Steven began to look through it. Prechet spoke as his eyes scanned the contents of the book. "He does a lot of writing on the historical warrior and revolutionary named Pandera. Some believe this warrior was the Jesus of The Bible." Her face contorted and she waved her hands as if she was shooing away a bug. "He ain't talkin' about the mythology of Jesus, or that never existing, white-long-haired hippie-wanna-be that most Negroes worship."

"You're vicious, for a pretty, little thing," Steven commented. "Any other suggestions?" he asked Prechet.

Prechet's eyes looked up from the book in Steven's hands to his locks, specifically the puffy, fresh growth in need of a wash and twist. It looked distinguishing, but if allowed to go too long it would be a mess. "Your locks need tightening," she suggested.

"Actually, Christine just did them," he said rubbing the top of his head. "Two weeks ago, or so. It's just this early heat." He attempted a joke. "Besides, you know my hair can sprout quick when I get the black, intellectual juices flowin'."

Prechet presented a motherly, caring smile. Her eyes fluttered as she noticed something through her peripheral. Her sight was pulled to the scene playing out between Carter and the woman. This time, the woman was clearly uneasy with Carter's presence. Prechet made it known to Steven. She nodded over his shoulder and said, "It doesn't look like things are going so well for the brother-from-another-planet."

Steven turned his head to investigate Prechet's claims. He watched closely. He was happy, but he suppressed a smile. Carter was losing his well rehearsed, charming hold on the woman. Carter looked up and caught the grin Steven believed he kept from making a facial appearance.

The two locked eyes.

It was just like old times between Steven and Carter—as recent as yesterday. The two had always been friendly-rivals since childhood. The stakes and the ego grew with age. They were cordial in their rivalry, but any behavior remotely mature was tossed aside. However, their brand of healthy competition never went too far to end their friendship.

Carter backed away from looking at Steven, continuing his pursuit of the woman, trying to regain ground. Steven faced Prechet. He feigned not being interest in Carter's dying crusade, trying to play it cool.

"You say they got Barashango's books?" he asked Prechet.

Prechet looked back at the shelf. Steven looked with her. "They have a lot of his titles," she answered Steven. "I'm surprised," she added.

"I'm looking for a specific title of his," Steven said as he scanned the books that were arranged alphabetically by author. "*Black Guardian Angel*," he revealed. "I think that's its name."

Prechet joined in looking for the specific title. Her fingers and eyes floated across the books by the late scholar Dr. Ishakamusa Barashango. It took no time for her to discover the book among the late scholar's works. *Afrikan Woman: The Original Guardian Angel* was the actual title. She removed the book from in between the other books, and handed it to Steven. He stared deeply at the book. He started examining its contents. He then looked over his shoulder at the other woman, removing Carter from his view. He looked down at the cover again, then again at the other woman.

"This is what I've been looking for," he said to no one in particular.

Of course Prechet could hear him, and she responded by asking Steven, "You gonna buy it?" She was trying to pry Steven's real intentions with the book.

"Nope," he said shaking his head. "This book is gonna buy me."

Prechet had no idea what Steven meant. She inquired, "Buy you?"

Steven nodded. "Yeah, buy me," he repeated, and then concluded, "a ticket to talk to that woman. I'm either going to break the ice with this book, or sink like the Titanic."

Prechet still did not understand what Steven was plotting, but she was still going to wish him, *"Good luck."*

Steven acknowledged Prechet's sentiments with another nod. He then inconspicuously paced toward the area of reading tables. He kept his gaze on the cover of the book in his hands. He took a seat at a table adjacent from the one seating Carter and the woman. He removed his backpack and placed it at the side of the table.

Steven could hear that Carter was not resigning to an easy defeat, though his confidence was fading. His continuing conversation was for the purpose of a shield, a stall tactic to look for the perfect moment to get up and walk away with his tail between his legs. The woman kept her eyes on her book, her real interest. Steven believed Carter and the woman's conversation was good for something. He listened closely, feigning to read the book in his hands. He picked up the woman's name.

Maithuna.

Steven caught the woman's name as it slipped from Carter's lips, slipping much like Carter's hold on the woman's interest. The one-sided conversation faded to a point where there was nothing Carter could do, except damage his ego further should he continue to speak. Finally, Steven heard Carter accept defeat, finding the perfect moment to get up and walk away.

The woman named Maithuna sighed relief. She could now concentrate on her book rather than entertaining anyone. She groaned and commented aloud, "What an annoying little—"

"Are you an angel?" Steven blurted the question at her.

The second Steven uttered the words he became torn between emotions congratulating himself for having the courage to speak—especially words such as these—and emotions berating himself for posing such a cliché, stupid question, which just seemed to pop out as if by reflex. The question jumped from Steven's mouth right toward Maithuna.

There was an impact.

Steven's words and voice made Maithuna flinch. Yes, she believed the line was a little corny, but it was spoken with so much grace, sincerity, and truth. It was as if Steven had become an innocent, nine-year old boy, gazing at the sight of a heavenly creature. Maithuna too was caught between entertaining another man trying out a line on her, thanking Steven, or take out the anger she felt for the last man on this new one. It was one masculine bombardment after another, but she decided to roll with this punch.

"W-what," she addressed Steven in a shaken voice.

Steven had her attention. *Good.* Steven thought. *It worked in the movie, and I'm glad it worked here. Now what's my next line?* Steven decided to go with what was in the script. "An angel," he spoke as if his tone would somehow give Maithuna a complete understanding.

Steven lifted the book in his hands. Maithuna looked at its cover, which was of a beautiful, black woman descending from the heavens, her hair wild and natural. The black angel's pink gown fluttered upward, wings attached to her back. Maithuna read the book's title to herself.

Steven added, "The book says they're descended from the original, black woman."

Steven's innocence amused Maithuna. It was cute, but little did she know it was a plan, calculated to precision. She tested the waters and asked in a defensive, yet playful tone, "Is that your best line to hit on me with?"

Steven paid no attention to her tone. He could sense Maithuna's playful, inviting vibe. He simply liked the fact she was not screaming at him after what she had been through with Carter. He was also amazed at himself for having the courage to engage the woman, corny and cliché as his first line had been.

But, Steven pondered Maithuna's question, and with quick wit, he feigned a perplexed look that played sincere to Maithuna as he asked, "Hit on you?" He thought about the words. "Goddess, if I was hitting on you I'd leave bruises. Why would I want to do that? Do I look abusive?" Steven wore a sly grin.

Maithuna sat back and sighed again. Her thoughts rekindled Carter. Steven worried that he had chosen the wrong words, his tonality coming off sarcastic. Maithuna answered him, "I don't know. The last brutha was *verbally* abusive. Interesting, but abusive."

Steven decided to push the envelope further by coolly sliding into a chair located at Maithuna's table. "If you don't mind me joining you—" he started to say when Maithuna cut him off.

"Not at all," she huffed. "At this point, I don't think I have much of a choice."

The comment stung.

Steven stopped halfway in his transition between tables. He looked at Maithuna with a curious eye. The woman realized her attitude was too much. She actually did not mind Steven's company. She was still suffering from Carter's. She waved the comment away and apologized. She extended a hand and a warm smile. Steven finished his journey, placed down the book, and accepted the woman's hand.

"Sorry," Maithuna said again as Steven joined her at the table. "I have a lot on my mind. I was trying to escape through this book." Prechet watched Steven's interaction with Maithuna. Her expression looked dull, detached.

Steven did not notice her. He continued engaging Maithuna, Prechet seeming to fade from his view. Steven suggested, "Maybe *I* should apologize." He decided to be honest with Maithuna. "It's just that…I've noticed you coming here for a while. I've been too busy—" and then he decided to divulge more of the truth as he rolled his eyes, smiled, and admitted, "—Or perhaps too much of a coward to introduce myself." Maithuna chuckled. She appreciated the honesty. "My timing is usually bad," Steven continued. "But you have to give me credit, sista. I went for mine."

Steven and Maithuna smiled at one another.

Prechet then appeared in Steven's view. The woman motioned to the door and mouthed the words *I'll be outside*. Steven nodded at her. Prechet disappeared beyond the doors. Steven looked back to Maithuna and introduced himself, extending his hand. "Steven Serge."

"Hello, Steven," Maithuna responded in a humble tone. She accepted his hand and said, "My name is—"

"Maithuna," Steven interjected. He pointed to his ear and explained, "I overheard. Carter was saying it so much I thought it was a mantra."

"Oh, you know him? You two are friends?" Maithuna rolled her eyes with the mere thought of the previous man who had approached her.

"Yeah," Steven admitted with a sarcastic, guilty smile. He understood that Carter was either seen as charming or arrogant, depending on which female personality he was engaging. *Maithuna must be a genius*, he joked to himself. "Carter? He's a character." Despite criticizing Carter's character, Steven too had plans—a gentleman as he was, he was still a healthy, heterosexual male. He put down another block in his conversation, building a string of interesting points to keep Maithuna engaged. "You have a pretty name. Speaking of characters, I actually used your name for a character in a short story."

Maithuna became interested. "Oh," she said intrigued. "You like to write?"

"It pays the bills," Steven said in a proud manner. "I freelance. I'm a copy editor and journalist for a local paper."

"Really," she asked curiously, "Which one?"

Steven answered, "The Block."

Maithuna's mind calculated the young man in front of her. "Oh, we got us a crusading brutha. You must be militant and all conspiratorial about The Man."

Steven shook a finger. "Now, see, there's the stereotype."

Maithuna pondered a moment. "I believe I've read some of your articles. You write under the name Serge, your last name. You're very good, I must admit. Your words don't seem as angry and paranoid as the other contributors. You give the paper legitimacy."

Steven nodded his head humbly. "Thank you," he said.

"I have a subscription," Maithuna informed.

"Thank you, again," Steven responded. "For your support, that is," he clarified. There was silence, but it was not awkward. Steven pondered the moment, and his next move. "Do you write? We're always looking for more writers, although there's little-to-no-pay for beginners. Probably bring you fifty bucks an article."

Maithuna looked away. Doubt clouded her mind and accompanied her words, "I don't think I could put my thoughts together correctly."

Steven cupped his hand, placing it at the side of his mouth, and whispered sarcastically, "That's why we have editors."

Maithuna giggled. She looked up at the ceiling and thought. "I do have a couple of ideas," she said in a more confident tone. "I mean, what I'm doing in this bookstore is research for a lot of questions I have." There came a shy smile as Maithuna admitted, "I'm at that inquisitive, pivotal crossroads that every black person comes to when pondering who we are."

"Then it's important that you have the right questions, find the right answers, and act appropriately," Steven said to her. "That's something many of us don't do." He then added in a lighthearted manner, *"Message!"*

Maithuna chuckled.

Steven sat back and said, "I'm not trying to whittle my way into your life, sista, but I could help you write your thoughts. You'd get full credit and pay."

Maithuna thought, doubt continued to battle her confidence, but it was not as strong as before. She shook her head. Steven could see she was almost there. Her face spoke of determination, but something in her spirit seemed to hold her back.

"I don't know," she said in a low voice. "You bruthas and sistas over there are pouring with knowledge. Something I'm lacking greatly."

Steven flapped his lips. He waved her comment away, and along with it, her doubts. There was energy in him that Maithuna was attracted to. "I've only been on this Know-Thy-Self kick for about two years. Studied, done the locks thing," he flicked his hair. "Wearing it is one thing, understanding it is another. It ain't somethin' a good read in a book won't fix. Plus, I got a study group I go to. If it makes you feel any better, I was a Padawan learner myself once. Someone helped me out. Now it's my turn to do the same. An each one, teach one kinda thing."

Maithuna was enticed, looking seductive in her curiosity. "Really?" she questioned. It was more to push her doubt aside than address Steven's comments.

"Yeah," Steven continued. "My friend Shabazz runs a program down in the city. They teach African Ancestry. They even get them good grassroots speakers. They got mad workshops."

Maithuna's concentration was fixed on Steven's energy. It gave her confidence. This was something Carter before him was missing. "All right," she replied. "It sounds beautiful."

Steven finally relaxed on the inside.

"It's gonna be all good, sista," Steven assured. "Trust me." He paused and then inspected Maithuna. She was beautiful in her desire to learn, and glowed even more as she overcame the anxiety to take a step in the direction she wanted to go in. Steven's eyes, looking Maithuna up and down, were undisguised in their intentions. But he was not admiring her physical features. He addressed her outfit, "I have to say, from a distance, you look like you already got that knowledge. The way you carry yourself, and all."

"Never judge a book by its cover," Maithuna replied sternly.

Steven accepted her cliché. He did not want the conversation to end on that note. Steven continued to speak. He asked Maithuna, "So what made you come full circle?" He was finally comfortable.

Maithuna exhaled. She thought for a brief moment about her answer, and then she replied, "Nothing I was being told about black people added up. I was happy when Obama took office. I wanted to see if his image was repeated in our history. My questions led me here, to this bookstore." She looked around at the store and then to Steven. She gave him a curious eye. "I've seen you as well. You're always talking to the books."

"What can I say," Steven said in a confessing manner, "the books speak to me."

Maithuna leaned close and asked, "What do they say?"

"They say, *'Don't worry, kid.* Someone *is as lost as you are'.*" He leaned close and added with a playful tone, "Thanks for provin' 'em right. I had my doubts."

They laughed and leaned away from one another.

"I have to admit," Maithuna began, "I'm not always this talkative." She cleared her throat and added, "At least not recently. Don't have much of anyone to talk to." Steven found the comment curious. "Most of my friends are getting ready for a nine-to-die job."

Steven chuckled at Maithuna's choice of words. "Nine-to-die," he repeated while still chuckling. "I like that."

"Well, that's just the way I see it as I get closer to looking for one as well," Maithuna admitted. "I'm already working at a school in Brooklyn. That's why I moved here. I'm originally from New Rochelle."

"You live here in Brooklyn now," asked Steven.

Maithuna shook her head, yes. "I'm on Putnam, between Stuyvesant and Malcolm X."

Steven nodded his head. "Okay. I'm on Decatur, between the same streets."

"Okay, now," Maithuna acknowledged. "You from Brooklyn."

"No," said Steven. "Queens."

Maithuna joked, "I forgive you." Steven put his hands over his heart, feigning being hit by an arrow. Maithuna slapped his arm playfully, and Steven took notice of the playful contact.

Maithuna backed away and continued speaking. "I work at the Charter School over on Macon. I chose teaching because, even before I was on this black conscious kick, I kept thinking I can *save the children!*" Her voice was loud, alerting several customers. They looked over in wonder. Maithuna chuckled, but still made an embarrassed face. She looked at Steven, leaned close, and the two laughed. She relaxed and said, "I actually can't wait for my student teaching to end. This school system, I tell you…"

"We deal with that in the next issue," Steven reported.

Maithuna paused and looked at Steven. She said appreciatively, "I love you bruthas and sistas. You got me."

"It's contagious," said Steven. "Most of the subscribers became writers. They went from paying to being paid. And they still subscribe, giving money back and circulating the dollar. That's how we employ and empower our own." Steven looked around the store and concluded, "Any Black-owned business can do the same."

"Like this store," Maithuna said. "Most of the people who work here frequented the place. They came so much it became a hangout and then—"

"They were working behind the counter," Steven finished for her. "And that's how we do it. Simple. We bring it back to our own. Like all the business over on Lewis." He looked around the store. "I wouldn't mind getting a job here. Writing articles doesn't take up much time." He then remembered the article he had to finish. "Which reminds me, I have some notes to put together for an article that's due real soon. You're in luck, Maithuna, I have to leave."

Maithuna spoke, low and to herself, "And it was actually becoming interesting."

Steven caught her words and took a chance by saying, "It can be continued another time."

Maithuna reacted quickly. "Tomorrow night? Dinner?"

"Your place?" Steven recommended. "I'll cook."

Maithuna was impressed. "Oh, a brutha can do that?"

Steven shook his head. "Not really," he admitted. "I just ain't got the money—" Maithuna covered her mouth to keep laughter from escaping. "—to be taking you out."

"OH-Kay!" she exclaimed.

Steven then added, "I'm kidding. Besides, taking someone out is synonymous with shooting them. Where I'm from, anyway."

There was something sincere in his tone, but Maithuna continued to hiccup laughter. "Then let's stick to dinner," she suggested.

Steven explained, "Seriously though, going out gets on my nerves. People feel the need to act different on a date. Let's just be ourselves in the comfort of a comfortable space. Your place?"

Maithuna was intrigued. Steven did not resonate with any danger, and Maithuna, as a woman, had the best of senses. She accepted Steven's proposal to her apartment…on one condition. "And you're gonna cook?" she asked for reassurance. Women in clubs took men home for much more. Maithuna wanted to prove his cooking skills, more than any other skills he wanted to present.

"Sure," Steven retorted. "You like Ramen Noodles?"

Maithuna pointed her finger, and blurted, "Now *that* better be a joke."

Steven pretended to be perplexed as he stated, "What? I can work that stuff up, cook it like heroin and have you addicted to the taste." He simmered down his jokes and said sincerely, "We'll make this a mutual thing. We'll work something together. It'll be an adventure in your kitchen."

"It's a deal," Maithuna agreed. She reached for her backpack and began shuffling through it, looking for her cell phone. "Give me your number. I'll give you mine."

Steven went to his bag, removed his cell phone and the two of them exchanged numbers, programming the digits into their cells. Steven gathered his bag and slipped it on his back. He pushed the Barashango book to Maithuna. "You can look at this. I'll get it another time." Maithuna accepted the book. Steven rose from the table and told her, "I'll get in touch with you when I finish the article."

Maithuna nodded her head and said to Steven, "I'll be looking forward to your call, brutha."

Steven said, "I'll be looking forward to making it."

"Peace, brutha," Maithuna bid farewell.

Steven nodded and walked away feeling a rush of emotions. He could hardly walk. He had to consciously make sure one foot was stepping in front of the other. He hoped he was subtle about it. He exited the bookstore, hoping he would regain his composure outside in the fresh air. Prechet was right there waiting. She could tell by his smile all had gone well. She jumped the gun and stated, "You'll need to get your locks tightened for your date."

Nothing could get to Steven. Not even his doubts.

"I think she's digging the rugged look," he said to Prechet as the two started walking back toward Fulton Park.

They reached Fulton Street and made a right to head back to the park. Carter appeared just as they passed Marcus Garvey Boulevard. His glare was noticeable. Prechet saw him first. "Oh, great. Lando," she warned.

Before Steven could do or say anything, Carter's mouth went on a verbal assault. "Why you no-good, woman-swindlin' thug."

Steven outstretched his arms victoriously. He said to his friend, "Hey, give me this one, sun. You're always gettin' the girl."

Carter walked up to Steven. The two were face-to-face, mocking an intense situation. Both did their best not to laugh at the other's silly, intense expression. The friendly rivals were locked eye-to-eye, their focus unbroken.

"I shouldn't even talk to you, after what you pulled in there." Carter could not hold it. His hidden smile made an appearance. "Whatchu doin' movin' in on my woman? What idiotic mess did you say to *my* girl?"

Steven's eyes went wide. "Your girl," he pointed to Carter. "Hey, you lost her to me fair and square," he quoted.

"Fair and square," Carter mocked the words. "Like there's any honor among you, *thief.*"

Prechet felt Carter's words. He was getting personal. She stepped to the side of him and Steven. Neither was focused on her. Neither could see her. But she had to remind them, "The woman the both of you are looking to 'conquer', is no *object* for thievery."

Steven barely caught the words. "Right," he acknowledged. "And, if there's any consolation, Carter, she thought you were interesting."

"Like a heart attack," Prechet said under her breath.

Steven heard her words clearly, but he kept focus, not breaking a smile or laughing. Carter did not hear Prechet's low spoken sentiment. Steven leaned toward Prechet and said into her ear, "Let me handle this, Goddess."

Carter smirked at Steven's gesture. "You got something to say to me, sun," he asked.

"Not really to you," Steven retorted.

Prechet just rolled her eyes thinking of the old adage that *'boys will be boys'*. She liked to add, *One day, maybe men.* She sighed and said, "Well, the two of you have fun fighting over something that's not either of yours. Keep that in mind." She turned and started away. "Steven, you'll know where I'll be." Prechet was gone, walking down the street.

Carter relaxed a bit. His smile became sincere and warm. "Whatchu up to now, man," he asked his friend.

"I got an article to put together," Steven informed. "And some things to clear from my mind."

Carter's eyes floated down the street in the direction of Prechet's exit. He looked at Steven. "You mean like Prechet?" He tapped his head. "You ain't thinkin' she'd mind you and Maithuna?"

A guilty feeling overtook Steven. He became jittery. "No," he said, his eyes looking everywhere but Carter. "She, uh, she's done for me…what she's needed to do."

Carter asked in a careful, yet teasing, tone, "So, you're not seeing her anymore?"

Steven lifted his shoulders. "I didn't say that. Our relationship is…complicated. Kinda."

Carter agreed. He sighed just thinking about it. He said to Steven, "Yes it is, brutha. But that's something you gotta work out in your mind and get straight in reality."

Steven lied when he replied, "Not to change the subject, but are you still considering writing for The Block?"

"Yeah," Carter said half-interested. "But just considering."

It was Steven's turn to attack. "Well, hurry up and make a decision."

Carter shrugged, "It's just with work and all."

Steven argued, "Hey, I got a regular gig editing for a publishing company handling textbooks, but I make this work." He then opened his arms and said, "But if you're out, sista back there is in. I asked Maithuna if she wanted to write. She said she was a subscriber."

Carter snickered. "From thief to crusader."

Steven did not like the comment. "Hey, lay off that, man," was his response.

Carter backed down, understanding. "Sorry, sun," he apologized. "But y'all down at The Block have been through some thangs," Carter expounded. "Ya'll got attacked for still talkin' about the problems in America during and after 9-11. I thought y'all revolutionaries would be better off wavin' a white-flag."

"That was before my time, sun," Steven reminded. "Jevon tells me of those days. I was sixteen and runnin' wild."

"I forget I got five years on you," said Carter. "Now y'all got Obama," he continued. "Do Black people have anything to complain about now?"

Carter was teasing, but Steven felt as if he was being baited. He simply replied, "There is much still to be done. You need to throw down an article on that."

Carter just groaned. "Words don't mean shit. Neither does the truth. Niggas won't listen, and niggas that do think it's about getting white people to approve. And don't get me started on these dumbass kids runnin' around here."

Steven persisted, "*You* need to write an article. Let some of that tension out."

"Maybe," Carter started to relax, even presenting a smile. "But how long will it take for you to get yours finished?"

"I got to put some notes together," Steven listed. "Then, I gotta write it. I actually wanna finish three, so I ain't got to worry."

"You better hurry up," Carter started. "Your deadline is gainin'."

Steven waved the comment on. "Hey! It's me," he said with a wide grin. "And besides, none of my *lines* are *dead*."

Clever, Carter had to admit to himself. He chuckled at Steven's sharp-wit. "I'm gonna stop by your place later, Mr. Poet."

"Just give me a ring before you do," Steven told him.

"Will do, brutha." Carter stepped closer and shook a finger. "And when I get over to your place, you gonna tell me your secret with gettin' Maithuna."

"Simple," Steven stated. "I treated her like a human being, 'stead of someone to flaunt a new line on."

Carter clutched his heart, playfully. He added to the gesture by dropping his head in shame. "Oh, that hurt."

"Really," Steven said excitedly. "I didn't think your ego could be. But if it can bleed, I guess I can kill it."

They burst into laughter.

"Man, I'mo bust yo' ass!" Carter yelled through his laughter. "You ain't even gonna make it to your date with this girl."

"Girl?" Steven riposted. "See, there's where you're wrong. Maithuna is a woman."

Carter flapped his lips. "Really? What kind of woman has a name like 'Maithuna'? What the hell does that mean anyway?"

"Well, let me kick a proposition." Steven leaned closer to Carter. "You go research it, write about it in an article, and hand it in."

Carter shook his head. "Damn crusader."

Steven backed away and exhaled. "It was worth a shot," he said.

"Don't worry," Carter said lifting his shoulders and throwing shadow punches. "I'mo get to my writing. I'mo handle business."

Steven stepped back. "Yeah, right. I'll believe it when I see it. Peace, sun. I'll see you later."

Carter engaged Steven in a farewell handshake. "Later," he said.

Steven walked up Marcus Garvey Boulevard, came to Decatur, and walked up to his apartment block. Prechet appeared. Steven knew she did not care much for Carter. He was arrogant, she thought. But Steven always tried to sway her away from the notion. Carter was an intelligent man. He was just doing things his way. All the excuses had no affect on Prechet.

"So," she said in a low tone to Steven. "Are things settled between your naiveté and Carter's arrogance?"

"I'm not worrying about him anymore," Steven assured her. "Besides he and I are good friends, despite our competitive nature." He then paused. Prechet could see he had more to say, and Steven noticed her gaze. For her sake, he continued. "But to tell the truth, Carter did bring up something interesting."

"What's that?" Prechet asked.

Though Steven built up the courage to address the issue, he could not get it out. He opened his mouth and just waited for the words. Slowly, they came. He said to Prechet, "Do...you have a problem with me seeing Maithuna tomorrow night?"

Prechet folded her arms. She rolled her eyes at Steven's question, and smiled only to keep from showing being offended at the notion. She looked at Steven and replied, "What do *you* think? Do you think it would bother me?"

Steven lifted his shoulders. "I don't know," he said. "I guess I'm looking for confirmation."

Prechet gently put her arm on Steven's shoulders. She said sincerely, "You have to stop imagining things between us will revert back to the way they were, Steven. It was fun while it lasted." She stated her next words gently. "It's over. We should *both* understand that. Start making up your own mind."

Steven stayed silent.

Prechet continued to console him. She assured, "I'm happy you pursued this woman. You're opening up again. See what you can find in this woman. Go on.

Get out and have some fun. Stretch your wings, baby. It'll do us both some good." Steven finally smiled; a gesture Prechet always knew how to bring out in him. "And whatever you do," she continued, "don't think of me. I'll be fine."

Steven nodded. He looked at his watch just to segue into his final words to wind down their conversation. "Well, let me get this article done so your brother doesn't kill me. I'll see you later." He took a few steps away from the woman, turned back, and asked, "I got your word? You don't mind?"

Prechet grimaced. "Will you just get going, Steven."

Steven waved his hands. "All right. We good."

He walked away.

Prechet stayed behind. The expression in her eyes negated her comforting words to Steven. Maybe something was still there. But that would be impossible.

Steven sat at the desk in his bedroom typing frantically on his laptop. His fingers, tapped into the speed force, did not slow down, and were precise and efficient. He was down to the last moments and clicks for his article, papers filled with notes piled next to his computer and on the floor. He saved the data once he was finished, sat back and exhaled. He was tired. It was late. He looked over at the clock. It was one in the morning. He had already called Maithuna at eight. She was doing fine. Their conversation was short because of Steven's dedication to work. He called simply to keep his promise of calling.

Carter on the other hand never called.

How typical of him.

Then the phone rang.

It was Steven's cell. He looked at it for a while before picking it up.

It was Carter.

"Peace, sun," Steven greeted. "Say, man, I was just wondering when you would call. I guess there's no time like one o'clock in the morning." Carter responded. Steven replied, "Well, I hope you don't come now, 'cause it's too damn late. It ain't Saturday night anymore. It's Sunday morning. I'm goin' to sleep. Keep yo' ass at home." Steven paused again, only chuckling at his own comment. Carter had his own retorts, then a question. "Yeah, I finished the articles," Steven answered Carter's inquiry. "Have you even started one at all?" Steven paused, adding quickly, "Coward." Carter did not catch the comment, or maybe decided to ignore it. Steven paused for Carter to get in some words. "Yeah, well one of these days you'll come around. 'till then, you give me a call when you start liking girls. Guess I'll be waiting for a while, huh?" Both of them laughed. Carter retorted immediately causing Steven to respond, "A'ight, Carter, simmer down a bit. I'll tell you how everything goes with Maithuna after tomorrow, a'ight? Cool. Peace, bruh."

Steven hung up the phone.

He exhaled again.

He needed rest.

He thought about Maithuna.

He thought about Prechet.

It was eight o'clock in the evening the following day, and Steven was on his way to Maithuna's apartment for what he had hoped was a wonderful rendezvous. He spoke to Maithuna earlier, walked to the grocery store on Marcus Garvey Boulevard, picked up a few items for cooking, and made his way to Maithuna's block, which was not too far from where he lived.

Steven had his locks tied back in a ponytail. He was dressed in tan slacks that were slightly baggy and were equipped with a drawstring to substitute for a belt. He had on brown shoes, and a black collar shirt. He paced down the street, came to Maithuna's brownstone complex, and buzzed her apartment.

Maithuna came down the stairs. Steven stared at her the whole way down. She was as elegant as ever, wearing one of her signature skirts. This one was yellow with a light brown, mehndi-like design woven into the fabric. Maithuna also wore a matching blouse. Her feet were bare as she made her way down the carpeted stairs. Her face, however, was dressed with a smile, beaming at Steven.

She opened the first door, came to the window of the second door, and joked, "Who's there?"

Steven played along. "The killer who wants to kill you," he said.

Maithuna looked at the groceries in Steven's hands. "Well, does the killer have food?"

Steven said back, "Well, how else can I get you to let me in than with a slick bribe?"

Maithuna opened the door. "It works," she said looking inside the grocery bag. She saw lamb patties, couscous, vegetables, juice, and ice cream. She was impressed. When she looked up at Steven she noticed he was concentrated more on ogling, but he was making it obvious.

"You look amazing, Maithuna," he complimented.

"Thank you, Steven," she said accepting the compliment in a shy manner. "You look handsome," she remarked.

"I'm just trying to keep up," Steven retorted. He bowed his head and answered humbly, "Thank you, sista."

Maithuna invited Steven inside. She looked at the bag. "This will definitely be an adventure," she commented.

"Or a disaster," Steven quipped.

"Disasters can be adventurous too," Maithuna noted.

Steven pondered the sentiment as he moved aside to allow Maithuna lead up the stairs. Maithuna chuckled whimsically at her own comment. Steven followed her laughter like an ethereal trail.

Maithuna lived on the third floor. She guided Steven inside a spacious, front room area decorated with fine furniture. A couch lay to his right, black and leather.

It faced the television. A large coffee table was in front of the couch, and the couch's matching loveseat was located near the window. The kitchen was directly left of the door. It was white, tiled, and had updated appliances. Beyond the kitchen was a short hallway leading into Maithuna's bedroom.

Steven followed Maithuna to the kitchen. He placed the grocery bag on the kitchen counter. They both began extracting the contents. "Lamb patties with couscous and vegetables," Steven announced. "You'll be my assistant in this operation."

Maithuna took out the ice cream from the bag and placed it in the freezer. "That Guardian Angel book was excellent, beautiful," she said to make conversation. "I bought it. It was a quick read. You can borrow it if you want."

"Thanks," said Steven sorting the ingredients in the bag. "Hey, do you have a roommate?" Steven asked.

"Yeah. But she's out for the night," Maithuna answered.

"Good," Steven said raising an eyebrow. "No one will be able to hear you scream," he removed flowers from the grocery bag and presented them to Maithuna. "When I give you these," he finished.

Maithuna accepted the flowers. She was wide-eyed, completely amazed at how Steven stored the flowers in the grocery bag. She hadn't seen them when she looked inside earlier. She inhaled their fragrance. "They're beautiful," she remarked sincerely. "You're a romantic. Or is that word too Eurocentric for you?"

"I ain't an uptight, psychotic conscious cat like that." Steven assured her. "Besides, the word 'romantic', coming from 'Roman' can be traced back to the Egyptian *Amen-Ra* or *Ra-Amen*. Their story of the twins Romulus and Remus founding Rome is no more than a retelling of the Egyptian Neter Ra and his wife Ra-t, as they suckled the energy from the star Sirius, the Dog Star or Jackal. Like the two twins suckle from a wolf. It also connects to the demon Ahriman in Persian mythology."

"And you don't think you have much knowledge?" Maithuna said with a raised eyebrow.

Steven just clapped his hands together. "Could I interest you in some fruit or desert to go along with that food for thought?"

"Please," she smiled flirtatiously. "Show me how well endowed with knowledge you are."

"My knowledge is long," Steven retorted, nodding his head and taking a step closer to Maithuna. "And I can kick knowledge all night long."

"Oh, shit," Maithuna exhaled sensuously, biting her lip. "Really?"

"Yeah," Steven said, low, drawing Maithuna closer to him and giving her a kiss.

Maithuna accepted Steven's advance. She pressed her lips closer to his and the two of them tasted one another. Maithuna felt as if a cool breeze passed through her, rising up through her spine. Her body tingled and shivered. Steven played it cool, controlling the kiss with his lips. It was an unexpected moment for Maithuna, and she giggled, breaking away from the kiss. Steven did not mind. He was amazed at himself for making such a daring move.

"Wow," Maithuna expressed in a low voice.

Steven felt the need to say, "Hey, sista. Let's just have fun. We'll save all the seriousness for another time." Steven's voice then became playful again as he said, "Y'know, like when we have to call the fire department to hose down your kitchen after we're done with it." Maithuna inhaled. She looked at the contents for their dinner, then to the stove in back of her, and then to Steven. He said to her, "Let's see what kind of damage we can do. Let's start cookin'."

"It looks like we were," Maithuna said in a coy manner.

Steven chuckled. "Yes. We broke that ice. Let's see if we can make dinner." He walked toward the contents of their uncooked meal and again shuffled them around. Maithuna prepared the stove. Steven opened the lamb patties and prepped the meat with seasoning. Maithuna put water in a pot for the vegetables. She prepared another pot for the couscous. She put a frying pan on the stove and lit the various burners.

The meal's preparation brought heavy conversation between Maithuna and Steven. There was laughter as the both of them shared childhood stories. The time passed, the contents on the stove coming along fine. Maithuna opened a bottle of wine and poured a glass for Steven and her. The apartment filled with the aroma of cooked spices and the growing chemistry between Maithuna and Steven.

The wine allowed Maithuna to share an embarrassing childhood story consisting of she, a bike, and her inability to keep her balance. Steven laughed at her story. She did the same, though she was still a little defensive.

"I was a child," she said trying to calm her laughter. "What would you expect me to do?"

"I guess embarrassing yourself is in the contract of childhood," said Steven over his shoulder, stirring the meat into the cackling pan.

"Like *you* never did anything stupid," Maithuna said to him.

Steven dulled the fire under the pan. "Hey, I'm still hiding out for some of the stuff I did when I was a kid," he said.

Maithuna was intrigued. She noticed Steven was careful about revealing his past. He talked about growing up, family, his current age. It seemed his teenage years were a blur. There was no mention of college. Her curiosity piqued. She asked, "And where did you gain all your insight from, Mister?" She was trying to sound playful. "Where did you go to college?"

Steven stiffened. He scratched his head as a diversion, and concentrated harder on the food. Maithuna waited. Steven spoke, "I didn't go to school here," he said. "I never went to college."

"R-r-really?" Maithuna had no idea why she was so surprised.

Steven said defensively, "Yeah…really."

"What were you doing after you got out of high school?" Her heart jumped with the question. Something was telling her to be quiet and just continue with the fun.

"I guess this is were we have to get truthful, or rather, serious?" Steven said, half joking.

Maithuna wanted to take back her question. She thought it was too soon. They had just talked, shared an ice-breaking kiss.

Steven inhaled. He could not get out of this. He stepped back toward the counter and leaned against it. He looked up at Maithuna and opened his mouth. No words came out. He gave an uneasy smile, dropped his head, and tried again. There were still no words. Maithuna took a step back, giving Steven space.

Steven thought about where he should begin.

How about just describing what you were?

"I was a mean sonava bitch growing up." Steven could see his words cutting through Maithuna. "Between the eighth grade, and up until two years ago, I wasn't…" He lost his words. He cleared his throat trying to push them back up. He relaxed, and started again. "My friends and I started off stealin' bikes. Then…we graduated to cars. We didn't care if the owners were still in them." He chuckled, reminiscing. It was not the sort of memories most people were fond of, but it was just the people he knew. The faces of past friends snapped into his mind one-by-one. Dead friends. Friends alive. Friends on the run. Friends in jail. It was like a slideshow of portraits. Most of the pictures he saw resembled police mug shots, lineups. These were Steven's friend.

"I fenced stolen goods," Steven continued. "Goods I stole. Goods other people stole." Steven shrugged, lifting his shoulders and contorting his face. "I went on runs to pick up money…I kept a percentage."

Maithuna then remembered something Steven had said. She hoped it did not really apply. She wanted to move away from Steven, but she did not move. Instead, she spoke, "So when you talked about taking someone out meant shooting them…?"

"I never killed anybody," Steven injected sternly. "I shot at some people," and then his humor came through. "But, hey, they were shooting at me." The joke did not make Maithuna comfortable. In fact, the first half of the revelation made her uneasy.

"That's not an excuse, Steven," she said in a low voice, her eyes dropping away from him. She looked back up and asked, "Did you ever…deal drugs?"

"I knew drug dealers," he admitted. "I hung with 'em all the way until they hung in jail. But I never dealt drugs. Never used or sold 'em. Materialistic theft, I always believed people could get that back. Sellin' drugs? That was like poisonin' people." He could see his so-called moral standpoint was not lifting the moment. "Did that make me a saint? No. I was still a bad guy…temper and all. And I'd knock the hell out of anyone who crossed *me* or a *friend.*" Old rivalries and unfinished business watered Steven's eyes.

Revenge.

Maithuna stared at Steven's face. It was like stone.

"B-b-but you're better now?" She asked, uneasy.

Steven wiped away his tears and memories. He remained stern. "You have nothing to fear, Maithuna," he said with conviction. "Believe me." His voice was then gentle.

Maithuna stepped forward and embraced him. She did not know why. She wondered if Steven could feel the intensity of her rapidly, beating heart. Steven's heart beat just as rapidly and intense as hers.

An hour passed in silence. Steven and Maithuna dined quietly at her table. They sat opposite one another. Steven did not like the silence, but he respected Maithuna's space, even if she had shut herself off.

Steven believed that his life was nothing special. He did not understand Maithuna's sudden behavior after he revealed the missing pieces to his story. He guessed that his life as a petty criminal was in stark contrast to his personality and the way he carried himself as of recent.

Steven then decided to escape as well. He thought about Prechet. He wondered what she would say in this particular situation. She was always strong, always supportive. Then her words came to him.

"This woman is no different than when I found you," Prechet's voice said to Steven. *Yeah, that's what she would say,* Steven thought. Prechet's voice continued, *"She's just looking for direction."*

Steven shook Prechet's voice from his head, trying to keep his promise not to think about her. But he sure could have used Prechet's wisdom at this moment. He looked at Maithuna. He decided to break the silence.

"You're awfully quiet over there," was the best he could say to inspire conversation. Maithuna stopped eating. She did not respond. She did not know what to say, but she felt Steven deserved a reply. Steven filled the silence by speaking more. "Does it bother you that much," he asked Maithuna. "What I use to do? What I used to be? There were marks that figured out I robbed them and had less of a reaction."

Maithuna wanted to laugh, but her current state of mind stopped her. She did, however, break her silence. "You just seemed so innocent."

Then, Prechet's voice billowed in Steven's head.

"You know it's not that," Prechet told Steven. He accepted Prechet's intrusion. He needed to hear her voice to relax him. He needed it to guide him. *Sorry,* Steven thought. *I have to break my promise.* Prechet continued, *"She's suffering from other feelings about you."* Steven adjusted himself in his seat. *"Get your mind out of the gutter, Steven,"* Prechet's voice scolded him. *"I mean she admires and envies the way you were able to change.*

She's looking to make a change too. This girl is having a hard time. To her, you seemed to have changed overnight."

"I did change," Steven addressed Prechet's ethereal voice aloud. Maithuna looked up at him. Steven relaxed as he and Maithuna's eyes met. Steven spoke sincerely, "I changed, Maithuna. I *am* different." He rolled his eyes. He knew what his next words had to be. "Thanks…to a beautiful woman…who's gonna kill me for thinking about her." He chuckled. Maithuna was confused. Steven explained, "I'm here because of her."

Steven's cryptic explanation did not completely diffuse Maithuna's confusion. She responded with humor in her voice, "To change what you were, this must be some woman."

Steven sighed. "She…is." He chuckled to scatter the tension inside of him. "Goodness," he said. "I'm breaking a promise."

"What promise?" Maithuna asked in a relaxed voice.

"A promise to a good friend." Steven took a bite of his food, chewed, and swallowed. His appetite was coming back. "Her name is Prechet. She's the sister to the Editor-In-Chief of The Block. She saved my life. Literally. Her and her brother."

Maithuna started to understand there were many surprises with Steven Serge. The surprises came in waves, and started with simple innocent questions. There was no need to stop with the surprises. Maithuna considered they made the night more interesting. Her initial shock was over. It was time to know the whole story concerning Steven Serge. "How'd you meet?" she asked.

Steven waved the question away. He responded, "Ah, it's a long story."

"It may be a long night," Maithuna retorted.

Steven liked Maithuna's answer and capitulated to the demand. Before he started his story, he adjusted himself in his seat. Then he mentally prepared himself, recalling where his life was prior to meeting Prechet. The story began shortly after.

"A friend of mine needed an extra man to go on a run with him," Steven started. "He was picking up money, and trouble as well. It was a setup. The people he was dealing with were no good. I don't know what the beef was between my friend and these cats, but they wanted blood. His blood, and the blood of any nigga he was rollin' with. That day it just happened to be me. I don't even know why he decided to get me, of all people. Or, at the very least, just me."

Maithuna did not even know what Steven was going to say next, but she jumped ahead and said, "You're lucky to be alive."

Steven shook his head. "Yes, I am, sista." He took a moment, and then continued. "All I remember was waking up in an alley after getting jumped. Prechet and her brother found me. I was bleeding."

Maithuna imagined the scene of Steven and his friend getting jumped, filling in the story's blanks. Blurry, ghostly shadows attacked him. Despite what she knew of Steven's past, she could not imagine why someone would want to hurt such a nice young man. "What happened to your friend," she queried.

"He actually got away," Steven answered. "Last I heard he was in Houston, layin' low. I know he's itchin' to come back up." He looked at Maithuna and tried his best to recall his attack. "Him running probably saved my life. They wanted him, not me. I can kind of remember these cats just swingin' on us. Luckily, there were no weapons involved. My friend ran. They followed. Four guys. I was left behind, unconscious and bleeding. I just happened to be across the way from Prechet's old apartment building."

Maithuna gasped, "You need to marry this woman."

"I suppose I do," Steven said, mostly to himself. "She and her brother got me back on my feet. I wasn't taken' to a hospital. It would've been complicated. The police would've gotten involved and my ass would've been in jail with my friend, and with those cats that jumped us. In prison, them crazy niggas would've finished the job. Or my friend and I would've wound up killing them just to be safe." He brushed the notion aside and changed the conversation's direction. "So, Prechet cared for me. Her and her brother got me back on track. Jehvon, her brother, introduced me to his paper. He promised me a job if I just kept out of trouble. I took editing courses. Prechet got me a regular gig at a textbook company where she worked. She gave me some Black History books to clean my head. She started my locks. And all this time, being caught up in this change, I never really thanked her."

Maithuna could feel Steven was leaving something out. She believed there was more between Steven and this woman. She was strongly convinced. But this time she did not pursue the matter, already feeling like a third wheel.

Steven almost flinched. He was able to keep his body still. He swore Prechet's image materialized behind Maithuna, and then it was gone. Steven shook the thought away. He wanted to keep as much of his promise as possible. He'd already failed enough. An overwhelming sense of guilt and sadness came over him. He kept cool on the outside. His body started to shake with small, barely noticeable tremors. He felt cold. The emotion stung his eyes, but he was able to keep tears from forming.

Steven realized there was something he needed to do.

He got up from the table. "I don't mean to…" He stopped his words and then asked, "Can you meet me in the bookstore tomorrow afternoon? After work?" He walked over to Maithuna, put out a hand, and gently raised her from her seat. He kissed her forehead. "Everything was lovely, trust me," he assured. "I know this is a little awkward, but I just have to talk some things over with—"

Maithuna raised a hand. "I completely understand," she said. "To tell you the truth, if someone had done the same for me, I would be in *their* arms right now."

Steven shook his head. "Like all relationships, it's a little more complicated than that."

"Just iron it out, brutha," she told him. "I'll meet you tomorrow at the store. After I get out from teaching. Tell Prechet to come. I'd like to meet her."

"…Sure," Steven answered in a nervous tone. He knew what kind of trouble that would be, actually. He was already between two women, and not in a favorable way. "I have work too. I actually edit for a publishing company that puts out school textbooks. I don't think I mentioned that. I said it a second ago, but…"

Maithuna smiled warmly. "You told me over the phone," she said.

"Oh, yeah," Steven said, sounding anxious. "Let me also hand in my article for the paper. Then I'll stop by the store to meet you. I'll bring Prechet…"

He gave Maithuna a sweet kiss on the cheek. He made his way to the door, Maithuna following him, her hand on his arm. Steven opened the door, and the young woman stopped him to say, "It *was* lovely, Steven. This night. We can have more. You're very interesting. And I apologize for my uneasy behavior."

"I didn't make it easy, though, sista," Steven said to her. "You're a very patient black woman. Most sistas would've kicked me out quick." He then joked, "Unless I was white. Then a sista would've given a chance, cuz black women give white men chances."

Maithuna laughed at the joke. "That's foul."

Steven said, "Peace, goddess." And then he left.

Maithuna walked Steven downstairs, guiding him out of the brownstone building. Steven stepped outside. He waved Maithuna goodbye and started down the street. The door closed behind him. He stopped halfway down the next block, dropped his head into his hands, and then slowly dragged them away, stretching his face. He exhaled. There was more to do. He headed home.

Inside.
Steven's apartment.
Front room.
It was late. Prechet was there. She had been watching Steven pace back and forth for the last twenty minutes. She thought he was going to wear out his floor. She felt the need to say something. Steven had been pacing without saying a word. She could feel the conflict within him.

"Steven," Prechet's voice broke the air. "Are you alright?"

He stopped.

He looked at her.

And just said it.

"I'm not all right. I…I'm in love with you."

It was the phrase Prechet feared from Steven, even amidst her desire to hear the words. She knew he would say them eventually. But not like this. Prechet's head dropped. She started to shake her head. "Steven…"

He jumped to her. "Come on," he fired. "That's the least I can do. The least I can *be* for what you've done for me." He paused. He waited for her to say something, but it was now her turn to be silent. Steven hated her silence. He wanted Prechet to say something, even if it was a protest for him to come to his senses. He continued to speak in place of hearing nothing. "I look up now, and all I can see is you. Even tonight, when I was on a simple date. I just kept hearing your voice. I even saw your image. I just imagined you were there."

Prechet finally looked up. There was a biting, sarcastic smile on her face. Following the smile were a set of words mirroring the same emotion. "Like us being together isn't part of your imagination, anyway."

The cut was deep.

Steven backed away slowly, his head hanging lifeless. Prechet realized what she had done. She reached out for him and pleaded, "Steven. Steven, I'm sorry. I was just—"

Steven dodged her grip. "Don't touch me," he said.

"I...I can't—" she whined.

Steven turned away from her, walking toward his kitchen. He was angry. "Can I, for once, try and make this up to you? Can I give you a simple 'thank-you'?"

Prechet followed him. "Steven, that's all you need to say," she told him. "But saying you love me?"

He turned to her, stepped, and was in her face. Close.

"Sista, what else am I suppose to feel," he asked her. "I spent two years avoiding that thought—giving you space." His teeth were grinding against one another with the intensity of his words. "I just watched on selfishly as you guided me to a better life. You gave me a job. You nursed my mind, body, *and* soul. You gave me lessons, books. You put my life straight. You *and* your brother!"

It came again. The sarcasm.

"You gonna confess your love for him now," Prechet blurted.

Steven almost bit through his lip. He was either going to kiss this woman or hit her. He just shook his head. "Will...you please...just..."

Prechet realized she was doing no good. She was only making things worse. Humor was not always the best medicine. Like any other remedy it had to be prescribed in the right doses and at the right time. This was not the right moment for it. The problem, however, was that Prechet did not know how else to handle the situation. She wanted times to be good. She wanted to laugh. She wanted to just have fun with Steven

But that would be impossible.

"Steven," she said his name in the gentle tone he loved to hear from her. "I don't mean to be rude. I just—"

"Got sick," Steven finished in a low voice. "You just...suddenly got sick."

Prechet froze. She did not want Steven to take on the burden of the words he was going to let fall from his mouth. The words would magically defy physics and drop from his lips, rise, and settle on his shoulders. She put her hands up and pleaded, "Steven. Don't do this yourself. Don't say anything you'll regret."

Steven ignored her. "I was forced to watch," his words were low, but loud to Prechet.

"Please, Steven," she begged.

There were tears in his eyes.

There were tears in Prechet's eyes.

"And I was unable to reach my hand out and help you," he stepped away from her. "I couldn't help you as you helped me."

"Okay, Steven. Stop! You made your point." Prechet's voice became fainter to Steven. "I love you…and…and…and I accept your love for me."

Steven stopped.

He looked up at Prechet.

He confessed, "That's impossible. You're not even here."

"Steven, please…"

He finally said it. "You…you've been dead for months now."

Prechet looked down. She looked frustrated, and then her image faded from Steven's sight.

Steven continued to speak, tears streaming down his cheeks.

"And…I just think about you so much, I believe you're still alive."

Steven turned down the hall, made a quick left into his bedroom, and dropped onto the bed. He buried his face deep inside the pillow. His tears were uncontrollable. He wanted to choke something. He wanted to hit something. He wanted to scream. Most of all, he wanted to hold a dear friend.

Every option was impossible to Steven.

His body quaked with anger.

He lied to Carter. He was still seeing Prechet.

He lay still. Exhausted. Lifeless. His imagination appeared from a shadow. She walked over to Steven and looked down at the young man, sympathy in her eyes. She leaned closed to him and whispered, "I will always continue to live, just for you, Steven."

She waited patiently. Maithuna. She was alone at her usual table at the Hour Heritage Bookstore. She sat with her back to the door, front facing the register. It was a way to stop her from looking up and wondering if the next person stepping inside the store was Steven. It did not help. She just kept turning her head every time she heard the door open, alerted by all the sounds of the environment outside that found their way into the store. She tried to lose herself in the book in front of her. That was no help either. Her concentration on the book was usurped by thoughts of Steven and the possibilities of this meeting. She also thought about the previous night.

She looked over her shoulder at the door again. There was movement. It was not Steven. Maithuna went back to reading. But as her eyes hit the book, Steven slipped into the seat opposite her. She looked around for Prechet. There was no one. She tried not to be obvious in her observation of Prechet's absence, but Steven noticed. There was no need to discuss it. Steven looked tired, and a little pale.

Maithuna felt the need to make conversation. "I was getting nervous," she said exhaling a sigh of relief.

"Work," said Steven. "Not my…nine-to-die, though. I was clearing things up with Jehvon." Steven continued to look down, his eyes scanning the table. "He said he would handle most of the copy editing for this issue. That's cool."

Maithuna felt something bothering Steven. Maybe it was just his heavy workload. "I can't imagine Jehvon not liking anything you write," Maithuna expressed, attempting to cheer Steven up, hopefully raise his level of vision.

"It ain't the article, sista," Steven said, eyes still down. "It was matters concerning his sister."

"Prechet…?"

Steven nodded. He looked up at her. "Yes. Those same matters concern you too."

Maithuna could not imagine how. She became stiff. What was Steven going to say next? She tried to prepare herself for anything.

"I have something to confess," Steven continued.

Maithuna could see Steven struggling to talk. She wanted to reach out to him, but she decided her voice could soothe him. "Steven, it's okay. Go ahead," she said.

Steven shook his head. "Nah, sista, it's far from okay." He raised his eyebrows and said, "Trust me." He paused again. He took a breath and said, "Prechet, the woman I was telling you about, she died."

Maithuna was taken aback. She wondered when it could have happened. Was it today? Yesterday? Regardless, it happened, and before she could even get to know Prechet. Maithuna felt emptiness and loss as if she had known the woman for a lifetime.

"Oh, my God," Maithuna gasped.

Steven explained further. "She died…several months ago." Steven dropped his eyes again.

Months ago, Maithuna wondered.

"You're gonna think I'm crazy, but, I constantly think about her." Steven's eyes watered. He bit his lip in an attempt to hold back his tears. He looked away from Maithuna, trying to hide his watery eyes. Something magnetic pulled him back to face the woman sitting across from him. Maithuna. He said to her, "I think of her so much, I actually believe I see still her."

Maithuna's stiff body melted into sincerity. Steven did not seem so crazy. "That's all right," she comforted Steven. "That's just a way to cope. She was someone special to you."

"No, sista, you don't understand." He cut into her words sharply. "I *see* her. As clear as day. I see her." He saw Maithuna lean away from him. Her eyes were wide. He was losing her. But he continued. "And she appears as real as you are in front of me, like a spirit. I'm talkin' some ol' Obi Wan Kenobi to Luke Skywalker stuff."

She appeared. Prechet. She stood behind Maithuna, standing over the woman. Steven looked at Prechet just as her image faded away. He put his eyes on Maithuna.

"She speaks to me," he told Maithuna. "Her spirit still guides me. But...I can't touch her. I mean...it's not a ghost...it's my memories putting her back together. That's her spirit." The words kept coming. They streamed from Steven's mouth. He needed to confess, to let it out. "Even last night, at your place, I saw her there. I heard her voice while we were eating. It's like anytime I feel uneasy, there go my memories putting her back together. There she is to tell me what to do or say next."

Maithuna continued to back away. She believed she had lost Steven, or he lost her. Either way she looked at him with new eyes, and she needed to get a full view of him. Steven was certainly complex. Every way she tried to figure him out, there was a new road. He was a maze.

Amazing.

"Do you see her now?" Maithuna asked, worriedly. She tried not to look around. However, she did not know what she would be looking for. Was she looking for Prechet, or just the other customers who might have been listening to them, making outrageous faces overhearing their conversation? Something told her it was more about seeing Prechet for herself. How would she react if she too saw something?

"I caught a glimpse of her. Then she left." Steven had to chuckle at how ridiculous it sounded. His laughter severed a very strong tension. He put his head down and laughed a little more. "I know that sounds crazy."

Steven's new lightheartedness eased Maithuna. She even contemplated what Steven was going through as not entirely crazy. Maithuna decided to make her speculation known. "No, no. Steven," she consoled him. "You care for this woman so much you bring her back to life. That's beautiful."

Steven lifted his head and joked, "Well, I'm glad you didn't study Psychology at school, 'cause that's actually called crazy."

Maithuna retorted with a sarcastic look.

"What?" Steven said, smiling raising his shoulders. "It is. It's crazy. I've accepted it."

"Steven," Maithuna drawled in a nurturing fashion. "If you weren't effected by this woman's death, somehow, someway, then *that* would be crazy. Right now, you are beautiful. Odd, but beautiful."

"I still feel that I'm some sort of sad case 'cause I can't function without her here. It's almost like having an imaginary friend." He rolled his eyes and sighed, his thoughts swirling around the situation. "Jeez! I have to bring Prechet back to life in order for me to continue with mine."

"What was she like, Steven?" Maithuna asked in a warm voice that strangely echoed Prechet's rhythm and tone.

Steven leaned back. The tears were gone. There were good memories filtering through Steven's head. "She was a woman," he listed first. "Beautiful. Diplomatic. Just. Balanced. Y'know? Whatever she did, it was executed with a dancer's grace."

Maithuna prompted, "Go on, Steven."

"She was, or rather is, a natural, beautiful black woman. She wasn't arrogant with her shit—excuse the saying. What she knew she taught to others. She was wisdom in its feminine frame. She gave people the confidence to be themselves. She was good at that."

Maithuna finally reached across the table and took Steven's hands with her own. "There's no reason to go through this alone. Whatever you started with this woman, you can finish with me. We'll continue to learn together."

Steven thought.

"All right. So, you want me to gather some books together, and we can start all over again? Dinner? Your place? No ghosts, or an overactive imagination?"

Maithuna switched seats to be next to Steven. She kissed his cheek. "We'll cook something," she said with a smile.

"And we can also start on your article," Steven said authoritatively. Steven saw Maithuna's face contort. "Didn't think I forgot, did you? Besides, I said I had business with my editor that concerned *you*." Steven winked.

Maithuna gave him another curious eye.

"What? If you prove yourself, you got a freelance job," Steven said to Maithuna as he leaned closer. "Now that Prechet is gone, the torch has been handed to me to teach. Which sucks, cuz I still got a lot to learn, sista."

Maithuna kissed his cheek again.

Steven returned the kiss, but placed it to Maithuna's lips. He backed away and said, "I'll be back. I got some books to purchase."

"I'll be here," she assured.

Steven got up and headed over to the bookshelves. He fingered through the books, looking for specific titles and authors. Prechet appeared at his side. He saw her, but did not look in her direction. He wanted to see her, though. He wanted to stop missing her by remembering her. He continued to look through the books, playing it inconspicuous. "You are beautiful, Steven," Prechet said to him. Her smile was bright. Her eyes were wide and beautiful. She was there.

"I would like to make peace with you, Prechet. Tonight." He barely moved his lips. His voice was barely audible. But even if he just thought the words, Prechet would be able to hear him.

She leaned close to Steven's ear. Her lips almost touched him.

"We *will* make peace tonight, Steven."

Steven took several books, turned away from Prechet, and walked back to Maithuna. He took a seat and a quick glance back at the bookshelves. Prechet was gone. He concentrated on Maithuna.

"Those the books you're getting?" Maithuna asked lightly.

"Yeah, sista," Steven answered in the same tone. "We can get together tomorrow night, right?"

"Definitely," Maithuna answered disguising a concerned tone. She was wondering what was wrong with tonight. She thought it might have something to do with Prechet. She did not bother to press the matter, respecting Steven's decision.

Steven read the concern in Maithuna's eyes. "I'll be honest," he said. "I just have some feelings to square away. I want to make peace with Prechet. I want to allow her spirit true rest. Got some rituals to do."

"That's fine." She was genuine.

The matter was pushed aside. They jumped into the books in front of them. Their new objective was to search for a thought Maithuna could shape into an article.

Night.

Steven's apartment.

Steven walked through the door. He was tired. It was late. He had spent a good deal of time with Maithuna. He tossed his bag on the couch, walked through his kitchen, and went into his bedroom. It was dark. There was no light. Steven made no move to turn any of the lights on. The only light came from the monitor on his laptop. The screen glowed, hummed, and illuminated the room. Steven sat down, folded his arms on his desk, and dropped his face down. He was exhausted. A ritual to cleanse his mind of Prechet would have to wait.

But the spirits were restless.

A woman's finger ran sensuously across his neck.

Steven jumped as he felt the touch. He turned around.

There was nothing there.

He slowly turned back to his desk, his eyes taking one last pan around the room.

He heard a woman giggling.

The sound was sensual, playful, teasing.

Steven's head lifted. He looked behind him again.

Something glided past the door.

He stood up, slowly. He walked from the room and looked around his apartment.

There was nothing.

Steven exhaled. He began to rub his forehead.

"This is where black people get killed in movies," he expressed. He took another look around. His eyes went to the door, and then to the open area.

A woman giggled behind him. Sensual. Playful. Teasing

Steven felt a kiss being planted on the back of his neck.

A light wind enveloped him.

He wondered if any of this was real, or if he was suffering from a 'beautiful mind'. Something lifted Steven's arms. Then he felt someone embrace him around the waist.

Imagination?

Or a Sixth Sensation?

Prechet faded.

Steven exhaled. Before he could react emotionally, Steven looked down the hall and saw Prechet's silhouette against the door. She was there. Her spirit. Steven was not scared. He embraced the moment and walked up to her. Prechet's was nude. He reached out. His heart jumped excitedly when his fingers touched flesh, silk and smooth. Steven stepped closer, leaning toward Prechet. His lips touched…Prechet's. He paused from kissing Prechet further. He put his hands on her face and kissed her deeper. Their lips massaged one another, open and beautiful. They spoke to one another through this kiss.

Steven dropped to his knees, leaving a trail of kisses from Prechet's lips, to her neck, down her stomach, and in between her thighs. He kissed her right thigh first. Prechet's legs opened. She, guided by Steven, lifted her right leg. It slipped over his shoulder, and he ran his tongue between her thighs causing Prechet to writhe with pleasure. Her body arched. She bit her lip and moaned.

Steven's tongue caressed the lips of her aperture, then deep into its core. The motion of his tongue ran straight across, tickling the most sensitive areas. His tongue ran down the center, then across again. Down, across. It swirled in a circle, diagonal left, back down and diagonal right. Down again, and three times to the right, then looped down and up.

Prechet was a current of electricity. Her leg tightened around Steven. She leaned her body into Steven's actions and waved her hips, back and forth like the flow of water. Steven actually believed he heard her speak. But it was calm, not excited.

"Can you imagine touching your imagination as it stands in front you?" she asked in a flirtatious voice, moaning from the pleasure Steven invoked in her spirit. "It's all right, because thoughts always come before you. And I'm holding thoughts of coming before you."

Prechet's spirit turned transparent. Her face contorted with the pleasure of Steven's sensual movements, made by his tongue alone. Her back arched, as if she was being pulled downward. Her spirit lost itself in Steven's pull. Her mouth opened and burst with a silent pleasure. She exhaled delectation, but no sound escaped, there was just the action. Her spirit drained. She climaxed and disappeared.

An ambiance entered Steven.

Steven placed his hands on the door.

Nothing was there.

Prechet was gone.

He rubbed his hands and exhaled.

Steven felt another spirit inside him.

And an eye attuned to spirits could not tell who was kneeling on the floor. Sometimes it was Steven. Sometimes it was Prechet. When the image faded back to Steven, he stood. He checked his pocket for his keys. They were there. He opened the door and left.

Maithuna opened her front door, answering the knock. She believed it was her roommate, forgetting her keys as usual. A woman she had never seen before lay on the other side of the door. The woman was tall and beautiful. There was a purple aura resonating from her flesh. She had locks, thick and long. They snaked far beyond her shoulders. They glittered with her aura and skin tone. Her eyes were wide, brown and hypnotic. She seemed to capture Maithuna with those eyes.

No wait.

Maithuna blinked.

It was Steven.

She wondered how he got inside the building. Perhaps when her roommate left, he entered. But then she wondered whom it was she saw first. Maithuna questioned the woman's appearance, then her own sanity. She definitively saw a woman, as real as she saw Steven in front of her now.

Maithuna let the moment pass. Steven was there. He had a determined look in his eyes. The look was not threatening. It was just as hypnotic as the eyes on the woman she had seen before Steven appeared. Regardless, Maithuna was surprised and happy to see him. She just happened to be thinking about him.

"Steven, come in," Maithuna greeted pleasantly.

Steven kept his cool stare on Maithuna. He said nothing. Maithuna observed his movement. Steven appeared to be walking on the wind, gliding by her. Maithuna stood in front of the door. Steven's back was to her.

"Steven, are you okay?" she asked addressing his silent manner.

There was the woman again, standing in place of Steven. She turned around and looked at Maithuna.

Split second, gone.

No.

It was Steven.

"Yes," he answered her. "I'm fine. I just happened to slip in downstairs. I wanted to surprise you." His eyes were wide with curiosity. He inspected Maithuna's hair. She was in the process of going natural. "I love when a Black woman wears her hair naturally, and studies what it means." His grin became wider. "Yeah, cut the lye out and let the truth grow. You gonna keep the process of losing the process?"

"Yes..." she said, her voice breaking. There was something about him. "Definitely," she added.

"Good. It's a step in the right direction."

Steven walked coolly. He stepped up to Maithuna. "Y'know, Prechet always use to tell me that we as black people do not define ourselves,"

There she was again, taking over Steven's image. This time she spoke, finishing Steven's statement. "We *divine* ourselves."

This time Maithuna reacted. She flinched. But when her vision fixed, there was Steven. He said to Maithuna, "Let's *divine* each other."

Maithuna stood still. She allowed Steven to come closer. Her heart raced, but she was not frightened. She felt as if she was at the moment of being opened and penetrated.

Steven kissed her. Maithuna accepted, her mouth open. Steven's tongue penetrated her lips and tasted inside her. He backed away from the deep kiss, planting smaller kisses against Maithuna's visage. She stepped back toward the door, her back pressed up against it. Steven lifted her arms, spreading them as if they were wings. He traced the edges of her body with his fingertips, and then glided them over her breasts. He resumed his deep kiss. As she was leaning more into his kiss, accepting him, Steven backed away. He grinned and just looked at her. Maithuna still had her arms raised. She looked angelic.

Steven stepped forward and whispered into her ear, "Would you like to know what it feels like to have your original, feminine soul, sista?"

Maithuna did not know whether she said the word 'yes', or just thought it. Steven still responded. Maithuna prayed her roommate would not walk through the door as Steven kissed her again.

The ritual resumed.

The straps of Maithuna's dress slipped from her shoulder. Her dress dropped. Steven followed it. Her altar exposed.

Knees against the floor, Steven treated Maithuna no different than Prechet's spirit. His tongue found her abyss, her space, her dark matter halo. Maithuna contorted and moaned sensually. Steven scribed a message with his tongue. It slowly glided downward, back up, looped to the right and diagonal downward and right. It went up again, crossed, went back down and crossed again. He then snaked left, over right, and left again, straight down, over right three times. Then, it was just a gentle massage.

Maithuna's fingers journeyed through Steven's locks, almost re-twisting them as a pleasurable and searing heat coursed through her. An electrical feeling ran along her spine like a writhing snake. Her fingers tightened around the natural, tangled and locked hair. Maithuna looked as if she had just stepped into a sun shower. Her head arched back, a smile painted on her face. It was as if she could feel the drops of gentle rain giving her kisses on her cheek. Something warm caressed her, slipping into her as she inhaled. Her body was a torch.

There were flashes of light. Maithuna felt an ambiance enter her body, exhaled by Steven. Suddenly, it was Prechet against the door receiving Steven's tongue, her spirit finding its way into Maithuna's body. And then, there was Maithuna. She gasped in quick breaths. Her body moved up and down on Steven's tongue. Her movement was rapid, and her rhythm precise. Her moans were louder, ultimately becoming fierce ancestral calls. She received the spirit.

It was Prechet again. Maithuna gone. The other woman was against the door. Her movements were the same. Her mouth hung open, exhaling exhilaration. But no sound escaped, until Maithuna stood against the door. Sound released.

Maithuna the body.

Prechet the spirit.

Together as one. Re-nude

Steven backed away, exhausted.

Maithuna slumped down and embraced him.

She kissed him to taste herself on his tongue.

Steven held Maithuna close. They lay against the door, rocking back and forth, coming to a pause. They said nothing, which spoke volumes. They knew this ritual was not about sleeping together, but waking up together. This was their story, come to a beginning, not an end.

Together.*

---

* Mai-thu-na (mie/thu/nah): The achievement of knowing the divine experience of spiritual, mental, and physical unity with a woman. *Afrikan Woman: The Original Guardian Angel, by Dr. Ishakamusa Barashango*

Vicariously Alive
How To Resurrect A Black Woman (Part Two)

There were only two ways to begin a story. Either someone walks into town, or someone walks away from it. What are the repercussions of this act? The story begins there. I'm Detective Rick Hunter. My job is to investigate the repercussions. That was one of the first things I read when I ordered and received the prepping kit and brochure: *'12 Steps On How To Become A Private Detective (and What to Expect)'*.

That's a joke, kid. Keep up.

The next thing I read about was the rules.

Rule one: People were going to walk into your life.

Rule two: Don't worry about when they walk away.

There was only one side of a story a detective had to worry about, and that was the walk in. Ironically, a Detective's mind had to walk backwards and cover the whole story, find out what happened prior to the walk in. You had to walk backwards through the story of a stranger, living another life in reverse.

Today seemed no different.

Someone walked into town.

Someone walked right through my office door, early in the morning. The sun was just beginning to warm the office when a disheveled, redheaded, Caucasian woman stepped in from the cold, gray hallway. That was a place the sun never got to explore. It was an area where people told others to stick it. The sun didn't shine in that hallway. No windows. The walls didn't seem like they wanted to be bothered. The lights that dared to illuminate the area were dim, as if they were giving a 'ho-hum' attempt at introducing light to an area of darkness it didn't want to be acquainted with.

This instant.

The woman holds a crumpled paper bag tucked in the cradle of her left arm. She's holding the thing as if she was nurturing a child. Her right hand manipulates the door. She finally turns to me, and I deduce that she's in her mid-thirties. She looks tired by experience. A lot of drama saw this woman. She's aged beyond her years. I understand. All the years of age couldn't do anything against a split second of trauma. Drama can bestow on a person an unflattering gift of age. *"Here ya go,"* situations say. *"Here's five more years in exchange for your confidence and faith."*

Now.

She closes the door slowly as if she's conducting a ritual. Maybe she's just stalling. Many people employing my services do that, especially the women. Women tend to take their time. Walking into my office meant you were accepting whatever was wrong, or entertaining a gut feeling that something was not right. The women always amused me. Women, who always had something to say, an emotion to express, and gossip to indulge in, appeared the most nervous about giving me the details of a situation they wanted me to solve. The men? They'd jump right into it. *"Can you kill a motherfucker for me?"* The guys would scream. *"At least find this cocksucker?"*

This woman fit right into the usual. I even notice her take that all-too-common last glance out the door before closing it. I used to think people were afraid they had been followed. Now, I just believe they're getting that last look at a normal life before engaging their problems, which will take them to the brink. *Jesus, this woman looks haggard. Sleep and her have been divorced for several days now.*

But I always entertain asking if someone is following them. It keeps me alert. So, whose life did she walk out on? Whose life did she enter? What were the repercussions of this act? It was always good to ask these questions and be a Detective before someone officially hired you, and it keeps you aware of the rules.

Then.

She fixes her hair, as if that would help her overall appearance. She wears gray jogging pants and a t-shirt. She looks up, her eyes on me. That's when the second part of the introduction ritual begins.

I almost roll my eyes when I see her eyes widen at the sight of me. I never get use to the fact that most of my white clients, and even some black clients, were always surprised to see a well dressed, well groomed black man as a Private Investigator. Friends always called me crazy for seeking this line of work. People didn't trust black people with finding anything unless it was their cars in a parking lot. *"Find me my car, boy. There's a good tip in it for you that you can bring home to your mammy."* Well, give me the keys to your life, and let's see if I can't pull up something interesting. I got a tip too: Go fuck yourself.

But being at this job was not as crazy as a friend of mine who works in Atlanta as an editor for a government agency. He always jokes that white people line up by the dozens to have their grammar checked by a black man. He says there's a line like Disneyland. He says he has to bat the white people back as they ask, *"Please, correct my English you black ebonix-speaking nigger."*

Of course, he's just kidding. They avoid him like the plague, unless there is absolute necessity to go to him. When they do need his help he says they ask, in what he calls 'a sweet voice', as if they're talking to a child, *"Is there anyone else here?"* or *"Are you the only one here?"* They don't ask him, *"Can you edit this document for me?"* I repeat, they ask, *"Is there anyone else here?"* or *"Are you the only one here?"* And he says they're talkin' to him like he's a sad puppy. He says their voices are so sweet he finds it hard to retaliate angrily, because he knows what they mean. White people play that defense real well. Just act nicer. Don't raise your voice. You won't look like you're a racist. Meanwhile, when the black man or woman gets upset, they'll look unstable and 'wrong' and 'mean'.

Oh, yeah. I almost forgot. This woman. I drummed up so much emotion I almost take it out on her as I give her a contorted look. *Yes it's me*, I'm thinking to myself, wanting to express it to her. *A black man. Clean cut. Dark skin. Nice suit. I just made thirty-six years last spring. Don't worry. It's legal for me to carry my guns.*

Now it's time for her white ass to get caught between the emotions of fear and having a sex fantasy about me.

I come back to my senses when I see the woman's lips begin to tremble. My anger subsides, and I begin to sincerely sympathize when I see her eyes swell up with tears. She sniffs them back, wipes her eyes, and then takes the seat in front of me. She lays the crumpled, brown grocery bag on top of the desk and lifts a hand, a signal for me to wait. As if I'm going anywhere. She begins speaking quicker than I thought she would. Her voice cracks with anxiety. "Give—give me a second."

"Of course," I say. "When you're ready."

Always the nobleman, I am. And I'm speaking from the experience of past lifetimes. Age ain't a thing to me compared to past lives. Yeah. I believe in that sort of thing, to an extent. I even took some courses in Paranormal Psychology. I'm always fascinated by the strange. My *complete* belief in them is so-so. I'm picky and choosy about the ideas the paranormal offers. One reason I became a detective was to encounter the strange. There were no ghosts, but some people harbored many skeletons in their closet, and the past could be haunting.

Again.

The woman looks over her shoulder at the door. She then looks at each of the four walls in the room. It was as if she was trying to stare beyond them. She continues to tremble, as if a threat lay on the other side of the walls. I'll be honest. I get a little nervous. Her eyes finally looking back at me didn't help either. "Detective Richard Hunter," she asks trying to make sure that's who I am. *"Are you the only one here?"* I anticipate to be her next words.

"Yes," I assure her gently.

Then she just drops her head, as if she's ashamed of something. "I know I have no appointment," she tells me.

I console her. "I have no cases for today." She jumps at the sound of my voice. Maybe I put too much 'black' bass in it. At first I think she's just startled by my voice, but then I notice something more about her actions. It was like I had spoken out of turn in a class that she was teaching. Annoyed by a student who she keeps telling to be quiet. I didn't care. I keep talking. "I came in to organize paperwork. You're lucky I'm here."

"My case needs to start immediately," she says like a strict command.

Everyone thinks they're so fucking important.

And I entertain their importance. I tell her, "It started the minute you walked in." She jumps again. I'm getting annoyed. I make sure my tone doesn't represent that. "Look," I say to her. My tone does border on aggressive. "I need you to relax. Give me your name and state your case. Let's start there."

She wipes her hair from her face. She takes a deep breath, closes her eyes. I wait for her to exhale. This is usually when all the bullshit comes flying at me. But it seems like she never does exhale. One intake of air held long, but then comes the reverberation of vomited words. She opens her eyes and tells me, "My name is Tamara. I'm looking for a friend of mine." She's deliberate with her words. She looks down. Then this woman, Tamara, darts her eyes all over the floor. It was as if the words had run from her mind, running crazy on the floor. She was looking to collect them, place them back on her tongue.

Silence.

Uneasy.

She becomes still.

She pauses in words and movement, and with the way she was moving her eyes and quickly speaking her words, bothered me. I've seen many crazy people walk into this office. I was once hired by a schizophrenic man to stop imaginary mobsters from trying to catch him. I took the case because he was offering a large sum of money. However, in the end, after learning the truth, I couldn't accept the money—if, of course, he even had the money to give.

But this woman was different. This was real. She was for real, and as crazy as she acted, she was not insane. I could tell. Something was rattling her.

I ask the obvious question, "Where was your friend last seen?"

Tamara looks up quickly and tells me something that makes the case interesting. "I know where she is," she yells.

I clear my throat and adjust myself in the seat. I ask pleasantly, trying not to sound too condescending, "Then why do you need my help?"

"People are keeping me away from her," Tamara says, tears crawling back into her eyes. I concentrate on her tears. Not the emotion, but mostly the sparkle reflecting the sun's glow. It's the first sign of life I actually notice in this woman, the first glow of warmth. She looks pale, otherwise. Not just white, as in race, but pale as in sickly. *Beyond dead, perhaps? Vampire? Paranormal activity?*

Despite the fact she's distraught over her friend, I can't help her until there's a situation that I'm legally obligated to take part in. She's looking for a friend that she knows where to find. But, I think the woman's too jumpy for reason and common sense. I decide to engage her with a series of questions. "Is she in danger where she is? Is there a jealous boyfriend of hers…?"

"No," Tamara hisses. "I need you to protect me."

People always get Investigators confused with hired guns or bodyguards. I ask in a serious tone, "Is someone after you?"

"Yes," she informs me in a very calm voice.

"Is it the same people who are keeping you from your friend," I continue to inquire.

"Yes," she answers again.

I begin to straighten the objects on my desk, moving things around just to create movement and dispense tension. I don't touch her paper bag. I clear my throat, switching around items on my desk as if I'm playing chess. I'm thinking about the situation that's in front of me. That's how I look at people. Everyone's a situation to me. Unfortunately, I can't get involved in this one. I finally look up at her and say, "Look, Miss…" I pause. Then speak, "Your last name?"

"My name is Tamara." That's all she gives me.

It makes me smile. I'm intrigued, and I tell her too. "Intriguing," I comment. "A woman with only one name."

She throws another riddle at me. "I have three if you look closely," she tells me.

My smile disappears. My eyes become stern. I want to tell her to push aside the mystique. My life's filled with enough mystery. I don't have time for clients being mysterious. It's bad enough I have to solve a problem for them.

But I don't say that. I just say, "Enough philosophy," that's the best I can do. I go on to inform her, "I just want to stress that I'm not a hired gun. I'm not a bodyguard. If there's something deeper going on, then I can escort you to the proper authorities."

"No police," she hollers.

"It doesn't have to be the police," I assure her. "I said *proper* authorities."

She insists, "You are the proper authority."

I take another moment. I need to relax myself from trying to relax this woman. I've never had a client this difficult. It's not always easy trying to drive sense into someone infected with hysteria, but she's beginning to throw me off. I choose my words carefully. "I'm not authorized to go around shooting—"

She interrupts me. Her voice sounds surprisingly authoritative. She speaks like she's thought of all this beforehand. "The cover is this, Mr. Hunter. You would be helping me look for a friend. In the middle of your search, three men tried to stop you. They began to use force. You defended yourself by killing them."

Her words, ironically, relax me, but I still had to keep rational.

"Let's start over," I suggest. "I need a complete rundown of your situation." I stand up and start to pace off the remaining tension. I stay behind my desk. I dedicate another thought to the situation. I'm in. I confirm to Tamara just as much. "I can't just let your case go. Your friend seems to be kidnapped. Your life has been threatened. Or so I can figure by what you've told me." I ignore direct contact with her harsh glare, but I know she's giving me one. I make a brave walk from behind my desk and stand in back of this woman as she continues to sit. She doesn't move. Her eyes follow me as far as they can go until I'm directly behind her. I ask, "What's the value of your friend that makes her such a precious item to hold?

And what makes you so much of a threat they don't want you near her?" I look at the desk and have an odd feeling she's looking in the same direction, anticipating my next question. "And lastly, what's in the bag?"

I make a complete journey around my office, sitting back in my seat. My eyes go from the crumpled grocery bag to Tamara. My movement says it all. I'm asking the question all over again with my eyes, and prompting her for an answer.

She sits still. I exhale. If she won't tell me, I'll use my superb detective skills and just see for myself. My hand goes for the bag, but Tamara snatches it before I can extend my reach. She puts the bag in her lap and opens it. She's slow, deliberate, presenting the whole ordeal like a ritual. She doesn't know how close she is to getting her head blown off.

I keep my eyes on her hand inside the bag. I don't move, but I ready myself to make a quick grab for my gun, should she draw one from the bag. My body is cocked slightly enough to the side to make a jump from my seat. The energy is coursing through my arm to bend, reach into my jacket, and go for one of my two guns holstered behind my suit jacket. I've made enemies over the years. I wouldn't put it pass one of them to disguise a gunman as a client.

But there's no gun on her end. Tamara removes a black object that looks as if it's carved from onyx. It radiates, absorbing the sun with its color and creating a glow. I inspect the object from across my desk. Scribbled on its sides, in gold, are ancient glyphs. It's erect, black and gold. Tamara holds it close to her face, lovingly. She caresses it gently with a single finger, and looks at the object with sad eyes. I start to feel like I'm intruding on something between her and the item.

Tamara puts it on my desk. She looks away and begins shaking her head.

"That's not mine to touch," she blares. Her voice trails away and then recuperates. "Not like this…"

I ignore her antics, my eyes still on the item. It's a tapering, four-sided shaft of stone with a top shaped like a pyramid. It looks heavy and strong while it stands upright. It was magnificent. Extending only twelve inches up, it still manages to touch the ceiling. It has me transfixed. Even the sun stares at its onyx and gold beauty. It's an Egyptian obelisk. I remember reading about their symbolism as the penis of Osiris. I start to question myself being so transfixed on the object.

Note to self, watch good, heterosexual porn tonight.

That aside, I begin to wonder what this woman feared from the object. Before I can ask her, she explains to me the obvious. "It's called an obelisk." She talks while still keeping her gaze away from the item. "In ancient times it was referred to as a Tekken."

"I know," I tell her, wearing my ego on an invisible chain around my neck. "What's so special about this one? You can buy these online or at any decorative shop. Is this authentic? It looks newly forged, not ancient."

"It belongs to my friend," she says, more tears hovering at the edge of her eyelids. The answer wasn't really compatible with my question, but I accept it.

"Is this what the kidnappers are after—holding your friend ransom?" I inquire this while coming to my own conclusion. I just need her answer to confirm.

"No," she answers, completely dissolving my deduction skills and placing my manhood on the table. Then she adds more mystery to the blaze by saying, "It's what my friend needs."

Good, black dick? Well shit, you've come to the right place, sweetheart. I clear the joke from my head and ask, "They want to keep it away from her?" Tamara answers affirmatively with a nod of her head. I feel better about my abilities as a detective. My eyes go back to the obelisk. I ask another question. "They're trying to keep you from giving it to her?"

Tamara tells me in a low voice, "They don't want you to give it to her."

I barely hear her. "What was that?" I ask. She doesn't answer, and I decide to brush the question away. I had another inquiry. "What is your friend, some sort of rare items collect—"

"All you need to know is that she's in trouble," Tamara answers me sharply. "And you need to understand that I'm serious about this."

I was again faced with Tamara's cryptic hysteria. This time, though, I address the issue. "I know you're serious, Tamara." Of course, my voice is still gentle. I don't want to run away potential money. But I don't think I could get rid of this woman if I tried. She seems hell bent on having me, specifically, handle this situation for her. I still enforce, "Enough with the cryptic banter, okay. I need a real answer. What's going on? The whole story. Where did your friend come across this item? What's its significance? And if it's so precious and valuable why aren't the people who kidnapped your friend asking for it as a ransom?"

"It's of no use to them," she answers quietly.

"Why not?" I demand.

I get nowhere. She doesn't seem like she wants to answer me. Tamara tosses the grocery bag back onto the desk. It lands directly in front of me. "The rest of the contents are yours," she says as if to shut me up. I take the bag, eager to hold it before she swipes it from me again. I look inside. There's enough money, all in hundreds, for me to retire. She's good. I'll shut up. I don't even wonder about where she got it. That's not my worry. She tells me, "It's yours if you can keep your mouth shut until we get my friend out of that house."

Like I said, I'm in. Sounds a lot like 'amen'. "So…you…do *know* where your friend is?"

"Do you want that money, Detective?" Tamara asks rigidly.

I capitulate. I'm ready to ask how much is here, when Tamara's emotions begin to pop like microwave popcorn. Tamara's suddenly alert. I jump back. She checks the four walls making up the room. She again appears to gaze through them. More so, she reacts as if she sees something. She aims her wide, panicked eyes at me, and she yells, "We have to get out of here."

I'm up quickly. For good measure, I check my guns tucked behind my jacket, holstered at my chest. Nine-millimeter firearms. I know my mathematics. I'm born again with these guns. They're the most reliable partners I've ever had. Coupled together, in my hands, I got the knowledge on how to build or destroy a situation, even under an honorable code when I handle them.

I'm compelled to say to her, "I know you want me to keep my mouth shut, but what the hell is going on?"

She doesn't answer, and it scares me that I'm starting to get used to this. She looks dazed, lost in staring at each of the walls. I'm unaware of what's happening. Paranormal events. She can see something appearing in quick flashes, pictures coming to her. She can see events lying beyond the walls. She's seeing three men, dressed in black suits and sunglasses, heading to my office. But I just thought she was going crazy. She brings herself out of her hypnotic gaze. Her lips tremble with fear as she says to me in an assuring voice, "They're not here yet." Well that was good, whoever they are. Tamara continues warning me, "We have…" Then her words disappear. She looks likes she's contemplating, or rather calculating. She resumes, "We have eight minutes before they destroy this situation. We have to get out of here. They know I'm here, Detective."

I'm stupid enough to want to ask more questions. As if bad guys understand time out, like we're kids playing games. "Tamara, I—"

"Grab the obelisk," she commands me. Now, it's me that's not in my right mind. "Put the money away," she shouts at me. "In your desk, or leave it out. They don't care about the money. Just grab the obelisk."

I play chess again with the objects on my desk, notably the obelisk and the bag of money. I reach for each item, making moves. I place the obelisk under my right arm. It taps against one of my holstered firearms. I shuffle the bag of money into a drawer. I move around the desk, and stop to wait for Tamara to get up. We both head to the door, she close at my back. I put my hand on the knob. She stops me from opening the door. I turn and look at her as if she's crazy.

Her eyes are sad.

She begs me in a whisper, "Please, believe my words."

I have no idea what the hell she's talking about. "R-r-right," I respond, patronizing her. "I trust you, and you trust me. Stay close. We're going to my car. We're going to take a drive." I want to say more, but I pause. I allow her to announce the next move.

She picks up my cue wonderfully. "We go find my friend," she says.

I nod. It's the first time we're on the same page. I turn the knob slowly, and I open the door. I instruct her, "We're going to walk casual, like everything is Cool and the Gang. But, I want to be alert. So who are 'they' and what do 'they' look like?"

She answers only the second half of my question. "They're wearing suits. Black," she tells me.

I say what I'm thinking, for once. "How original."

I'm shocked at what comes next. It's not an attack. It's not a gunshot, or a scream. Tamara actually smiles, and then makes a lighthearted joke. "Original they will never be. They can't wear that black suit like you." *That's an odd statement.* I actually wonder if she's flirting. I even look her up and down, checking her out. I don't know if I'd actually hit it. She looks a mess, and sickly. I decide not to make a retort. Why ruin the moment? But, it only takes a second before Tamara decides to drift back into her mundane, serious tonality. She gives me more of a description. "They also have tattoos on their cheeks and forehead."

Now that's *original.*

The information is collected, and then I ease my way through the door, looking left and right, making sure we don't have tattooed, black suit wearing visitors. My eyes ingest the dull, gray scene of the dimly lit hall. There's nothing. It's clear. I motion for Tamara to follow. She's cautious too, checking the hallway. It's a little annoying. Hadn't she hired me for trust? But, there's nothing like a second set of eyes.

We make our way down the hall. We're inconspicuous. We're just leaving. We take the elevator. It takes its time to come. That makes me nervous, but I don't go for a gun. I just hope no one has the elevator occupied, especially not tattooed, black-suits. The elevator opens. It's empty. We get in. I push for the lobby. It's silent. We don't speak. Not even a breath could be heard, nor the hum of the elevator's descent.

The elevator door opens. We make our way through the lobby of the office building. We're outside, out into the daylight. I look for my car. Tamara pans three hundred and sixty degrees. There's nothing in sight, but she looks like she's looking beyond sight, beyond what's there. She appears to be more preoccupied by what's *not* there.

I keep our pace, leading us to my car.

"Get in," I command roughly while placing the key into the lock, and turning it to unlock all the doors. Tamara grips the handle, pulls the door open, and slides into the passenger's seat. I'm right beside her, slipping into the driver's seat quickly. I slam the door and toss the obelisk into her lap. I put the key in the ignition, and I start the car. Tamara's looking at me, observing my mannerisms. "Calm yourself," she says gently. "You don't have to prove you're a man."

I don't even know what the hell that means, and my expression at her does more than just question her choice of words. I'm on pause simply to give her this sneering gaze. She makes one in return, and doesn't back away. She thinks she has a point to make. I make mine first, verbally, anyway. I lean close and bark at her, "Look, sweetheart, on blind faith alone I'm extending my services to—"

Tamara's eyes go wild. She's not looking at me, responding to my outburst. She's looking over my shoulder, and I don't need her mysterious, sixth sense to know what's got her spooked. I turn to get a look at these guys, wondering if I can actually bargain to hand her over to them. This woman's getting on my nerves.

I'm taken by surprise when I see only a single man.

Caucasian. Early thirties. Dark hair. Sunglasses. Black suit. Tattoo on his forehead. I can't make out the design. Doesn't matter. This guy is one of three men I've been warned about. He's nearing my car, walking slowly. He's clearly seen The Matrix too many times. But I'm not worried about him. I'm worried because he's one of three. There's two more, according to my quirky, cryptic informant.

"What kind of crazy cult is this, Tamara?" I ask her. "Should I arrest him?"

"Get us out of here," she hollers.

I turn the key in the ignition. I'm a little confused. I thought I had already started the car. Uncertainty aside, the car comes to life. Then it dies. Now I'm a witness to speculation.

I turn my head to the approaching Black-Suit. His hand is outstretched. He looks like he's reaching for something. He twiddles his fingers and the car doors unlock—all of them. I waste time staring at my lack of control inside my own car. I share my expression with Tamara. She's unfazed, because, y'know, this type of thing is apparently typical in her line of business, which goes with my initial thought.

Has she seen this before?

Then.

At the passenger window.

There's another Black-Suit. It's a different guy. Looks the same. Dress. Composure. But he has a different tattoo, and it's placed on his right cheek rather than his forehead. It's a circle with lines curving from the top, resembling horns. This is all happening in a split second. I take the information in, but decide to digest it later—if there is a later.

Action is too quick for me to think.

Slow enough for me to narrate.

The door's open. I can't react verbally or physically. The Black-Suit has his arms around Tamara, pulling her from the car. Chalk it up for another reason to wear your seatbelt. Tamara's last independent action is to grip the obelisk.

I open my door, remove my guns, and aim one at the Black-Suit still approaching from the left, and aim the other at the Black-Suit grappling Tamara. My eye is on the Black-Suit approaching. He's got a sly grin on his face, which has me wondering why.

There's action going on with Tamara and her Black-Suit. She hits him, slamming the base of the obelisk in his face. It doesn't look like much, but it drops him as if he's taken a hit from Ali himself. He clutches his forehead at the area of the impact from the obelisk. I watch the staggering Black-Suit closely. Something catches my eye.

Is there steam *coming from his face?*

I don't give it much thought. My heads turned around, looking back at the oncoming Black-Suit. The smile's gone. He's stopped dead in his tracks, his expression fighting fear and frustration. I start to believe he realizes I have the upper hand, holding a gun in each hand. But something gets me thinking. I contemplate, *This guy didn't seem to be afraid of a gun just a second ago...*

Maybe it's his staggering, burning friend. I look at Tamara for an answer, and I find one quickly. She's holding the obelisk out toward the approaching Black-Suit like a holy cross to a vampire. It's working.

I holster my weapons and ask, "What next, Tamara?" This is rare in my experience. I'm not use to this kind of situation. All of it. I'm waiting to wake up, but I know that option is just a dream. This is reality. This is all real, and I'm part of it. I've got what I wished for. Paranormal activity.

"Just get in the car," she tells me.

One Black-Suit is staggering. The other is stopped in his tracks. I don't see the third. I calculate I have enough time to make small talk with Tamara. "On one condition," I sneer.

Tamara checks on our staggering, smoking friend. He's slowly recovering from her attack. Tamara's eyes come back to me. "What condition?" she asks impatiently.

"You explain to me who these bastards are," I demand.

There's no time to argue, or at least our time is running out. "Deal," she agrees. "Just get in and start the car."

I hope I can. I jump back inside my car and turn the key to start the vehicle. Tamara keeps the obelisk aimed at the Black-Suit, buying time and keeping the mysterious fellow at bay. She quickly ducks into the car and closes the door. I hit the gas before the Black-Suit can display his magic tricks. I drive forward, then hit reverse, shift again, and exit the parking lot at high speeds. I make a quick right at a red light. This ain't the time to obey traffic laws, and I won't feel safe until I'm miles away, out onto an open road barren of stoplights. When I get to my open road destination, I decide it's time to get real answers.

"What's going on," I ask, my voice surprisingly calm. "Who are those guys? Are they the kidnappers?"

"Yes," she answers. I can tell there's probably more, but she's just making it quick. I don't mind.

But her interrogation isn't over. "Is your friend, or you, or the kidnappers in some kind of strange cult?" It's the only question I can come up with that keeps what I've been through grounded in reality.

Tamara tucks the obelisk under her seat. "Their mysticism would take lifetimes to explain. Let me sum up." *That's all I ask for.* "The tattoos they're branded with are four signs of the zodiac." I give her quick, contemplative glances, but I also keep my eyes on the road. "One of them has the tattoo of Taurus—" *The circle with the horns. Got it.* "—One has Scorpio. Then there's Leo. I've only seen three, but there are four Cardinal Signs. There has to be another. A fourth. Aquarius."

"There are twelve zodiacs, sweetheart," I remind her. There's no need to speculate that there's four when we might see twelve. I don't need surprises.

"But only four corner signs," she barks at me. "They represent the four elements. Water, earth, fire, and air." *I'm aware of the elements. What about the fifth, ether?* "This is where we get the word ATLAS from. Aquarius, Taurus, Leo, Scorpio. A-T-L-S."

"You're forgetting another 'a'," I scold. Again, no surprises. I don't want a second Aquarius popping up.

"You must think ancestrally," Tamara points out. "Vowels between words didn't often exist in ancestral times. Either way, it's these four signs, as Atlas, that hold up—*or rather make up*—the world."

"These guys seem to be bent on dropping it," I say matter-of-factly. I make a quick glance at Tamara and ask, "Or am I working for the wrong side?"

She doesn't even give me a glimpse. "You're all right," she assures me. "These beings are not part of the Zodiac proper." *Oh, of course not,* I think as she explains. She continues. "They're reversed. In my studies they were called the Devil Chakras."

"I'm a Taurus," I say with a slight smile. "Does that mean anything?"

She surprises me by beaming another warm smile. "No," she answers.

"What are you?" I ask.

"Aquarius," she tells me in a deep, otherworldly voice.

I hit the breaks!

We're both jarred forward by the sudden stop. Tamara sits back and tells me in a soft voice, "Relax. It's just a coincidence. I'm kidding with the voice, Detective." I take a moment before driving forward. Tamara reaches for the obelisk and holds it firm. "Besides, I wouldn't be able to hold this if I was a part of them...and I'm not."

I dig for information that I can understand. "Are you and your friend investigators of the paranormal?" I ask her. "Are you two some type of archeologists? Treasure hunters? Rare items collectors?"

Tamara doesn't answer. She looks sad, overwhelmed. I let her have her time and space. If she's been through on a daily basis (for God knows how long) what I've been through in just minutes, she deserves a rest. She looks out the window and asks me, "Do you know where thirty-three Pine Hill Drive is?"

"Pine Hill Drive," I repeat, using my inner GPS. "That's right near the school."

"Go there," she commands in a soft voice. "Your answers are there, Detective. Hopefully, so are the answers to my prayers."

"And your friend," I inquire for the purpose of keeping this case heading in the same direction.

"She's there," Tamara says. She sounds detached from reality. I can't blame her. I myself have just been separated from all I thought I knew. "She's…there…"

And if her friend is there, if we're going to see her, so will the Black-Suits. Most likely, plus one, or plus two. Which ultimately means there will be a fight. And it's going to be shoot to kill. These thoughts stay with me as I guide the car back onto a main road. My eyes dart from mirror to mirror. I cover all directions. And it's not for the purpose of being a careful driver. I ain't worried about the traffic. I got Devil Chakras to worry about. Having two eyes and a conscience makes a quick believer out of people, and my eyes ain't ever deceived me. Those guys made the car stop with an invisible power. They made the doors unlock. They feared an ancient symbol.

Please, wake up!

Of course, this wasn't a dream. I understand that. Guess I'm gonna have to ride this train and see what comes next? Tamara stays silent for the rest of the car ride. She continues to look longingly out the window. My thoughts keep me company, and they're not exactly much help in relaxing me. The tingling anxiety arrives just as I pull up to the house. It looks empty, abandoned, run down. It's sticks out among the rest of the well-kept houses on the block, and I wonder how the neighborhood allowed such a thing. The paint on the house is faded and peeling. The front door's open. Grass seemed to grow in sporadic spurts, here-and-there. The patches of dirt that kept itself clear of grass were the color of rust.

Tamara grabs the obelisk from under the seat. She instantly ejects from the car just as I slow down and stop in the driveway. She opens the obelisk at the bass as she comes over to my side. I open the door and get out, meeting her.

"Here," she says holding out her hand. "Take these."

I open my hands and accept her gift. It's individual items, small. There's a bunch of them. I take a look at what's in my hand. They're mini obelisks. I give Tamara a curious look, perplexed.

"They're bullets," she informs, addressing my curiosity. "It'll stop them. If it's anything that can stop them, it's these bullets. Regular bullets won't do."

Who am I to argue? I take a peek down the street, both directions. All's clear. I lay the bullets on the roof of the car. I quickly substitute the bullets in my guns for the obelisk-bullets. I have no idea if this will work, but again, no time to argue. Guns are loaded and holstered. I take Tamara's side and wait for the next set of instructions. She's sad again. She says, "Thank you. Thank you for believing me. Thank you for helping me."

"It ain't over yet, Tamara," I state. My eyes become fixed on the house. I try to indulge in the trick Tamara pulled back at my office. I try to look beyond the walls, dig into the interior to find whatever it is Tamara's looking for. Considering some of the façade is opened up, I don't believe I have to possess magic powers to pull off my sight-beyond-sight. "Your friend's in there, right?" I ask her.

"Yes." She then warns me, "Prepare yourself."

I remove my guns and bring a whole new meaning to the phrase 'dressed to the nines'. I hold my guns tight, almost caressing them. My mentor called this 'a nobleman's grip'. I call it the grip of a well-prepared individual.

We pace forward, slip through the opened front door, and into a dark hallway that reminds me of the hallway outside my office. The sun don't shine here. Eerily so. But, ironically, this darkness is calming, peaceful.

The abyss.

The kitchen is the next room. The sun's tendrils crawl through the window like fiery spiders, illuminating the room, bringing light to this dilapidated area. I see real spiders and other crawling phenomena sifting through cracks in the floor. Dirt cakes the room like a second coat of paint.

Then.

I take a step. The floor creaks. Something snaps. But there's another noise, coming from my left, in the dining area. The room looks just as smashed as the kitchen. The chairs lay in pieces. An entertainment center is knocked over, all its contents spilling onto the floor, broken, surrounded by glass from the case. The table's cut in half, one of its legs missing. God knows where.

But.

What was that noise?

"Hold yourself," I tell Tamara.

I make a slow pivot to control the creaks in the floor. I don't want to alert whatever, or whoever, is also making sounds.

There's scratching.

Scraping.

I take a look back at Tamara. "You need a gun?" I ask in a low whisper. She pretty much has to read my lips to know what I'm asking. I figure if she can see other scenarios playing out by staring at walls, she can read my lips. She nods her head, no and mouths back, "I couldn't bring myself to pull the trigger."

Fine, sweetheart, more for me. I place my eyes back on the dining room. I can hear more scratching, more creaking that I'm not involved with. I feel a breeze. The wind whistles. I make my way into the dining room, aiming my eyes and guns in every direction, making a sweep of the place. My eyes and guns settle on the curtains. They're ruffling up against a plant and a curtain rod. It's the breeze playing the music of itching and scratching. I exhale the chorus in relief. I turn back to Tamara.

My smile fades quickly.

Tamara's gone.

I begin to run back to where she was standing in the kitchen. I take two steps, and then I stop. My eyes are darting back and forth. "Tamara," I call loudly. I regret opening my mouth. But it doesn't matter.

I feel his presence.

He's right behind me.

I make a quick turn. My speed is intense. Spider-Man and The Flash would be proud. Quicksilver too. With each degree in my pivot, I lift my firearms. But it's no use. This guy is an overachiever. He's all over me, grappling me. The Black-Suit's crumpling my suit jacket's collar. He's got a firm grip, amazing speed and strength. He uses all three to lift me up and toss me to the other side of the kitchen, passed where Tamara and I entered. I crash against the floor. The impact only jars me. It doesn't hurt much, but my back jams into the floor, breaking up more brittle tiles. I lose the grip on the gun in my right hand. It slides away.

Black-Suit's standing over me. Like I said, he's quick. His foot comes bearing down on my arm. He stomps my wrist. My fingers unfold with the pressure. There goes the grip on my other gun. I decide to look Black-Suit in the face. I wanna know who it is I'm gonna beat the shit out of. But he looks no different from the others I've faced. And truth-be-told, because of the placement of his tattoo, I can tell it's the same one from the parking lot that had the twiddling fingers and magic trick. We're up close and personal. I guess he has something to prove, a score to settle from before, back at the parking lot.

I can see his tattoo more clearly. It's like a horseshoe. The ends of the symbol curved upwards, aimed toward the horseshoe's arch. I don't know which Zodiac symbol it is, nor do I care.

I kick my right leg up. The tip of my shoe slams into the Black-Suit's back. He fights strong, but he takes a hit like he's soft. The force of the blow pushes the Black-Suit forward. His face crashes against wooden panels nailed up to block the opening to the front room. His sunglasses break.

I'm free. I got him stumbling. I make my move, left arm and hand numb from the attack. I don't take time to think about all that. I'm just aware of it. I twirl around, and scoop up my gun with my right hand. I get on one knee, aim, and fire four bullets into the Black-Suit's back.

Fuck honor.

It's either him or me.

I get up and stand over him. I put another bullet in him, dead center in the back of the head.

The Black-Suit falls.

Still.

Dead.

I take a step back. He's not the first guy I've killed. I've done this so many times that I don't feel the gun's kickback. I take a look at the hallway where we entered. I see the obelisk just inside. I walk over to it and snatch it up. Before I forget, I snatch my other gun. I see someone standing in the dining room doorway. He's still, just watching me. It's another Black-Suit. I pretend not to look at him, still bent down, gun firmly in my grip. I take a peek toward the one I just offed. He's still there, lying lifeless. Good. That makes this other one someone new.

He's just standing there.

Watching.

I haven't made it known that I'm aware of him. I'm cautious, but confident. These guys are strong and fast, but they can die. I stand up and take a look at my new friend. He's the same, just different tattoo. Left cheek. Different design. It's a cursive capital 'M', the last curve turning up into an arrow.

He's just standing there.

Watching.

This was going to be easy.

I raise my gun, aim, and smile. I'm too damn confident. My father always said fear a man that doesn't appear frightened by the weapon in your hand. I remember that lesson too late. The Black-Suit lifts his hand, opens it, and my gun jumps from my grip into his.

My smile's gone.

…A little confidence too.

But I admire my opponent. Not too long, though. I try an idea, and then lift the obelisk up just like Tamara back at the parking lot. No good. The Black-Suit smiles at the gesture. He raises my gun and cocks it.

I dive into the hallway seconds before he shoots. If those new-fangled bullets can take out these guys, they'll definitely make short work of me. After all, regular bullets can kill me. I've been shot before. It ain't like the movies.

Damnit! My grip opens as I jump. I lose my other gun. It stays in the kitchen as I dive into the hall and duck a shadow and lay low. I'm covered in darkness. The Black-Suit walks to the hallway's kitchen entrance. I swear he's looking right at me, but it seems he can't see through the darkness. He looks perplexed. He steps into the hall. He comes closer, stands right next to me. I'm wondering if my heartbeat will give me away.

I rotate the obelisk around in my grip, holding it with the pyramidal point aimed downward. I got a new hunting knife. I rise slowly, ready to pounce. The Black-Suit cocks his head. I think he hears me. I pause and wait. He does hear something. I hear it too.

There's scratching.

The Black-Suit turns around and walks away. I let him go, simply for the fact that I'm bringing a knife to a gunfight. I'm not too sure how effective stabbing him will be. All he needs to do is recover for a second, even if he starts to smoke up like the other guy. If he gets a good shot off, this story's over. He gets a pass, for now.

The Black-Suit heads back to the dining room. I think he can lead me to Tamara. I take a second before emerging from the dark hallway. I peek around the corner. The coast is clear. I retrieve my gun that's still lying on the kitchen floor. I follow the Black-Suit's path through the dining room. He's gone. I wonder where Tamara is in all this.

I remember she's an Aquarius. I cock my gun and think, *She can get some too. Fuck around and watch me do somethin'.*

I walk to the next room. It's on my left. It's a study. The room is surprisingly untouched by the whirlwind of fury and chaos that ransacked the dining room and kitchen. The room doesn't look like it belongs in this house. Books lay neatly on shelves that are carved from fine wood. A desk holds an unlit lamp and an open book. The neatness and order is short-lived, confined to this room. Next is a living room. There are broken and splintered pictures, chairs, and cracked mirrors. Ripped sofas and shattered statues decorate the room.

Where is Tamara?

This room led back into the dark hallway. I notice again that even with the open door leading outside, no light flickers into the hall. The abyss. There's a staircase across from me. I stand at the base and call up, "Tamara!" My gun is aimed toward the top of the stairs. I look down the hall at the kitchen. My eyes go back to the top of the stairs. I ascend, declaring in a whisper, "I dare somebody to jump-the-fuck-out at me."

I press my back against the wall and climb the stairs further. My gun stays aimed upward as I climb. My eyes go left and right. I watch my back and my front. I skip the last two steps and arrive at the top. There's a door right there in front of me. It's closed. I keep my back against the wall, take a peek down the upstairs hallway, tuck the obelisk under one arm, and then try the door.

There's no resistance. The door isn't locked. It creaks open. I stay outside to investigate the room. It's empty, glowing with sunlight coming through the window. All that decorates the room is the word G.O.D. written in black paint. I don't bother to step inside. Instincts are good, heightened.

Then.

Something tickles my neck, like a mysterious wind.

I can sense the presence at the end of the hallway even before I look. There's a shadowy frame covered in another blanket of darkness. There's the sound of a cackling flame. It's a low noise, like a match. The sound swirls with the faint babble of hissing. I could have sworn the sound was a low chuckle coming from the shadowy figure. My gun's up and aimed. I move into view. Tamara comes from the shadow. A Black-Suit has her gripped.

I step to my left. I got the two of them dead center. Tamara looks frightened. "Let her go," I yell at the Black-Suit.

This is the same Black-Suit that had her hemmed up back at the parking lot. His grin widens. I think I can get a good enough shot to put a bullet through his sly smile, blow it off his face. I line the shot, and that's when I get attacked.

It seems the Black-Suit with my gun was standing inside the room at the top of the stairs, standing just left of the door. He and I plummet down the stairs. It hurts like hell, different stairs jamming into my ribs, and all along my back as I tumble with this idiot over me. In the attack, the obelisk gets tossed away, dropping against the floor in the upstairs hall. I see a flash of bright light. I think nothing of it. I actually think the light comes from all the knocking around that I'm suffering while falling down the stairs. I'm lucky I don't break my neck, or my gun doesn't go off. I'm unlucky that the Black-Suit doesn't break his neck, or his gun doesn't go off…well, maybe I'm lucky for that last sentiment. The gun could easily go off in my stomach or face.

But the light came from the obelisk. Its brilliance blinding the Black-Suit wrestling with Tamara. They're engaged in a good fight. I'm still tumbling. We finally hit the bottom of the stairs. The Black-Suit is quick on his feet. He jams his foot into my ribs. Nothing breaks, but that doesn't mean nothing hurts. I've lost my gun. He's kept his. He stands up straight and aims.

I don't know what's happening between Tamara and the other Black-Suit, but I see the obelisk come flying down the stairs. It lands on the Black-Suit straddling me. It looks like lightning strikes his body when the obelisk bounces off his back. He arches, throwing the gun into the dark hallway. Looks like I should've stabbed him earlier when I had the chance. He would've been all types of fucked up.

I feel lucky until he recovers quickly. The tip of his foot cracks against my sternum. His knee splits my lip. His hands are quick. My head is lobbed back and forth, volleyed from one fist to another. I taste blood, warm and salty. I don't know if it's the blood from the cut above my eye, from mouth, my nose, or all three.

I'm able to see the obelisk resting behind him. I don't know how, though. I swear my eyes are closed. I reach for it and he backs away. I slam the object into his shoulder. He screams. The lightning comes back. It does nothing to me, but it makes my friend dance an electric jig.

I take the advantage. Now it's his head and face being volleyed between my left and right fists. He drops to his knees. I keep swinging until I feel his cheekbone break. But it seems this guy can take a beating. He looks like he's just resting until I eventually get tired. Maybe he's like a werewolf, and only one thing can stop him. I jump to the hallway and find my gun. I turn and put several shots into the Black-Suit's chest. He's done.

I run back to the stairs and look up, taking witness to Tamara being shoved against the wall by the remaining Black-Suit. *Tamara said there could be a fourth one…be careful.*

I aim my gun to make the score 3-0.

The Black-Suit becomes aware of my presence. He stops his attack on Tamara and reacts quickly. He aims an opened hand at me. My gun soars up the stairs before I can pull the trigger. I run after it, moving quicker than when I was a kid. Being desperate to live gives you good reflexes. This sonava bitch gets more than my gun. He gets my whole body crashing into him at top speed. I knock him through the open door, into the room at the top of the stairs. The Black-Suit never gets a grip on my gun, but it lies next to him on the floor. I stomp his face. Once. I go to do it again. He catches my foot. I use my heel to scratch his face. I jump back, out of the room, closing the door.

I yell to Tamara to jump down the stairs. She doesn't argue. She jumps. I follow. Bullets puncture the door and whiz past our heads. We land hard at the bottom of the stairs. I tumble into the hallway, recover, and search for my other gun. I find it. Tamara removes the obelisk from the dead Black-Suit.

I grab Tamara and return fire up the stairs. The shots are just shields, and they buy us time to keep the third Black-Suit at bay. Tamara heads back to the kitchen. I follow.

Back.

In the kitchen. We're not being followed. Not yet. I stay alert. Tamara moves the dead Black-Suit aside and begins kicking the set of wooden boards covering the entrance to the front room. I take a moment to help her. The rotting boards are broken. I notice another set of boards on my right, next to the hallway entrance. I just guess there's another passageway behind them. I ask Tamara, "What about these?"

"Not yet," she answers. "This way first."

I continue. I'm alert. My senses are heightened. I feel as if I can see every room in the house, and feel every presence. I can't see or feel the Black-Suit with this extrasensory vision. I take a look at the one I'd slain earlier. I keep him in view, just in case. *Get up and I got more bullets for you!*

We bust through.

This area was also well-kept. It was large, stretching horizontally. There was a piano directly in front of us. There was a fireplace to the right. The room was furnished with bronze trophies, rare paintings, books, and an elegant chandelier. Tamara walks in. I post up right at the entrance, gun aimed at the dark hallway.

I'm ready.

Tamara comes up behind me.

"I have it," she exclaims with an excited smile.

I look down at the object in her hand. It's flat, black, and oblong. There's a square in its center. I look at the obelisk in her hand. It looks like it fits. I already know that these two objects were meant to come together. Join.

"Keep your gun up," Tamara instructs as she passes me. She starts kicking the second set of wooden panels. She breaks through quickly. I can see a set of stairs leading to the cellar. She walks down casually.

I mumble to myself, "This white woman is gonna get me killed."

I follow. The stairway is dark, but short-lived. A faint electrical light burns in the cellar, located around the corner of the stairs. The basement's small and unfurnished, save for an oak table in the center of the room. There are two closets. The writing on the wall catches my eye. It spells *Y-T O.K.* followed by eight periods and a question mark. I have no idea what that means, but the phrase is everywhere. It's written in white paint, written as if it has the rhythm of a nursery rhyme. The only thing that takes my eyes off the continuing phrase is the sleeping beauty resting on the oak table. I didn't see her at first, but now I do.

Tamara's been staring at her the whole time. Her eyes are dotted with tears.

The woman on the table is black and beautiful. She's wearing a decorative, flowing dress, its blue and gold colors flowing into one another looked like water and gold making illustrious patterns and designs. Her dress appears to glow amidst the cellar's darkness. She's alive with color. Her face is dark and smooth. I'm reminded of when I first saw the obelisk on my desk. Radiant, I believe is the word. The woman's hair is coiled into locks. They're thick, and bubble from her head like strong tree branches. They're at her sides, draped elegantly passed her waist.

"Oh. My. God," escapes from my mouth. I can't control the verbal jailbreak. What else could I say? Silence seems like sacrilege. I'm drawn to the table. I look down at the woman and ask Tamara, "This is your friend?"

Tamara's silent.

"Tamara!" I call.

Tamara just says, "So beautiful." I turn and see her crying. Her watering eyes, becoming more and more flooded, drop tears onto her face. "Now...I realize that," she continues. "You were so powerful. I'm...I'm sorry...I'm sorry I did this to you."

Did this to her?

I put the gun in Tamara's face.

"You mind repeating that last statement?" My teeth are grinding. I'm angry. I feel like I have more of an obligation to protect the sleeping beauty than the woman who hired me to find her. "You did this to her?"

Tamara doesn't even flinch. She pays the gun no attention. Her head drops in shame. "I did this to myself."

There's noise from upstairs.

I make a quick glance in the direction of the sound. I look back at Tamara and demand in a rough voice, "Whole story, sweetheart. I want it all."

Tamara continues to look away. "I have three names," she declares through a burst of tears. "I am Tamara. Ta-Ma-Ra." She cries heavier. She yells. "I am the balance of earth and the sun. I am Africa."

Who is this white woman foolin'? Africa?

I cock the gun. I wanted an answer! I get this? She did this to her friend. Then she says she did this to herself. Then she declares she's Africa. She needs to sell what she's smokin'. She'd make a killing.

And then I get it.

I look at the woman on the table. I look at Tamara. I have my doubts, but I also have my conclusion. And as weird as this mystery has been, I'm still a great detective. But doubt let's me ask one more question. *There's no way...was there?* I feel foolish. I've seen my reality flushed down the toilet for the past hour or so, and I got a problem with this? I take another look at the woman on the table, then again at Tamara.

There was noise coming from upstairs.

Louder.

Closer.

God! Please, wake up.

I lower my gun. I want to say something. Tamara beats me to it.

"The world made me feel so ashamed of who I am," she says to me like a confession. "They made me fear myself. My power. What I could do." I'm listening. I'm even ignoring the creaking on the stairs. "Without the proper guidance my power grew. It was out of control. Everywhere I walked I could hear people's thoughts. I could touch their souls or even the depths of their emptiness where a soul was supposed to be. The things I learned through my power...even I feared them. It got to be too much."

The creaking stops. Someone is waiting around the corner.

I'll kill him when he steps inside the room.

Tamara finally looks at me.

"My power was so intense, and I was so afraid of myself, that I could only live in other people's bodies." She says it. "I could only see through another's eyes. I could only live in another's mind. And sometimes, I was the only soul someone had."

Can you arrest someone for stealing another's body?

"Why not?" Tamara hisses as if she could hear the question asked in my head. "So many have stolen my dreams and my faith. But I got them back. I studied. And I can live again as me."

"Where do the Devil Chakras come in?" I ask in a low and cautious voice.

Tamara just hands me the black disc and the obelisk. I accept them, holstering my gun. "Let's worry about them later," she says. "I have a destiny with my real body." I stare at the two items. An obelisk and a black disc. Tamara instructs, "Place the obelisk on the table, above my body's head. Then slide the black oval onto it. The obelisk must penetrate through the oval."

Sounds suggestive, but, "Okay..."

I do exactly as I'm told. I place the obelisk at the head of the unconscious, black woman lying on the table. I slip the black disc over it. The woman I've shared the adventure with drops to the floor. I don't move. She looks like she's fainted, body crumpled atop itself. Even if I wanted to move, I couldn't. The combined objects hold me in place, my grip around the obelisk. My body begins to vibrate. The ground shakes. I can feel a surge of energy ride up my spine. My back arches. The woman on the table does the same. She writhes and contorts, breathing heavy like she's about to have an orgasm. To be honest, I feel the same. The sensation is erotic. The black woman opens her eyes, life and spirit slipping back into her, and I can feel it happening.

We're having a moment.

A strong wind billows around the room. I feel the wind massage me. My entire body feels relaxed, like I'm bathing in warm water. I'm still shaking. The wind condenses into a black cloud. It separates in two, and each half of the ethereal blanket slips into the pours, nostrils, and in between the lips of myself, and the woman on the table.

The sensation stops.

I exhale heavy breaths, but I'm not exhausted.

Tamara's no longer trapped in another body. She sits up on the table and examines her original physique. I do the same. It's a helluva sight. She jumps from the table and wraps her arms around me. She looks different, but I know it's the same person. Her spirit is a little brighter. She feels more alive.

"Oh, God," she exclaims. "Thank you. Thank you so much, brutha."

I hold her tight, like I've been looking for her all my life.

"Nothing to it, sista," I assure her.

Tamara backs away. Her dark brown eyes glow with life. A rich smile on her full lips. There was spirit inside this woman. My eyes absorb the sight. I'm smiling, wide, like a fourteen-year-old schoolboy eyeing his crush. Tamara still has some concern. "There are two left," she reminds me. She's talking about the Devil Chakras. "Taurus and Aquarius are near." She grabs the obelisk and the oval from the table. "They want to destroy consciousness," she tells me. "They want to smother the natural elements that make up this world. I came across them when I was trapped in her body." she points at the limp and lifeless woman lying on the basement floor. "I cursed myself. I did not feel the same in her body—in any body. But I was trapped inside her. I couldn't escape. And it took me some time to get control of this woman's body. It was a struggle." Tamara manages to smile and laugh at herself. "Can you imagine?" She says looking at me. "I was fighting to be someone else?"

"Go figure," I exhale. I share the light moment. It's needed. But my eyes catch something, even in the darkness. I can see wavy lines magically being etched into the fallen woman's forehead. I take a split second to see if Tamara notices too. Then I go for my gun.

It's too late.

The woman's up! Her arms are wrapped around Tamara. The joined items of obelisk and black disc drop from Tamara's hand and bounce away. The Devil Chakra's face is wild! Now I can see her tattoo clearly. I remember her telling me she's an Aquarius in the car. I remember the voice that spoke. It was deep. Otherworldly. It wasn't Tamara's voice that spoke those words. It was something else. Now the real entity inside that woman had *its* body back.

I raise my gun. "I don't think so," I tell the Devil Chakra.

The Devil Chakra opens her hand. There's a glowing and writhing red aura billowing in the palm of her hand. It gathers like a furious storm. I see Tamara close her eyes. She looks like she's concentrating, and I hope she can work it out quick. She does. Tamara spins around, loosening herself from the Devil Chakra's grip. She opens the palm of her hand and releases an invisible force. The Devil Chakra's body lifts through the air. I waste no time and fire my gun into her stomach as she soars through the air. The Devil Chakra crashes near the basement entrance, and quickly jumps back to her feet.

She's up. Unfazed. And I put four obelisk-bullets in her.

Tamara looks just as confused. We both notice the other Black-Suit walk into the basement. It's Black-Suit-Taurus. Tamara gets in front of me, shielding me.

The Black-Suit aims his gun.

Bullets don't fly. The gun does. From his hands and into Tamara's. She gives it to me. *Fuck you, Black-Suit boy.* Tamara gets behind me. I cock, aim, and fire both guns. It's a parade of bullets. The female Devil Chakra spins around, several rounds of bullet fire tearing at her. She's tossed into the wall. Black-Suit Taurus fairs a little better. He executes a trick, opening the palm of his hand and deflecting my gunfire.

Devil Chakra Aquarius slithers up the wall. She's unscathed. She takes the Black-Suit's side. I dispense more rounds until the guns are empty.

My targets still stand. They're unharmed.

I holster my guns and charge forward, fists balled for action. It's time to go old school. Black-Suit Taurus grabs my neck. I'm nervous he's gonna snap it. Instead, he just tosses me across the room, over the table that Tamara's original body rested on. I hit the floor, but there's no pain. The wall cracks. My body is contorted uncomfortably. I regain stance in time to see Tamara swipe her arm at the Devil Chakras. Both fall back. They look like the force of a speeding train hit them. Tamara runs to me. She asks if I'm okay.

"Rick." Her voice is soothing when it speaks my name. "Are you all right?"

I pick a fine time to become infatuated with her presence. I just stare at her. She's dark, rich, and beautiful. "Yeah, I'm all right."

Then.

I notice the two forms standing over us.

Damn, they're quick.

Tamara can see the concern in my eyes. Her power paints the picture of the spiritless forms standing over her and I. She doesn't need to turn around. She knows. I hope she has a blast of power ready should they come any closer.

The Devil Chakras grope at us.

I pull Tamara closer to me, and I wrap my arms around her to keep her safe. Tamara wiggles her right arm, loosening my grip on her. She aims her hand out and magically calls the conjoined obelisk and black disc into her hand.

Tamara pushes my grip completely loose. My arms open. She turns around and jams the obelisk deep into Devil Chakra Aquarius' chest. Tamara lets go of the object as the woman jerks wildly. Her spastic body slams into Black-Suit Taurus, knocking him to the floor. Strands of purple light jump from the Devil Chakra's wound. It wraps around her like an electric squid. The woman's flesh cracks and begins to recede. The scene is grotesque. I'd say I wouldn't wish it on my worst enemy, but I believe it's happening to my worst enemy. Her insides melt, bubble, and then turn into dust, spilling from her mouth and nose. Her body eventually does the same.

The obelisk hangs in the air, hovering magically over a pile of dust that was once a female Devil Chakra. Tamara calls the object to her. Black-Suit Taurus is on his feet. He looks determined, but not as much as Tamara. She's got the gaze of a warrior on the hunt. I'm rooting for her. I'm also scared of her more than I am of the remaining Devil Chakra, even with his hand glowing with that red energy. He might be Shonuf with the glow, but Tamara's got that Bruce Leeroy thing going.

Black-Suit Taurus does what he has to. He jumps forward, but he doesn't attack Tamara or myself. He slams his glowing fist into the floor. The house shakes on impact. Tamara falls against the floor. She manages to keep the obelisk in her grasp. My body, on the other hand, jumps up and down like a Mexican Jumping Bean. The house's quake is intense.

I see Black-Suit Taurus' body become consumed inside a red aura. He explodes. There's no force with the explosion. The house ceases to quake. Tamara and I stand up.

"Wait," I order sternly. "Just wait. Don't move."

A loud sound echoes from upstairs. The house shakes again, but not with the same force. My ears catch something. Creaking. The floor. Upstairs. It ain't footsteps. It's pressure. The house is caving in. The crashing noise echoes again. The roof and the top floor don't exist anymore.

"Reverse the last command," I quickly correct. "Run like hell."

We make our way to the stairs. There's another rumble and a loud crash. Our exit is blocked by debris made up of the upper levels of the house. I move Tamara out of the way just as another monstrous scream echoes and more of the house collapses inward. I guide Tamara to the farthest corner of the basement, and we wait.

Tamara holds me tight. I hold her.

An overwhelming feeling of guilt gets to bury me before the debris from the collapsing house. "Buried alive, huh," Tamara says in a sad tone.

Debris crashes in.

I sigh and tell her, "Sista, I've been through a lot today. And as much as some of the things I've witnessed have been strange and horrible...they've been amazing. I don't think this is the end." I look at her and smile. "I'm pretty sure you got some sorta power that'll help us get outta here."

More debris falls in. It looks heavy. It should kill us instantly when it reaches our corner.

"I don't," Tamara answers me.

The graffiti lining the wall starts to glow a dark red. Spirals of light, the same dark red color, reach out from the wall, tearing it open. Large piles of the house's debris tumble in. We hold one another tighter, if that's possible. Tamara concentrates, focusing her power to reverse the flow of the debris and mend the ceiling. It works for a while, but she becomes exhausted, overwhelmed. She goes back to holding me tight. I close my eyes and try and concentrate.

The debris stops

I did it!

The ceiling collapses. The house's debris attacks us, rushing in, screaming. I close my eyes and hold tight to Tamara. I anticipate the heavy debris, and at least a split second of intense pain before my body snaps and is crushed by the fall…air?…The cool air? The breeze?

Outside.

We're somewhere, in the middle of nowhere, embracing on the grassy, earth floor. We're far from the collapsed house. We're far from thirty-three Pine Hill Drive. I lift myself from the ground, but not before I kiss it. And it's more like launching myself to my feet. I help Tamara up before enjoying a quick breath and dusting myself off. I turn to her and grin, "Like I said, amazing."

"Thank you," she commends me, congratulating me with a hug and a gentle kiss on the cheek. I accept. Who wouldn't? She's gorgeous. "Thank you for getting me out of there."

I tell her she's welcome, anytime. Then I look at the joined obelisk and the black disc lying in the grass. "I guess you should thank these magical items. It got you back to where you belong, took down the bad guys, and even got us here. Where ever here is." Tamara backs away. She looks at the objects and then at me. She has a curious eye and a smile. I return the gesture and say, "Unless, that was you who managed to blink us free from that place. Either way, you can make the check out to Richard Hunter."

"No," she says holding her smile in place and aimed at me. "It wasn't me."

I take another breath. "Well, now we gotta find our way back." Tamara returns to her old ways and becomes little-to-no help. She sits on the grass, basking in the sun, feet outstretched. What the hell, huh? Might as well relax too. We got time. No Devil Chakras after us, I hope. I take a seat next to her. "Feels weird to be you again, doesn't it?"

"Not really," she says. "It feels warm, natural. It feels like…me."

I just snicker and give her some helpful advice, "Well of all the lives you jumped into—"

"Why did it have to be yours," she finishes prematurely.

That's not what I was going to say. She's not too much of a psychic. I shake my head and conclude, "No. Why did it have to be some crazy wench partnered with three thugs equipped with telepathic powers, and had the ability to trap you in her body?"

Tamara chuckles.

"Maybe it was destiny," she says.

"So I gotta look for him?" I joke. "This Destiny character."

Tamara ignores my comment. She adds, "Maybe it was for me to know who was going to try and stop Kem Wer."

Oh, great! A new word. More cryptic banter.

She looks at me with a stern face. "It's happening, y'know," she says in a matter-of-fact way. "Kem Wer is coming."

"Just let me know if that's a good or a bad thing," I request.

"It's a good thing," she informs me. She plays with the grass and then says, "I know you're frustrated with all the cryptic banter." She leans closer to me, armed with a beautiful smile. "I am psychic, y'know?"

"Great." I roll my eyes.

Then she stands up, just as I'm getting comfortable. "Kem Wer is something we'll study together." She extends her hand. "Do you need a partner Detective? I say again, my resume lists me as a psychic."

I take her hand and lift. I brush the dirt off my pants and declare, "*Psychotic,* maybe. And I don't need a partner. I need a car. I'm gonna need one to get us out of this place."

"No you don't," she tells me in a proud voice.

"You wanna walk…g-goddess…?"

Hey, that's just what she looks like.

Tamara steps toward me, shaking her head.

"Neither myself nor those idols 'blinked' us out of that basement, *Detective,*" she announces.

I raise an eyebrow, point to myself, and mouth the question, "*You mean me?*" She confirms with a positive nod, and my entire reality gets completely ripped apart. Tamara cups my hand. "My King," she says in a musical tone. "Walk with me, hand-in-hand. I am Aquarius-Proper. We have work to do."

I take her other hand. Our foreheads meet. I'm breaking the rules. Someone is walking into my life. They're staying. Most likely, we'll be walking together. Forever. Hand-in-hand.

I tap into that new power.

She and I vanish.

Gone to another story.

TALES OF THE DJEDHI

Though there were dark times, the tales of the Djedhi had no sunset.
Their stories of adventure were numerous and ongoing.
This is but one.

The desert sands glimmered as they exhaled waves of blistering heat. The pregnant dunes seemed to give birth to a mass of mounted warriors, an army trudging over the horizon, coming from the east. The army was foreign, made up of current conquerors occupying East Africa. The indigenous tongue spoke of these conquerors as *Tamahu*, descendants of the Macedonian named Alexandre. They were more horde than organized militia, and they were on a hunt, tracking down the remaining warriors defending Africa, and all its knowledge.

The army's leader was a clean-shaven man, bald, wearing a warrior's cap, leather armor, and an assortment of knives. He was mounted on a chariot dragged by horses. He had a round head, and he possessed sharp features. His skin blistered a deep, sweaty red, having never truly adapted to the African climate, though he was raised in Egypt—the land where his army had come from.

He surveyed the vast sandy sea in front of him, his sharp eyesight catching the activity of a settlement lying in the distance. The army found its prize. The leader gazed deeper. There were no women and children running around the settlement. It was just men. Ngr warriors. The outlaws sought by the foreign rulers. The leader considered that if the Ngrs were true warriors, they would have stayed for a real fight. The Ngr warriors were cowards to him, but he was delighted that his expedition into Africa's interior did not prove fruitless. He put his hand on his sword and moved his chariot out in front of his army. This was his position of command. His keen eyesight again narrowed on the camp in the far distance. He removed the sword from its sheath and signaled his troops by lifting it high into the air. He screamed a command and battle cry, his sword pointing straight toward the settlement. His chariot was the first to charge. His men followed fast in pursuit.

The cavalry was only several strides into their attack when the leader noticed the desert sands magically open up in front of him. Large amounts of small circles of sand swirled, and dropped into the earth creating open pits. Laying wait inside, and emerging from the sandy terrain was a regiment of Ngr warriors. Judgment day had arrived for the foreign occupiers. It seemed like the dead rose from shallow graves. The Ngr warriors, buried for attack, now rising up to strike.

The warriors' faces were as black as the night, black like death. The weapons in their hands signaled they were prepared to deliver death's message to Africa's invaders.

There came their collective scream!

The scream echoed and reverberated on invisible walls, tearing into the eardrums of the invaders' mounts. The beasts bucked. Riders were cast off. The foreign army's advance ceased. Their mounts bucked wildly, jarred by the attacks just as much as the riders. From the southern horizon came Ngr bowmen. A garrison of arrows was launched at the foreigners. Each arrow met a mark.

The infantry of Ngr warriors advanced on the foreign army, even through the shower of arrows launched by the bowmen. Lances, spears, and swords cut down the foreign army. The Tamahu soldiers' last glimpses of life saw advancing on them robes the color of sand. Black faces and sharp metal were the last images the foreign soldiers' eyes captured. Not even nature supported them. The desert winds lashed them. The African heat intensified, almost as if nature itself was magically at the command of the Ngr warriors.

The sky poured arrows for rain.

The invading army was consumed.

The Ngrs suffered no casualties.

The bowmen receded from the horizon as the robed warriors glided like ghosts back to the camp in the distance. They were like sand wraiths, warriors of the desert.

Tedros was surprised to hear his name called. He was finally assigned a solo mission. He was excited. His wife's head quickly lifted from his shoulder. Tedros sensed her eyes on him. Her grip around his arm tightened. He turned and kissed her. He stood up and bowed to the elder who had just called his name. The elder, named Mazi, commanded him to sit. Tedros obeyed. He knew that after the council was held, there would be a private meeting between he and Mazi. His wife embraced him again, her grip tighter. Her head was heavier on his shoulder. She wanted to hold him so tight and close that he could not escape, not leave her side.

Tedros kissed her hand.

"It will be alright, Sauda," he expressed to her. She only responded with a teardrop on his shoulder. Mazi then adjourned the meeting. The other Djedhi dispersed into their tents. Tedros stood up, guiding his wife to her feet. He looked at his wife, Sauda. Her dark skin absorbed the afternoon sunlight. Her watery eyes absorbed Tedros. He wiped her tears away and kissed her again. "This is a chance to really show me how strong your protective magic can be."

Sauda's somber mood broke into light laughter. "I'm sure you'd like that," Sauda said wiping her remaining tears away. She was skilled in tantric healing arts.

Tedros felt better knowing he could still make his wife laugh. He reminded her, "Besides, I go into battle almost daily. This won't even be half as dangerous." He saw her contemplating his words.

It was at that moment when a fellow Djedhi warrior walked up to Tedros and whispered into his ear, "I'll ready your weapons for the task." It was not exactly the news Tedros needed his wife to hear, and Sauda heard every word the messenger relayed. Tedros thanked his fellow warrior in a sarcastic tone. He looked back at his wife who was staring at him with one raised eyebrow.

Tedros explained, "The weapons are a necessary precaution...for when I travel." Sauda remained silent. Her expression intensified, purposely and amusingly so. Tedros smiled at her. "I believe you're jealous that I'll be going back to Kemet."

Sauda looked away, her head down. She shook her head in agreement and then looked back at her husband. "A little," she admitted. She stroked his cheek and requested, "Go by our apartment."

Tedros stiffened, anger stirring. "Why, so I can see savages living in our quarters?

"No," Sauda said, forcefully. "For me. For us." She hugged him.

Tedros commented, "Maybe Mazi should've picked you to go."

Sauda leaned away and told Tedros, "You should go see him. I want to know exactly what this task is."

"I know what it is," Tedros shrugged. "He wants me to decode a card. And then he's going to ask me to find scrolls on the subject matter." Tedros pulled his wife back into his embrace.

This was the new life for the Djedhi Khepri, the Wisdom Keepers. For several grand cycles, calculated at twenty-five thousand years, they were the guardians of knowledge, wisdom, and understanding. The Djedhi Khepri was an ancient order dedicated to freedom, justice, and equality. Every land, in and outside of Africa, called upon the Djedhi Khepri to guard their learning centers, libraries, and all branches of government. Their main operation was in Kemet, also referred to as Egypt. The land was not a kingdom, as many perceived. It was a learning center, a place where many traveled to study. Kemet housed the most ancient doctrines dedicated to all forms of study, which came from all corners of the ancient globe. The Djedhi Khepri made Kemet their home. They guarded all knowledge, and now, they were retrievers of the very knowledge decoded and documented for many grand cycles. The Djedhi had been outlaws in their own land, removed from their home settlement by foreign invaders.

The Djedhi Khepri fended off the intruders long enough for another regiment to escape with as many women, children, and scrolls of knowledge as they could carry. The barbarians never attacked in a single crushing wave. They came in spurts. That gave the Djedhi enough time to decide what to do. Some would flee, taking a good deal of the population and scrolls. Others stayed to defend. Those who escaped fled in every direction, even fleeing in the direction the barbarians invaded from. The Djedhi Khepri dispersed to the east, west, north, and south.

Tedros, his wife, and the regiment they escaped with, settled west. Their encampment rested outside a small village south of the Libyan border. The village was filled with people from the urban centers of Central Africa. The village was made up of students conducting the life-study of their chosen paths. Before anyone could attempt a profession, it was necessary to journey out to nature and get to know its every degree. The group of students welcomed the band of Djedhi, but was disturbed by the news they brought with them. Kemet had been invaded.

That was four years ago.

Tedros opened his eyes, surveying the small camp. "I'll go by our apartment," he told Sauda, kissing her forehead. "And then I'll return to you."

Sauda returned a kiss, placing it on Tedros' cheek. "I'll be satisfied with your return. Everything else is extra." She patted him on the shoulder and stepped away. "Go to Mazi and get your assignment. He's waiting." She disappeared into their tent.

Tedros made his way toward the elder's tent. A guard lay outside. He allowed Tedros entrance, announcing through the curtain that Djedhi Tedros had arrived. Mazi stopped all manner of activity. The elder turned and greeted Tedros. Tedros bowed respectfully, but his eyes could not help but notice a second person in the tent. It was another Djedhi named Paki. He was not just any Djedhi. He and Tedros had formed a friendship ever since the two had been classmates, entering the Djedhi temples in the same year. Tedros was surprised to see him. Paki had been on assignment in Kemet, gone for two months. Tedros believed he would be gone longer. He was not worried about his friend, but he was excited to see he had returned.

Paki waved to him nonchalantly, as if no time had passed.

Tedros ran up to Paki and greeted, *"My ngr!"* Paki stood up. They threw their arms around one another. Paki greeted Tedros the same. He stepped back and examined his friend. Tedros bombarded Paki with questions. "What did you find? How does the land look? How are the people?"

Paki lifted a hand as if parrying the flurry of questions. "The land is fine," Paki assured. "It's not in flames. Most of us live in the upper regions of Kemet, settled closer to Ta-Seti." He informed, "We still govern ourselves. It's hard, but manageable." He looked at the elder and then back to Tedros. He began to explain, "The lower region, toward the Nile's flow out to sea, is governed by the invaders. It's a very mixed population there. The government presses hard on the people. They believe telling people what's best for them equals government. This has caused uproar, especially with the continuing…debates." Paki barely breathed life into the last word. Tedros almost missed it. His ears caught it, and barely processed it.

"Debate," he questioned his friend, almost to make sure that was the word Paki pronounced. "What debate? What's there to debate?"

Then Mazi sighed, stepping away from the two friends, heading to the back of his tent. Paki and Tedros watched the elder walk away somberly. Tedros put his eyes on Paki, anticipating an answer. Paki remained silent. Mazi spoke instead. "They still argue over the validity of Serapis."

Tedros looked at Mazi and Paki. "I can end the debate for them," he said. "Serapis is not real."

"Let them debate," the elder commented with a thunderous voice. "It is within this confusion where we can sneak in and obtain more scrolls, or make new cards glyphed and abridged with their knowledge." Both Djedhi straightened their posture and bowed respectfully toward the elder, even though his back was turned. Mazi was not being rude to the younger Djedhi. He was merely contemplating other moves for the entire unit of Wisdom Keepers. After some time, he turned to Paki and spoke, "Show Tedros your card."

Tedros looked at Paki with a wide-eyed expression. "You created a card," he said surprised. There was a smile on his face. He was ecstatic about the news.

Paki nodded humbly. "Two, actually," he corrected, but still with complete humility. The Djedhi opened the pouch strapped to his shoulder. He removed two parchments etched with drawings. He presented them to Tedros who held the cards carefully. "I'm going to the nearest city to get them etched by professionals," Paki continued. "I'm also going to get them pressed to tablet."

The intricate designs etched onto the cards were magnificent. Paki captured deeper meanings with colors, angles, and layout. Years of study, and a wide range of lessons, were condensed into a single drawing. One drawing depicted a tall, mighty tower. A violent bolt of lightning was striking it. A man and a woman were being tossed from the top of the tower's window. The second drawing was of an amalgamated creature. It had the physique of a man, with the breasts of a woman, the head of a goat, and the wings of a divine being. Its legs were folded, in the lotus position. The creature pointed up with one hand, and down with the other. He pointed to a yellow crescent moon above him, and he pointed to a black crescent moon below him. Atop the creature's head was a long-necked, three pronged crown that sprouted fire. In the center of the creature's forehead was the symbol of a five-pointed star. On the creature's lap balanced the Uraeus, a pole with a ball at the top, with two winding snakes whose mouths opened to swallow the scepter's topmost point.

Tedros was in awe, looking back and forth to each picture. They were powerful in appearance, but he had to admit they were also a little bleak, gloomy and fatalistic. Paki read the concern in Tedros' eyes. He spoke when Tedros looked back at him, "I know. They're creepy. I was instructed to make the designs look horrifying."

"That's the point," said Mazi, answering the unspoken question of 'why' that was expressed in Tedros' eyes. The elder continued to clarify, "We need some of these images to look as malicious, bleak, and as horrifying as possible. They must frighten away *and* be misinterpreted by the average mind." Mazi stepped closer with each word spoken. "These symbols, art, and etchings will be for the initiated and the ready-of-mind." He tapped a finger against his head. "It will be for those willing to put balance back to this world, not for those willing to disrupt natural order." The elder turned his back again. He spoke aloud after contemplating, "There will be those who abuse our lessons—just as there are now. There will be those, even who are direct descendants of us that will fear what they see. Their minds will be wrapped up in a programming and indoctrination that is unalike in their nature. A programming that will tangle their thoughts."

"It's already happening," said Paki, addressing that the future Mazi spoke of was taking shape in their present. "Most of the ancient ways and lessons are outlawed. If their so-called god, Serapis, does not will it, then it's deemed unholy, regardless of the lesson...or common sense."

There was silence. No one spoke. Even nature's sounds, and the sounds from the settlement outside the tent, were silent. Each of the Djedhi contemplated the situation they were in as a people. They each wondered how it would continue long after they were gone. Tedros broke the silence, asking, "What's my assignment?"

Mazi faced him with stern eyes. The elder drew another card and handed it to Tedros. In the Djedhi's hand was the etching of a robed woman sitting between two pillars. "This is your assignment. Decode this card. Find the scrolls that are based *only* on its *surface* meaning, not the deeper aspects of its symbol."

"Yes, *A-Sir*," Tedros complied.

Mazi raised a finger and said more. "Wait, Tedros. I am not finished." Tedros stood tall. Mazi's words had a way of bestowing pride into his students and subjects. "That is the first part of your assignment," he said. "Next, you are also to bring back the *Scrolls of Enoch*. It is a recent scripture, but it documents, through symbols, the terrible events of four-thousand years ago, as well as higher sciences."

"Yes, *A-Sir*," Tedros said as he bowed.

Mazi returned the gesture, and then he concluded, "Your journey begins in three days. Let your wife assist you in decoding. Use your resources. She's a brilliant woman."

Tedros nodded. He handed Paki's cards back to him, and kept the one he received from Elder Mazi. Paki said to him, "I leave the same time you do." Paki clarified, "To the urban center."

Both warriors looked at Elder Mazi. He gave them approval to leave his tent. There was nothing more he wished to discuss. "If you have any further questions, Tedros, I'll be here," said the elder. Both Tedros and Paki bowed toward their elder. Mazi politely guided them to the exit, stepping outside into nature's warmth. "Return to me when you have decoded the card. I'll critique your answer. Then you'll be off."

"Yes, *A-Sir*," Tedros addressed. He and Paki walked away, blending in to the settlement's daily activities.

"Your assignment shouldn't take long," Paki told him. "All you need to do is find scrolls, not draw a glyph."

Tedros calculated the potential time his assignment would take. "It'll still be more than a month's time." He then began to list the tasks, "Travel—back and forth. I have to get into the temple, sneak around, and find the specific scrolls. I have to review them. I have to decide what to take, what to leave." Tedros exhaled. "How did you fair with all that, plus having to draw a glyph?"

"When I stowed away inside a temple, I was there for days," Paki began, a slight smile on his face as he recalled his adventure. "Being inside the temples will be your best cover. The invaders don't enter the temples. I think that's a political move. It makes it look as if they respect the area." Paki paused, and then he added, "Of course, our people can't enter the temples either, so I don't know how much respect is really there." Paki continued as the two walked to the outskirts of the camp, heading to a distant dune. "But, I didn't always rest in the temple. I got out. I traveled to where our people's settlements were, and I joined in festivities. I never revealed my identity, or why I was there. I just blended in. I took up at an inn. And I met a woman who I intend to go back for."

Tedros then joked, "Is that the inspiration for your drawing—" Paki playfully struck Tedros on the arm. He ducked and swiped away another salvo of playful strikes. "And here I thought *Banebdjedet* was your inspiration. I'll at least know what to look for."

The punches ceased.

"Look for," Paki questioned.

Tedros rubbed his arm, feigning injury. His laughter cooled into a smile. "You just stay right here, brother. Give me this woman's name. I'll get her for you. I'll bring her back."

Paki shook his head, no. "I'll do you one better, *ngr*." He then propositioned, "I'll meet you there *with* Sauda. With all the time passed, she will have missed you. I'll introduce you to my woman. Then, we'll travel back together." He looked over his shoulder, his eyes on the camp. His sight found Mazi's tent. "I'll clear it with Mazi and the other elders." He looked back at Tedros. "If it can't be done, then we'll go with your plan."

"A deal," Tedros agreed. They shook hands to honor the friendly contract.

"You should get to your decoding," suggested Paki.

"Right," Tedros acknowledged. He inspected the card Mazi gave to him. He bid his friend farewell and then walked back to camp. Paki stood alone, his gaze reaching out over the horizon. His thoughts turned to the beautiful Nuba woman he met while on his assignment. "I'll see you, again," he spoke his promise into the air. He hoped the desert winds would catch his words and deliver his message to the Nuba woman who lived far off.

Hours later. Inside his tent, Tedros examined the card imparted to him by his elder. He stared at the card without thought, just taking in the picture lying in front of him. The task of deciphering its meaning was just a test. The Council of Djedhi Elders put forth a mental test before sending out their Djedhi into the field. If the mind was prepared, then too was the body. The card lay on a table inside Tedros' tent. His gaze turned contemplative after some time. He tried catching a glimpse of the surface allegory the card displayed, not the deeper meaning of the etching. But the more esoteric and occult science, symbolized in the card's drawing, screamed and jumped out at him. The card's deeper secrets constantly caught his attention. He batted them away with mental hands; parting them like the mythological character Shu-Anhur did the sea to lead the fallen stars, jewels of the cosmos, back into heaven.

Tedros took a breath. He closed his eyes, concentrated, and then opened them. He first observed the woman etched onto the card. She sat on a bench, dressed in a light blue gown and robe, the goddess crown atop her head. She was between two pillars. Tedros understood the woman was a representation of the goddess Auset, also called Isis. The two pillars were masculine principles, phallic. They guarded her, much like the Djedhi Khepri guarded all forms of wisdom. They were symbols of her husband, Ausar, also called Osiris, and her son, Heru, also called Horus. The pillars were strong, powerful, unmoving in their task to guard the woman.

Was Tedros being asked to find scrolls on the *Foundation of the Woman*, the knowledge as to her importance and why she must be protected?

No. He thought.

Tedros wanted to seek his wife's opinion, but she was meditating in another tent, secluded as she prepared her body to anoint Tedros with her protective magic. Sauda did take a glance at the picture before she left the tent. She remarked the woman reminded her of Tedros, to which Tedros felt a little offended, emasculated. How could his wife think of him as a woman and not a man? Sauda laughed sweetly at her husband's ignorance. She corrected her husband by saying the woman looked as if she was guarding the scroll in her hand, a keeper of wisdom. It seemed she was on the very same assignment as Tedros. Sauda then departed.

This thought sparked a revelation. He believed his wife unintentionally gave him the key. He observed the scroll in the woman's hands. He noticed an inscription scribbled on the parchment. *Ta-Ra*, it read. It was two words compounded into one. Tedros whispered the words, contemplating. "Ta-Ra," he said. It meant *From Earth to Sun*; low to high; a royal pathway. "Ascension," Tedros questioned. He cursed, "Damn. Thinking too deep. There's a million ways to go. Why do Wisdom Keepers have to be so damn knowledgeable?"

His eyes again focused on the scroll. Then he uttered, "Secrets." A thought started to grow. He announced, "Symbols. The secret art of symbols." Tedros stood up, proud. He spoke, "There are five books on the language of symbols. Each one designated to an element."

Tedros snatched the card and exited the tent. He walked through the Djedhi settlement, making his way to Mazi's dwelling. Again, a guard blocked the entrance. Tedros bowed to the guard. The Djedhi guard informed Tedros that Mazi was busy. He would have to return in the morning. Tedros did not put up a fight. He instead bowed gracefully, and then returned to his tent. He placed the card on the table and lay on one of the cots. "The five books," Tedros said to himself. Everything about his assignment became real. He was leaving. He was returning to his home. He was going to miss his wife.

Sauda entered shortly after. She lay next to him, cuddling close. Tedros felt her warm hand touch his cheek. She kissed him. Tedros leaned close for more, but his wife backed away. "I'm gaining my strength to give to you," she reminded him with a coy tone in her voice. "You'll have me tomorrow night."

Tedros exhaled melodramatically. He revealed to Sauda, "I know what I'm looking for. I decoded the card. With your help, of course."

"My help," Sauda pondered, her eyes closed.

"Yes," Tedros said. "The answer was in the scroll the woman was holding."

"So, what do you seek," Sauda asked folding her leg over her husband.

"The five books on symbols," Tedros answered, his voice cracking. He squirmed as he spoke. He then addressed, "Sauda do you have to flirt without promise or delivery?"

His wife smiled teasingly. "I'm saving my energy," she purred. "So you can be well protected, brave Djedhi."

Tedros cleared his throat and stuttered, "At the moment, I'm well *erected*."

Sauda chuckled, hitting Tedros on the chest. She then held him tighter, wanting to absorb him. "Maybe I should've stayed until my magic was completely energized. I feel like a snake." She writhed over his body sensuously. Sauda was exciting Tedros. Her voice was music, and she rubbed her body up against him with a remarkable rhythm. "Turn over," she commanded him. Tedros did not hesitate. Sauda got to her knees and said, "Take off your shirt and lay on your stomach."

Tedros complied only arguing as he lay flat on his stomach with his shirt off, "Aren't I facing the wrong way?"

Sauda did not respond. She straddled Tedros, and then pressed her fingers against two pressure points located on Tedros' back. Tedros jumped immediately. The shock stung him. "I thought this was going to be pleasurable," he moaned through clenched teeth.

"It will be," Sauda assured. "But that little maneuver was punishment for the silly comment." But she apologized quickly by leaning over and kissing Tedros on the shoulder. "*That* is for your bravery, Djedhi." She straightened, and then began pressing her fingers against Tedros' back, running over specific points, treating her husband as if he were a musical instrument. Her fingerwork relaxed his muscles, quickly dulling the pain she delivered to him earlier. Sauda's massage made Tedros believe he was levitating. Tedros could no longer feel her hands. Sauda touched every nerve only to numb them. Her massage allowed Tedros' pores to exhale stress from his body. Relaxed, he fell into a deep sleep. Sauda lay down next to him, her arms wrapped around Tedros tightly. Her embrace was like a cocoon.

Tedros woke up. It was early in the morning. Sauda was gone. She returned to meditating inside another tent. Tedros lifted from the cot. He put on his shirt and robe, took the card from the table, and stepped outside. He returned to Mazi's tent after a quick wash using water harvested from an oasis and after applying a scented spray. There was no one on guard at Mazi's tent. Tedros announced his entrance, and then turned around, his back to the tent's opening. He walked inside, backwards. "Elder Mazi," he called.

"Turn around, Tedros," the elder commanded in a delightful tone. "My wife and I are fit to be seen."

Tedros turned around. He bowed to Mazi and his wife. He presented a distinctive bow to Mazi's wife, small choreography that male Djedhi offered to women, especially one of her stature. Mazi's wife was named Qalhata. Her age and wisdom made her beautiful. Her locks were gray, ashen as if her hair was made of a magical mist. Tedros admired her. Each lock of hair that looped down her physique seemed to hold inside it lessons from every year she endured. Qalhata was pure wisdom. She was also one of the deadliest Djedhi to touch a lance. She was refined as a woman at her heart, but to cross her as an enemy was sudden death. Even without a lance, her bare hands, used within her elegant, dance-like style of martial arts, commanded lightning's speed and thunder's might, regardless of her age.

Qalhata smiled warmly, accepting Tedros' bow. He performed it gracefully. Tedros observed the elder woman's smile. He admired the female warrior, gracefully deceptive as she could be. Deadly. There was nothing more deadly or equally enticing than a woman's smile. Tedros knew that too well. His wife got her way many times just because of a smile, and every once in a while, because of a lot of whining.

Qalhata excused herself from the tent. Tedros approached Mazi when Qalhata departed. He placed the card on the table and said proudly, "*The five books on symbols.*" Mazi was also proud. The young Djedhi decoded the card. "I didn't study all those years for nothing," Tedros added.

Mazi nodded, smile remaining. But then his expression changed. "The test is over," he said in a stern voice. "We can begin preparing you for your task. Have you decided on your weapons?"

"My lance and short sword," Tedros answered.

"Good," said Mazi. "That's safe. Those are a traveler's weapons. Not too suspicious." He walked from around the table in front of him and added, "You will be given common clothes. The urban center is supplying us. You will also be fitted with a common robe."

Tedros nodded.

Mazi balanced on one of his swords as if it were a cane. He rubbed the hilt with his thumb and continued to speak. "Your task should take no longer than two months to complete, possibly shorter. Paki discussed with me his wish to bring back a woman he met. Once he goes to the urban center, he will meet you there."

"Will Sauda accompany him?" Tedros asked.

"If she wishes," Mazi sighed. "I don't like having too many of us on excursions, especially all at once. But I grant the leave." He stepped closer to Tedros. "Don't overwork yourself during weapons practice. Your combat should be minimal, if at all. You've seen heavy combat in the last month. I recommend rest. Practice at noon. Two hours. Plan your rendezvous with Paki. He also has encoded parchments to give you."

"Encoded?" Tedros was surprised. "With what," he asked.

Mazi raised a kind hand, trying to halt the young Djedhi's excitement. "Don't worry," he said. "The parchments will be legible to your Djedhi eye. They're written in our code. They will be unintelligible to anyone who may interrogate you." Mazi took a moment, watching Tedros relax. The elder continued, "On them you will find the coordinates to the location of the two temples in Kemet that house the five books on symbols and the *Scrolls of Enoch*." Mazi put a hand on Tedros' shoulder. "Fortune favors the bold, Tedros," the elder informed, his voice a whisper. He shook his finger and added, "On this journey, do not falter."

"I won't," Tedros assured.

The elder pulled Tedros into a single arm embrace. He shook Tedros happily. "I have faith in you," he said. "I know you will brag about this assignment to your parents. I grant you leave when you return. Visit them in the urban center. I too should journey into the city. I must thank its governors for taking in some of our population, and allowing us to live among their students."

Tedros thought about his older sister. She always believed he would make a wonderful Djedhi Khepri. He was elated that he was able to get her and her husband and two children out of occupied Kemet, his younger brother too. His mother and father had left years before, worried about the incoming marauders.

Mazi continued, "Tonight will be a special night for you, Tedros. You will feel your wife's magic like never before. Tomorrow morning you will feel as if you can take on the world. I'm sure her magic has blessed you before battle." He whispered the next sentiment. "But locked inside her is the understanding that her husband will be gone for a long time. Her magic will make sure you come back to her." He continued to keep his voice low as he relayed, "And she *will* get better with age." Mazi's eyes locked with Tedros'. Both men had a grin on their face. "And if you think my wife is a fierce warrior in battle, imagine when she takes that ferocity to," he cleared his throat before adding, "another level."

Tedros laughed. Mazi let go of him. The elder grabbed his sword, again balancing on it for support. Tedros commented, "So, the two of you know how to cut loose?"

Mazi said in a lighthearted tone, "We didn't have eight children for nothing." He laughed again. "Oh, I know I can play the part of the 'wise old man', but I would like to emphasize that I am *still* a man. And Qalhata is very much *still* a woman. She is skilled with a lance, but she surrenders to mine." He cocked his head and an eyebrow toward Tedros. "If you know what I mean."

Tedros liked when Mazi shed his duties as a 'wise old man'. It relaxed him, and he needed to be, considering the task ahead, and the amount of time he would be away from Sauda. He suggested to Mazi, "When we return we'll all go to an urban center and have a beer."

Mazi looked at Tedros with a surprised expression.

Tedros brushed it off. "I know, I know. I don't drink anything stronger than water. But when I pull this off, it will be cause to celebrate."

Mazi beamed. "Yes, of course." He did not want to hold Tedros any longer. He instructed the young warrior, "Be off. Prepare. Get a good meal. Keep the outline of your preparation in mind. It is time for your weapons practice."

Tedros exited and walked over to a large tented area where meals were being served. Trades came across their settlement. Lamb and beef were sold to them, traded for goods and supplies. Tedros inhaled the aroma of the finely cooked meat and vegetables. Cooked egg yolk was also served. Tedros sat with Paki. Other Djedhi flocked around them, asking questions about their assignments. Paki received the most attention, the questions aimed at him concerning Kemet's politics. Tedros received more congratulatory statements, handshakes, and pats on the shoulder. This was the normal ritual that accompanied Djedhi having returned from their assignment, or assigned a mission.

Tedros finished his meal and then returned to his tent for meditation, allowing his breakfast to digest before engaging in practice. He lost himself in the thought of returning to Kemet. He imagined going on his journey, his wife by his side. He believed, through her protective magic, she would be. He opened his eyes and stood up. An hour had passed. He took a peek outside his tent. He watched the warriors in his settlement scurry about. Some were eating. Others laughed, played, and even argued—disputes settled gracefully. Baths were being taken under certain tents.

They were displaced, thought Tedros, but they were still a community.

The weapons instructor, Oman, caught his eye. The man waved for him to come into his tent. Tedros lifted his hand, signaling for Oman to wait. He walked back into his tent and scooped up his lance and short sword. He slipped from his quarters and then made his way to the weapons instructor's tent. He walked through the traffic of fellow Djedhi warriors. One grabbed his arm and said, "We celebrate your leave tonight."

"Not too late," said Tedros. "I have to rest tonight. I leave a day early. I decoded my card quickly." The Djedhi congratulated Tedros and continued on. He entered Oman's quarters. The teacher waited patiently. His tent was an armory, lined with all manner of weapons: short swords, bolas, spears, javelins, and bow and arrows.

Oman greeted Tedros, giving him the proper salute. He congratulated Tedros for being selected for the mission and asked if he were ready for practice. Tedros answered, "Yes." Oman examined Tedros' weapons and equipped himself with weapons of the same type. They saluted and bowed toward one another again, then walked from the armory and away from the encampment. Oman made small talk as they proceeded to a secluded area. He said, "It's been a long time since you've taken instruction from me. But, we can always use practice."

"I don't believe I'll come across an enemy as fierce as you," Tedros remarked.

"While that might be true," Oman started, "you will be up against killers without honor. They won't be swift killers. They'll be out for blood. Brutal, wild, and thirsty." When they reached a far dune Oman pitched his lance into the ground. He instructed Tedros to do the same.

Tedros complied.

Both warriors discarded their robes, and before the garments hit the sand, Oman attacked. Tedros blocked! Oman spun around and swung again, a deadly strike. Tedros backed away. He shielded himself from the strike using his short sword. The Djedhi spun, imitating his instructor's strike. Tedros' blade only struck against Oman's short sword.

Tedros backed away. Oman did the same.

"I will go easy on you, trust me," Oman assured. "I'll make sure you're not bruised or killed."

"Good to know," Tedros replied.

The words were barely a breath when Oman struck again. Tedros blocked. Both men became mixed up and intertwined in a whirlwind of attacks and parries. Oman screamed an order in the middle of the fray. "Lance at the ready," he yelled.

Tedros tossed his sword away. Both Djedhi launched toward their pitched weapons, removed them and swung at each other in a martial rhythm. Oman was excited to see Tedros had developed his own style. Oman admired Tedros, however, being the expert on weapons and style, Oman could see Tedros' weaknesses as well as strengths. The instructor calculated Tedros' moves as he engaged him. At the height of their clash, Oman yelled, "And finish!"

Tedros stood straight, his lance at his shoulder just the same, point facing the heavens. Oman stood opposite him. They were mirror images. "Sit," Oman instructed. Tedros took a seat on the sandy floor, legs crossed. He pitched the blunt end of his lance into the dune. "And rest," Oman concluded.

Tedros exhaled.

The instructor sat down with him. He talked to Tedros about the strengths and weaknesses he noticed in his fighting style. He also expressed how much he admired Tedros' growth. In the middle of his congratulations, Oman screamed an order to resume the fight. Tedros was back on his feet. It was hand-to-hand combat now. The rhythm of rest and practice continued for two more hours. Tedros was well exercised.

The Djedhi's nightly festivities did not carry on long. The participants retired to their residences. Tedros waited anxiously in his tent. His wife was still away. She did not attend the festival. Tedros could not possibly imagine what magic his wife had readied for him. He took seat on their cot, legs crossed. Candles provided light. Tedros breathed slowly. The rhythm of his breathing eased him. He was alerted to his wife's presence, hearing the sway of the tent's flaps parting. Sauda summoned a breath of nature's air, which opened the tent. She stepped inside, beautiful. She was dressed in the flowing robes and gown of a priestess. Her forearms were adorned with gold bracelets and bangles. Each piece of jewelry dangling from her was designed to enhance her rhythm, her movement.

"Stand up," Sauda commanded her husband. "Remove your clothes."

Tedros did as his wife asked. Why argue with such a command? His clothing was shed. All he wore was his crown of hair that burst from his head like a black, vibrant fire. Sauda removed her robe and swiped her hand downward, palm open, an elegant, silent command for Tedros to drop to his knees. The movement was graceful, like a dance. Tedros obeyed his wife. Sauda stepped closer. He hugged her waist and placed small kisses on her thigh. He could feel Sauda's body vibrating with energy.

She directed, "On your back, my love."

Tedros complied. He positioned himself on his back, lying on a wide rug.

Sauda stood over him, bestriding Tedros. She lifted her dress. Tedros became erect. Sauda lowered herself onto his erection. Tedros penetrated into her, opening wide her warm aperture. His hands grabbed her waist. Sauda stretched out her arms like wings, the palm of her hands facing upward. She leaned her head back. Her eyes were closed. She moved her hips to nature's song, gyrating smoothly. She started slow, and then she gradually increased her hips' sway. Each gyration took Tedros up into her. Energy entangled Tedros. He felt as if a blanket wrapped around him. He believed he could see and feel spirals of light flowing into and out of his body. They jumped from his body and connected to Sauda. He could see other strands of light jump from Sauda's body and connect to his.

Tedros matched the rhythm of his wife's hips, thrusting up inside her. He looked at his wife. More magic occurred. Her short, cropped crown of hair began to grow spirals of locks, glowing energy. A light show of magic was in front of his eyes, growing from the top of his wife's head. Sauda retracted her arms and placed fingers at strategic points on Tedros' chest. She pressed against sensitive points on him, typing a love letter, increasing her husband's pleasure. With one press against him, Tedros let go of his wife's waist. His arms lay outstretched on the floor. His body jerked and twisted, and though he opened his mouth to shout, no sound escaped.

Sauda kept her eyes closed. She tilted her head down. She could see Tedros even with her eyes closed. She could see his chest. She continued to type, thrust, and type. Her fingers danced on Tedros, playing him like an organ while she played his organ. Sauda composed a sensual symphony. Her hands went flat against Tedros' chest. Her hips were wild. In the last waves of her love she tightened her muscles, squeezing Tedros inside her.

Tedros ejaculated.

His body jerked. Energy snaked from the base of his spine to the crown of his head. He could hear the electric hiss of the snake climbing him.

The candles in the tent blew out.

Sauda leaned forward and kissed her husband, breathing her magic down his throat. Tedros tasted her energy on his tongue. Sauda stood up. She opened the tent's flaps wide, fixing them to stay open. The wind swirled inside the tent like a ghost. Sauda grabbed a thick blanket. She returned to her husband and wrapped the two of them tightly inside the blanket.

Tedros could feel himself small, inside his body. He was in the pit of his own stomach. Then he began to grow. He reached the build of his body but continued to expand. He seemed to grow larger than the tent, the desert sands, the continent, the world, and then he equaled the size of the universe. And there was Sauda, the other half of the universe, lying next to him. The two were wrapped in a blanket the color of their skin. They were the All at the beginning of time. Dark matter, the mother. Dark energy, the father. Folded as one.

Tedros felt an intense heat enter his body. He opened his eyes and realized he was in a strange position on the floor of his tent. His legs were straight, the left leg atop the right leg. The blanket was no longer around him. He was naked, and the sun beamed in from the outside, hitting him directly on the chest. Sauda lay at his waist, consuming his erect penis in her mouth. Tedros inhaled. He locked eyes with his wife. The origin of the heat was not in the sun's rays, but in his wife's moistening lips wrapped around him. Once again, he was at the mercy of his wife's magic. Tedros wanted to caress his wife's hair as she ingested him, but his arms, lying outstretched to either side, could not move. Sauda hit a pressure point while he was asleep, fixing Tedros to this position. More of the sun's light stabbed him. The palms of his hands blazed like fire. Tedros stiffened as he expelled his seed again.

He could move once he ejaculated.

Tedros closed his eyes and fell back to sleep.

When he awoke again, his wife was gone. Tedros did not know how much time had passed, but the sun had shifted away from his tent. Next to him were his traveling suit and robe. He stood up. He smelled the perfume coming from his body. He had been washed while he slept. He put on his clothes, his body feeling as if it were molded from fire and cosmic energy. He believed a magical dome surrounded him, humming in the tone of his wife's voice. He was protected. Tedros stepped from the tent. His wife was there to greet him. Sauda handed him his short sword and lance. Tedros kissed her and whispered, "I can take on a thousand men thanks to you."

"I love you," she replied placing a necklace that was adorned with a protective amulet around his neck. The necklace had been anointed by her feminine magic and a sweet perfume.

Tedros sheathed his sword and strapped his lance across his back. In front of him was Paki, holding a sitting camel by the reins. The camel was fitted with provisions. Tedros mounted the beast, and it stood up. Paki handed Tedros a pouch. Tedros placed it over his shoulder.

"The card and the two scrolls are in there," said his fellow Djedhi. "And some quick food for your travels. Your mount's food is strapped to him, along with more supplies, currency, water, and additional rations for yourself."

"Thank you," Tedros told Paki. "We'll rendezvous in two months."

Paki nodded affirmatively.

Tedros commanded his mount to go forward. He walked down a path made up of two lines of fellow Djedhi, standing to his left and right. At the end of the path was the council of elders. Mazi stepped forward. Tedros stopped his camel and told him, "I will make every elder proud."

"You already have," Mazi assured.

Tedros bowed his head. "Well, let's see if I can't increase the pride." Tedros slapped his camel with the reins and dashed away, leaving behind bursts of sandy clouds. Tedros and his mount became a tiny silhouette, drowned in the waves of dunes on the horizon. The crowd of Djehdi dispersed after he departed.

Sauda smiled, continuing her gaze in the direction of Tedros' departure. She loved him. She was confident in her magic. He was protected. She would travel to be reunited with him in time. With that comforting thought, Sauda turned and entered her tent. She lay down on the cot, placed her hands on her stomach, and began to meditate. Tedros was inside of her. They were still connected, though apart. She would protect him from here.

Travel was easy. The only problem Tedros incurred came at the border of Kemet. It was an hour passed noon, two days after leaving the Djedhi camp. Twelve guards lay in front of him, blocking the entrance to one of the country's outer rim cities. The guards quickly surrounded him, brandishing weapons as he approached. Tedros remained calm throughout the ordeal. They were just doing their job, according to him. The circumstances demanded that Tedros do his. His only worry was the language barrier.

"Identify yourself," one ordered. This man was most likely the captain.

Tedros understood the phonetic and common language. The accent was thicker than he imagined, but he had little trouble understanding the men. "My name is Tedros. I'm a traveler on business."

"From where?" the same man asked.

"I'm from Abyssinia," Tedros identified.

The man approached Tedros. He inspected the camel. "What's your business," he inquired.

"Trade," Tedros answered matter-of-factly.

The man looked in the distance from where Tedros approached. He looked at Tedros. "Shouldn't you be with a caravan," he wondered.

Tedros casually replied, "I'm just inspecting the goods here, carrying the news back to my employer."

The guard nodded and said, "I see."

"Would you like to inspect my pouch or other sacks?" Tedros politely invited.

The guard waved the comment aside with his hand, playing right into Tedros' hand. The Djedhi understood the tactic of being polite and inviting, which would prompt the guard-captain to display such an action in return. The guard's pride quickly came through his response. He wanted to show he was in control.

"Did you come across any nomads in your travels," the guard continued to interrogate.

Tedros decided to be honest. "Yes," he answered.

"Were they Ngr warriors," the guard queried.

Tedros became tense. The word *ngr* was only for Djedhi to use. It was a sacred word to define brotherhood and sisterhood, and only an initiated Djedhi could speak its blessed syllables, save if an African was a leader of a nation; the Neggur or Neggura. Tedros wanted to strike the Tamahu man dead for such insolence. He kept his composure, however. There was a mission at hand.

"There were nomads," Tedros answered in a courteous tone. "I was invited into a camp. I rested there. The people were lovely."

The guard continued to question Tedros. "Did they seem like warriors? Were they savage?"

Tedros acted as if he had no idea. "They were polite. Civilized. I'm sure they had a warrior class among them. They greeted *and* welcomed me with all the hospitality one could ask for." *And I dare you to try and attack them*, Tedros thought to himself. He played to the guard's ego again and added aloud, "I've never been treated better." He leaned closer and joked, "And you're not really trying to be in contention, are you?"

All twelve guards gripped their weapons tighter in reaction to the comment. The guard-captain broke out into laughter. He pointed his thumb over his shoulder, aimed at the city. "Go on in," he permitted.

"Ah, I did hear good things about you, Captain," Tedros commented with a smile. He then asked, "The closest inn, please?"

The guard-captain responded, "You'll see it when you step through. It's a wondrous place."

Tedros galloped off. He shook his head and replied to the guard-captain's sentiment in a low voice. "I doubt it," he grumbled.

Captain Agil Oster watched Tedros make his way into the city. When the Djedhi was far inside, the guard-captain looked at his men and ordered them to keep watch on the city's new visitor. He instructed a guard to ride off and follow the stranger. Tedros, at that same moment, made it to the inn. He paid for his stay and settled himself inside one of the inn's suites, his camel placed in a stable.

He unpacked his provisions and unraveled the parchments in his sack, inspecting the code scribbled on them. He already decoded the language and the numbers on the scrolls. The third scroll was newly inscribed. Paki had drawn it. It was a key to help him decode the first two parchments. It was all a map, the first two parchments. They were parts, drawn in code, making up a larger map. Tedros looked from the first two parchments to the third, re-examining the encrypted map. He studied all the symbols, his eyes seeing again what the code was hiding. He saw that the temple he needed to get into was located on the other side of the city, on the outskirts. Tedros thought about his strategy. He decided he would find the temple tomorrow.

He would also lose the guard trailing him.

For now, he rested, opting to explore the city when he awoke. This was not his home city in the country of Kemet. He was far from home, at least a day's travel away. He promised his wife he would go by their old apartment, and he made note to see it after he found the temple. Hopefully, it would still be standing.

Tedros' rest lasted three hours. He became restless, stirring from sleep, though he was still tired. He left his room at the inn, packing into his pouch all the belongings that could incriminate him as anything other than a trader, and set about the city streets, observing the population. Most of the people were foreigners. The indigenous African Kamites mingled in small clusters. The city guard kept close watch from mounts, and from strategic points of the city, on foot or from rooftops. There were carriages offering rides for a fee. Other than the enclosed chariots, Tedros understood that unless a citizen's travels were outside the city, they were regulated to travel on foot.

Tedros inspected the buildings around him. He was satisfied that most of his peoples' original architecture remained. The war-torn buildings had indigenous African Kamite workers putting them back together. Tedros' real observation was the man following him. The Djedhi turned his head from side to side, keeping the guard in his peripheral, feigning interest in the scenery around him, looking inconspicuous to his tracker, who was not the best at his job.

Despite only feigning being a tourist, Tedros could not help but calculate his surroundings. He sighed. *Behold now, something has been done which has never happened before*, Tedros thought to himself as he panned the environment. He saw a Tamahu man exit from an apartment and he thought, *He who never slept on a plank is now the owner of a bed.* The man was dressed in business robes; the clothes once adorned the accountants of Tedros' people, most likely still manufactured by indigenous hands. The man stepped over two African men who lay near an alley, dressed in tattered clothes. *Behold, the owners of robes are now in rags. But he who never wove for himself is now the owner of fine linen.* The Tamahu's consort was a Tamahu woman. She held a mirror to her face, admiring herself. *Behold, she who once looked at her face in water is now the owner of a mirror.* [1]

Tedros waited for the Tamahu to pass. He stepped up to his fellow countrymen. The two African men stood up quickly. Tedros was about to offer them currency when both men issued pamphlets.

"Hello," Tedros greeted properly.

Both men smiled at Tedros. The one on the left began to speak. "Hello back, brother. Take this. Keep it concealed. It is a pamphlet that talks about resisting the Tamahu ruling over us."

Tedros took what was offered him, inspecting the parchments. There was writing on it reflecting the proper language of the indigenous people. This put a smile on Tedros' face. The top of the parchment read *The Demotic Chronicle.* He scanned the writings and found romanticized histories of early rulers, and history pertaining to the freedom and culture prevailing in earlier times. Tedros paid the two men. They thanked him and carried on, roaming the streets pretending to be vagabonds. Tedros felt good to know he was not the only one on an assignment and in disguise. You did not have to be an initiated Djedhi to be a Wisdom Keeper.

Tedros continued on. He glanced around, catching the guard in his peripheral. Tedros waved down a taxi. He stepped into the back of the enclosed chariot and was greeted, "Where to?"

"To the Grand Hall and back," Tedros ordered politely.

"You know that's across the city," spoke the man. "You want me to take you there *and* back?"

Tedros confirmed, "Yes. It's not a problem. I have the money," he assured the driver.

The chariot started forward. Tedros sneaked a look behind him, pretending to take in the sights. He saw the guard duck around the side of a building. Tedros did not think he would follow him any further. It would take him too long to get a chariot. Tedros also knew the guard wanted to remain inconspicuous. He would just have to wait for Tedros to return. The guard would probably scout the inn. Tedros clutched his pouch tighter. If the guards searched his apartment, they would not

---

[1] Italics, quotes from *The Admonitions of Ipu-Wer*

find anything. Tedros had also setup a trap at the entrance of his rented room at the inn. He would be able to tell if anyone entered his rented abode. But Tedros did not expect this scenario to go that far, at least not yet.

Tedros removed the pamphlets give to him by the two African Kamites. He began reading *The Demotic Chronicle*, glancing up every one and a while to entertain the Tamahu driver pointing out new buildings in the city. They were in honor of Serapis. Tedros observed their architecture. The temples were shambolic in design. The foreigners were definitely trying to imitate the style of the ancestors and their indigenous descendants. But when it was mixed with the foreigners' ideals the design became haphazard. The symbolic mathematics and layout of the temples were nowhere to be found; the spacing and the numerical length were absent. The design twisted without rhythm. The Tamahu were trying to add their influence, but it was not, according to Tedros, spiritually, cosmically, or mathematically grounded. It just was. Tedros put his eyes back on the parchment when the driver finished. When the coach stopped, Tedros lifted his head. The driver turned to him and stated, "We're here."

"Wait for me," he said as he exited the coach. The driver assured that he would. Tedros scoped his surroundings, looking both ways. He did not believe he would spot the guard pursuing him, but he was cautious to look for him—again, remaining inconspicuous. He journeyed through pedestrians and stopped at the Grand Hall.

The building was much of the same design as the new temples. It was big, but it lacked the spirit of precise mathematics. The Hall was not Tedros' interest, however. He walked to his left and spotted an alley that led to a path out of the city. Tedros looked around, making sure he was not being watched. He slipped through, casually, coming to the back of the Grand Hall and the edge of the city. Behind the Grand Hall, in the distance, was a graveyard of buildings and temples. The Grand Hall did mark the city's boundary, but it was not located at the edge of the city. It was at the center of a much larger urban center that had been wracked and decimated, not by war and invasion, but on the authority to erase a culture's history.

The temples were untouched. They were locked shut, closed. However, they were not toppled, unlike surrounding buildings. The foreign rulers may have banned the people from using the temples, but they allowed them to remain, a gesture to show mercy, as reported by Paki. The contents were untouched as well. At least Tedros hoped.

Having memorized the map, Tedros walked along the coordinates he remembered and stood at the base of the temple that held the five books on the language of symbols. He made a mental mark on the whereabouts, turned to his right, and began to wind through the graveyard of buildings to find the temple with the *Scrolls of Enoch*. After locating the second temple, and making another mental note, he walked back into the alley and blended seamlessly into the ebb and flow of city traffic. He climbed back into the coach and instructed the driver, "And back, good driver."

The coach started.

When Tedros neared the area he departed from, he instructed the driver to take him to the inn. At his destination he exited, paid the man fairly, and walked to the door of his room. In the corner of his eye he spotted the guard who had been following him. He was making small talk across the street, trying to be inconspicuous. Tedros opened the door to his apartment. As he pushed it forward, his lance fell over, having been kicked outward, away from the door. That was Tedros' trap and test. He had set it up purposely. If anyone had entered his room, they would have knocked over his lance, and most likely placed it straight up against the wall, next to the door. But no one had disturbed his space.

Tedros walked inside, shut the door, and swiped the lance from off the ground. He placed the weapon against the door. He took his pouch from around his shoulder and dropped it on the ground. He tossed *The Demotic Chronicle* on the bed.

Today was an adventure, he thought, exhaling. He then pondered a plan to get rid of the guard. It would have to be tomorrow. After he got the guard off his back, he would have to stowaway in the temples, and then retrieve what he came for. There was a slight problem, however. Tedros figured that once the guard was taken out, and he showed his face again, he would be suspected by the guard-captain.

Tedros looked at the two *Demotic Chronicle* pamphlets on the bed. A plan formed in his mind as the image of the parchment came closer and closer in his vision.

Tedros smiled. He had a plan.

The next day Tedros exited his room equipped with short sword and pouch. His lance was strategically arranged in the position at the door. He walked to the public stables housing his camel. He retrieved his mount and assured the stable-keeper he would return. The man informed him that he would keep his spot open. Tedros had already paid for a week's use. Tedros took his camel and made his way to the edge of the city. As he mounted his ride, Agil Oster, the guard-captain, approached. The same guards as the day before, including the one who was trailing Tedros, surrounded him. Tedros believed this was the guard-captain's unit. He wondered if he was one of many guard-captains, and if he possessed more soldiers. This must have been his district to patrol too.

"So you're off," Agil said with surprise. He tried his best to hide his tone, but it came through in his words.

"I'll return." Tedros told the guard-captain. "Just some business in another city."

Tedros galloped away. Agil looked at the guard he assigned to Tedros. "Follow him, Gretes," he ordered. "Get your mount. Never lose him, but keep a distance in your travels."

"Yes, captain," replied Gretes. He went for his horse and provisions and then exited the city.

Tedros took his time when traveling to his home city. The lag in his travel was purposeful. He knew the guard was tracking him. Tedros rested for a night, pitching camp to meditate. Before the night was over, under the cover of the night's darkness, Tedros tracked down the guard's campsite. The guard was asleep. Tedros watched him, observing the guard's supplies. The guard was alone. Tedros hoped there would be more sent to pursue him. But, Tedros was satisfied with the one.

He returned to his campground, his mind now anxious to return home. He could not wait. It would be glorious to him. It was the smallest of all the country's cities, but it was home. Kom-Ombo. When he returned to his site, he forced himself to sleep. In the morning, he continued to Kom-Ombo, Gretes following him.

Like the city Tedros had left, Kom-Ombo's interior structures stood, mixed with the contemporary temples and buildings of the foreigners. And also like the city Tedros had come from, Kom-Ombo had Tamahu guards stationed at its perimeter. Tedros dealt with them in the same manner he dealt with Agil and his soldiers. He was permitted entrance and took rest at another inn.

Tedros waited until nightfall. He left his apartment and walked out to get re-acquainted with his home city. He quickly ventured to his old apartment. He walked the streets as if he never left. Near the old temples was the layout of the Djedhi housing. He felt as if the building reached out and embraced him. The Djedhi was flooded with memories. He could see the past in front of him. He then thought of his wife, Sauda. She would have loved this, thought Tedros.

He found their old apartment and smiled. Memories stirred, but his thoughts were interrupted. There was a noise behind Tedros, alerting.

The Djedhi cleared his throat, feigned a cough, and looked around while pretending to wheeze and catch his breath. He spotted Gretes. Tedros made his way to an alley. Gretes followed. The alley was a winding maze that stretched around the Djedhi housing complex. Tedros ducked to his left. The maze was part of his training. Every turn and twist was locked into his memory. He could feel the guard behind him. Tedros lost Gretes, exploiting the maze's confusing layout. Tedros circled around, ending up behind Gretes. Tedros removed his short sword. He approached the Tamahu guard, his footsteps quiet.

"Where are you, ngr," Gretes said in a low voice.

Tedros whispered eerily, "Right here."

Gretes turned around. Tedros swiped his short sword at Gretes' neck. The tip of the blade cut the guard's throat open. Gretes' clutched his throat, eyes wide with surprise. Blood seeped through his fingers and gurgled from his mouth. Tedros stepped back and stabbed Gretes in the stomach. He removed his sword and watched the guard drop dead.

Tedros backed away from the body. It would be days before the body was found in the winding circuit of alleyways around the old Djedhi housing. Tedros cleaned off his sword, returned to the inn, and rested for the night. In the morning he purchased supplies and rations for his travel. At noon, Tedros began his trek back to the first city. He decided to enter the city from an abandoned section. He would go straight to the temple. He would be perceived to still be gone. The Tamahu guard too. The guard-captain would not become suspicious.

Tedros arrived at an abandoned area of the city, slipping in undetected as he planned, guiding his mount through the undisturbed area. Though he remembered where he could find either temple, he referenced the coded language on the scroll that formed into a map, and saw that both temples could be entered through a secret chamber. The Djedhi led his camel around the first temple and found the chamber. He dismounted, opened the secret passage, and led his mount inside. The chamber was long, and at first declined at an angle until leveling off. The camel became restless as the darkness became greater. Tedros calmed the beast. He came to an incline and went into another room filled with sunlight. It was a stable. Tedros locked his camel inside a booth and moved to the next chamber. The next room was empty, lit with sunlight. Tedros continued on, exited the room, and then came to another long hallway that ended abruptly. It was dark. Tedros felt around and touched a solid wall blocking his path.

He knocked on the wall three times.

The wall slid opened.

Tedros stepped into a room stacked with scrolls and books. Windows positioned high on each wall provided light. The room was twice the size of the stable, but it was stacked with papyrus, bound and unbound, and scrolls. It was hard for Tedros to navigate through. There was no space. He had to look and sort every piece of writing here, and he feared this was not the only room. *Maybe this* will *take over two months*, he thought to himself. But he did not worry. He only wondered whether he had enough food for him and his mount.

Tedros waded through the piles of books, scrolls, and loose papyrus. He needed to find five books lost among the chaos. He reached the other side of the room where there was another door. He opened it and saw another room identically stacked with books and scrolls. "*Gafdamnit*," he cursed. Tedros exhaled his frustration. "Well, there's no time like the present to get started."

The Djedhi went back to the first room and shuffled through the collection of works. He re-stacked the books and scrolls into a pile consisting of books and scrolls he came across. He was looking for bound papyrus, books, not a single scroll. That thought was comforting. He was hoping the *Scrolls of Enoch*, which would be found in the second temple, was actually a single book. From what he could remember, the *Scrolls of Enoch* was a compiled and bound set of scrolls. It was a book.

Hours passed before he found two of the five books. The books were titled *The Fire Language: Stars and Suns* and *The Language of the Wind*. He carried the large tomes back to the stables, resting them in front of his camel's booth. He returned to the first room that was filled with books and scrolls. He resumed his search until nightfall. He fell asleep atop a pile of works, waking up when the sun tickled his eyelids. He had slept, but he was exhausted. Before he resumed his search he returned to the stables and fed himself and his mount. He returned and continued looking for the other three manuscripts.

Hours passed again. Tedros believed it was noon. He took a long look around the room and felt confident that he searched the room completely. He entered the second room and repeated his process. Another several hours passed before Tedros felt winded again. He took another break, went back to the stables, and dined with his camel. After the meal he returned to the second room of scrolls and books. He became bored with his search rather quickly. He found another passageway, walking through a corridor, and ending up in the temple's main hall. He looked around at the glorious site. Once again, windows that had been strategically placed provided light. The windows were designed to make full use of the sun's light, no matter the season or position of the sun during the day. As long as the sun shined, there was a marvelous display of light. This was mathematics.

Tedros walked over to a set of stairs and ascended them. The stairs led to a section that offered more stairs. Tedros found several bedrooms on the second floor. When the Djedhi occupied the temple, only the Grand Masters lived inside. Tedros picked a room that was untouched. Even the bed was made, welcoming. There was no window. Only the natural light from the hall illuminated the room. He went into the room and permitted himself a comfortable sleep in a nice bed.

There were only several minutes of sunlight left when Tedros awoke. He cursed himself for not preparing a lamp, his supplies left at the stables. He did not want to use a lamp while searching for the remaining books. He was afraid he would start a fire. But he considered that he could use the light now as he rested from his search. He lay back and went over the next part of his plan. His thoughts then turned to his wife. Tedros clutched the medallion around his neck.

"I'll see you earlier than expected, Sauda," he said raising the amulet to his lips. "I hope you're well." He began to think about the days long passed, training as a Wisdom Keeper. He thought of the small adventures he, Paki, and other friends were involved in, including Sauda. He thought about their fates at the moment. Tedros' thoughts eventually subsided, and he fell asleep.

Tedros returned to the stables as soon as the sun peaked over the horizon. He made breakfast and fed his four-legged companion. Both he and the beast could have used a bath. Both used the stables to relieve themselves, and Tedros did not keep company with his mount long, the smell unbearable. His search continued in the second room of books and scrolls. He shuffled through the parchments, scrolls, and bindings, and within an hour came across a third script. It was *The Dark Language: Invisible Speech.* He placed the book aside and sorted through the rest of the room. An hour later he picked up *Earth Symbols.* He rested the book atop the other, and went back to find the last.

Hours later, Tedros found nothing. He hoped there was another room. He took what he had to the stables and rested the books atop one another in a single pile. Tedros decided to take a break. He walked back to the front hall. He felt free inside the temple. There was no stress. No one knew he was here. He did not have the guards on his back or foreigners looking at him as if he was a stranger in his own homeland.

He noticed another room across the hall. He went inside. It was packed with scrolls and bound papyri. It was as grand as the other two. Tedros did not mind. He could take his time looking for the book. He did not want to move on to the second temple until nightfall, so he could be concealed by the darkness. If he found the book early, he would use the time to explore the temple further, for nostalgia's sake

Tedros sifted through the room looking for the final book of symbols. In three hours time he only found his way across the room and into another room of literature. Tedros continued his search in this new room. His search ended an hour later. In his hands was the final book. *Liquid Swords.* Tedros smiled. He had retrieved all five books, the language and symbols of the five elements. He returned to the stables and propped the book on the pile. He rewarded himself with rations.

When Tedros finished his snack, he grabbed his sword, stood up, and walked back to the temple's front hall. He surveyed the scene. By way of his imagination, Agil and his remaining eleven guards entered the room. Tedros flung his robe off, tossing it to the side. With his sword gripped firmly in hand, he charged at the imaginary figures and battled them. He executed moves whereby his imagination witnessed several guards stab each other while trying to attack him. He engaged in battle with two more, cutting them down quickly. Tedros' imagination allowed the guards no fighting chance. He saved Agil for last, and gave the Guard-Captain a spectacular sequence of blade against blade. He fell his imagined enemy and exhaled, his exercise over.

"If it even comes to this," he said, his voice echoing in the chamber. Tedros' heart skipped a beat. His voice seemed loud. He knew no one came near the temple, but he made a note to keep his voice low from now on. Other than that, Tedros found the emptiness soothing. Usually it was a Djedhi who made an offering to a temple, now the role was reversed. The temple was offering Tedros freedom and the chance to feel at home. Tedros prepared himself as night dawned.

Tedros had his belongings packed and a lamp fixed. He exited the first temple, leaving the same way he came in. He escorted his mount by the reins, walking back through the secret entrance and out into the graveyard of buildings. Tedros could hear the city's night activity in the distance. He walked carefully through the winding abandoned streets, stepping quietly. When he found the second temple, he entered and came across a similar layout. There was a secret entrance and a long tunnel. The journey through the passageway was just as uncomfortable for the camel as in the first temple. The mount struggled with Tedros.

"Easy. Easy," Tedros said, the beast becoming a burden as it used its weight to try and wiggle free from the Djedhi's grip. Tedros did not let go. He held the reins of the mount firmly and trekked on. "We're almost there," he assured the beast as it regained a calm demeanor.

The tunnel declined, and then straightened out for several strides. Tedros felt as if he was underneath the temple. He came out into an unlit room. Tedros lifted his lamp to shine the light around. It was another stable, and it smelled better than the one he had just left. The Djedhi locked his camel in a compartment, and then searched for a way out. He used the lamp, the light like a knife cutting into the dark. His hunt for an exit was short. He found a door that opened to stairs ascending up. At the top of the stairs was another door. Tedros opened the door and went through, ending up in a short hallway.

At the end of the hall was an opening in the shape of an oval. Though he was equipped with light, Tedros kept his arms outstretched, walking cautiously, feeling in front him. His hands brushed against fabric when he came to the oval-shaped opening. It was a tapestry. Tedros moved it aside and journeyed out of the short hallway and into a council chamber. It was bare of chairs, but a long wooden table still existed at its center. Tedros exited to the front hall. It was as glorious as the first temple, though Tedros could only see little of the room because the small flicker of light could not illuminate the entire area. But, Tedros could see the outline of a grand room. He also saw stairs, which he made his way to, ascended, and found a master bedroom. The Djedhi felt safe inside the second temple. It was the same comfort the first temple offered him. He dropped his robe, climbed into the bed, and went to sleep. He left the lamp burning, the candle flickering at the foot of the bed.

Tedros awoke the next morning. He ate and explored the temple, finding two rooms filled with scrolls and books. The rooms were located across the hall from each other. Tedros searched the room closest to the council chamber first, shifting back into his routine of check and separate. He found his prize within an hour, a cluster of bound scrolls titled *The Scrolls of Enoch*. He did not let his search end there. He took the rest of the day sifting through both rooms, being careful that there was only one volume of the work. There was nothing. He possessed all that was written for *The Scrolls of Enoch*. Tedros' mission was complete, for the most part.

He rested for the night, ate rations, and fed his ride. The following night, Tedros packed up his belongings and all that he confiscated, strapping the literature to his camel, and left the second temple, again guiding his mount by the reins. He slipped through the alley beside the Grand Hall. He walked across the city to the stables. There were few pedestrians, but there were many guards, including Guard-Captain Agil Oster and his crew. They swarmed around the area located near Tedros' inn. The Djedhi cursed his luck. He grimaced and thought to himself that he should have just left the city through the abandoned area. Despite the Guard-Captain's presence, Tedros remained calm. He made his way to the stables. He noticed the guard-captain and his crew interrogating the men that sold him the *Demotic Chronicle*. He believed the guard-captain noticed him.

Tedros fashioned a plan. He stowed his camel at the stables, leaving the confiscated literature strapped to the mount, and then he left the stables to return to his room at the inn. The guard-captain, flanked with troops, blocked his path. Tedros was calm, but alert. "Hello there," Tedros greeted politely.

Agil replied in an inquisitive tone, "So, you've returned."

"Ah, yes." Tedros kept his composure. "Only minutes ago, Captain. I arrived through the southeast entrance." He took a breath and stated, "I'm very tired. Excuse me, if you don't mind. I don't mean to be rude. You understand?"

Agil said nothing. He and his guards did not move. Tedros figured the guard-captain was probably wondering where his assigned man could be. Tedros spotted the two men who sold him the *Demotic Chronicle* in the distance, over the guard-captain's shoulder. They watched closely the exchange between Tedros and Agil. Tedros grimaced in their direction when he noticed the two men approaching, their faces serious. Tedros did not want trouble. He fixed his face into a smile and said to Agil and the other guards, "I have only two days left, Captain. My business will be finished then." Tedros wished the guards a good night and walked away from them.

Agil whispered an order to one of his guards, "Find Guard-Captain Atanas. Ask if any civilians entered from his area of the city." The guard saluted and was off to complete his task. Agil said to the others, "Spread out, but keep his abode under surveillance." The guards dispersed, following orders.

Tedros approached the two revolutionaries. He walked by them quickly. One of them spoke, "We saw those Tamahu guards harassing you," he said. Tedros continued walking. The men followed. "They were asking us about you, brother. My name is Sol. This is Om."

Tedros made a quick glance behind him. Agil and two guards were still watching him. "Look," he addressed Sol and Om in a low voice, barely moving his lips. "If you have any sense of discretion, keep quiet. Follow me. I've been looking for you. Act as if we're old friends."

Om and Sol started to pat Tedros on the back, smiles beaming. He shook their hands and hollered a greeting. He embraced both of them separately, taking an inconspicuous look at Agil and the other guards. They were still looking at him, but Tedros did not know if they were believing his act. He continued with it, leading Sol and Om back to his apartment room. Tedros whispered to his new acquaintances, "I've been looking for the two of you," he said opening the door to his room. "I need your help."

"Indeed, young man," said Sol.

The door to his room opened with ease. He closed the door and lit the lamps around the room. The room was in order, though Tedros knew it had been searched in his absence. The lance was stationed upright beside the door. Someone had knocked it over and placed it in its current position, not at its angle. Tedros invited Sol and Om inside. He dropped his pouch at the foot of the bed. He closed the door, taking one last look outside. No one followed. Tedros revealed his identity, explaining to Sol and Om his assignment as a Djedhi Khepri. Both men were taken aback, becoming excited. Sol and Om, bursting with admiration, shook the Djedhi's hand. "How may we assist you," Sol asked.

"I've taken out one of the guards," Tedros explained. "He was assigned to follow me when I visited Kom-Ombo. I don't know if he was on orders to take me out, but I brought him...into my world. I engaged. I'm alive. He's not." Tedros took a peek at the door. He looked back to Sol and Om and continued, "That guard-captain is waiting for his return. I'm sure he won't allow me to leave before that happens." Tedros picked up his pouch, sifted through its contents, and removed a map. "I need one of you to follow this map to the Djedhi settlement. Ask for a man named Paki and tell him to meet me early at our rendezvous."

Sol nodded. He turned to Om and ordered, "You handle that task." He looked at Tedros and suggested, "I'll help you handle the guards. I'm a trained soldier. I come from a line of Nuba warriors."

Tedros agreed. He looked at Om for his reply.

"It will be done, Djedhi," he assured.

"Good," Tedros said quickly. He handed the map to Om. "The confiscated lessons are strapped to my ride. There are also provisions for rest. It's not too long of a journey."

Om nodded his head.

"Do either of you have family," Tedros asked. "A wife? Children?"

"My wife died in a riot three years ago," said Sol. "She was protesting the closing of the temples. My sons and daughter are safe elsewhere. I do this for my wife, Djedhi."

Om said while folding the map handed to him, "My wife is in Kom-Ombo. The rest of my family fled west."

Tedros acknowledged Sol first. "I'm sorry for your loss." He turned to Om and stated, "We will locate your wife. We will take the three of you in. We must execute this plan now. Is that a problem?"

"Not at all," Om expressed.

Tedros pointed toward the door. "The guards are probably watching this place as we speak. I'll leave first." He started gathering his equipment. "They'll keep their eyes on me. Meet me at the stables. Om, you will leave on my mount. Sol and I will lure the guards to the temples." He sheathed his short sword and grabbed his lance. "The stables, meet me there. Ten minutes."

Tedros left the inn, making his way to the stables. The night could not conceal him. The moon's light was dazzling. There were very few pedestrians on the streets. Agil's guards watched him closely. Tedros did not mind, as long as they did not see Sol or Om. He kept a casual pace toward the stables. He entered quickly upon reaching the building. The two revolutionaries entered moments later. Sol stepped up to Tedros, Om behind him.

"Agil and the guards are outside," Sol informed. "They're trying their best to look casual."

"I don't think they suspected us," Om added. "Either way, they look set to arrest you."

Tedros huffed. He led the two men to his mount and asked the man on duty for his mount to be removed. The man opened the gate and gently removed the animal, handing the reins to Tedros. The Djedhi gestured to Om. "To this man," Tedros instructed the stableman. "He just purchased this fine creature from me."

The man gave the reins to Om. The revolutionary mounted quickly. All three men walked back to the main door. Tedros looked at Sol and told him, "We go to the Grand Hall. We'll use back alleys and remain in as much shadow as possible."

Om guided the camel to the exit and dashed away.

Tedros and Sol exited the stable, waiting a moment after Om's departure. Citizens gathered in one area, a group of aristocrats returning from an outing. Kamite servants surrounded them. Tedros and Sol blended in for a second, getting lost in the crowd. It was enough of a camouflage for the two men to slip into an alley.

Agil, keeping a close eye, blinked rapidly once his subjects disappeared from view. The guard-captain surveyed the area. Nothing. He asked for a guard to search Tedros' room, and moments later the guard returned reporting the room was empty. Agil remembered Gretes informing him of Tedros taking a chariot. It headed to the Grand Hall. Agil wondered. He knew that behind the Grand Hall were the abandoned temples. Guard-Captain Atanas sent word of no strangers entering his section of the city. Agil grimaced. He commanded his guards, "Mount up. Horses. Now." The men scrambled to meet their orders.

At that very moment, Tedros and Sol were hopping from alley to alley, sticking close to shadows. Other guard units were on patrol. They dodged detection, and finally came to the Grand Hall. They kept close to other pedestrians when they emerged from an alley, making their way closer to the Hall. Tedros grabbed Sol's shoulder and quickly pulled him into the alley on the side of the Hall. Sol was amazed at the young, nimble man's strength. Once covered by shadow, secure inside the alley, Tedros asked Sol, "Lance or short sword?"

"I'll take the lance," Sol answered. "I practice a staff. The lance is closer to my weapon of choice and skill."

Tedros handed Sol the weapon. "It will be eleven against two. Are you ready for that?"

"We'll see," said Sol. "You don't believe he'll call more of the city's watch?"

Tedros shook his head. "No. This man wants this capture—or kill—for himself." He looked at Sol and said, "A Djedhi Khepri and a revolutionary? He'll have a great promotion for this." He then ordered Sol to move further down the alley. Sol complied. Tedros kept his back tight against the wall, body hidden in shadow. He waited for Agil and his troops. The guard-captain, with his entire unit, galloped into view. He panned the area, looking closely at the Grand Hall.

Tedros clutched the amulet around his neck. He lifted it to his lips and gave it a kiss. "Protect me well, Sauda," he said. He spoke a Djedhi prayer and then made a move from one side of the alley to the other, purposefully catching the guard-captain's eye. He saw Agil point in his direction. His mounted troupe pressed forward, waving off fellow guards and their units. Tedros scurried down the alley.

Agil and his guards formed a single line as they entered the alley. They walked all the way down, out into the abandoned city, the graveyard of buildings. Agil looked in all directions. The moon was great assistance, but Tedros and Sol wanted to be seen. Agil spotted them darting away to the right. He moved his horse forward. "Stop," he yelled at the two of them. "You are under arrest!"

Tedros and Sol made their way to the center of the buildings. Agil and his guards dismounted their horses, the mounts becoming a burden in pursuing their suspects. Agil and his men continued on foot, the captain at the lead. Their heads looked left-to-right, searching, peeking down abandoned alleys and streets.

There was a sound like a gust of wind.

A dark cloud grabbed the guard in drag. The cloud jumped from one alley, scooped up the guard, and disappeared into another. No one noticed. Agil continued, stopping suddenly when he came across the corpse of the trailing guard who rested against a building, his throat open and bleeding. Agil froze. He wondered how the guard stationed at the back of his troupe was now lying dead in front of him.

Agil received his answer when a voice spoke, "You might want to leave before the rest of you end up the same way." It was Tedros. The Djedhi was nowhere to be seen.

"He has magic," whispered a guard.

"Nonsense," replied the captain.

All the guards stood still, one with his back to the secret entrance to one of the temples. It opened. Something grabbed him. A hand wrapped around his mouth, smothering his scream. The guard was dragged inside. The door closed.

"You really think you have an advantage over me in my land?" Tedros' voice reverberated.

"I knew you were a Ngr Warrior the minute I saw you!" the captain shouted into the air. "I count on arresting you and killing your entire band."

"You better *count* your men, Captain," Tedros retorted. "They seem to be disappearing at an alarming rate."

The captain overlooked his crew. Another was missing. He screamed into the night, "You coward! You'll be dead."

Tedros walked from around a corner. The captain looked at him, Tedros was shaking his head. "You don't sound confident about that, Captain."

The temple's secret entrance opened. Sol stepped out, lance in hand. The captain gripped his sword. "The two of you are outnumbered."

Tedros took a fighting stance. It was an elegant, swordsman's pose. "Then why is there fear in your voice?"

Agil trembled with anger. "Kill them," Agil commanded.

Three men charged Sol. The revolutionary slammed the butt of the lance into one of the attacking guards, twirled it around and slammed it against another. Both men fell back unconscious. Sol twisted his body, continuing to twirl the lance, and jabbed the third attacker in the stomach. He flipped the lance again and ran the blade across the man's neck. The bleeding guard dropped to the street, dying.

The captain engaged Tedros. The Djedhi took two steps toward the captain, ducked, and slammed his shoulder into the captain's stomach. Swiftly, Tedros raised the captain up and tossed him over his shoulder. The captain rolled onto the street. Tedros turned and kicked him in the face.

"Behind you," a voice warned Tedros. It sounded like his wife.

The Djedhi turned around. The guards attacked. He faced them, crouched like a cat. He sprang forward. He parried a guard's blade, spun his body around, and then sliced the same guard's stomach, cutting deep. The wound was fatal. Tedros swiped his sword upward at another guard. His blade hacked the guard from belly to neck, under the chin. Sol lanced a guard who almost managed to strike down the Djedhi.

Three guards stood, ready for attack.

The captain jumped to his feet and commanded again, "Kill them!"

The three guards advanced. Sol stood firm. Tedros turned and saw the captain dash away. "Stay on that one," Sol yelled. "I'll take these three."

Tedros followed the captain, Agil heading for his horse. Tedros ducked down a side street and found a shorter path to the guards' mounts. Agil slowed his approach and cursed as he spotted Tedros. He gained his composure and attacked. Tedros parried. The captain was sloppy, clouded by anger and frustration. Every miss and parried swing only made the captain angrier. There was an aura around the Djedhi. Nothing was going to touch him.

The captain swiped at Tedros' head. The Djedhi ducked the swing, countering with a swipe at the captain's chest. Agil was cut, deep. He backed away, panting. He lifted his sword to charge Tedros but was suddenly stabbed through the back by Sol's lance. Sol removed his weapon. Agil fell dead.

"The other three are taken care of," Tedros asked.

"Five," Sol corrected. "Earlier in the fight, I only knocked two unconscious. They got up. So, I knocked them back down. They won't get up this time."

Both men took a breath before clearing the abandoned streets of the bodies. They buried the guard's bodies inside a secret chamber in a temple. They took two horses and made their way out of the city to meet Paki, Sauda, and Om at the rendezvous point. They stayed among the Ta-Setian people for several days before Om returned with Paki and Sauda. Tedros kissed his wife deeply, thanking her for the protective magic. He greeted his friend Paki with a secret, Djedhi handshake and a brotherly embrace. Paki introduced Tedros to a common woman named Olah, the woman he fancied and wish to bring back to the settlement. Tedros had not met the woman, though he had been among the settlement for several days. Tedros gave the woman a polite bow.

Paki informed Sol, "Your friend Om was almost slain. But reason pushed aside paranoia."

Tedros asked Sauda as he gave his wife a tight embrace, "Did you think he was going to bring news of my death?"

"Absolutely not," Sauda replied. "I never doubted my magic."

Tedros took his wife aside and said to her, "I saw our apartment, Sauda. It looked okay."

Sauda smiled. "Maybe while we're here, we can go relive that past. We'll take a day to journey there and then head back to our settlement. Besides," Sauda added, "the young man that delivered your news says his wife lives there."

"To our future," Tedros said kissing his wife again.

Sauda snuggled deep into Tedros' arms. "Mazi wants some of us to move into the urban centers. I suggest we do. We can raise children there." Tedros agreed. And so it was. Tedros, his wife Sauda, and their companions stepped into the future. Though there were dark times, the tales of the Djedhi had no sunset. Their stories of adventure were numerous.

This was but one.

HEADLESS

It was November. Late night. The year was 1798. The road to North Tarrytown was dull and dreary from the inclement fall weather. Nature exhaled a low breath of moisture that condensed over the road and surrounding environment. The fog was thick, the trees reaching through, and the end of their branches piercing the mist like the last, desperate reach of a drowning man. James Williams watched with haggard eyes as the scenery swirled by the carriage window. He was tired. He had been riding inside the carriage for the last two hours, coming from New York City. He was getting cold, he was hungry, and more than that, he was anxious to attend to the business ahead of him.

James' brother accompanied him on this business trip. His name was Kumi. He wore a fine suit, presentable for the business that needed to be handled upstate. Kumi sat up straight, his eyes closed. His body was still, unmoving even in the midst of the carriage waving up and down over the road. James found the sight more fascinating than the scenery outside. He looked over at Kumi, leaned close to him, and asked, "Are you okay?"

"I'm fine," Kumi said, his deep voice reverberating in the carriage's cabin. He adjusted his glasses but did not open his eyes. "I'm just preparing myself." His tone was curt.

James exhaled a low sigh. He sat back and returned his gaze out the window. "We won't be there long, I assure you, Kumi," he informed. "Four days." He looked at his brother again and concluded in a hesitant tone, "There will be no blacks there. Their servants are white, but they'll be use to someone like you."

Kumi's left eye opened. It spotted James. "*Someone like me?*" The eye looked away after Kumi spoke. He hid it again behind a closed lid. "What about you," he questioned. "Do you believe they'll be accustomed to doing business with a mixed, free store owner from New York City?"

The path's terrain became coarser. Kumi was unaffected. James tried to adjust himself to the turbulence. "They think I'm a white man," James said to his brother. Kumi did not reply. James too said nothing more. Both he and Kumi shared a father, a man far darker than most mulattos. James' mother was also a mixed slave. Both parents were the products of African women raped by their slave masters. The brothers' father was a strong and durable man, and because of these traits he was made a breeder several years after James' birth—taking him away from James and his mother. The first woman he was bred with was Kumi's mother, a sixteen-year old African slave girl. The first time she held Kumi was also her last. She was taken south, sold. Their father was sold off as well. The two of them were raised by James' mother who was in service to the wife of a white storeowner in Washington D.C. The storeowner's name was Arthur Williams. He moved his business from Washington D.C. to New York City, opening a large store.

The move to New York City produced a remarkable twist in destiny's plans for the two enslaved brothers. Local street gangs killed both of Arthur Williams' older sons. James never knew if the two boys were involved or innocent victims. Their disposition was always polite. But Jeremiah, the oldest of the two boys, loved to gamble. He had run into trouble at various times with accusations of being a cheat. James figured one imputation led to his fatal stabbing. Carl, the younger brother, was either trying to defend Jeremiah or just killed for association. Though this particular scenario was never proved, it was how James considered it played out, but he never voiced his opinion aloud to anyone but his brother.

Master Williams was never the same afterward. James helped Master Williams with the store business. Ironically, because James' skin was so light, and his features were aquiline and sharp, people figured James was another of Arthur's sons. There was never any question. James' hair was light brown, though peppered with loose coils, which were not tight and dark like Kumi's hair.

Then, Arthur Williams' wife became ill. The disease wracked her body for a year before she died. Arthur Williams passed just a year later, leaving the store in James' care. James was eighteen. Kumi was thirteen, and he helped James by running errands in the city. James' mother kept Kumi close, caring for him as if Kumi was her own child. James deduced Kumi probably reminded his mother of their father, whom she called Talisman. James' mother was always haunted by her separation with their father. Kumi's presence was like a memory in the flesh.

Kumi was darker than his father, though, because of his mother's full African blood. But, he had the same strong features as their father, even at a young age. He had his father's athletic physique, low haircut, and sharp instincts.

Both James and Kumi carried the presence of leaders. James taught his brother to read when Kumi was ten. He tried to teach his mother, but she refused. *"All I need is my spirit,"* she would say to James. *"It's been my spirit that has governed this house. It's been my magic that has always surrounded you and given you this store. Never forget my magic. And make it your own."*

James' mother died when he was twenty-five.

That was five years ago.

Though his mother passed, her magic did remain. Business was never better. Their journey to North Tarrytown was for the benefit of the store. A client requested to see some of the goods James sold. Word spread all round that the Williams' store was stocked with the best goods. North Tarrytown was in need of keeping a fresh supply for its small population.

James watched the fog thicken, and the carriage became absorbed by the mist at the edge of town. The ghostly cloud stayed heavy even as the carriage exited the hollow. James could make out the faint glow of lampposts barely blazing through the fog to illuminate the night. James could not see the town's layout. He trusted the riders guiding the coach. He took his face from the window and looked straight ahead. He spent time fixing his suit, straightening his appearance as the coach took several turns and then eased its travel. It stopped in front of a small tavern. The riders jumped from the stage and opened James' door. James stepped outside, the fog addressing him just as quick as the riders.

"Your party is in there, Mr. Williams," said the rider, his hand aimed in the direction of the tavern.

James thanked the man. He turned around and commanded sternly to his brother, "Kumi, come." Kumi slid from across his seat and exited the coach. He watched the fog ensnare the environment. He heard James inform the driver, "We will return shortly." The man bowed politely. James tipped his silk hat to the driver, and then he and Kumi walked into the tavern, encountering an almost barren atmosphere. The only occupants of the tavern save the barkeep and two barmaids, were three well-dressed men sitting around a single table. James leaned to his brother and said, "Stay by the door."

"I know," Kumi retorted in a low, irritated whisper.

James replied just as sharp, "And remember—"

"—We're not brothers," Kumi finished. "I'll remember my lines, *Masta Williams.*"

James looked at Kumi with a face contorted by frustration. He hated having to act in such a manner, but this was what society demanded. James took a deep breath, exhaled his anger, and walked toward the table feigning a smile. The three men at the table stood up and reached out their hands as James approached. James extended his hand to the eldest gentlemen there. He was of average height and build. His hair had receded, but left enough patch of gray to add to his age. He introduced himself as Jacob Goldman. James smiled and replied that it was a pleasure to do business. Jacob introduced the others as James shook their hands.

The man in the middle, tall, burly, and built for war, dirty-blonde hair atop a pudgy, circular face, was introduced as Campbell. James guessed he was in his early forties. His musket leaned against his chair, and a hunting dagger was sheathed at his hip. The last man was the one James was here to do business with. His name was Talbert Koningswinter. James had met him before. He was the youngest of the three, in his late thirties, though his hair was showing signs of gray.

James bowed at the neck and took a seat.

Jacob pointed to Kumi and remarked, "A fine neggar you have at the door." He leaned over and slapped James' shoulder with a quick hit. "You even have him dressed proper. He's damn near wearing the same suit as you."

James laughed and retorted, "Your property must be a reflection of you."

Jacob swallowed a cup of air and then let out another laugh. "If I dressed all my neggars that nice I'd be broke. You must have so few."

"Not many are needed in the city," James explained substituting a nervous laugh with a nervous smile.

The conversation carried to Kumi's ears. His heart felt as if a long needle had pierced it, followed by an attack of hundreds of wooden splinters. He clenched his teeth, but kept his composure. He had heard worse before, even from James as he sweet-talked various white men soliciting them for business.

Jacob ordered a drink for James, and the small talk quickly dissolved into negotiations and commerce. James informed the men that his shipment of goods was arriving tomorrow. In the meantime, he was here to inspect the town and Talbert's stock of goods at his farm and ranch. In the course of their discussion the gentlemen struck a deal. James' goods would be exchanged for money and other goods. Trade would also remain exclusive between James and Talbert. Jacob Goldman expressed his vision for a line of trade that would reach Canada. Goldman was the mastermind behind the larger picture, with investments that would ensure travel linking one store to the next. A Chain. One name. One business. Many stores. An alliance of tycoons. It came up that Campbell was an ex-soldier employed in Goldman's service as an overseer for black slaves. Campbell was ordered by Jacob to describe his army service, fighting in the Colonial Wars against England. Talbert emphasized that it was men like Campbell that made the country free for all men.

The deal was unofficially finalized with a toast. After taking a sip from his mug, Jacob asked James where he was staying. James answered, "A local inn." Immediately he was met with jeers and scoffs, Talbert waving away what he felt was a nonsensical notion.

"You'll come to my ranch," Talbert invited. "You can see our stock houses. We have plenty of room." He lifted his mug and made a motion toward Kumi. "We even have room for your neggar."

James peeked over his shoulder at his brother. His eyes went back to the three men in front of him. He felt he needed to make an argument, and one that did not give away too much information hinting at Kumi's relation to him. He stated, "I want my property to be well kept. I don't want my property placed in damaging conditions. Neggars can be as fragile as any animal."

"He'll be as well-kept and treated as my favorite horse," Talbert assured.

Jacob added in a relaxed manner, "I brought twenty-two neggars with me. They've been in fine conditions for two days. And they give help around the stock house." He peered at Talbert. "You Northerners. So damn proper. I keep telling you to invest in some neggars."

Talbert shook his head. "Too much trouble," he huffed taking a sip of his drink. "It doesn't fare well. It's expensive and overwhelming. There's not much room for it up here. I keep my business in my family. No neggar is going to learn through experience how I deal with my business. They're a sneaky lot. We've already had an unruly incident with those two Negresses."

"My neggar does fine with helping my business," James said matter-of-factly. He felt the need to speak and interrupt what was brewing between Jacob and Talbert.

Jacob jabbed a finger in James' direction. "You see there." He said to Talbert. Again, he leaned toward James. "If anything happens to your neggar I'll replace it with a fine buck."

Talbert expressed to James, "I assure you, Good Man Williams, our stables will hold him fine."

The comment stung. James wished he could protest another area for his brother to rest, but he could not think of where. He could not suggest whatever room he was going to be in. And he definitely could not ask for Kumi to have his own room. James only hoped Kumi could sustain the conditions for the next four days. More so, James hoped his brother would forgive him. This was only business. James nodded his head and said to Talbert, "Thank you."

The men finished their drinks. Talbert stood up and reached into his pocket for coin to leave on the table. Jacob grabbed Talbert's wrist and kept it in his pocket. "You've done enough. I'll pay," he told Talbert.

Talbert lifted his hands and said, "I will not argue." He knocked on the table and told James, "My wife has a fine meal prepared. I'm sure you're hungry."

Everyone stood up. Jacob left several coins on the table. The men made their way to the door. Kumi immediately opened the door for the approaching men. He bowed at the neck as each man passed through the door, addressing each man as sir. His smile was forced. James was the last to pass him. Kumi did the same for him, exiting behind his brother.

Outside, Kumi overheard Jacob tell James to follow their coach. The man's breath condensed in the cold air, adding to the creeping fog. "I know the air is thick, but just keep close."

"We're on the other side of the town," Talbert informed. "To the north. We're just at the edge of the hollow."

The carriage's driver opened the door for James as they approached. James waved Kumi to step inside first. Kumi slid inside the coach while his brother finished up small talk and business with the three men. There was a joke thrown out by Campbell that produced laughter and a volley of condensed breath from their mouths. James remarked they would converse more when they reached the ranch. With a smile and a dying laugh, James turned to the coach drivers and told them to follow the others. He hopped inside, shutting the door behind him.

Kumi watched his brother. James fixed his suit. "Business over, boss?" Kumi sarcastically asked James. The coach bucked as the riders started forward.

"Business is far from over, Kumi," James said ignoring the sarcasm. "We have several more days of playing this act." He removed his coat and handed it to

Kumi. "You'll need this tonight. You'll be in the stables." Kumi accepted the coat without fuss. His frustration was exhaled in a heavy sigh. James could not ignore his brother's feelings. "I tried to keep us at an inn. Believe me." He gave Kumi a sincere look. "This is not the life we come from. This is not the life *you* come from, even as a servant to Master Williams. We're different. You're different. Yes. But both of us are a huge exception to what rules."

Kumi rolled his eyes. "It's easy for you to say such a thing." He pointed forward, motioning through the barrier and at the coaches they were following. "Look at the role you adapt yourself to."

"Business calls for this," James hissed. "It will only be a few days."

Kumi turned his head toward the window. "What about when these people are your full time partners?"

James' face froze. The expression melted from shock into total perplexity. He never thought of that particular notion. How long could he keep the secrets he had? He only had one answer. He spoke it aloud to his brother. "I'll get Alan to make up legal papers to have you freed. Simple as that." He leaned against the window. The feeling of exhaustion re-surfaced.

The ride out of the small town uncomfortably dragged on in silence. There was a haunting of unresolved emotions, a tension as thick as the fog outside. James was relieved when the coach finally came to a stop at the Koningswinter Estate. He sat up straight when the door opened for him. He was surprised to see a black slave on the other side of the door. He was the same age as his brother, and he wore faded and worn clothes. James guessed he was one of the slaves owned by Jacob. He held out his hand to James and escorted him from the ride.

A black slave too greeted Kumi, opening the door and holding out an assisting hand. He helped Kumi from the coach. The black slave took a step back and inspected Kumi's apparel. He was impressed with the way his fellow black was adorned. "You must be a free man," the black slave exclaimed in an excited, appreciative voice. He was middle aged and portly. The hair on his face, from eyebrows to beard, was fading from black to gray.

Kumi fixed his sullen look, replacing it with a warm smile. The man added warmth to the chilling atmosphere. Kumi appreciated it. "No," he answered, his voice low, nervous about making small talk in front of the white company and his brother. "My Master keeps me well." It was hard for him to speak the words without gritting his teeth, but he kept his emotions behind his smile.

"Well, he must be a good man," the slave retorted. "You must be his only child." The expression caught Kumi off guard. He flinched and was unable to recover with words. His face was stuck with an incredulous look. He more-or-less doubted his hearing than the slave's words. The black slave continued to speak, not missing a beat, only Kumi's expression of surprise. "Masta Gol'man dresses us well," he said as if apologizing for being too overcome by another Master's kept property. "But he got too many of us to throw God's sweet money our way."

Kumi and the slave walked to the front of the coach. They grouped with James, the other slave, the three businessmen, and two white servants holding bright lanterns that turned the fog into an orange haze. Jacob ordered the black slaves to escort Kumi to the stables. Talbert mentioned that Kumi was to be well kept, and he was to be treated well. James wanted to say something, but his voice failed him. His words went from his mind to his throat, and just settled there, never stirring to reach his lips and tongue. He coughed, trying to clear his throat and give himself the courage to speak a departing word to Kumi in front of the three businessmen. But he believed anything he said would embarrass his brother, or worse, excite Kumi's pride to state anything that would put them both in danger.

James' dilemma was unnoticed by the white men in attendance.

Kumi was dragged away like a prisoner, the two black slaves on either side of him. He looked over his shoulder to throw an expression that would cast guilt onto his brother. Instead, the medallion dangling around Jacob's neck distracted his gaze. It was a talisman that looked much like a cross. It had a loop for a head instead of a straight stalk. Kumi remembered James' mother speaking of such a talisman. She called it an ankh. It was a symbol forged in Africa. Kumi's gaze was held so long on Jacob that he noticed another talisman around the businessman's neck. It consisted of two equilateral triangles overlapping one another. One triangle pointed to the heavens, and the other pointed to the earth. Kumi also knew of such a symbol, recalling that his mother told him it was actually called a merkaba, and that it too had its origins in Africa. But, Judaic Europeans called the symbol the Star of David, though only the spiritualist, and not the majority of the faith's European followers who argued against incorporating and using a symbol that held occult origins.

Kumi noticed the same medallions were worn by the other men, none of which, for one reason or another, he believed were Judaic. He wondered why men of such stern business fashion were strapped with superstitious devices. But before he could wonder any further, the fog swallowed the images of his brother and the businessmen, the orange glow of the lanterns bubbling from the thick, earthly cloud.

The wind howled, carrying through the dense, low, hanging mist. Kumi looked to either side of him and inspected the black slaves flanking him. The black slave on his right looked passed him to the other and suggested, "We could escape in this fog." He looked behind him and could see nothing but a smothering dense cloud. Even the orange glow cast by the lanterns was faint and distant. "They even let us go alone."

The wind howled again. A wild animal joined in nature's song.

The black slave on Kumi's left shook his head, disagreeing. "Don't mind those thoughts, now," he said in a low voice. "If Good Man Campbell don't find you, the woods will. It's already done swallowed up some boys. It's a better guard than them soldiers."

"A devil's lie," the young black slave argued. "Them boys returned just today."

The one on the left retorted, "And they ain't look the same. Lifes is missin' from they eyes." He tugged on Kumi and warned, "Don't listen to this fool."

Kumi beamed and assured the older man, "I wouldn't dare leave the life I have. It's not as hard as most of…ours." His smile faded. He became uncomfortable with his words. He did not want to seem condescending or conceited.

The younger black slave on his right picked at Kumi's sleeves. "I knows you wouldn't want to give none of this up, boy. You sho' is treated well. You seen this here," he asked the other.

The older black slave smiled. "I sho' did. He ain't goin' nowhere."

Kumi felt the need to tell both men of his status as a free man. But he knew that would be a death sentence for he and his brother. He kept his secret buried. There was heat at the base of his spine. Kumi was frustrated with his inability to speak the truth. He decided to take the conversation back to a statement made by the black slave on his left. "You said life was missing from their eyes. What did you mean by that?"

The man chuckled at Kumi's speech. It was proper, sounding educated. But he did not comment. He just brushed his laughter aside and answered, "Somethin' evil got in them. I tell you boy, it's the woods."

"Just the same," the other interjected. "Good Man Campbell beat them hard, is all. Them boys just actin' right. They lucky they wasn't killed."

"I just don't know about that," retorted the older black slave. "Nobody know what happened to Miss Sally and Miss Kendra. They ain't been seen at all."

Large, fiery eyes glowed through the fog from the far left. It was the ranch house, indoor lanterns glowing through the windows. Kumi knew that James was enjoying a warm meal, and a climate made moderate by a fireplace and the burning lamps. Kumi thought about the comfortable bed his brother was going to enjoy. Kumi's body started to ache from the long travel, but at the moment he would have preferred to sleep in the coach than the stable. He looked straight ahead. The fog began to part, and he could see the stable in front of him. Kumi started shivering from the cold. He buttoned up the coat James provided him. He witnessed the other men becoming affected by the air's cold sting.

"And where do you two sleep?" Kumi asked the men.

"Here, with the rest," answered the younger slave.

The stable doors seemed to jump out from the fog as they made their final approach. The black slave on Kumi's right opened the doors. The fog was forced away and a wave of air escaped the stables. The air made a deep thunderous moan and carried with it the stench of waste. The air was warm and smothering. Kumi stepped inside and noticed burning lamps made of jars filled with wax and a thick candlewick. The black slave on his left closed the doors once they were in. Kumi observed the other black slaves lift their heads from their hay-constructed beds to see who was coming through the door. There were low mumbles and voices asking for identification.

"It's just us," said the younger black slave. "Zephon and Melchiah." He pointed to the black slave on the left and commanded, "Go and fix this boy's space, Zephon."

Zephon walked to a ladder and ascended to the stable's second level. The ladder wobbled, the hefty black slave's weight challenging its stability. Kumi observed many black slaves huddled into compartments. A bucket used for waste accompanied them. Melchiah led him to the ladder. They watched Zephon descend.

"You lucky, boy," Zephon said. "You all by yo'self up there." He reached the ground and added, "But it's a little colder too. There's a thick blanket, though."

Melchiah tapped Kumi with his hand. "You still treated well," he chuckled.

"Thank you," Kumi expressed.

Zephon quickly shook his head. "No, no, no, boy. It ain't us to thank, now. It's Masta Gol'man and Masta Konswintah that done all this."

Melchiah rolled his eyes at Zephon and said to Kumi, "You welcome." He shook Kumi's hand. "I serve the blood." He then gave a frustrated eye to Zephon. "You just keep secrets." He let go of Kumi and told him. "Go on and rest, boy. We on alert to work your Good Man's first shipment of goods arrivin' tomorrow."

"Whole lot," Zephon exclaimed. "I hear yo' Good Man got good stock."

Melchiah started to speak. "Prob'ly why them bastards—" he then laughed, "—see now, boy, that's what I call them. But, uh, them bastards Jacob and Talbert want him for trade. That's the reason, now," Melchiah said proudly, as if teaching Kumi something he was blind of. He pointed to his ear and clarified, "We hear when they don't think we listenin'."

Kumi liked Melchiah. He shook his hand again. He felt the urge to confess that he could read, but Kumi did not trust Zephon. He expressed being tired, and wished both men goodnight. He ascended the ladder and came across his bed atop the stable's rafters. There was a pile of hay for bedding and a thick, lightly tattered blanket. It was colder up in the rafters. There was a chill, but not quite as piercing as the outside. Kumi crawled to the blanket and rolled himself inside tightly. He removed his glasses and eased himself to sleep.

A vivid dream came to Kumi. The dream took place in the morning, and inside the stable. The stable doors opened. Jacob Goldman walked inside. Next to him was Zephon. The black slave looked at Jacob and asked, "Who you want?"

"There are only eight left that need branding," Jacob said in a cold manner. He ordered, "Pick from them." His voice echoed eerily, waving like the dreamy vision Kumi witnessed.

Zephon hustled on Jacob's command. He separated two black slaves from the stock, an elder man and elder woman. Their names were Melvin and Sara. Zephon and Jacob escorted them from the stable. The doors closed with a loud thud. Kumi's dream turned black, and then dissolved to another image. The stable doors opened. Sara and Melvin were escorted back inside. Where life flowed through them before, there was nothing now. Their expression was blank. Jacob and Zephon stood at the stable doors watching the two black slaves return to their compartment without escort. The two black slaves went to sleep.

"Let them rest, Zephon," Jacob ordered.

The stable doors closed again. All, again, went black in Kumi's dream, but not for long. Darkness faded into another image. It was night in the stables. Zephon stirred from his sleep and slipped out of his compartment. He crept cautiously toward Melchiah's compartment near the door. He shook the young man awake.

"We gon' leave now," Zephon whispered.

"Is you crazy," Melchiah hissed. "You gon' yell about *not* leavin' at all and now you talk about headin' off?"

"I don' trust that new negga they done brought here," Zephon explained. "He live a good life. He don't want to leave. You heard him."

Was Kumi awake?

"I *had* to say those things," Zephon continued. "He could turn us in." He pulled on Melchiah's arm. "Now I know a way out. Let's go. We'll be free. Miss Sally and Miss Kendra already gone. That's why we ain't seen them. They gone."

"But I ain't ready," Melchiah pleaded. "Why didn't you say somethin' before I rested that you was just talkin' nonsense?"

"Boy, you want to leave or stay?" Zephon asked forcefully. "Any negga in they right mind is always ready to leave. Now let's git to gittin'."

Melchiah considered his offer. He leaned close and asked in a stumbling voice, "Campbell?"

"With a good meal in him and some drink, that man is out for the night." Zephon said in a rough whisper. "Ain't no other guards. This is the time. Fog is still thick too."

Melchiah was inspired. He felt strong and refreshed by the mere notion of freedom. He lifted himself up. Quietly, the two men made their way to the doors, opening them just enough to slip through. The wind barked its way inside the stable. Zephon peered back to see that no one was disturbed, sound asleep. Zephon closed the doors and the two men were gone.

The dream followed the men outside. They moved quietly through the estate. Zephon miscalculated nature, unpredictable as she could be. The fog had dissipated some, but that which remained was used as cover. Melchiah and Zephon sneaked their way to the misty woods surrounding the ranch and stock house. The foggy hollow was a spider-web of interlocked branches and trees. The two black slaves winded their way through the intricate and organic maze. Zephon took lead, snapping twigs out of their path and finding the least dense areas to move through. The further they trekked, the darker it became.

Zephon started to slow up as fatigue overcame his heavy physique. He gasped for air, bending down. One arm leaned on a tree. His tongue hung low from an agape mouth like a dog panting for air. Melchiah stood next to him. The young man was anxious, wanting desperately to continue. He grabbed Zephon's arm and tugged, trying to stand the older black slave upright.

"I need to rest," said Zephon. "Give me some time. I'll be back to—" A twig snapped. Zephon immediately stopped talking. Both men were still. Something else was disturbing the woods.

The brush rustled as something moved it aside. Dried fragments of twigs and leaves lining the ground, crackled as someone walked over them. A sharp sound cut the air. Something was carving a path for itself, hacking away thicket. Melchiah crouched low, trying his best to use the night as cover, to blend in with the winding environment of brush and trees. He cursed himself for not having a practical plan. And here they were. Trapped. Campbell, who they thought was submerged in a drunken sleep, on their trail, tracking them down.

The sound of woodland debris crunching grew louder. Strangely, the possibility of their pursuer being the soldier Campbell started to subside. It was something else creeping through the night, moving in a slow, rhythmic manner. There was an icy hissing sound echoing. Melchiah noticed the fog lift. Stories of the woods infiltrated his thoughts. His heart raced. He was warned about the woods. He heard they were swallowing the citizens of North Tarrytown. He turned and saw Zephon beginning to shake.

Kumi was frightened, the emotions resonating in his dream overtaking him. He tried to wake up. His body started shaking and sweating. His eyes did not open. He tried to scream and warn the two men. He could see what was coming toward them. He could see its large, black form melting in and out of the shadows, turning into a black mist and filtering through the intertwined branches. Then it condensed into something solid, big. It looked human. It had arms and legs. Hands. Gripped tightly into each hand was a long, hooked blade attached to a short wooden handle.

Sickles.

Death was coming closer, hovering over the two black slaves. There was something attached to the figure, black and watery, flowing in waves from its back.

A cape.

Kumi's scream was smothered by sleep. All he could do was watch.

The figure stood over the two men, tall and ominous. It was behind them. They sensed its presence, turning slowly to gaze on the specter. Zephon grabbed Melchiah's arm and sprinted through the woods. He crashed through the brush using his weight to tear through any of the brittle obstacles in their path. The figure pursued them, its clothing clanking as if it wore armor. The figure swiped at the brush, cutting it down in an angry attack. Zephon screamed to Melchiah, telling him they needed to cross a body of water for the spirit to cease its pursuit of them. But Zephon, despite his plan, led Melchiah into a clearing. With Melchiah's arm still in his grip, he swung Melchiah ahead and let him go. Zephon looked up and saw Jacob standing there. He wore a black cape, a black suit, a silk hat, and a smile.

"Here he is, Masta Gol'man," Zephon announced.

Jacob waved Melchiah closer. "Come. Be the last two."

Melchiah was out of breath, but not without words as he inspected Jacob Goldman's attire. He cursed, "You bastard. You ain't no Baron Samedi. Dress all in his clothes, you ain't ever gon' be the Baron."

The large, shadowy figure weaved its way from the woods, gliding through the night and into the clearing. Its ghostly black form hovered over Zephon and Melchiah. Zephon's eyes went wide. He pleaded with Jacob, "But I thought he was the last."

"Good servant, join him," said Jacob.

"Please, Masta Gol'man," Zephon screamed. "No." He turned and watched the figure lift his sickles. "No," he yelled again. "No!"

Kumi lifted from the pile of hay. He inhaled rapidly.

It was morning. Kumi was awake. Kneeling at his feet was his brother James, shaking his leg. "Come on," he said. "You have to help the others unload the cargo. It arrived early this morning. Everyone is out there." Kumi looked over the side of the rafters. All the black slaves were gone. He looked at his brother wide eyed. James asked Kumi, "Are you okay? Did you sleep well? Were you cold? If you have a fever, I'll get you excused from the work."

Kumi ignored James' questions. He reached out his hand and asked in a quavering voice, "Are…are those two men who brought me here out there?"

James wanted to question Kumi again, but instead he answered him, "Jacob's slaves are all accounted for. I'm sure they're outside." He lowered his brother's hand. "You okay?"

Kumi relaxed. He exhaled, "Just a bad dream, I guess."

"Come then," James ordered standing up. "Get yourself together. I don't need these people getting suspicious of you or my relation to you. I need you together. Now, come on. There will be a meal for the slaves once this is done. You'll be given time to bathe. Warm water."

Kumi stood up, James' sentiments not as comforting as his brother presented them. He followed his brother down the ladder and out of the stables. The morning was cloudy. Fog still populated the area, but was not as dense as the previous night. With the fog thinned, Kumi absorbed the sight of the ranch and stock house. Truthfully, there were two stock houses, and they were as large as mansions. Between them stood an E-shaped ranch house. Two large wagons, filled with boxed goods, stood outside the stock house on the left. The black slaves were already unloading the goods and taking them inside. Campbell stood guard. Five other men stood with him. Jacob and Talbert conversed pleasantly. Beside them was another white man named Alan Reynolds. Kumi knew him. He was James' lawyer. Alan had a handsome chiseled face with a dark, thick patch of well-groomed hair atop his head, at the moment covered by a silk hat. A thin, dark mustache lined his face. He was dressed in an expensive suit.

Kumi grouped with the regiment of black slaves that were unloading the wagons. He noticed a second stable as he traveled toward the black slaves. It was located behind the stock house on the left. There were two fenced areas for livestock constructed near the second stable. No animals occupied the areas. Close to the fenced areas was a small shed.

Kumi joined the working line of black slaves. He spotted Zephon and Melchiah. They were alive and attending to their duties. Kumi heard Talbert saying to Jacob that his wife was complaining the Negresses were cluttering the house, apparently taking away her duties as a good woman. Kumi also heard that Talbert's two sisters-in-law, however, appreciated the Negress slaves' helping hand. Both men commented there was nothing finer than a Negress in the kitchen. Kumi kept his face from contorting. His stomach twisted from anger held down. It rumbled, bubbled, and reminded him of his hunger. Kumi heard Jacob speak about the Negresses preparing rice, beans, and bread for the slaves once they finished with unloading the wagons.

"Kumi," James called to his brother with an authoritative voice. "Get in line and help with the other neggars." It was unnecessary for James to shout any order, Kumi thought, considering he was already in line and assisting James.

James' lawyer, Alan Reynolds, was surprised. He exclaimed, "You have Kumi doing work?" He put his hand out toward Kumi and added, "In those fine clothes? That's a waste of money and stitching."

"He spoils that damn neggar," Jacob noted, elbowing James while giving him a wink. "I can't believe I'm doin' business with you two." He pointed to Talbert and said, "This one won't invest properly in a set of neggars; and this one invests poorly. At least you both know trade."

The businessmen erupted into laughter.

Kumi bit his lip inconspicuously. The bite was hard, almost enough to draw blood. Kumi felt he needed to hurt something. Someone. Even himself. There was a heavy feeling in his chest. He could barely breathe the anger was so strong. He had nowhere to put it. He grabbed a case of goods instead and walked into the stock house, the inside of which was spacious, though already filled with other cases of goods not brought by his brother. The other stored crates were stacked haphazardly, and the black slaves worked to organize them in neat rows and lines. They worked in unison, systematically. Kumi stepped inside the rhythm of his fellow workers. He put the crate in a proper place and went back for more. He managed to find Melchiah, greeting him kindly. Melchiah returned the greeting. He sounded tired. Kumi waited until the two were deep inside the stock house to warn him, "If you plan to escape, don't. You'll be caught. And don't trust Zephon."

Melchiah reacted slowly to Kumi's words, his head lifting in a lethargic manner. His eyes were droopy. But there was something more to Melchiah's demeanor. Rather, according to Kumi, there was something less. Lifeless.

"I wasn' thinkin' on runnin'," Melchiah said in a hebetudinous tone, his words sluggish. He faced forward, trekking back to his duties. Kumi noticed Melchiah was walking hunched over.

Kumi quickly caught up with Melchiah and asked, "Are you okay?"

Melchiah smiled without looking at Kumi. "I'm fine, good sir. I just have my duties for Masta Gol'man. Theys got to be done. You best get to doin' yo duties too."

"Oh," Kumi said starting to understand. "We'll talk later," he whispered. Kumi looked over his shoulder to see if they were being watched. Campbell and his company were too busy with the other black slaves. The other two guards walked into the stock house and took either side of the door. They were armed with muskets.

Kumi resumed his duties. He became more anxious for time with Melchiah than the meal promised after their duties. Kumi and three other black slaves were dismissed from the stock house and escorted to the ranch by the two guards. Their duty was to carry the prepared pot of rice and beans from the kitchen to the stable. They entered the front hallway through the door and continued straight into a small cooking area. There were several black women huddled inside the room. A bubbling vat of beans and another of rice simmered near the window. From around the corner peeked Katherine Koningswinter. She looked older than Talbert, and she had long brown hair. She watched the black slaves closely, suspiciously.

Kumi stood still as the other black slaves stepped forward to attend with carrying the large cauldrons. There was an inquisitive look on his face as he heard the loud sobs of a young girl coming from another room. He started to tremble. The sobs were eerie, yet melodic. The sound was icy, like the hiss of the creature in Kumi's dream. Kumi guessed the little girl was ending her crying.

Kumi must have been concentrating on the sobs too long. A guard asked him in a forceful tone, "Is something the matter, neggar?"

Kumi jumped at the sound of the guard's voice. "Sorry, Good Man. I's just heard the li'l girl sobbin' in the otha room is all?"

The guards gave one another a look. They looked at Kumi simultaneously, raising an eyebrow. "Little girl?" The same guard questioned. "Ain't no little girls here. There's only the good women of the house, neggar. That's Miss Katherine Koningswinter and her sisters."

Katherine's innocent examination of the slaves dissolved. She came from around the corner huffing. She pointed an angry finger at Kumi and shouted to the guards, "Please, get that neggar to work!"

Kumi noticed the scar on Katherine's face, though it was partially covered by her hair. The scar went from her chin to above her eye. Kumi looked away, feigning shame as the woman continued to scream at the guards.

Katherine ordered angrily, "And get my husband in here this minute!"

"Yes, Miss Koningswinter," both guards said politely. One left voluntarily. The other stayed behind to watch the slaves.

Every black slave in the room tightened with tension.

Katherine started to wave the women away. "Go on! Get out of here! The rest of you, get your food and leave."

The women shuffled out, holding a basket of bread. Kumi helped with the large vats of beans and rice. Despite the cauldron's weight, the black slaves moved quickly, scattering from Katherine's exasperation. Kumi tried to keep his eyes aimed toward the stable as everyone left the room, but his gaze wandered to the other guard who now spoke with Talbert Koningswinter. Kumi's heart raced. He knew there was going to be trouble between he and James. But Kumi pushed his worry aside when the aroma of cooked food writhed from the large, heavy pots. The redolence filled his nose. His stomach tightened with hunger pains, grumbling. He had not eaten since yesterday afternoon. His footsteps were now motivated by sustenance.

The women entered the stables ahead of Kumi and the male slaves. They held open the door as the men passed through. The second guard was right behind them, musket aimed. He stopped at the door watching the slaves closely from the outside. The men lay the pots down in the center of the stable. A female black slave explained they would begin when the others returned. Her accent was thick. Her words sounded garbled to Kumi, but he still understood her. He liked the way she spoke. It sounded African.

The other black slaves drifted into the stable. Kumi felt as if he had been waiting forever. He was hungry. He watched the other black slaves rush to their compartments, gather small wooden bowls supplied to them by Jacob, and then form a single line to receive their rations. The black slaves bowed appreciatively, one-after-the-other as the women dumped food into their bowl and gave them a slice of bread. Kumi went to the ladder to climb up to the rafters and retrieve a bowl he hoped had been set for him, unseen by last night's darkness. James walked into the stable before he could take a step. His brother called for him. Kumi turned around and saw the incensed look on his visage. James motioned Kumi toward him by wiggling a single finger.

"Now," he said adamantly.

Kumi exhaled. He knew what was about to transpire. James grabbed his arm tightly and took Kumi around to the side of the stable. He threw him against the wall and slapped Kumi with a force that left a throbbing stinging sensation on Kumi's cheek. "You called Miss Koningswinter a little girl?" James yelled slapping Kumi again.

Kumi recovered from the barrage of slaps. He felt the side of his cheek and said, "No. I heard a young girl crying. I just pointed it out when I was asked—"

James slapped his brother again. "Ain't any goddamn other women in that house! Her sisters left for town for the day."

"But I heard—"

"Goddamn your hearing!" James said hitting Kumi so hard his lip split.

Blood started to flood Kumi's mouth. He stood firm and clutched his fist.

James looked down at Kumi's balled fingers. "Don't you dare," he hissed. "Loosen yourself, now! Are you crazy? Do you know what trouble you will get us both in? Do you know the business you will ruin?"

Kumi relaxed. "You think I don't know my place," he expressed through pressed teeth. "You know this isn't the first time I've had to shuffle my feet for white folks? You think I just forgot all those years with Master Williams? You think I forgot how he sold my mother and *our* father as if they were—"

"His property," James protested. "He was the figure who had complete authority over their lives. They were no different than his livestock!" He looked Kumi up and down and added, "And he treated us well. He died for you. He gave you the good life you have. We have his store. He left that to us. You remember that. And you remember how to act." His voice was low when he addressed his brother next. "Do you have a problem because this is me? Because it's me you have to take orders from? We're just pretending. We're tryin' to get a deal—"

"This ain't the first time I've had to shuffle my feet for you either," Kumi reminded as he wiped his mouth and chin of blood. He was not bleeding as hard as he imagined.

James caught his breath. "Get in there and get somethin' to eat," he commanded. "And don't say a goddamn word. Just keep your mouth shut."

Kumi bowed and replied in a sarcastic voice, *"Yessir, Masta Boss Sir."* He made his way back around to the front of the stable and walked inside. He went to the ladder and climbed up. He found a small bowl, climbed down, walked to the line of black slaves, and finally received his portion of food. He thanked the woman as she gave him a hand of bread and a spoon. He turned around and made his way back to the ladder. Melchiah, enjoying his meal in a compartment, caught his eye. Kumi walked over and joined him. He knelt down next to Melchiah and asked, "You think we can talk now?"

Melchiah looked up at Kumi, his face still dreary. "I ain't speakin' no mo' 'bout up and leavin'." Melchiah's voice was drained of its enthusiasm and youth. He dragged his words as if he multiplied in age and exhaustion. The sight of the changed Melchiah shook Kumi's senses. He believed Melchiah would let go of his act. But Melchiah was just as he was in the stock house. Melchiah continued, "All that there is nonsense talk. Talkin' 'bout runnin' off."

"I don't want to run off," Kumi corrected. "I have a good life, remember? I just thought to warn you."

"You ain't got to warn me," Melchiah smiled. "Here is where I'll be." The black slave lifted his bowl up at Kumi. "And I'll be plenty fine if I can find some time to eat."

"Sorry." Kumi nodded his head and stood up. He pivoted and headed toward the ladder, climbing up with his bowl and bread balanced in his hands. Once atop the rafters, he huddled on the bed of hay with his blanket. As he ate, something below caught his eye. It was the sight of two familiar faces.

Sara.

Melvin.

Kumi looked closer at them. It seemed unreal. He had never before seen them, save his dream. But here they were in reality, and there was something unreal about them, lifeless, just like his dream.

They ate. They did not speak. Not to each other. Not to anyone.

Kumi then noticed there were no conversations at all. Black slaves were just eating, minding themselves. Kumi was forced to do the same. He finished his small meal. His stomach could have used more. There was not enough food for seconds. He lay down and wrapped himself in his blanket. He fell asleep.

Images flashed.

The first image lasted for no more than a second, and then all went black. The image came again, spliced with a moment of total darkness. Every time the image appeared, the sound of a girl crying could be heard. It was the same sobs he heard inside the Koningswinter ranch house. Then came the scene again. It stayed. There was a thirteen-year old mulatto slave girl tied to a bed. She lay naked with a man forcing himself on her. The man's hand covered her mouth. He let out a roar with every penetrating thrust into the young girl. The image was like a flood. There was no intermission of darkness. The girl's features were much the same as James'. She had light skin, with soft patches of brown swirling on her skin like clouds stretching and dissipating. She had light brown hair, almost blonde. Her light brown eyes, watered with tears, dared to open when she became tired of the darkness. Kumi felt her name. The wind cried Sally.

The man atop Sally was Talbert Koningswinter. Surrounding him were four other men waiting around the bed to engage the girl once Talbert was finished with her. Campbell and Jacob were in the room. Kumi did not know the other men, but his dream gave him insight. The tall, blonde man was named Seth MaGruder. He wore the same ankh medallion around his neck that Kumi saw on Jacob when he first arrived at the ranch house. This man was a trader, and he was part of the line being formed by Jacob and Talbert.

The second man was a burly ex-soldier named Sonny Hollister. He was extremely pale, but not for any reasons concerning health. His hair was a mess, wild, stringy and oily, but his mustache and beard were finely trimmed.

The scene flashed again.

Each cut showed another man atop the thirteen-year old girl. Her sobs echoed and remained even as the scene faded and opened up to the kitchen area of the ranch house where Kumi had been earlier that day. Black women stirred food for the slaving black men outside. There was a young black woman named Kendra. She had brown skin and brown, exotic, almond shaped eyes. Her hair draped past her shoulders in an alluring tangle and net of soft spiraling locks. Most would have called her hair a mess. Kumi's consciousness was attracted to its wild display. He found her beautiful not just because of her physical traits, but because of her actions.

Kendra's face was wracked with tears as she listened to the muffled cries coming from the thirteen-year old girl trapped in the master bedroom. Anger and grief tormented Kendra as the voices of the men chanting, taunting obscenities and slurs disturbed her ears. The same emotions choked Kumi. He felt as if water filled his throat. Kumi's body convulsed. Kendra's emotions possessed him.

There was another flash.

The men were finished with Sally. Talbert pulled on two handles at the side of the bed. The underside pulled out as a long drawer. Hollister wrapped cloth around Sally's mouth as Campbell cut the ropes binding her to the bedpost. The men handled her. She jerked her body to escape, her hands and feet now bound together. But Sally's actions were to no avail. She was tired, overwhelmed. The men lowered her into the large drawer and pushed it back into the side of the bed.

Kumi heard Kendra scream, pulling the images back to the scene concerning her. The black woman reached down and snatched a piece of charcoal. She charged toward the front door. The other black women backed away from Kendra as Katherine Koningswinter raced after her, a knife in hand. Katherine caught Kendra by the hair and slammed her against the door. The force was so strong, and Katherine was so possessed with anger, that she dropped the knife. Kendra swiped it, stood, and slashed the side of Katherine's face. The mistress clutched her bleeding wound and screamed to her husband for help. Kendra stood up and darted through the door. She dropped the knife and made her way to the stable. Hollister and Seth MaGruder were close in pursuit.

The dream shifted. Kendra was locking herself in a shed. She shut the door and, using the charcoal, began to draw symbols around the door's handle. She huddled up into the corner while crying and breathing hard. The shed's door jiggled. The handle shook. MaGruder lay on the other side. He smiled thinking of the pleasure he would receive chastising Kendra. The symbols made from the charcoal burned brightly, but did not spread to affect the wooden shed. The heat instead writhed through Magruder's hand, traveled up his arm, and clutched his heart. MaGruder froze. His eyes went wide, his mouth hung agape. Pressure formed around his heart and it imploded as if crushed by a mighty hand. Blood jumped from his mouth and spattered against the shed. MaGruder's body coughed one final time. He then fell backwards, dead.

The other men gathered outside the shed. Jacob took Seth's medallion before the man concocted a torch to burn the shed. Before Seth tossed the burning wood, his body burst into flames, disintegrating instantly. Jacob was pushed away by the force. He slowly stood up. He backed away from MaGruder's body and called for several black slaves to bring the corpse back to the house. Jacob whispered to Talbert to leave the woman inside the shed and let her die of starvation.

Everyone walked away.

Everything went black.

Kumi heard a feminine voice whisper in an icy tone, *"Help me."*

The voice pulled him from his dream. He lifted his body up. Kumi's eyes opened to darkness. It was nighttime in the stable. Several candle jars glowed below him and he could see that all the black slaves were asleep. Kumi was still trembling. His brow was drenched with sweat. The stable door opened and the wind rushed inside bringing with it a voice and message.

"Help me," the icy wind whispered.

Kumi was still. He closed his eyes and tried to breathe in a relaxing rhythm. But the wind interrupted him. It glided up to the stable rafters and whispered into his ear, *"Help me."*

Kumi opened his eyes. He removed the blanket from around him. He crawled to the ladder and worked his way down, and then out of the open door. Kumi peeked his head outside. There were two guards. One was asleep. The other was awake. Kumi lowered his head and knocked on the door to stir the guard's attention. Startled, the guard lifted his musket to Kumi. He shook his head negatively and aimed his thumb toward the inside of the stable. He said, "If ya need to piss or shet ya got a bucket inside near your bed, neggar."

"I just need some fresh air, sir?" Kumi said humbly, his head still low. "I's won't take long, just a little while. You can watch me. I ain't goin' nowhere."

The guard continued to inspect Kumi suspiciously, a single eyebrow raised. He understood that Kumi was not the property of Jacob Goldman but of the other businessman, James Williams. Mister Goldman had given the guard full right over the neggars he owned. All forms of discipline were acceptable. However, James Williams had not given the guards full sanction and warrant over the treatment of the single neggar he dragged with him from New York City. Kumi was thinking the same notion. And he hoped the circumstances would yield to him.

The guard huffed. His breath, condensing in the cold air from his nostrils, resembled a dragon's puff. He lifted two fingers. "Ya got two minutes, neggar. One, two."

"Yes, sir." Kumi stated. "Thank you, sir."

"I've got a watch to keep time."

"Yes, sir." Kumi nodded his head. "And you can watch me too. I'm gon' stays right here."

The guard grumbled and removed a dingy pocket watch.

Kumi panned his vision to find the shed he saw in his dreams. He knew there was one near the stock house, but he figured there was another. He remembered his dream clearly. His memory was clearer than he would have liked. The feelings were still there. Grief. Torment. Pain. His memory recalled Kendra running toward the stables. The men chasing her had the ranch house at their backs. Kumi figured the shed must be behind the stable. He stepped forward, trying to get a view from around the stable.

The guard tightened his grip on his musket. "Watch your move, neggar."

Kumi replied humbly, "Yes, sir, Good Man."

Kumi peered through the darkness, straining his vision. He could see nothing from where he stood. He could see the silhouette of the trees swaying in the light wind. They were barely visible. There was very little light to make out anything. The movements of the trees were just a faint shadow against the night. There was not even moonlight. The branches swayed in the wind. They reached out from the consuming darkness. Then, Kumi saw something that paralyzed his movement.

A shadow separated from the darkness. Kumi just watched, as if this was his dream. The specter walked ominously toward the stable. A low, clanking sound played in Kumi's ears. It sounded like chains dragging and rattling against a cobblestone road. The heavy pace of boots mixed with the clanking. Kumi's eyes narrowed on the instruments the creature gripped in either hand.

Sickles.

The specter's cape billowed like a watery black wave. Kumi noticed the one missing attribute from this foreboding phantom menace. It had the physique of a man. It was built like a warrior and carried its shadowy frame like a suit of armor.

But there was no head.

"All right," said the guard. "Back inside, neggar."

Fear loosened its grip on Kumi's ankles. But instead of sinking back into the ground, fear jumped into Kumi's legs and made them shake with every step he took back to the stable. He took a loud, deep breath and almost passed out. He exhaled and said to the guard, "Thank you, sir." Kumi slipped back into the stable and closed the door. He ran to the ladder and ascended to the rafters. He cast his blanket over him and lay down. He tried to close his eyes but they continued to tremble, remaining open.

Kumi listened. Everything was still. There was a loud gust of wind. The sound woke no one. Kumi heard the guard outside slumping to the ground. The specter must have claimed a life. Lives, considering both guards.

The stable door opened and the black shadow glided inside. It swirled like a small tornado, and then formed physically into the headless figure. Kumi stared down at the apparition, lying on his stomach, peering down through a set of beams. And though it had no head, Kumi knew it was somehow staring back at him. Kumi's eyes started to water, his body trembled from a sudden chill. He slowly lowered his eyelids. He could not run. He could not scream. He did the only thing he could. He tried to keep his eyes on the situation.

Kumi opened his eyes, his gaze aimed at the stable doors. The creature was gone. This was not a reason for Kumi to celebrate or relax, especially since he could feel something standing over him. Kumi did not face the specter. The chill in the air became heavier, as if disturbed by the creature's presence. Kumi's body felt the weight of the creature's proximity. It was close, bending down to inspect Kumi's still body.

Kumi heard the phantom grunt. Air seethed from out of the area where the neck and head were missing. The figure exhaled a cold breath that fell on Kumi's neck. Its exhalation was like speech. The creature rubbed Kumi's cheek with the tip of one sickle blade. Kumi started to chant a simple African phrase taught to him by James' mother. The chant called for protection. Kumi also balled his fist and opened his other hand. He was ready to strike quickly, grabbing one sickle and punching the creature in the chest.

But the creature stood up before Kumi could react. It stepped away, swirled into a shadow, and disappeared. The weight of its presence lifted. Kumi looked over his shoulder and saw nothing. He closed his eyes and breathed in a rhythm that relaxed him until he was asleep. There were no vivid dreams, just a peaceful darkness. Shouting forced Kumi awake. It was morning. Kumi stood up, exhaling hard, his heart racing. Campbell, along with other guards, stormed into the stable. They gathered Jacob's black slaves and forced them outside. Campbell ordered each one to line up. James followed the guards inside, pacing past them and ascending the ladder to Kumi.

"Outside," he said in a loud and stern manner. *"Now."*

Kumi jumped up at his brother's command and descended the ladder, following James outside into another cold, dreary day. Kumi saw every black slave lined up, standing tall and firm. James reached around and grabbed Kumi tightly by the arm. He led Kumi to the end of the line and placed him a good distance from Jacob's stock of black slaves. Kumi looked on in concern. He had no idea what would follow. He kept his eyes on James who jabbed a finger in Campbell's direction. The ex-soldier addressed the black slaves, "Last night, Good Man Tierney was found dead. Good Man Tierney was standing guard outside on his shift while Good Man Meyers slept next to him."

Kumi's heart raced. He pressed his teeth hard against each other trying to slow his heart's pace and his growing anxiety.

Campbell continued to scream, "Good Man Tierney was choked!" He shook his finger at every slave. "And there will be a good disciplinin' to this entire company of neggars if there are no answers."

Kumi noticed Melchiah looking at him. Kumi put his eyes elsewhere, but his anxiety increased when Melchiah lifted his hand and was allowed permission to speak. The black slave informed, "I seen Masta William's son, Kumi, walk outside in the middle of the night."

Kumi was caught in the crossfire between James' and Campbell's sudden glares. Campbell stepped to him quickly. "Is there any truth to this, neggar?" James also stepped in front of Kumi.

It took Kumi time to answer. He was shocked. He never suspected Melchiah informing on him. He expected such behavior from Zephon. Kumi decided to speak rather than contemplate Melchiah's change in behavior.

Kumi put on his act, defending himself in a humble voice. "I's was awake. I's couldn't sleep. I came out for air." James' face contorted, grinding his teeth behind an angry expression. "Good Man Tierney," Kumi continued, "He let me get some air for two minutes." He turned to James, thinking addressing him to be safer. Kumi added urgently, "Good Man Tierney was alive as you and me when I came back inside." His next words were dangerous to add, but he felt the need to explain simple common sense. "If I was gonna do somethin' to Good Man Tierney, sir, why would I's stay and not run?"

Campbell advanced on Kumi. The guard was angry. James stepped in his path, his back to the guard and his eyes on his brother. Campbell aimed a finger over James' shoulder. "I have to take this neggar in."

James said over his shoulder, "He's my property. You have no legal authority to seize it." He faced Campbell. "And he's right. Why kill a man and stay around to be apprehended for the crime?"

Campbell overlooked the line of slaves. "Then one of these neggars is responsible for—"

"Lock the neggars in the stable," James suggested. He looked at his brother and ordered, "You will come with me. And Campbell—"

"Yes, Mister Williams," the burly overseer asked humbly.

"Round up Mister Goldman," James answered. "Tell him to meet me here."

Campbell and the guards guided the black slaves back inside the stable. The overseer and the other guards then marched toward the ranch house. James looked back at his brother, the guards far in the distance. He did not need to speak. His expression demanded an answer.

"I did not kill that man," Kumi said in an eased manner. There was no need to be emotional with his statement. "There's something strange at this ranch house. And I need you to see something for me."

James did not know how to react. He looked back at the ranch house, making sure no one was heading toward them. James needed time to speak before Jacob, or anyone else approached. He felt the need to ask, "Do you know something?"

Kumi contemplated how he would address his brother. The situation was too unbelievable for even Kumi to grasp. The dreams. The spirit. "I need you to do some things for me."

"What's that," James asked slightly annoyed.

"Just two things," Kumi clarified. "See if there's a shed behind this stable, and then check the master bedroom."

James lifted his shoulders. "Is that all?"

"No," Kumi stated. "There's more to the bedroom."

"What's in there?" James tone wavered from being annoyed to cautious.

How could Kumi explain this? "I've never seen inside the ranch house but the front hall and the kitchen."

"So what am I looking for?" James said as his frustration returned. "The girl you heard crying?"

Kumi became irked with his brother's sarcastic patronizing of his earlier statements. Kumi said in a low angry voice, "Don't do that. Don't belittle me."

James' huffed. "Just tell me what's going on."

Kumi spotted Jacob and Campbell heading in their direction. He spoke quickly. "Just hear this. The master bedroom has a bed with a large drawer built into its side. There hangs a painting of Miss Koningswinter's father; he's a soldier who served under the command of George Washington himself. Also in the room is a fine dresser-drawer with a large mirror. There is also an antique armoire and a—"

"Why are you telling me this, Kumi?" James interrupted him.

Kumi saw Jacob and Campbell coming closer. He said to his brother, "Because I have never been in there before. I've only seen it in a dream. And before I can tell you anymore you need to see the room."

"I still don't know what I'm looking for," James whispered forcefully as Jacob and Campbell paced closer to them.

"The girl is tied up and gagged inside the bedside drawer," Kumi revealed. "She's a slave, as mixed as you."

"Watch your tongue!" James hissed.

Kumi gave an inconspicuous signal with his eyes. James straightened himself. Jacob and Campbell finished their approach. James faced the men and notified, "I know we're dealing with a situation. I need to speak with my neggar."

Jacob smiled warmly. "There's nothing wrong. It seems Mister Campbell may have jumped the gun on his analysis of the body. He is not a doctor. We will have a doctor in town examine the body." He gave a stern eye to Campbell. "Who's to say the guard didn't have a heart attack?" The old man suggested. "There's no need to rattle our livestock."

"But my neggar was out of place, though the guard permitted it," James spoke out. "I'll need a moment for a talk." He grabbed his brother's arm. "We'll be in my coach."

Campbell and Jacob nodded their heads. James carried Kumi to the coach they arrived in, still parked at the side of the ranch house near the gated area. James dismissed the riders hanging around the coach and shoved Kumi forward to open the doors. Kumi opened the side door and then waited for his brother to wave him inside. James stepped in after Kumi. He slammed the door.

"Exactly how do I get into that room?" James said quickly. "And what will all this prove?"

Kumi fixed himself before he responded. "If you see for yourself something that I have only seen in a dream, then you will understand something is not right with this situation." He looked at his brother with a serious expression. "And you will heed the warnings in my dreams. There is much more to tell you. There is so much more I have seen."

James did not have the energy to argue. He capitulated to his brother's demands. He asked again, "How do I get into that room?"

"Remark that the ranch house is a fine house," Kumi answered. "Tell Talbert that it beats living in a storehouse. Get at his pride. He'll then show you around the house."

"And, so what if he has a mistress?" James remarked lifting his shoulders. "He's entitled to the use of his property any way he sees fit. Let his romance continue."

"But it's not his property," said Kumi. "It would be this man Jacob's."

James rolled his eyes. "Just the same." He jabbed his hands forward and added, "He's an old man. Let him have his romance."

Kumi was perplexed at his brother's words. He sighed and felt alone. "I need you to separate me from the other slaves."

"What?" James questioned.

Kumi raised his hand and stated, "Say that you want me separated to keep me out of trouble."

"And put you where?" James' indignation was starting to boil over.

"The shed behind the stable," Kumi answered.

James rolled his eyes again. "We don't even know if there is one."

"Trust me," Kumi pleaded. "Just get me in there."

James opened the door angrily and slipped out of the coach. He aimed a single finger to the ground and commanded Kumi, "Out. Now." Kumi followed his command. James looked over his shoulder and spotted a guard. He pivoted and yelled, "You, there. Good Man. Come here." He grabbed his brother's arm and dragged him toward the guard. "I need my property separated from Mister Goldman's livestock. There's been trouble."

"And where should the neggar be taken," the guard asked politely.

James turned back to his brother. He looked back at the guard after taking a deep breath. He said, "I believe there's a shed in the back of the stable. That will do."

The guard shook his head as he apologized. "I'm sorry, sir," he said stepping closer. "But people aren't permitted near that shed. It's off limits, especially for neggars." The guard took Kumi's arm. "I'll take him to the other shed near the stock house."

James let his brother go. "Lock him in good," he said as the guard departed with his brother. "And then take him his provisions from the stable. You'll find his things up on the rafters."

"Yes, sir," spoke the guard.

"Thank you, my good man." James started walking toward the ranch house. Jacob met him at the front door, a wide smile on the businessman's face. James sighed toward him. "I apologize, Mister Goldman." He aimed his hand at Kumi's relocation. "He isn't use to the proper ways of behavior. He's a city boy."

Jacob looked away, disappointment in his eyes. "Well, you do spoil your property. Clothes. Spectacles." He listed. "I guess the neggar is more adapted to the city. But there are ways to keep him in line."

"I told you," said James, "I don't want to damage my property. He's a good worker."

Jacob chuckled at James' naivety. He stepped closer, shaking his head. "No. No. No. No damage would be done. Nothing physical." His smile faded. His expression and manner became serious. He raised an eyebrow at James. "Neggars are a superstitious animal," Jacob stated. "If he gets out of hand you warn him that the other Masters will raise all the sleeping ghosts of the woods to haunt him for the rest of his life." Jacob spoke with all the melodrama he could muster.

Jacob was serious. James could not help but snicker. "Kumi—my slave's name—I don't believe he's the superstitious type. He won't believe in ghost stories, or tall tales, or legends."

Jacob's smile returned. It was devious instead of warm. "Oh, Mr. Williams, he will believe in the legends of this territory. He will believe in the legends of the woods. It's what the locals call Sleepy Hollow." Jacob patted James on the shoulder and then walked inside the ranch.

James refrained from rolling his eyes or smirking. He kept a straight face and followed Jacob inside. Talbert approached them in the front hall accompanied by James' lawyer, Alan. "We were just coming for you both. Is everything fine with the neggars? No matter. My wife has a fine breakfast prepared. Come." Talbert led them to the dining area.

James took a seat at the breakfast table and commented, "This is a lovely ranch house." His voice stumbled, his words breaking as he acted his part. But James recovered and continued. "It does beat living in my apartment above the storehouse in the city."

James felt like everyone was staring at him as if he was absent of clothes. His thought was not the reality. Talbert was smiling. He thanked James for the compliment. "I've been such an ill mannered host," Talbert expressed. "I haven't taken you around, James. And with two days already passed."

"The dining room and the guest room is all I need," James joked. The others laughed on cue. "Seriously, though. I would love a simple tour."

"Alan and I are heading into town," said Jacob. "Some business needs to be taken care of." A black slave woman put a plate of food in front of him. "The two of you can conduct your tour while we're gone." He took his utensils and began eating. "Before you leave here, James, we will initiate you as a partner." He reached over to Alan and slapped his hand, shaking it. "And you as well. You will be a part of our law department." He lifted a drink and the others joined in. "To a new country, a new government. A New World Order."

They clanked their glasses against one another. The men eased back into their breakfast. James fell into deep thought. There were two more days left for him to finalize the deal with these businessmen. He would commission a black slave from Jacob. He would train the black slave and declare his brother a free man. The paperwork would take time. This would defuse the tense situation Kumi was creating. His pride would not cloud his judgment, nor would his actions look awkward if he was legally free, James considered. He would still need to understand his place. Being free would not give him the power to make suggestions about the store or its business. He would be given actual monies for his work as well as room and board.

Jacob moved his empty plate forward and stood up. He looked over at Alan. He said to the lawyer, "Whenever you're finished." He aimed his gaze at the entrance as Campbell entered. "There he is. Campbell, I'd like for you to accompany Mr. Williams' lawyer and myself into town. "

Alan scooped the last bits of his meal into his mouth and joined Jacob at his side. Jacob asked Campbell if he had already eaten. Campbell responded, "Yessir. I ate earlier." Jacob called for them to leave. Alan took lead as the men walked from the dining room. They departed with goodbyes and a promise of return at sundown. When James and Talbert were alone, James asked, "Has there been any conclusion on Good Man Tierney's death?"

Talbert swallowed and wiped his mouth before he spoke. "Two other guards took him into town. I thought Campbell was going with them. I guess not. But, we'll know soon enough."

James cleared his throat. "My neggar was wandering around—"

"I know," said Talbert. He raised a hand to relax James. "If there is foul play, we will not hold it against you." He smiled and took a bite of some egg. "You're a fine businessman. You have the best of stores in the city and great contacts. Money is what this growing country needs, along with proper trade and expansion. Guards and neggars are a dime-a-dozen. They can be replaced. We'll put the neggar down if he's the culprit, suit you with another."

James trembled at the thought. He paused in eating, returning to his meal only to not raise suspicions about him. He and Talbert finished their meals. Talbert rose from the table and motioned for James to follow him through the house. From the dining room they headed into the study area. It was a room that James had already been in. It was where business was concluded every night, starting at the dining room and ending in the study. Talbert introduced James to the other guest rooms, which looked no different than his own. The house was actually rather dull. James figured his apartment and storehouse was more furnished and lively. But Talbert seemed proud to show it off. The master bedroom was the last room they explored. The door was closed, where the others were opened. Talbert did not hesitate to reveal the contents of the room inside. James stepped inside as the door swung open. The room was exactly as his brother described. He concentrated on the large drawer built into the side of the bed.

James stiffened.

A cold chill danced on him.

James felt as if Talbert was eyeing him suspiciously, though in reality Talbert held a large, proud smile on his visage while showing off the room. James felt the need to speak. He pointed to the painting of Katherine's father and asked, "A relative of yours?"

"Yes," Talbert answered. "My father-by-law. He's a good man who fought for our freedom." Talbert nudged James in the side and added, "He even served under General-turned-President Washington."

"Wow," said James. His eyes went back to the drawer on the side of the bed. "A captain's bed?"

"Yes," Talbert replied quickly. "There is no mattress inside. We just store old items in there. Come along."

James swept his eyes around the room again. Everything seemed fine. He turned around and suddenly heard a thud behind him. He spun around, reacting to the noise. "Did you hear that," he asked Talbert.

Talbert cupped James' arm. "A slight embarrassment on my part," said the businessman awkwardly. "There are mice in the walls. My wife is on me about fixing the problem. I'm just so hung up in business. Come, now."

James stood still. He listened closely. The noise never repeated itself. He moved his feet slowly and allowed Talbert to lead him from the room. Talbert closed the door and let go of James' arm. He heard James curse and asked, "Is something wrong?"

James looked at Talbert apologetically. "I need to consult with my neggar," he explained. "I just need to know if certain boxes at the store are in order." He softened his pace to not look too anxious to leave Talbert.

James exited the house and crossed the field to the shed near the stock house. A single guard stood outside. James tipped his head politely and excused the guard. He opened the shed and walked inside. The tools were removed to insure that Kumi would not use them as a weapon. Kumi was huddled up in the corner, his blanket from the stables wrapped around him. There was a lit candle jar in front of him. A waste bucket sat several feet from him. James closed the shed door and knelt in front of his brother. Kumi sat up. He looked anxious.

"They'll probably feed the slaves soon," said James. "I'll have a bowl brought to you."

"The room?" Kumi inquired, ignoring his brother's comment.

James sighed. He turned his head before confessing to Kumi, "Just as you described. He looked back at Kumi and said, "There's more." James saw his brother's piqued expression. "A sound came from the drawer in the bed. It was a thud."

"Sally..." Kumi spoke.

James narrowed his eyes on his brother. "Is that the girl's name?"

"Yes," said Kumi looking away. "Everyone had their turn with her. She was crying."

"It's Jacob's property," James rationalized. "She was probably a gift to celebrate the business between—"

"She's a thirteen-year-old girl," Kumi protested. "If she's a gift to anyone it's her mother and father, or this earth." He then blurted, "I saw a headless spirit in my dream. It attacked two slaves. I think it killed that guard. There is something scary about the woods, this town."

James waved his arms. "Enough," he exclaimed. He jabbed a firm finger at his brother. "My mother preached such nonsense. Magic. It's made up." He turned toward the door, took a step, and then turned back to Kumi. "The real magic is the deal between me, these men, and the money that will be made. I sign the papers tonight. If you keep out of trouble, this deal will provide us with stability, and it will give me the power to buy your freedom. You just sit still for two more days, and you forget about those neggars out there." He stood over Kumi and added, "You saw for yourself they ain't good. They just tried to sell you out, stab you in the back. You ain't them, and they ain't you."

James pivoted and walked out.

Kumi watched his brother leave. The door closed. Kumi looked around the room. He had just one hope left. Himself. There were still two more mysteries to solve. There was the headless spirit and the mystery of the black woman in the shed. Kumi calculated there was only one specific moment in time to investigate both of these phenomena.

Tonight. Tonight. Tonight.

Kumi chanted the single word until the sun went down and the night bloomed. Two meals were brought to him in the time he waited. Each meal consisted of a single bowl of rice and beans and a hand of bread. Kumi made a conscious effort to see the outside and memorize the field when the door was opened. He took note of the guard's position; he always stood to the left of the door. But as time passed he wondered how any of this would help his situation. He was not going to harm the guard, nor was he planning an escape. He started to think of the business his brother James came for. Kumi reflected on James' disappointed look and started to feel guilty. James just wanted a secure life for both of them, he considered. James even promised Kumi freedom papers. He would no longer have to engage in this act. Kumi sat back and sighed. He closed his eyes and fell to sleep. Nothing was going to happen tonight.

Then the air became cold, and not from the night. Something controlled the autumn winds. There came the low, icy breath. The cold breeze lassoed the shed and Kumi wrapped himself tighter in his blanket. The cold intensified. Kumi opened his eyes, but it was not in reaction to the uncomfortable cold. He felt the desire to see what his ears could hear. There was something walking close to the shed. Its steps were slow, but heavy. There came the sound of breathing, an icy breath. Kumi reacted. He turned his head, looking at the wooden wall next to him. The marching came closer. It was directly on the other side of the shed. Something started to scratch the wood, a sharp instrument grinding alongside the wall. The sound suddenly stopped right next to Kumi's ear.

Kumi moved his head away from the shed's corner. He moved slowly to conserve sound. He went to lay himself flat on the floor when a sharp blade from a sickle penetrated the wall and blocked his path. The tip of his nose lay against the blade. Another blade broke through the wall above him, the flat end lying neatly on the top of his head. Kumi observed his environment for a split second, his head being between two blades. He jumped to his right and lay flat against the floor. He crawled toward the door, his body flat against the floor.

The blades retracted.

Kumi heard the figure advance around the shed. Its pace was quicker. Kumi did not move. He stayed low and watched the door. He heard the locks on the shed jingle and rattle. Slowly the front door of the shed opened. Fog invaded. Kumi watched anxiously. He moved backward.

"What's that noise you make in here, boy?" The guard jumped inside, musket aimed at Kumi. His hands trembled, jiggling the musket. Kumi feared being shot because of the nervous guard's shakes.

Kumi put himself upright and told the guard, "I's don't make no noise, sir." He swallowed air and continued. "I's thought that was you."

The guard's eyes examined the shed. His jaw quivered as his breathing became rapid. He panned the muzzle of his musket around the room only to place it again on Kumi. The guard's eyes were wide. He was anxious.

"Sir," Kumi said in a voice implying the guard to calm down. "You could move me to the stable and take position over there with your fellow—"

"You're to stay here, neggar," the guard hollered. "But you a smart neggar, ain'tcha?"

"Sir?" Kumi asked.

The guard answered, but seemed to be talking to himself aloud. "Yeah. I'm gon' lock you in this shed and move myself to the stable." He backed up toward the door. His musket aimed at Kumi, hoping he would not make any sudden moves.

But Kumi did move. His eyes. They shifted to look over the guard's shoulder, wide with horror. And what Kumi saw, the guard backed into. It was headless, black, and ominous. It towered over the guard, gripping its sickles. The specter's chest pumped as if it breathed. It looked tense, anxious, and ready to strike. Its body bent down as if it had eyes to view the man in front of it. The guard turned around quickly. The expression on his face changed dramatically, mirroring the exact terrified look etched onto Kumi's visage. Whether or not the guard heard the next phenomena that penetrated the shed was not Kumi's concern. But, there it came again. It was the sound of the icy, feminine voice from the night before, whispering the same message, *"Help me!"*

The guard's mouth hung agape. His head cocked back to get a complete view of the headless specter in front of him. The phantom attacked when the guard's neck was exposed, bent back to observe his killer. A sickle was swiped. The guard's neck opened. Blood gurgled from the wound and the guard's mouth. His scream was muted, as it was lost in the mix of bubbling blood from the mouth.

The guard's musket dropped. His arms hung low. His body crumpled onto the floor, his knees and life giving away. The headless warrior stepped over the guard's corpse. The specter's cape flowed in a wind created by the creature itself.

Kumi crawled back to the corner, keeping his eyes on the headless entity in front of him. It stepped closer, trapping Kumi in the corner of the shed. Kumi stood up, slowly. He opened his shirt, snapping several buttons from his apparel. He bared his chest to the creature and screamed, "Send me to the next world, if that is your duty. I'll meet you there and hurt you in ways I cannot here." The creature stepped closer. Its body made a gesture, bending its knees, rising and lowering. Kumi believed the headless creature was somehow inspecting him. Kumi kept his chest out. "It's not death if you accept it. Trust me."

And then came the icy, feminine voice again.

"Help me!"

The creature stood up. It turned around and marched away, stepped over the guard's collapsed body, and exited the shed. Kumi buttoned his shirt while following the creature to the outside. He witnessed the creature disappear into the fog, heading in the direction of the shed behind the stable.

Kumi had the ranch memorized. With the fog acting as another cover for him, he could sneak to the shed behind the stable. He charged through the fog, racing. He came to the side of the stable and slowed his pace, careful not to alert the guards outside. He placed his back against the wall and peeked around the corner. One guard was awake, the other asleep. Kumi looked toward the other end of the shed, taking his eyes off the guards. His ears, the second his eyes left the men, picked up the sound of gutted flesh and snapping bone.

Kumi looked around the corner. His heart raced and his body felt as if it was glued to the side of the stable wall. His eyes spotted a guard bleeding to death on the ground. He held his stomach with both hands, trying to dam the massive waves of blood pouring free. The dying guard had no stamina to scream. The other guard sat with his neck twisted and broken. His mouth was agape. His eyes looked caught by surprise.

Kumi turned his attention to what was in front of him. There stood the headless killer, the fog swirling around him. He was watching Kumi without eyes. Kumi defied the cold and started to sweat. He longed for the comfort of the shed and the ignorance of everything around him. He wanted to forget. He wanted to become what his brother wanted him to be.

The creature stepped out of the fog and raised a sickle.

Kumi closed his eyes, prepared to die.

But there came the icy plea, *"Help me."*

Kumi's eyes opened. The headless entity swiped at him. Kumi bent his knees. The blade crashed into the stable wall, skimming Kumi's shoulder. Kumi slipped from the attack and ran to the other end of the stable. He turned the corner and beheld the shed from his dream. He felt something over him, ready to strike. Kumi increased his speed, closing in on the door to the shed. Several strides into his rush, his foot twisted. He dropped, tumbling to the ground. He saw the headless specter above him strike as he rolled. He pushed himself, continuing to roll, and just missing being gutted by the creature's sickle. Kumi lifted himself with another strong push and ended his journey to the shed. He stood there looking at the door's handle. Behind Kumi, the entity struggled to pull its sickle from the ground.

Kumi examined the door's handle. He was hesitant to touch it, remembering what happened in his dreams to the man named MaGruder. The man had died instantly. Kumi turned around and saw the headless spirit gliding his way. He turned back to the door. He looked at the handle and inhaled. He had no choice. Kumi grabbed the handle. Nothing happened. He was too short of time to revel in relief. He pulled the door, but to his dismay, nothing happened again.

The door was locked from the inside.

Kumi jiggled the handle, frustration building. He banged against the door. "Kendra," he called putting the side of his face against the door. "Kendra, please. I'm here to help you."

Something clinked and clanked on the other side of the door. The door swung open and there stood the woman from Kumi's dreams. Kendra. She grabbed his arm and rushed him inside, closing the door on the headless shade. It dissipated into the fog, frustrated that its prey eluded it.

The shed was smaller than the last, but it felt like another universe. It felt safe. Kendra locked her arms around Kumi. Tears streamed down her face. "She's dead," the woman cried. Her voice was coated with a heavy accent that Kumi did not recognize. He understood Kendra's words, however. But he knew not many could. He wondered if she was even speaking English. But he questioned how he would know the language she spoke. "That little girl is dead," Kendra said, continuing to sob. "Little Miss Sally. They killed her."

Four flames flickered in each corner of the shed, floating in midair. There was no wick or oiled table that kept the flames burning. The ambience in the shed was magical. Kumi held Kendra tightly. She was warm and alive. She was far different than the outside world and the people who inhabited it. Kumi did not want to let her go. They were both trapped inside the shed, but they were freer than anyone they could imagine. Kendra's next moves surprised Kumi. With a tight grip around Kumi's waist, Kendra bent down. Kumi followed. The two on their knees, Kendra tossed Kumi to the ground with a frenzied push. Kumi lay flat against the floor. Kendra crawled up Kumi's body inhaling his scent.

"My spirit has not smelled my man in a long time," said Kendra in a low, breathy, sensuous voice.

Kumi tightened. The young woman attacked him with maturity beyond her age. She spoke with a voice of wisdom, understanding, and experience. Kumi had never been in this situation with a woman, but he invited it. She undressed him, pulling Kumi's pants to his knees. Kendra lifted her dress and straddled Kumi, resting on his erect penis. He penetrated her. Kendra moaned with the feeling of Kumi inside her. Her hips raced and writhed. She called out, "Clean me." She hissed, her voice warm and enticing to Kumi. "Clean me of their foul touch."

Kendra was like a wave Kumi wanted to be drowned by. She was the fire he wanted to burn in. She was warm air he wanted to be wrapped in. She was the earth, and a heavenly body. Kendra was everything natural above as it was below. Kumi saw flashes of the very symbols Talbert and Jacob wore as talismans. The images of the ankh and merkaba swirled together until came the image of the headless specter. The symbols landed on its chest, glowing. And though it was without a head, it screamed!

Kumi was thrust back into reality. He and Kendra were no longer locked in sexual embrace, though she held him close, his head against her chest. They cuddled in the corner. Kumi was dressed. He did not know where time went, but he did not question the reality Kendra and he shared. The woman stroked his cheek and kissed the top of his head.

"The spirit is no monster," she told Kumi as she rocked back and forth. "It protects the woods and the land."

"It tried to kill me, good woman," Kumi said to Kendra, his eyes admiring her as an image above him, holding him.

Kendra shook her head. "No," she disagreed. "The spirit can't think for itself. Those men control it with talismans. The spirit actually wants to help us." Kumi closed his eyes to focus more on Kendra's voice and accent of words. It was ethereal. "It serves this land and carries the souls of the indigenous slain. These men are using the spirit to control the slaves' thoughts. They are kept docile and obedient."

Questions bombarded Kumi's mind and then escaped through his lips. "Why did they let you live? And, what manner of magic surrounds you? Who are you Kendra? And, why me to help you?"

Kendra's lip curled into a smile. "Who knows why you were chosen," she answered. "But my calls fell on your mind. And the manner of magic I practice comes from the very dark pavilion where Christians say their God resides." Kumi marveled at Kendra's intelligence. Once again her words were a blanket of warm air, smothering the autumn cold. "I am no longer scared to express my power. All that's been done to me, all that I've seen to impregnate me with fear, have been aborted. No one but our blood can touch that door handle. I marked it with a protective spell. And no one can come near this shed with bad intentions." She lifted her shirt and bared her stomach. Kumi looked down at the young woman's stomach. There were symbols on her navel of whose meaning he had no knowledge. They had been scribed with charcoal. "The symbols add sustenance. I don't need to eat."

Kumi rubbed her belly and Kendra laughed playfully. "You may have to put those symbols on me," he said.

"I will." Kendra kissed the top of Kumi's head again.

Kumi expressed a concern, "They might use the headless spirit to open that door."

Kendra's eyes went from Kumi to the door. "That's fine with me," she said with a nurturing voice. "There is no god nor spirit that is locked on this world that will protect them. And with you, Good Man Kumi, even higher powers need my permission to act." Kendra took a breath. "When we step through those doors, the slave masters will fear us. And so will their spirit. I promise."

The warm atmosphere stroked Kumi to sleep. Kendra's arms were more comfortable than any bed, and she provided more warmth than even the sun. And when the morning came, the jealous sun competed by making the day unusually clear and warm for mid-November. James stood on the other side of the shed. He stared blankly at the small outbuilding, his head cocked to one side. He was mesmerized by a faint glow he saw coming from between the wooden panels making up the shed's walls. A haunting song came from the house. It was a woman's voice singing a ballad of love in a language James did not understand. The voice giggled sensuously, causing James to smile.

"Watch your proximity," warned Jacob, sneaking up from behind.

The old man's voice cleared James' head. The music ceased and even the light slithering between the wood panels died. James shook his head, jarring himself back to his senses. He gave Jacob a perplexed look. Campbell, a guard, and Talbert approached.

"The bodies have been rounded up," Campbell reported to Jacob. "There's no sign of Mister William's neggar. But your stock checks out."

Jacob nodded his head at the information delivered to him. He raised an eyebrow at James. "We'll do a wide search of this area, but first we need every place checked. And we don't want your neggar to disturb what's in that shed." He waved James toward the shed like a father to a child. "Go on, James. If he's not in there, we'll search the woods."

James felt like confessing that Kumi could not have committed the ghastly crime of slaying the two guards posted outside the stable. James wanted to confess he believed this because Kumi was his brother. James wanted to tell Jacob he was as black as Kumi. He wanted to tell Jacob everything he was hiding from him. And then James wanted to tell Jacob to go to hell. He wanted to tell Talbert to go to hell. He wanted to tell Campbell to go hell, and even his lawyer Alan Reynolds. But last night he signed legal papers that bound him to a duty promising service for the growing trade routes. It appeared that James was already in hell with the men in front of him. He signed a deal with the devil. The least he could do was honor it.

James turned away from the men and stepped slowly toward the shed. Campbell put his mouth over Jacob's shoulder and whispered, "There's a good chance he'll die, Mister Goldman."

Jacob waved the guard away. "I don't think so," he said. Jacob looked at the other guard and nodded. The man lifted his musket toward James. Jacob said back to Campbell, "He signed the papers last night. We have nothing to worry about. We'll still have our spot in the city." He kept a curious eye on James. "And I suspect something about our friend."

James felt as if the shed was approaching him rather than the other way around. It became larger than life, overpowering. It provided no music or warm glow. It was like a mouth waiting to swallow him. He wasted no time placing his hand on the handle of the door when he finished his approach. He tried to open the door, but it was locked.

James looked back to Jacob and the rest. "It's locked," he told them, feeling relieved. "It won't open."

Jacob's vision became a furious red. His eyes zoomed in on James and he sneered at the young storeowner. Jacob bit his tongue and shook his head as he decided how to handle the situation. He rolled his eyes and told the guard, "Shoot him."

The musket fired!

James was pushed up against the shed by the force of the small, cylindrical bullet tearing through the upper left of his chest. He slumped to the ground clutching his bleeding wound. He inhaled air rapidly. His vision blurred. Blood choked him, spitting up from his throat. It dribbled from his mouth. Most of his energy went to the perplexed face and emotion he aimed at Jacob and the others. He could see Alan coming behind them. Two other guards escorted him.

James screamed, *"Kumi! They shot me! Help me!"*

Jacob cupped the talisman around his neck and in hurried steps walked forward. He could hear Alan inquiring what was going on as he approached. The closer Jacob approached, the more a heavy weight came over his body. He gripped the talisman harder and chanted. The weight eased only a little. Jacob stood over James and shouted toward the shed, "You're a clever witch! I'm sure only someone of your black blood could touch this door. I don't see why I didn't figure it out before." He spit on James. "You goddamned neggar." He turned around and screamed at Alan. "Did you know your client was a neggar passing as a white man?"

The guards aimed their muskets at Alan. He shook his head, no. James squirmed as he lost feeling in his arm. The left side of his body was cold. "He never knew," he said, his voice barely audible.

"What about that neggar in there?" Jacob screamed. "Is he a goddamned free man?"

James trembled as the cold and pain intensified. He scowled at Jacob. "He's my brother," he confessed.

Jacob grinned. He told James, "You'll live. We'll be able to fix that wound. But you won't remember any of this. You'll serve us forever, like these other neggars." The old man turned to the others and addressed Campbell, "Go and get us a neggar so we can get this door open." He looked at Talbert and raised his talisman. "Let us raise the spirit of the wood."

Talbert nodded and cupped the talisman around his neck. Both men lifted the medallions to their lips and whispered a chant. The invisible weight that rested itself on Jacob lifted completely. Black fog swirled from the edge of the forest. It twisted into the form of the headless, sickle wielding spirit. The specter walked forward in its slow, rhythmic manner.

The shed's door opened.

Kumi stood in the doorway.

His eyes narrowed on Jacob. The old man was smiling at him.

"Where's the witch?" Jacob asked.

Kendra passed through Kumi as if she was a ghost. Kumi felt her essence filter through his physical body, and then solidify, standing in front of him. "I am the Wise Woman you seek," the woman said in a strong voice. "A Witch, as I am anciently known." But Jacob did not understand her words. Kendra's language was foreign to the slave master, but she continued to speak. "You are only a master to those called slaves. I am not that."

Jacob backed away from Kendra. His eyes moved to the left to check on the specter's approach. The headless spirit walked closer, but not fast enough for Jacob. James' fading eyesight went from the headless entity to Kendra. Kumi knelt down and held his dying brother.

"Stay with me, James," Kumi demanded, tears filling his eyes. "Stay."

The guards trembled as they aimed their muskets toward the scene. Their eyes never left the awesome and frightening sight of the headless man making his way toward Jacob. Alan turned to run, but as he turned, his nose tapped the barrel of Campbell's extended pistol.

"Don't move, lawyer." Campbell warned. "Stay put."

Alan faced the scene again. The headless man stood in back of Jacob, red smoke coming from the hole where its neck and head should have been. James' eyes went wild at the sight of the headless, black-armor clad figure.

"M-m-m-magic…" James exhaled weakly. Anger flooded his senses. He took a large gasp of air and exhaled for the final time. Kumi held his brother close and tight. Tears crowded his eyes.

From James' lifeless body came a ghostly image. The spirit jumped from James' body and lunged at Jacob, screaming. The old man stepped away from the attack, and James' spirit was absorbed by the headless specter. His soul was lost inside the black figure's body. The headless creature bucked and writhed! A scream somehow escaped from the headless apparition. From the empty space atop its body came a head. It formed out of nowhere. It was a knight's helmet. Black. It turned its head to Jacob, eyes glowing with a purple radiance. It swung both sickles at Jacob and separated the old man's torso from his legs.

The black knight hollered! It raised its arms and shouted to the sky. Kumi ran to Kendra and wrapped his arms around her. The black and mighty figure peered down at both of them. It turned quickly and faced the guards, Talbert, Campbell, and Alan.

The muskets fired!

Kumi took Kendra into the shed and shut the door.

The black figure charged forward, swiping at the guards and businessmen.

Inside the shed, Kumi and Kendra closed their eyes and held one another tightly. But they could still see the scene outside. The black figure cut down everyone at the ranch house. It screamed and assaulted the inhabitants with an unbelievably, ferocious wrath. Not even the slaves could escape the sickles carried by the black armored spirit. It took the lives of those too fearful to understand that the armored spirit was there to free them. It took the lives of the slaves who believed the spirit was best respected only in the service of the slave master.

Only Melchiah and four other black slaves were spared. The young man, returned to his senses, and dashed toward the shed where Kumi and Kendra lay. He opened the door to find Kendra and Kumi still locked in an embrace, kneeling. The two of them looked up slowly.

Kumi smiled. "Melchiah?" he asked.

Beside him were three women. One was the elder Sara. The two others, Kumi guessed, must have been no older than sixteen. There also stood Melvin, a strong, older man with light brown skin. Kumi stood up with Kendra in his arms.

"The guardian returned to the woods," Melchiah explained.

Kumi and Kendra walked outside. The field was plagued with blood and corpses, appearing as if a small battle had taken place. Guards. Slave Master. Mistress. Slaves. Kumi noticed his brother's body was gone.

"We're free," said Melvin. "Until the authorities come lookin' for us, that is. They gon' blame us for all this."

Kumi thought quickly. "There are goods we can store for ourselves," he told everyone. "We'll pack up a coach and head further north."

"There's a Black Salaam settlement a day's travel to the north," said Kendra wondering herself how she knew such information. It just came to her. "We'll go there."

Melchiah nodded. He and the older black man turned around and headed for the stock houses. The black women followed them close. Kumi and Kendra took their time. They looked over the area, their eyes keeping a close watch on the edge of the surrounding woods. Kendra put her head on Kumi's shoulder and a hand on his chest.

"My Good Man Kumi," she addressed him. "Your brother is safe."

"I know," Kumi answered.

"And if any trouble rises between here and our destination, I believe he'll protect us well," Kendra continued.

Kumi saw a shadow gliding through the woods. "I know," he answered.

"And if for some reason his new spirit fails to protect us, my magic will." Kendra assured Kumi.

"I know," Kumi repeated.

The seven Blacks, now free, entered the stock houses and gathered what goods they could store into two coaches. They took utensils and blankets from the ranch house. It took an hour to stock the coaches completely. Afterward, they left. Kumi looked through the back window and saw everything disappear. The stock houses, the ranch, the sheds, the stables, and the bodies faded like a mirage. All that remained was an empty plot of land that was slowly covered with fog. Kumi looked out the window to his left and saw a shadow gliding through the woods.

Kumi felt safe.

There was a black magic woman to his right. His brother was on his left.

In front of Kumi lay a road to freedom.

Ah, Moor
Or The Woman Who Wore A Veil
But Had Nothing To Hide
How To Resurrect A Black Woman (Part Three)

It was night. Nazirah stood at her window listening to the people gathered in the square reciting their poetry and song. Her dark skin glistened in the moonlight and her eyes twinkled just the same. Her body reflected the universe. Dark. Her eyes, casting back the moon's light, shimmered like the stars above. Her silk nightgown flowed in a light breeze, as if it were a galactic cloud dancing like a jovial, celestial spirit. Nazirah's eyes observed her festive, Moorish people. Wherever her people went they carried their culture with them, making every place like home. The thought made the Moorish woman reflect on her birthplace, Africa. It was hundreds of miles away, across the straits that were once the waterways for the great General Tarik ibn Ziyad who conquered this land known as al-Andalusia. Exotic scents from her homeland permeated her living quarters.

Nazirah had not been home in five years. She decided to continue her studies at a University in al-Andalusia. Her parents provided financial support for her education and stay. Al-Andalusia was extremely beautiful, according to Nazirah. The land's beauty seduced her to stay. Nazirah was able to compare the Moorish Empire to the many places her travels and study propelled her to visit. She had been to Egypt in her travels, and although the country was a spectacular sight, al-Andalusia seemed to be the new form of that ancient land, which she properly referred to as Kemet.

While Nazirah's senses of sight and sound took in and appreciated the music below, the aroma of wild African flowers permeated through vents that brought in and perfumed the outside air. The sweet aroma tickled Nazirah's nose. Incense and myrrh danced with the flowery flagrance that perfumed Nazirah's living quarters. The aroma, much like the breeze, swirled underneath Nazirah's silk nightgown and licked her amorously on her thigh like a lover's gesture.

Nazirah rubbed her knees together.

A young man reciting his poetry in the square outside Nazirah's window also inspired the sensuous sensations. He recited words as if he were doing back flips, a verbal gymnast. His poetry swirled between Arabic and African languages, to even Italian and Greek. This dazzled the crowd and kept their ears close, even with every shift of language between lines and stanzas. The poem was mostly made up of an Afro-Arabic language. The other languages were to incite puns, and tongue-and-cheek word play. A word in another language reverberated humor and irony to the poem.

The young Moor was of an average height and had rich, brown skin. He was dusk, brought on by the roughish features of a growing beard. He was dressed in billowing, black pants lined with a blue trim, and boots to match. His hair was in a wrap, but Nazirah could see the twisted forms of woolen locks seeping between his wrap. He wore a light blue silk shirt covered by a black vest. The young man recited his poetry with passion and fervor making allusions to astrological equations that added to the Godliness of his ability to recite and entice. He was arrogance praised and encouraged by the crowd's 'hurah'. He was the Sun. The crowd was his solar system, orbiting him to catch the warmth of his stanzas. Nazirah felt as if she was a distant Moon. But, she was one that caught every aspect of this Sun's heat.

The Moor's words carried in the night air. They lifted and caressed Nazirah's legs. Their ethereal state solidified into a physical hand that lifted her nightgown, all done by way of Nazirah's imagination, swept up in the rhythm of the words. This ghostly hand, made from the syllables of the poet's lexicon, swept over her thighs and tickled her bush of hair, penetrating her as if the hand stiffened two fingers. Nazirah began to sweat love between her thighs. She swore she felt the young Moor's words kiss her lips, then her neck. The ghost of the same tongue that spoke these elegant words was between her legs reciting their own poetry and rhythm. Heat began to build up in her navel.

Nazirah put her back against the wall adjacent to the window. She lifted her leg onto the sill, her fingers playing between them, eyes closed. She put her head back, opened her mouth, and let passion escape from deep within her. Her body quaked with a sensuous tempo. Nazirah's fingers, playing her organ, excited the heat in her navel to jump two points to her heart. The heat, in her throat, escaped with a loud, passionate cry.

The poet's words stopped.

The crowd looked up toward Nazirah's window. The square went silent. Nazirah put her hand over her mouth. Her continuing exhilaration mixed with hiccups of laughter. Nazirah cleared her throat and came into view at her window, a coy smile on her face. "My apology," she said looking out at the city square. She tried to get a glimpse of the young Moor who was reciting the poetry. She did not see him. Nazirah explained to her audience, "I dropped a vase." The woman fibbed. "It was a rare artifact, a gift from an old suitor. It was the only thing he was good for." The crowd laughed. Nazirah closed the window. The young Moor finished his words without Nazirah's ears to amuse and penetrate. His voice, however, stayed in Nazirah's head. And, she had unfinished business with herself. She extinguished the candles in her quarters and took herself, and her overactive imagination, to the bedroom.

In the morning, Nazirah would hold the handsome Moor in the palm of her hand. Maybe she would dance with him. Tonight, however, the image of the Moor would stay on the tip of each of her fingertips, and she would use them to stimulate a song of sensuality and fantasy.

Morning. His name was Aswad. He was a soldier in the Night Army, a city guard. The sun, at its morning angle, glistened and spotlighted him like the spectators in the square the previous night. He was now wearing a tanned cape and cowl. His attire was much the same as last night only differing in color. A sword was strapped to his back.

Aswad, always willing to apply his training in the name of adventure, used his skills as a soldier to maneuver through the mass of people crowding the city streets. He twisted his body gracefully, narrowing his way through small pockets of space between the people. He zigzagged and tunneled through the maze of citizens as if he was in the middle of an assignment, tracking someone. He was conscious of his flight path, his exercise through human obstacles. It was a way for Aswad to turn everything into a game, a mission, and an adventure. His trained eye spotted his destination in the distance, Commander of the City Guard, General Khushtar.

General Khushtar was dark, tall, and in his late fifties. He was a retired Moorish General, now turned Commander of the city watch, allocating his skills as a leader, fighter, and strategist for the safety of the city. He had bushy, black hair, with no signs of gray, and a long pointed beard. His clothes were relatively the same as Aswad's, but all white. A sword too was strapped to his back. He was purchasing a large set of groceries at the moment, and Aswad took advantage of Khushtar being distracted. But, as silent and graceful as Aswad's approach was, the well-trained General sensed him coming. Swiftly, the General cradled his grocery bag in one arm, and reached around and grabbed Aswad with the other. Khushtar pulled him to his side.

The young guard's eyes widened with disbelief. "How…?" he asked.

"Did I see you coming," The General finished, letting go of Aswad. "There are waves of people walking with the horizon. But suddenly my peripheral spots something coming at me, out of place with the picture. I react." Khushtar let out a haughty laugh. He began to shuffle more goods into his bag. "Just 'cause I'm concentrating on what's in front of me, doesn't mean I can't see in back of me."

"I would've suspected the food had you fixated," Aswad joked.

"Fixed! Hah!" Khushtar continued to laugh and scoop several more goods into his bag. "Nothing neuters my attention. I'm Commander of the City Guard and General in the army."

"And a rotten drunk," Aswad added teasingly.

Khushtar stopped his activity. He looked at Aswad with a stern eye. Raising a heavy finger he stated, "You will never find me rotten." Then he burst into laughter as he concluded, "Especially when I'm drunk."

Aswad's heart never made a nervous flinch. Khushtar was too much of a playful spirit. Aswad anticipated his Commander to drop the stern façade and roll into laughter. Aswad continued to joke. "You won't find me rotten either when you're drunk," he said to his Commander. "You become lousy at chess. And my purse increases its coin with every uninhibited bet you place."

Khushtar scoffed, "Ridiculous. I can beat you at chess with my hands tied behind my back."

"I don't doubt that, Commander," Aswad retorted politely. "Just not when you're drunk."

Khushtar continued laughing. "In that case, pay for my groceries," he ordered. "It's my money anyway." Khushtar kept a smile while walking away from the vendor's stand. Aswad was left with no choice but to drop a fair coin for purchase. He quickly caught up with the General. Khushtar assured him, "You can make your pay back with extra guard duty tonight."

"Extra duty?" Aswad exclaimed.

Khushtar then turned serious, his emotion not a façade. "I know you're supposed to have three days off," he told Aswad. "But the vacation is going to be cut short."

"The vacation was already short," Aswad commented.

"Everyone is on watch tonight," Khushtar said sharply, his jovial persona swiped and replaced with his persona as leader and Commander. "There are people perpetrating as snakes out there."

Aswad and Khushtar continued forward, enveloped into the mass of people filing through the streets. Although conversations ran abound, the two guards were able to keep each other in earshot, and they lowered the conversation to their own hearing. This was not information to let loose to arouse the public.

"Exactly what," Aswad inquired.

Khushtar sighed. He answered Aswad with information the young guard did not want to hear, though it was necessary for the job "Three nights ago, a twelve year old child was kidnapped," Khushtar reported. "We found his body late last night." He sighed again. "He was dead. His fingers were missing. All of them cut off."

Aswad hated this part of the job. He gasped and shook his head. "A child? Who could've done such a thing?"

Khushtar adjusted the grocery bag he cradled. "Cultists," he answered in disgust. "People taking the sacred arts and degrading them with frenzied, literal interpretation."

Aswad contemplated the Commander's words. The young, Moorish guard deduced that the sacrificing of the child was a literal interpretation of an esoteric lesson. Instead of killing the inner child and becoming a man, the monsters perpetrating this crime decided to literally kill a child in order to display manhood. Aswad's next question, reflecting on the crime scene described by Khushtar, escaped his thoughts, ran along his tongue, and across his lips. "But taking the child's fingers…?"

"I'm not trying to figure out the rituals of this cult," Khushtar declared. "I'm just here to stop them."

Aswad replied in a determined and loyal manner, "I'll help you snag 'em."

Khushtar smiled lecherously. "Speaking of snagging," the Commander began, "how many ladies did you snag last night with that onslaught of words?"

Aswad gave Khushtar a cynical look. "Is everyone going to hound me about last night?" Aswad's shoulder collided with a passerby. "Excuse me," he said politely. The man he bumped into just nodded back, acknowledging Aswad's politeness.

"I didn't know a fierce adventurer could deliver such words," Khushtar teased. "Astounding. You are full of surprises."

Aswad pleaded, "As long as all my fellow guards understand I'm an equally good swordsman, and not tease too much."

"They might tease," said Khushtar in a fatherly tone. "Understand that it's out of admiration." Khushtar saw Aswad shake his head. The young guard lightly uttered an agreeable acknowledgement. He did not want to be seen as too much of a brooder.

Then, Aswad gave a light laugh. "Well, I scored many female admirers," he said addressing the original question. Aswad's skin blurred with a dark, red tone. "There was just one in particular. The woman in the window. Her reaction…"

Khushtar put up his thumb. "A beautiful woman. Her name is Nazirah." Aswad became excited that his Commander knew the woman. He became eager to know more, and the expression of excitement failed to have any form of stealth. Khushtar informed, "She's an al-chemist. She makes perfumes and medicinal concoctions. Takes after her father, a wonderful doctor."

Aswad was impressed. "You know this woman and her family?"

"I'm Commander of the City Guard," Khushtar reminded. "It's my duty to know the citizens in my district, and its visitors." He concentrated again on the path in front of him. He and Aswad slipped deeper and deeper into city traffic. "We had to escort her father several days ago. He's a prominent physician, like I said. Al-chemist. Medicinal. He was here for a short visit. Two days. Then he was gone. Back to Africa."

"Did you meet Nazirah?" Aswad asked. There was a noticeably boyish excitement in his voice.

"I met her only once," Khushtar stated. "Besides, as of last night, you've had the most important information to meet her."

"Where she lives," Aswad answered, a mature detective's tone in his voice. His maturity melted into a sly grin. "Trust me, I took note of that." He looked at Khushtar. His face contorted. "Of course, you foiled my plans to intercept her tonight, extra duty assigned."

Khushtar chuckled. "My apology," he said as he stopped near an alleyway. He pivoted and addressed Aswad. "Your guard duty begins at seven, ends at midnight. The child was found two streets down from her apartment. I'll have you stationed there."

Aswad crossed his arms and contemplated aloud, "Morbid. But I guess I should be thankful."

Khushtar leaned close and reminded Aswad, "There's always the seven hours you have before guard duty begins."

"She's not home," Aswad answered immediately, implying that the stunt of intercepting Nazirah in the morning hours was already tried with no success.

Khushtar snickered deciphering the hint Aswad displayed. "You can find her at the University," Khushtar said. "And I won't be offended if you left my presence in haste."

"Good," Aswad said with a raised eyebrow. "I'll see you at the meeting tonight so you can officially assign my post?"

"Yes," Khushtar answered, his stern, authoritative personality quickly eclipsing his jovial self once again. The Commander continued, "Though you know where you'll be assigned—we have to keep professional. And when you're on post, keep a sharp eye out."

"I will," Aswad assured thinking of the macabre crime recently committed.

"Now be off, Aswad," waved Khushtar. "And may your sword penetrate its mark," he jested. Aswad winked, turned, and disappeared into the city's crowd. He was on his way to the University. But, he would be disappointed there too.

Nazirah was elsewhere.

Nazirah traipsed carefully through the woods that lay outside the gates of the city. Her focus was on the brush and flowers in front of her. In her hand was a book given to her by her father, presented by him when he had come to visit. The book was the sole purpose of his visit. It contained new formulas. Some writings in the book contained formulas on fragrances. However, most of the book was scribed with medicinal formulas.

A year ago, Nazirah sketched many particular al-chemical equations containing specific herbs, roots, and flowers. When her father came to visit, that same year, she handed over her writings to him. He was the only one who could make sense of her formula, and also correct any errors. Nazirah admired her father's medicinal excellence, and the genius to understand her work. Her father spent exactly a year editing and revising her equations. He composed the book. He visited often, wondering if his daughter had come up with anything new, and to report on his progress. Nazirah spent time with her father building new formula and helping him revise the equations. Several days ago, Nazirah's father handed over the book. It was now time to put her formula into practice.

Most of the formulas were designed through study. Nazirah was often boxed into one of the many libraries scattered throughout the city. She was usually jumping from book to book, scanning the archives of ancient medicines, shrubbery, herbology, roots, and wild flowers. And while the architectural structure of the libraries and University she attended were a sight to behold, being outside was a blessing. She could feel the life around her. Each blade of grass, flower petal, and undergrowth she beheld, her mind translated into equations. It was as if she could see the particular life ingredients locked inside the Earth and all that blossomed from it.

Nazirah's ears picked up something else. There was a succession of twigs snapping, pressed by the weight of someone walking on them. The woman turned her head and took notice of the guards assigned to her. They kept a perimeter around her. One apologized for disturbing her studies. Nazirah smiled and told him not to mind.

Two of the guards approached one another, making small talk. Nazirah caught the laughter of the one on the left, after the other had made a comment she was unable to hear. But he too started to laugh, increasing the volume in his voice. Nazirah heard his final remarks. "Aswad really knows how to flow with those words," he said. "He truly is as good a wordsmith as he is a swordsman."

Nazirah became interested in their conversation, her focus on gathering flowers and herbs distracted. She was now farming for clues. But there were many poets last night, Nazirah decided. These guards could have been talking about anyone. However, if this was the man she was seeking, she knew his name was 'Aswad'—and these guards knew him as a swordsman, most likely, she deduced, a fellow guardsman. Nazirah continued to listen, waiting for an opening to join the conversation and become interrogative. Until then, she checked her book for ingredients, keeping both ears open to the guards' conversation.

Then it came, the final clue. The two guards ceased their laughter. Nazirah had to approach closer to listen. The guards described the techniques of their friend 'Aswad' in accordance to his poetry. There was his content, astrological and spiritual. There was the flow of his words and the languages he skipped around and plucked at for irony and excitement. Nazirah grabbed her basket and stepped closer, book closed and in hand.

"Excuse me," she said in a polite voice. "I was listening to your conversation, forgive me. I was wondering if the poet you were speaking of had any," she thought about her choice of words and decided to say, "strange effects on the women of the crowd."

Both guards turned to Nazirah. They bowed graciously and then stepped forward. "Well, young *mora*, not anyone in the immediate crowd. But there was a woman watching the festivities from her quarters."

"She seemed to be really shaken," the second replied with a low chuckle. "No one believed she was concerned over a vase, not with that sensuous holler."

Nazirah gave a coy smile. "I'm not embarrassed," she said revealing herself as the woman in question. "The gentlemoor's words brushed against and excited me." She leaned against a tree, dreamily. Nazirah embellished the emotion, making it sarcastic. The guards' mouths dropped. Nazirah's emotions quickly went back to normal and she added, "Is this 'Aswad' a friend of yours?"

"Yes, *mora*," said the guard on the left. "He's in the City Guard. He's part of the night watch. He had last night off." He stepped closer and spoke, "It was no surprise to see him in the square performing. Aswad loves being quick with a word, and a sword. He's a self-proclaimed Adventurer."

The guard on the right chuckled. "Yes. He's a focused swordsman, to say. He has only come across three city scuffles in his five years on guard." He looked at the other and concluded. "What type of adventure is that? He always states that his life is full of adventure," the same guard carried on. "I just see him do his duty, practice, then slip away into his quarters to script."

The guard on the left assured, "But as much as we tease, *mora*, he's a good friend."

Nazirah asked, "Where can I find him?"

Both guards lifted their shoulders.

"He could be anywhere at this time of day," said the guard on the right.

"You could check the Guards' Quarters at the center of the city," continued the guard on the left. "We could escort you."

"I do have to get back to the University to finish up my studies for the day," Nazirah admitted with a contorted face. She had never been this annoyed at her studies, or more interested in something outside of them. "That will take too much time." She looked at the forest floor and contemplated. An idea struck her. "Tell him to meet me at my window tonight."

"We've all been assigned extra duty tonight, *mora*," the guard on the right informed. "Aswad was supposed to have more time off. But, I believe he will only be on duty until midnight."

"Then I will get sleep early," Nazirah exclaimed. "I will then rise before midnight to meet him. Tell him my name is Nazirah."

The guards bowed gracefully. "It will be done," they said simultaneously.

Nazirah, finished with her fieldwork, gathered the remainder of her things, and was escorted back into the city and to the University. Nazirah entered the University through the southern entrance. Aswad waited for her at the Northern side.

Nazirah saw Aswad first. He was sitting at a bench. His sword leaned against him. The tip of the sheath angled against the ground. Nazirah's heart thumped an extra beat, but she remained calm on the exterior. Her eyes were fixed on Aswad as a crowd of people exiting the University camouflaged her. Nazirah walked up to the young guard, taking a seat next to him. Aswad looked up immediately. He knew who she was. Nazirah was shorter than he imagined, but dark and voluptuous just the same. Her hair was made up of woolen braids, and her garments flowed and moved with her body as if she carried a visible form of the wind. Aswad smiled and said, "*Mora* Nazirah," he addressed her as if he had known her all his life. "I've been waiting for you."

Nazirah blinked. She was surprised he knew her name. She wondered if his fellow guardsman had already spoken to him.

"*A-Sir* Aswad," she addressed him in return. "Have your friends of the City Guard already spoken to you? I thought we were meeting at midnight, on your watch."

Aswad then jumped. He was surprised she knew his name. He wondered if Khushtar had already spoken to her.

Aswad answered her, "I haven't spoken to any of my fellow guardsmen."

"Oh," Nazirah said awkwardly. Her face contorted with confusion. "Then how do you know my name?"

Before Aswad answered, he admired the sight of the beautiful woman, eyes scanning her. He focused on her expression and her question played again in his head. This time it was coherent. She wanted an answer. And here he was with his mouth open and a silly smile still formed on his lips. He blinked and then answered, "My Commander escorted your father several days ago."

"Khushtar," Nazirah answered pleasantly. "Yes. I remember meeting him."

Aswad leaned closer to the woman, a sly smile on his face. "I interrogated him for all information concerning you."

"A detective," Nazirah said flirtatiously.

Aswad teased her, "It seems you've done some interrogation of your own."

Nazirah's smile widened. "I talked to some of your guardsmen, *A-Sir.*"

Aswad blushed playfully. He leaned away and waved her comment on. "There's no need to address me as *A-Sir*," he told her. "I'm far from being a knight," he concluded.

Nazirah looked at Aswad admirably and said, "Well, you certainly have the knowledge of a knight. The words you use, how you use them. It's exciting."

"So I've heard," Aswad chuckled continuing to tease Nazirah. "Your reaction threw me off."

Nazirah bit her lip as she smiled. Her eyes narrowed in on Aswad's sword. "Are you studying for knighthood?"

"No," Aswad shook his head. "I'm just an adventurer. I'm in no need to become a soldier in an army. I'll stay around the city." He contemplated and then added, "For now, anyway."

Nazirah erupted into laughter. Aswad's statements seemed ridiculous enough to tickle her. "Do you have *any* ambitions?"

Aswad was a little offended, but he liked the fact he was sitting with the woman he sought. "My ambition is to find and survive the next adventure."

Nazirah considered Aswad interesting. She asked him, "And what brought you to this adventure? Were you born in al-Andalusia?"

"Yes," Aswad answered quickly. "I've been all over, though," he admitted. Reflecting back to the origins of his adventurous life brought back the pain on how it began. The adventure started with the death of his mother who had been ill for a year. Aswad remembered the event, watching her die. He was eleven. He tried to speak about the incident quickly, to brush past the memory. He confessed to Nazirah, "My father took my brother and I on a grand travel from here to Arabia after my mother died. I was eleven."

"Oh," Nazirah said low, becoming sympathetic. "You have my deepest sympathies and blessings."

Aswad nodded, acknowledging Nazirah's sympathy. "We were a gang. We followed legends to treasures. We robbed the corrupt. We protected dignitaries. Went after bounties, and had bounties placed on our heads." The young guard's smile returned. "Life became an adventure with the three of us."

"And the other two?" Nazirah asked. "Where are they?"

"My brother sold out and got married," Aswad joked. "I guess it's a whole new adventure. He's in Mauritania. My father went back to his birthplace in East Africa." Aswad gripped the hilt of his sword. "He's writing a book of our travels and adventures. All fourteen years."

Nazirah surveyed the young man. He had experienced so much, she considered, and there was still years to go, more energy to exercise. She could also see a hint of sadness in Aswad. If his adventures would continue, it would be alone. Before Nazirah could ask Aswad another question, the young man spoke first. "I hear you're an al-chemist," he said.

"Yes," Nazirah said politely. "I too have traveled side-by-side with my father, all the way into Arabia." Aswad was impressed. His eyes were almost as wide as his mouth. But, Nazirah shook her head and brushed away any implications that her travels yielded any form of adventure. "Oh, it was all in the name of studying. There was no high adventure. No sword fights, no tussles."

Aswad leaned closer to the woman and explained, "My adventures just included guard duty in other kingdoms, treasure hunting that did not lead to the greatest fortunes—as legends can be exaggerated. There was bounty and pirate hunting. But I just love the travels, the interaction with new places and people."

Nazirah still disagreed, knowing completely what her travels consisted of. There were no signs of pirates or marauders. She continued to be playful and keep a smile, careful not to create tension. "Well," she began with a sweet feminine laugh, "my interactions have been with exotic flowers, flora and fauna. I've even traveled to the Islands of Amenta."

Aswad's mouth hung open, wide with awe. "And you believe you've had no adventures," he questioned. "My goodness! The Islands of Amenta?"

"It was all in the name of science," Nazirah proclaimed. "Medicinal and fragrance." She laughed at her own joke. Aswad was too busy admiring the woman and her travels. Nazirah simmered her jubilance to watch Aswad as he continued to chant and praise her exciting voyages. Nazirah reached out her hand and placed it on Aswad's shoulder. He ceased his speech. "Talk to me in your second language," Nazirah asked of him. "Poetry," she specified.

Aswad took a deep breath, and then he spoke to the woman as commanded. His enticing, sensuous, sentence structure gathered a crowd. He spoke of Nazirah as the world, every continent a piece of her, and how he would like to visit every corner of her globe, making pilgrimages to several sacred areas on her landmass. Nazirah was not embarrassed by the strong words and declaration. She did not shy away with a coy smile or even blush. She was wide open to Aswad's suggestive language. She wanted everyone to see her. She loved the energy of his voice, and its mere sound did everything Aswad described through innuendo. The metaphors traveled on her body, exciting sensual nerves, and journeyed through her world. She felt open to Aswad. She dripped sensuality again, and rubbed her knees together. Nazirah inhaled Aswad's voice, his every word. When Aswad ended his flow, Nazirah felt completely refreshed, as if bathed and perfumed by one of her own chemically arranged scents. Nazirah exhaled. The crowd exhaled as well. They applauded.

Aswad stood up and took a bow.

Nazirah waited for the crowd to disperse, each person congratulating the young Moor. Finally, when it was just the two of them, she leaned closer and kissed his cheek. "You just took me on an adventure," she complimented. Her eyes went to her book of formula. Nazirah looked at Aswad's sword. "I could use you," she said putting her eyes back on him.

"And I could use you," said the poetic swordsman with a sly grin.

"Your skills at being a guard, I request," Nazirah emphasized in a sarcastically stern voice.

Aswad tightened the grip on his sword. Though Nazirah joked, Aswad detected sincerity and urgency in her request. "Are you in any danger, *mora?*"

Nazirah looked around. Her eyes searched the crowd for anyone who appeared to be listening in. The traffic around them flowed in and out of the University, into the city streets. When Nazirah was sure no one was concentrating on them she looked back at Aswad and answered him, "Possibly."

"By whom," Aswad pressed. "You do know there've been rumors of cultists in the city? They're active, and they've made a strike"

"Yes," Nazirah acknowledged. "That's why my father required escort."

"Do you believe yourself a target," He asked Nazirah as she inspected her surroundings again. She became uncomfortable. Aswad stood and slung the strap of his sword over his shoulder. He reached out a hand and lifted Nazirah. He suggested, "Maybe we should talk elsewhere."

Nazirah agreed. She led Aswad to her place of residence. It was not far from the University. Aswad followed Nazirah inside her apartment complex, up two flights of stairs, through a hallway, and into her living quarters. The place was well decorated, refined. Exotic scents warmed the room like a blanket. The first area was for dining and sitting. The room was a garden, decorated in exotic plants from various areas of the world. The plants were neatly placed, arranged and spaced to recreate the wild environment from which they sprang. There was a canopy above made of entangled stems and leaves. Nazirah was Mother Nature in this apartment turned weald.

Nazirah walked over to the window where she watched Aswad recite his poetry the previous night. She sat down and exhaled. "Your words were so comforting, Aswad," she said. "I've been through a lot of stress." She remembered his words from the night before. Even as a memory they calmed her, her body filled with a warm wind.

Aswad pushed aside his admiration for Nazirah's apartment. Her words alerted him to duty, and he remembered the specific reason they came to her apartment. Aswad took a step toward Nazirah. He could see the Moorish woman was fighting an onslaught of distress. He bent down and placed his hands on Nazirah's knees. He looked up at her and spoke her name. "Nazirah." She looked at him. "We're safe now," he said in a calm voice. "You can speak."

Nazirah said while smiling beautifully, "There is still magic left in this world." Her eyes were not focused on Aswad. She continued, "It's locked inside the science of plants, trees, and the entire Earth. It can be calculated through mathematics." Nazirah hesitated. She again exhaled, believing Aswad thought her foolish. Aswad hung on her every word, however. He was intrigued. "I have unlocked such magic," Nazirah spoke again. "My father and I discovered a formula for herbs that can heal wounds instantly. The calculations are written down in that book of mine. My father revised my formula and brought the book to me when he came. We're still working on a formula that will work against disease."

Aswad was completely amazed at Nazirah's revelation. He took a breath and inquired, "And there are people after you for this formula?"

Nazirah nodded, yes. "They're cultists, a small group. They are tawny Moors. But, I have a feeling they are just soldiers. I suspect they're hired for a larger body of people named The Brotherhood of White Light."

Aswad thought about Nazirah's words. He was shook. He looked as if someone drenched him with a bucket of water. "You discovered magic," he said in a hushed voice.

Nazirah chuckled at Aswad's choice of words. "Re-discovered, truthfully, tapped into its final moments," she said running a finger along his face. "There's a science to it. That's all we have been reduced to. Magic does not shimmer with the same light as it did for our ancestors. Magic exists only in small pockets of the Earth. It exists in all the natural things the Earth produces. It's now up to us to decode the Earth through calculated science and uncover the magic she still holds inside her." Nazirah rubbed Aswad's lips with a single finger. "It's like the science of your poetry. It too can produce magical results. It is in the calculated reverberation of your speech, your tongue's timing to wind your words into the wind, and make the thunders envious. I can be reborn through the mathematical rhythm of your poetic science, much the same as you could be reborn through the science I've discovered. That is magic."

Aswad raised himself enough to kiss Nazirah on the forehead. The gesture was caring, appreciative rather than romantic. "We must go to General Khushtar," Aswad notified. "I will have him assign me as your personal bodyguard." He stood up and turned around. He kept his hand locked around Nazirah's and lifted the woman to follow him. The two of them re-traced their steps, going from the apartment, to the hall, the stairs, and out of the complex.

Aswad led Nazirah through a winding path of streets, then shortcut their route through an alleyway, ending up in front of the City Guard's barracks. Khushtar was outside speaking with three guards. Aswad let go of Nazirah and quickened his pace up to the Commander. Nazirah traipsed behind him, keeping up. Khushtar spotted the young guard in his peripheral. He turned and smiled as Aswad finished his approach. He noticed Nazirah behind Aswad and gave the young guard a congratulatory wink.

"I see you've found your prize," Khushtar commended.

Nazirah blushed. Aswad, however, was too caught up in his duty to entertain the comment. He caught his breath and then told his Commander, "This woman, Nazirah, is in danger." Khushtar stiffened. He turned to the other three guards and waved them away for privacy. He gestured for Aswad to continue. "There are cultists after her," Aswad reported. "Possibly the same group of people who murdered the boy."

Khushtar inspected Nazirah with a raised eyebrow and a stern glare. Nazirah informed, "That is the reason my father needed close security for his stay." The woman waved her eyes around to inspect her surroundings. "He came to give me something, a book. These people, called The Brotherhood of White Light, are after that book."

Khushtar considered the information. "I will not ask you what kind of information the book contains. That is not my concern."

"But you should know," Aswad shouted, wanting for Khushtar to revel in the information Nazirah and her father discovered.

Khushtar waved the notion away. "Nonsense," he huffed. "If it's that profound I may assist them." The joke went over fairly well, producing smiles and lightening the tension. "No, I'll keep my job as Commander of the City Guards." He put an arm around Aswad and relayed his strategy, whispering into the young guard's ear. "I will assign you guard over the woman. Your assignment will last until these men are caught." He looked over at Nazirah. "This may mean he has to take rest in your apartment."

Aswad gave Khushtar a quick, light punch in the ribs. Nazirah laughed and bowed. "It would be all right, General."

Khushtar continued to tease Aswad. He whispered into his ears, "Now, remember to *guard* her body." Aswad again punched Khushtar lightly. "Relax," Khushtar said tapping Aswad's shoulder, chuckling the whole time. "I jest. Now, I'll also assign Anik, Bari, and Yunus over there to stay on guard *outside* the building."

Aswad looked over at the three guards Khushtar had been speaking to before he and Nazirah arrived. He knew the guardsmen well. He trusted their presence. Nazirah walked around to face Khushtar. She bowed and said, "Thank you, General."

Khushtar took his arm from around Aswad. He took Nazirah's hand and kissed it. "Please, I haven't been a General for years. I'm just a Commander now."

"A Commander who reminds his company that he was once a General," Aswad said rolling his eyes. "And still has us address him as such from time-to-time."

Nazirah laughed.

"Damn right," Khushtar exclaimed. His smile faded. Aswad and Nazirah noticed this and felt compelled to straighten up. "Listen, the both of you. To be completely serious, be careful. There has been another incident."

Nazirah placed her palm over her heart. "My goodness, no."

Khushtar shook his head sorrowfully. "Unfortunately, yes. An elder woman has gone missing. Her sister reported it just an hour ago. She's been missing for two days." He looked at Aswad. "Now, you're on your duty. Stay sharp."

"As my sword, General," Aswad assured.

"Right," said the old soldier. "I'll send those three to your place in an hour. I don't want it to be too obvious." He looked at Nazirah with distress. "I don't mean to alarm you, *good mora*, your pursuers may be watching you as we speak. Do not go anywhere alone." He waved a finger to Nazirah and Aswad. "The two of you get back to the complex. They may try an ambush."

"Yes, General," Aswad acknowledged.

"You'll have the three with you," Khushtar reminded. "I'll also post several guards around the street. It's in the square, so guard presence will be high. Now, go."

Aswad and Nazirah bowed toward Khushtar. Aswad took Nazirah's hand and guided her back through the shortcuts and pathways leading to her apartment building. There was no ambush or signs of disruption inside her apartment. The cultists would have found nothing, Nazirah keeping her book on her person at all times.

It did not take long for Aswad and Nazirah to settle into a simple routine. They played off the security aspect of their coupling by just pretending it was all a courting process. Aswad ordered the other three guards to find the finest café and bring back its best meal. Aswad gave them a hefty sum of money, trying to impress Nazirah. When Anik, Bari, and Yunus returned they delivered the meal and took their guard outside the building. Accompanying the feast was a bottle of wine and two pitchers of water.

Dusk. A single candle burned. The outside world dissolved away in the wide brilliance of night. Nazirah and Aswad, while they dined, shared stories about life and travel. Aswad rekindled an adventure in which he, his brother, and father were involved. The adventure took place in Arabia. They were guards for one of the Governors. An advisor took advantage of their status as outsiders. The advisor began stealing precious jewels and gold coins from the Governor's treasury and blamed Aswad, his brother, and father. It was easy to point the finger at three wanderers. Aswad's brother exposed the Governor's advisor. Aswad and his brother and father tracked down the advisor on command of the Governor. They arrested the thieving advisor and returned the stolen valuables.

Nazirah marveled at Aswad's stories. She wanted to hear more, but her curiosity forced her to ask Aswad how he knew Khushtar. Aswad answered that Khushtar's family was acquainted with his mother's family. Khushtar's sister and Aswad's mother were best of friends. Aswad's father, a swordsmith, met Khushtar while crafting swords for the city's army. He met Aswad's mother through Khushtar, and always marveled at Khushtar's stories of adventure. Aswad recounted that his father use to say, that one day, he would follow one of his swords into an adventure while holding its handle. Unfortunately, his adventures would begin with the death of his wife, Aswad's mother. He would carry his sons along for the ride.

Aswad grew tired of hearing his own voice and was anxious to know about the wonders of the world Nazirah had seen, especially the Islands of Amenta. Nazirah's narratives intrigued Aswad. The woman described the lengthy sail to the Islands. It was clear, peaceful, only one day of storms throughout the entire travel west from Africa. Nazirah described the islands as a paradise while defining them by their lush greenery, blossoming flowers, and exotic growth. She described the inhabitants as a humble people, inviting to visitors. Some were of African descent, with varying features. Other inhabitants were mixed with African and Mongolian blood. The islands were used by the inhabitants of the main continents much like the tribe-nations of Africa. They were a people creating a relationship with nature before going back to their nations and taking their respective professions among their people. Nazirah said she never traveled to any of the Continents of Amenta, only the tropical islands. Despite Nazirah feeling her stories did not match up to Aswad's swashbuckling adventures, the young guard was enamored by her storytelling.

Aswad slid closer to Nazirah. "Maybe we should take you there to get away from your pursuers," he suggested.

Nazirah disagreed. "I don't believe so," she said taking a sip of wine. "It would do no good. They could go after my father, who still has the rough copies of my formula, and a book for himself." She shook her head again. "No. Perhaps we'll visit after all this has passed."

Nazirah requested another story and a poem from her bodyguard. Aswad obliged under the condition she gave his locks a wash and fresh twist. Nazirah laughed, she did not mind the fee. Aswad serenaded her with a story, and then composed a poem speaking of the sensation of her fingers filtering through his hair, plucking him like a guitar to sing with a smile, song, and poetry. Afterward, the sleeping arrangements for the first night were simple. Nazirah slept in Aswad's arms. A kiss was exchanged between them after the candle was blown out. They slept on a wide, comfortable cushion resting in her front room, a blanket over them.

In the morning, Aswad and Nazirah left the apartment to check with Khushtar. Yunus and Bari accompanied them, Anik staying behind. Across the square, peeping from an alleyway, were three tawny Moors, members of the Brotherhood of White Light. They watched Nazirah's apartment from their vantage point. They watched Anik guarding the building. He was intimidating, despite being the only guard. Anik was stocky, built like an Arabian horse, and looked athletic and strong for a forty-two year old man. He had brown skin, a baldhead, and a stubble of hair on his chin.

The three members of The Brotherhood of White Light came from the alley and walked around the square, keeping an inconspicuous eye on Nazirah's apartment building. Farraj, Dharr, and Hilal were their names. Farraj was the leader of this Brotherhood outfit. He was of average height, but his lanky physique gave the illusion that he was taller. He was swarthy, with a hooked nose and mustache. Farraj was ferocious, and deadly with a blade. He was not to be crossed, quick-tempered as he was. Dharr was the muscle, but had an intellect for strategy and combat, especially fisticuffs. He was tall and muscular, and preferred a straight brawl rather than the use of weapons. Hilal was a simple soldier and the youngest of the group. He worked mostly for the money, rather than the power and legendary, magical objects The Brotherhood of White Light sought.

They did not stay in the square for too long, ducking back into the alley to keep watch on Nazirah's apartment. They calculated the time it took for Aswad, Nazirah, and the other two guards to return. The Brotherhood unit disappeared down the alley, returning later, during the night to watch Nazirah's apartment. They were hidden by shadows. The light of the flickering street lamps never threatened to expose the three cultists. There was little pedestrian traffic. The three guards stationed outside Nazirah's house took shifts. Two guarded while the third slept. There was not much else to see. The scenario's rhythm was closely observed. Satisfied with what they observed, the three cultists returned to their inn.

The Brotherhood scouts repeated their routine the next morning. They watched Nazirah and Aswad leave, once again escorted by two of the three guards. There was no aggressive move made on Nazirah's apartment, just another reconnaissance. The cultists returned at night to watch the apartment building. This drill continued for two weeks, the cultists learning their targets' pattern. But there was one day where the cultist did not observe Nazirah's apartment at night. The cultists returned to their inn to perform a ritual after a long day of surveillance.

The cultists' room at the inn was rearranged from its template. The furniture was pushed back to the walls, which created a large, open space in the middle of the room. A cooking pan lay in the center of the open space, placed atop a cackling, makeshift fire. The floor was caked with dried blood. The fluid originated from the body of the old Moorish woman lying in the corner of the room. Her name was Ahlam. She was seventy-two years old, and in the last moments of her long life, she was brutalized. The cultists' torture lasted for two weeks. Ahlam was selected specifically for capture and torment. She was a professed seer. Her dreams gave her insight. The morning of her capture Ahlam informed her sister that it would be the last time they spoke. She told her sister that she had no dreams, signifying nothing more to come in her life.

It took two weeks to break Ahlam down. She was strong. But though she had no more dreams to see, keeping her from sleep tore Ahlam apart emotionally. Sleep was where she found solace. Separated from her calm, dark, slumber, the woman's sanity broke. The cultists killed her at the height of her insanity, retaining some of her blood in a vial, and putting it to ritualistic use.

The pan's contents started boiling, a powdery substance already added inside the pan—the ash of a twelve-year old boy's fingers. The cultists, for this disturbing ritual, needed the vitality of youth, stirred with the blood of a mad crone, and an offering of their own blood to create intent.

The three men formed a triangle around the hearth. Dharr pulled a dagger and cut into the palm of his hand. His blood dripped into the pan and he handed the weapon to Hilal who did the same. The young soldier passed the knife to Farraj who repeated the actions of his fellow cultists. He then poured the contents of the vial into the pan, and he stirred the ashes with the blood. He spoke an incantation. The pan's contents dried quickly and became a gray dust. The fire was extinguished. Farraj gathered the gray dust, and the cultists then rested, returning to Nazirah's apartment in the morning.

The cultists were surprised to find their marks' routine had changed, and to their advantage. They observed: Aswad left the apartment complex. Nazirah remained inside. Yunus and Bari stayed on guard. Anik followed Aswad. After a moment, Bari went into the building located next to Nazirah's to fetch a pitcher of water. Farraj knew there was little time before Bari's return, as well as Aswad and Anik's. He commanded Dharr and Hilal to remain inside the alley, and then trekked over to a vendor selling flowers. He dropped a fair coin in exchange for a wealth of flowers. He walked toward Yunus and stopped in front of the guard.

"A present for the lady," said Farraj.

Yunus shook his head with a sly grin. "Aswad sure has no trouble expressing his fondness for this woman," he said.

Farraj chuckled. He lifted his shoulder and said, "You know love." He reached out and tapped Yunus on the temple. A patch of dust was left on the side of the guard's head. "It really gets into your head," whispered Farraj in an eerie voice.

Yunus could barely smile at the man's remark, a sudden fatigue overpowering him. Yunus dismissed the sensation as his nightshift duties on guard, coupled with this morning's shift, beginning to affect him. He pushed the weariness aside and reached for the bouquet. "I'll take that to the lady," Yunus said to Farraj.

"No need, good guard," said Farraj pulling the bouquet away from Yunus' reach. "Stay on your duty. I'll take this to the young lady."

Yunus formulated words to object to Farraj's demands, but they never manifested audibly. He wanted to state that his order was official by way of City Law, but he never did. Yunus' hands wanted to reach out and take the bouquet, but all this was somehow negated. Yunus found himself saying in a monotone voice, "Lady Nazirah is on the second floor, fourth room on the left." Farraj thanked Yunus and walked inside the apartment complex. The scenery turned upside down from Yunus' perspective. It cracked and split before he passed out in the street.

Farraj scaled the stairs to the second floor, walking cautiously to the fourth door on the left. He knocked and said, "A present for the lady." The door opened. Nazirah stood in amazement at the bundle of flowers held out toward her. A wide smile appeared on her face as she took the flowers into her arms. She praised Aswad aloud and then moved the large body of flowers away from her to look at Farraj. Nazirah wanted to thank the man for delivering the flowers, but he spoke first. He told her, "There's something more."

"What is that?" Nazirah asked with child-like impatience. She could not wait to see what Aswad had planned.

Farraj opened the palm of his hand and revealed a gray, powdery substance. He blew the ash into Nazirah's face. The ash burned Nazirah on contact. She buckled, bending down to clutch her face. The flowers dropped to the floor, spilling into the hallway. The ash stung Nazirah's eyes. She slumped to her knees and then dropped to her side onto the floor. Nazirah tried to scream, but her jaw was locked in place, paralyzed. Nazirah's scream was smothered in her belly. She struggled to yell for help. Farraj casually stepped over her and inspected the room. His eyes searched for Nazirah's book of formula. He walked to the window and saw Bari holding the unconscious Yunus in his arms. A crowd started to form around him. He saw no signs of Aswad and Anik. But with the growing commotion below in the streets, he knew he had little time to find what he sought. Farraj eyed the door to Nazirah's bedroom. The door was closed. He hurried to the room and tried to open the door, but it was locked.

Farraj cursed. He turned around and sneered at Nazirah. He watched her roll on the floor, her gown crumpled. Her hands remained curtained over her face. Her body quivered as if cold. She struggled to open her mouth and catapult a loud scream to alert Aswad and the other guards.

On the street below, Aswad and Anik penetrated the small crowd gathered around Bari. The two guards removed their swords and aimed them at the crowd. "This is guard business," said Anik forcefully. "Clear the area." The citizens departed, backing away slowly. Aswad and Anik knelt down next to Bari as he held Yunus' unconscious body. "I just found him like this," said Bari. "He's alive."

"What do you mean 'found'?" Anik asked in a stern voice.

Bari explained, "I went to get a jug of water from that building there. When I returned—"

"Goodness," Aswad scoffed. "He must be exhausted from all this guard duty."

A scream! Female. Coming from Nazirah's room. Aswad jumped to his feet, rushing inside the apartment complex, darting up the stairs in several strides. He came to the second floor and noticed Nazirah's door open, a bundle of flowers sprawled out in the doorway. Aswad raced to the room, sword extended. He saw Nazirah on the floor with Farraj straddling her, on his knees. His hands dug in and out of Nazirah's dress. Aswad calculated that the villain was searching her person not violently assaulting her. It did not matter to the young, Moorish guard.

"Let her go," Aswad commanded.

Farraj turned his head and peered at Aswad from over his shoulder. He stopped moving, slowly lifting from off Nazirah. He put his hands in the air, showing they were empty. He turned around to face Aswad, brandishing only a devious grin. He started to put his hands behind his head. Aswad was careful to watch every movement the perpetrator made. The young guard's close inspection of Farraj's movements saved his life. The cultist tossed two daggers in Aswad's direction. The young man swiped one with his sword and dodged the second. When Aswad regained stance, Farraj had already opened the window and dived from the building. Aswad followed Farraj to the open window, but pursued no further. He saw Farraj land, roll, and then spring on all fours past Anik and Bari, like a cat dashing away. He jumped to his feet in several strides, and continued his escape. Anik chased the cultist.

Aswad backed away from the window and sheathed his sword. He cradled Nazirah's body and asked, "Are you okay, *mora?*" Nazirah shook her head, yes, though her hands still covered her face. "Lock yourself in your room," Aswad commanded her. "I'll be right back." The woman shook her head again. Aswad helped Nazirah to her feet and then left the apartment. He kicked the flowers away and closed the door as he left.

Nazirah took one hand away from her face. She was weeping. She walked over to a pot containing a large growing plant. She dug her fingers into the soil, pulling out the key to her room. She opened the door and walked inside, closing the door behind her and locking it. She walked over to the basin of water in the bedroom's corner. A mirror hung overhead. Nazirah splashed some water onto her face, the burning sensation already cooling. She dried her face with a towel and looked in the mirror.

Nazirah's eyes widened with terror as she saw her face change before her eyes. Her image split and cracked in the mirror. Aging lines ripped and receded her flesh. Her skin decayed and peeled. Nazirah's eyes faded from dark brown to light blue. Even her hands suffered the same fate as her visage.

Nazirah shut her eyes from the horror. She trembled, frightened at her own image. She mustered the courage to open her eyes again. She kept her vision aimed at the water, then slowly panned up to face the mirror. Nazirah's heart skipped. She was still decayed. Nazirah gasped at the sight reflected in the mirror. There still remained the folds and wrinkles of her decaying flesh. She was withered beyond age. She was the sight of death laying six feet beneath the dirt. She lifted her hand and felt the jagged areas of her face magically peeling, receding, and withering further. She covered her eyes with her hands and started to weep harder.

Suddenly, there was a knock at the door. Aswad's voice came from the other side. He delivered news that her attacker, and the attacker's partners, escaped. Nazirah looked around the room, her eyes wide. Aswad could not see her like this. Her heart started to race as she heard his words asking for her to come from the room. She rushed to the door and made sure it was locked. Nazirah said, "Aswad, I am not presentable."

"Nazirah," the young Moor questioned. "Are you okay? Is something the matter? Are you hurt?"

"No," said the woman. "I'm...I'm just not presentable," she explained. "I'm not fit to be seen. Just give me time. I need time...to catch my breath."

Nazirah scanned the room as she kept her hand on the doorknob. Her vision spotted a dress lying across her bed. She hurried over to the garment and tore the cloth. She ripped a wide, rectangular piece of cloth from her dress, and then searched through her drawers to find a wrap to wear around her head. She put on the wrap and twisted her hair up into the folds. She took the cloth ripped from her dress and covered her face, making a self-designed veil. Nazirah turned back to the door. She hesitated, trying to relax her breathing.

Nazirah returned to the door. She put her hand on the knob and beheld the grotesque disfiguration of the melting flesh dripping from her hands. She ran back to her drawers and searched through them. Nazirah found a pair of gloves and covered her hands quickly. Her heart raced again, her breathing became erratic. She relaxed her breathing when she neared the door. She took a deep breath and then unlocked the door, walking through.

Aswad was standing in the front room, waiting patiently for Nazirah, his back to her bedroom door. He turned his head when Nazirah exited. Aswad spun his body around, ready to approach her, but he froze when he saw Nazirah veiled. He was perplexed. Aswad inspected the veiled woman in front of him; his head went up and down, eyes taking in her sight from head to toe. Had it not been for the attack, Aswad would have thought Nazirah was seducing him. He shook the surprised expression from his face and asked, "What's this?"

Nazirah rushed passed Aswad. "You should stay outside," she hissed. "From now on."

"Nazirah," the guard questioned.

The woman shook her head. "I am not fit to be seen," she expressed. Aswad walked over to her. He went to put a gentle hand on her shoulders. Nazirah ducked away from Aswad's touch. "No," she protested. "I am not fit—"

"Good woman," Aswad pleaded. "What's wrong?" Aswad was relieved that he could still see Nazirah's eyes, though he did not like their reaction to him. Nazirah's eyes went wide as she shivered, appearing to be frightened of Aswad. He took a breath and relaxed his demeanor. He lifted his hands, wanting to hold her, but afraid she would refuse his touch. Aswad's hands hovered. "I'm sorry, *mora.*" Aswad apologized. "I'm just as flustered as you from all this," he admitted. "You're my heart, and you were attacked." He stepped closer toward the veiled woman. "A friend of mine passes out for no reason, and this man gets through our guard. I'm sad to report, the attacker got away."

Nazirah turned her back to Aswad. "You have to leave," she dictated sharply.

Aswad was in disbelief of Nazirah's words. "But I have guard duty…"

"Then attend to it outside," shouted Nazirah, her words breaking as she started to cry. "I am not fit to be seen."

Aswad did not move. He was angry, frustrated with Nazirah's sudden change in behavior. He wanted to hurt someone, anyone. He put a stern gaze on the woman in front of him, and then recanted about wanting to hurt anyone. He did not want to strike her. He wanted to comfort her. He wanted to hold her. Aswad cautiously put up his hands and walked forward just the same.

"Nazirah," Aswad said her name with gentle sincerity. He said her name as if it was the only true way to express love. The resonance of his voice ceased the woman's tears and trembling. "I'm going to put my arms around you, *mora*," he said like a warning. "There's a saying, in the birthplace of our ancestors, that in order to calm a woman, the man must place his arms around her and take in the energy that ails her."

Nazirah remained still.

Aswad cautiously cloaked the woman with his arms. Nazirah trembled for only a slight second, and then she relaxed inside his embrace. "What's wrong, Nazirah," Aswad whispered into her ear. Nazirah turned around, still in Aswad's embrace. He looked at her veil and made the foolish attempt to lift it. His gesture was accompanied with a sly smile, a single, gentle finger lifting the veil. Before Aswad could see what Nazirah had become, the woman rushed from his embrace. She was as quick as the wind, fleeing from Aswad.

"No," She yelled. "I'm not fit to be seen."

The line's repetition started to weaken Aswad's nerves. He grit his teeth, angry with himself for making such a forceful move on Nazirah. He relaxed. "I'll leave you be, *mora*," Aswad capitulated. "But I have to report any happenings, including your attack. If something is the matter, I say with complete authority, it must be reported to me now."

Nazirah hesitated, but eventually turned toward Aswad. She reached for her veil, her hand raising and pausing as it made its way up to her face. Finally, she folded her fingers over her veil and started to remove it. Aswad held his breath, his teeth grit again. He braced himself for the worse. Aswad worried less about the possible scarring on Nazirah's face, how she looked, and more about the possible brutality that he would inflict on the woman's attacker.

Nazirah unwrapped the veil from her face and slowly took it away. Her eyes lingered to catch Aswad's expression. They were as slow and hesitant as the rest of her movements. But Nazirah finally looked up at the young man in front of her. Aswad looked perplexed. Nazirah's heart stopped. She gasped at her lover's quandary at what he beheld. She cried out and ran to her room.

"I'm unclean," Nazirah screamed. "I've become ugly! They have scarred me!"

Aswad shook the look from his face and ran after Nazirah. But the woman was too quick. She shut and locked the door. "Nazirah," he called.

"Go away, Aswad," The woman yelled from the other side of the door. "Go away, please."

Aswad did not move, not even his lips. He could not say anything, though there was much to say to Nazirah. He just stared at the door. He heard Nazirah demand he take post outside on the street with the other guards. Aswad walked to the window. He looked down and saw Anik standing guard. Bari had taken Yunus to the guard barracks for medical attention.

Beyond the door barring Aswad from Nazirah's room, the woman sat on her bed, weeping. She returned the veil to her face, covering her shame, her disfigurement. Her eyes were wide, sweeping the floor looking for answers to her dilemma. Nazirah shifted and felt the answer was under her. She was sitting on her book of formula. She pulled the book from under her and held it up like a treasure she had sought for many years. Nazirah opened the pages and shifted through her equations, writings, and exact methods to find her chemical formula to heal the wounds inflicted on her face. Nazirah found the equation, the page corner folded, marked off. She had gathered most of the ingredients the other day when Aswad escorted her to the University. One single ingredient remained. It was a flower that grew just outside city limits.

Marwan-Zuhr.

Nazirah jumped from the bed and rushed to the door. "Aswad," she called. She heard footsteps approach the door. She knew him too well. He was too stubborn to leave. Nazirah was both relieved and frustrated at Aswad's predictability.

"*Mora*," the other called.

"I have a command for you, my guard," she told him. "You must obtain a flower for me. It is called *Marwan-Zuhr.*"

"What," he inquired.

"Please," Nazirah responded. "It is the last ingredient I need to heal my scars."

"But Nazirah—" Aswad pleaded.

"Aswad, I command you as my guard," she said with great authority.

Aswad stopped. He stood at the door, gaining his composure. "But Nazirah—" and then, for a reason he did not know, he changed the words he wanted to speak. "But Nazirah, I can't leave my post. The search for this flower can only be conducted *after* your attackers are caught. And even then we have to make sure there are no other members of this cult after you."

"I understand," Nazirah yielded. "Until then, look through my books and find a colored sketching of the flower. And then take post outside."

Aswad backed away from the door and bowed politely. "Yes, *mora*," he said turning around and conducting his search. It did not take long for him to find a colored sketch inside one of Nazirah's books. He asked for permission to tear the page from the book, Nazirah granted consent. Aswad took the page, folded it, and put it in a pocket. He stood up and walked from the apartment and down to the street.

"How is she," Anik asked.

Aswad stood next to his friend. "She's wearing a veil," was all he reported. His voice sounded sad.

"A veil," Anik wondered. "Well, some of the women are beginning to cover themselves more, including a veil, so as not to be snatched up by wandering Europeans looking to kidnap them for use."

"It's not that," Aswad insisted.

Anik continued his interrogation of Nazirah's strange behavior. "Does she study Monophysitic philosophy, or is she a Monist Mohammedan? Does she follow al-Arabi? I believe his followers wear veils."

"No," said Aswad forcefully. "It is for no religious or cultural reasons. Her attacker has her wearing a veil, covered up."

"Is she scarred badly?" Anik asked concerned.

Aswad looked at his fellow guard. His voice was low to escape detection. Nazirah's window was open, and they stood just below it. Aswad did not know if the woman had come from out her bedroom with him now absent from her apartment. "She showed me her face, Anik." Aswad tightened his fist. "What he did to her…"

"My goodness," Anik said trying to imagine what the beautiful Nazirah looked like after a brutal attack. "She's torn apart then? We need to get her to a physician."

To Anik's surprise, Aswad revealed, "There is not a single scar on her."

Aswad was wide eyed, he too in disbelief.

"What?" Anik was perplexed.

Aswad glanced quickly at Nazirah's window. He put his eyes back on Anik. "Her face is as clear as the sky we stand under," he informed. Anik looked up at Nazirah's window. "There is absolutely nothing wrong with her," Aswad continued. "But she's mad," he hissed. "Nazirah insists she's unclean. She says her face is scarred, and that she's unfit to be seen." Aswad waited for Anik to look back to him before he spoke again. "We are dealing with cultists. They have this woman under a spell of some kind."

Anik looked at Aswad incredulously. "You really think this the work of magic?" he asked, his tone mirroring the expression on his face.

"Not what we define as magic, but as magic exists in these times." Aswad put his palms together and shook them as he explained carefully. "They must have concocted a hallucinogen."

Anik looked down at the street and responded, "That's what must've made Yunus pass out." He folded his arms and shook his head.

Aswad said vengefully, "I want these men punished. I want them dead."

Anik put a hand on Aswad's shoulder. "I understand, Aswad. But we need you calm, levelheaded. Justice will be—"

Aswad took a deep breath that cut into Anik's words. The young guard then said, "They will attack again. That will be their mistake and our advantage. They're after something Nazirah possesses." Anik listened attentively. He motioned for Aswad to continue. Aswad spoke, "Nazirah is an al-chemist, medicinal. She has concocted a formula that can heal wounds."

"Brilliant," said Anik, a look of excitement on his face. "And they're after her for this?"

Aswad nodded. "Yes," he answered. "She wants me to find the last ingredient for her medicine to fix her scars," informed Aswad. "But she suffers from an hallucination not anything physical."

Anik lifted an eyebrow. "Perhaps it'll still work. It might heal the hallucination, fix her sight, her mind." He searched for more rationalizations, but had none. "Those are just my guesses."

"I can't search for the ingredient," said Aswad, his tone cursing the situation. "I'd have to leave my post," he explained.

"Then do so," Anik told him confidently. "These cultists will return, but not soon. They'll need time to regroup their thoughts. If they do choose to strike tonight, it's because they'll think we've been rattled. They'll come harder. It's like when a fighter knows he has his opponent stumbling. He strikes again, instantly, to knock him down. They're clever," Anik said, contemplating. "And if they're cultists, they're cunning. If they come, so be it. Like a good fighter, we let them come to us." Anik balled his fist.

"And we swing hard," Aswad concluded.

"Right," Anik acknowledged slapping Aswad on the shoulder. "I'll hold fort here," he said. "You don't worry. Just get Nazirah's remaining ingredient."

Aswad saluted his fellow guardsman and then flagged down the nearest public carriage to taxi him outside the city. Wearing the robes of a guardsman allowed him to find transportation easily. He climbed into the carriage and stated his destination. His trip did not take long, traffic light toward the city outskirts. Aswad commanded the taxi's driver to stay at the edge of the forest as he searched the woods outside the city walls. He exited the public chariot, made his way into the woods, removed the sketch of the flower, and continuously put his eyes on the paper and then the shrubbery in front of him.

His eyes desperately scoped the area. His search took him deep inside the woods. He also kept a cautious eye over his shoulder, and on his surroundings. He did not need to be attacked here. Aswad believed he could slay as many cultists as there could be with his anger bubbling. He kept his mind on the hunt, which did not elude him. Toward the center of the forest he saw a patch of wild marwan-zuhr flowers. He picked several of them, not knowing how many he needed. He turned around, made his way back to the taxi, and gave a command to return to the city. The cost of his trip was put on the City Guard's tab. Aswad also added a heavy tip—a nudge at Khushtar for making him pay for the groceries weeks ago.

He returned to Nazirah's building. Anik still kept guard. Bari had not yet returned, and there was no news on Yunus' condition. Aswad displayed the flowers to Anik who patted him on the shoulder for a job well done. The young guard then took the bouquet to Nazirah's door. He knocked and the woman's voice immediately answered.

"Your flowers are here, *mora*," he told her.

"Put them at the door, and then take leave," Nazirah insisted.

Aswad's heart sunk at the command. He put the flowers at the foot of the door, bowed graciously, and then pivoted to walk away. He returned to Anik. His fellow guard could see the frustration on his face. Anik said nothing, which was more comforting than any words. Anik understood Aswad wanted to be with his thoughts. Upstairs, Nazirah worked rigorously to put her research into an alchemical brew.

As the sunlight dwindled, so too did the crowd flourishing through the square. Yunus returned to his post, recovered. Aswad determined that whatever was used against Yunus was only enough to lull him unconscious. A curfew was initiated because of the recent activities consisting of the twelve year-old boy's murder, the kidnapping of an elderly woman, and the reported attack on Nazirah—all thought to be the work of the same people. The officials hoped the curfew would reduce the number of total crimes, and also help apprehend the lurking cultists. Aswad and Anik did not call for more guards. It was their trap to bait the cultists into another attack. They wanted to appear vulnerable.

It was long after sundown. The city square glowed orange by way of the flickering lamps stationed around it. Aswad sat down, his back against Nazirah's apartment complex. His eyes were heavy, and he realized how difficult the guard duty had been for his other three companions over the past two weeks. He had it easy, until this morning. Prior to the day's events, his duty consisted of resting and cuddling in a beautiful woman's arms, and enjoying candlelit dinners with her.

At the moment, he panned the area across the square. He was not on duty. It was his time to rest, but he was anxious. Yunus rested pleasantly. Bari and Anik kept watch. Aswad's distress was overwhelmed by weariness. He realized he needed sleep when his eyes started creating shadows out of nothing, or when shadows wiggled into physical bodies. Aswad closed his eyes and rested. He could at least dream of being in Nazirah's arms, and her no longer suffering from hallucinations.

Aswad's desire rippled in front of his eyes, putting him in his own welcomed hallucinations. He dreamed of Nazirah, holding her, kissing her, exploring her world as he described weeks ago in stanza. But Aswad was quickly shaken from sleep. His eyes opened wide, his heart raced, and he inhaled the air. Anik stood above him, urgency drawn on his face. "There are two men in the alley across the square."

"Other guards," Aswad asked.

Anik shook his head. "Not sure. I thought if it's our perpetrators, you might want a crack at 'em. You and Bari go investigate."

Aswad stood up, dusting himself off. He checked his sword and started across the square with Bari next to him. Yunus and Anik stayed behind, keeping close to Nazirah's building. Aswad could see the two figures leaning against the opening of the alley. He squinted, focusing. Aswad still struggled with fatigue. The street lamps were becoming dim, and the darkness was growing. One of the men folded his arms. Both men turned their heads away from the approaching guards.

"Excuse me," called Aswad. "No one is to be in the square at this time."

The two men continued to speak to one another, ignoring the guards. Aswad and Bari held tight to the hilt of their sheathed swords. "A curfew was initiated," said Bari. "The streets are not safe, even for men like you. If you refuse to move we'll have to place you under arrest."

One of the men unfolded his arms. He turned slightly and made a sudden move. A throwing knife cut through the air, Bari its target. The guard ducked away from the projectile. He unsheathed his sword in the same motion. The attack brought Aswad to his senses as he tossed aside his exhaustion and pulled his weapon. His eyes recognized the knife thrower as the man who attacked Nazirah earlier in the day. Farraj and Hilal ran away, Bari and Aswad close behind them. Anik and Yunus witnessed their fellow guardsmen run into the alley across the square. Anik grabbed Yunus' arm as the young guard started forward.

"Unfortunately, our duty is here," said Anik.

But a fight stalked them as well. A large mass of ferocious muscle stepped from an alley located two buildings away. The massive figure moved toward the guards, his movement spotted by Yunus who alerted Anik. Dharr reached down and grabbed Yunus by his robes. He tossed the guard aside as if he weighed nothing. Anik backed away. He removed the scabbard from around his body and dropped his sheathed sword on the ground. Dharr grinned and cracked his knuckles. The two men circled one another.

"I know you," grumbled Dharr. "Anik El-Gabry, once champion world fighter," he chuckled. "You look old and tired."

"I've hurt people bigger than you while at this age," Anik retorted.

Dharr charged the pugilistic guard. He crashed his massive fist against Anik's cheek and quickly followed the attack with a punch to Anik's ribs. Anik back-stepped, less from the impact and more to gain stance. He countered with a hard punch to Dharr's abdomen. The attack was devastating to the giant. Anik's blow was a strategic strike. Dharr was a lot taller than him, and Anik needed to get the giant at eye level. The strong hit to the stomach bent the giant over, placing him eye-to-eye with Anik. The old fighter swung at the giant's face. His punch knocked against Dharr, and the giant buckled, extending his arm to the street to maintain balance and keep his body from falling. Anik swung again. His second hit caused Dharr to stumble completely.

But the giant recovered and swung his fist. His strike collided with Anik's chin. The hit lifted Anik off his feet. He soared through the air and landed hard on his back. He rolled on his side and looked up at Dharr. Yunus leapt onto the giant's back, his arm wrapped around the brute's neck. The guard was armed with a dagger, and preparing to strike. The brute reached over his shoulders and grabbed Yunus before the guard could strike with the weapon. Dharr dragged Yunus over his head and held him out in front of him. He reached for Yunus' hand and twisted his wrist, causing him to let loose the knife. Dharr slammed the guard to the ground, lifted his foot and brought it down on Yunus' chest, cracking several ribs.

Anik jumped to his feet and rushed Dharr. The giant put his shoulder down and slammed the oncoming Anik with his body. Anik tumbled back to the road. Dharr swiped Yunus' dagger from the ground. He brought the blade down into the guard's stomach, blade to the hilt. He added a hard punch to Yunus' face. Dharr stood up and made his way into Nazirah's apartment. Anik leapt to his feet and ran to his wounded friend. Yunus painfully pulled the dagger from his stomach. Blood leapt from his mouth following a loud, agonizing scream. Despite his painful cry, Yunus assured Anik, "I'll be fine." The tone in his voice showed nothing but pain and suffering. The wounded guard clenched his teeth and inhaled heavy. He gave the dagger to Anik, his hands trembling. "Protect the woman," he said.

Anik took the bloody dagger from his injured friend. He stood up and rushed into Nazirah's apartment. Yunus put his head back against the pavement, his wound gushed more blood with the dagger absent. Yunus put his hand over the tear in his stomach and breathed slowly, trying to remain conscious.

Up in Nazirah's apartment, Dharr had broken through her front door and made his way to the bedroom. It was locked. Dharr's ears picked up Anik approaching as the guard quickly made his way up the stairs. Dharr shoved the weight of his body forward and rammed Nazirah's door open. The woman was sleeping on her bed. She did not wake, her sleep induced by the medicine she concocted. The book of formula rested on a nightstand. The lamp burning on the table provided a spotlight for Dharr's desired object. He stepped inside the room and swiped the book. He came face-to-face with Anik when he attempted to exit the room. The pugilist lunged at the giant. Dharr again lowered his shoulder and crashed into Anik. He pushed the guard through the door and knocked him into a mess of plants and shrubbery. Anik rolled across the floor and got to his knee. Dharr backed up, an electrifying pain pulsing on the side of his abdomen. He looked down and noticed the dagger jammed into his side.

The giant admired Anik's move. He also figured he now possessed a weapon. Dharr reached for the blade, removed it, and then charged Anik to return the violent favor. The guard caught Dharr's forearm in mid-swing and threw his fist into the giant's face. Dharr's head turned with the impact. Anik kept a grip on Dharr's forearm, and punched him in the stomach. Dharr lowered his face, his body buckling with the impact of the blow to his body. Anik hit Dharr again across the face, letting the giant's forearm go. Dharr stumbled, Anik's assault taking its toll. But Anik's next move was a fatal miscalculation in strategy. The pugilist slapped the knife from Dharr's hand instead of hitting him again to knock the brute unconscious. This gave Dharr a chance to recover from the punishment Anik delivered. The brute blinked and shook off the heavy effects from the attack. He countered by grabbing Anik's neck with his free hand. He lifted the guard off the floor and tossed him through the open window. Anik hit the ground. His arm snapped on impact.

Dharr took a deep breath and then casually walked from the apartment, down the stairs, and then out of the building. He walked back into the alley and slipped into the shadows. Anik crawled to Yunus. He screamed an alerting cry. The howl filtered through the square and streets. Other guards stationed in the vicinity rushed to the aid of their wounded guardsmen.

Elsewhere, Bari and Aswad winded through streets and alleys tailing Hilal and Farraj. Their chase turned another corner, ducking into another shadowy alleyway. Bari took the lead, sword extended and at the ready, but his preparation for a fight was not enough. Two knives hit his chest, and another caught his throat as he turned down a backstreet. Bari dropped instantly, his breath and life gone. Aswad, alerted to the danger, spun from one side of the narrow street to the other. A barrage of knives ejected from the backstreet. Aswad lay flat against the side of a building. He saw the two cultists move into another alley. He approached cautiously but quickly. He peeked inside and watched Hilal draw more knives to toss. Aswad took the time to strike. He jumped from one alley wall to the other, left leg planted against the left wall, and then right leg planted against the right wall.

When he had enough air, he jumped forward and sliced Hilal down the chest. Aswad flipped over the cultists, turned, and ran his sword along Hilal's back, killing him.

"A wonderful display of gymnastics," Farraj teased as he stood in the middle of the alley. "Who would've guessed that you were as nimble with your sword as you are with words?"

Aswad turned around to face Farraj. "I'm also a sketch artist," he said sternly.

"Really?" Farraj questioned.

"Yes," Aswad answered walking forward. "After I *draw* my sword," he lifted his blade, "I *draw* blood."

Farraj cocked his head. "Clever," he responded. Farraj countered Aswad's action by unsheathing and lifting his sword.

Aswad and Farraj rushed one another. Their swords clashed! Each swordsman tried to gain the better ground in the narrow alley. Aswad was young, quick, and more experienced than Farraj had given credit. He was able to parry attacks with his back turned, sword drawn over his shoulder, and gain the advantage almost as swiftly as Farraj was able to take it away. But Farraj truly controlled the scuffle. He was calm, where Aswad was enraged and filled with deadly intent that took him out of focus, but Aswad was still able to keep up with Farraj. The cultist back-stepped and swiped his sword. The attack was only designed to move Aswad back and make him duck. Aswad executed the very moves Farraj intended. Farraj took the moment to turn and run, disappearing into the shadows, a designed escape concocted earlier.

Aswad sheathed his sword and ran back to Bari's body. He knelt down and held his fellow guardsman close. Aswad screamed for help. Aid appeared minutes later, citizens and other city guard surrounding Aswad. The guards lifted Bari and took him away. Aswad made his way back to Nazirah's apartment. Anik and Yunus were gone. They were substituted with four other guards who informed Aswad of Anik and Yunus's conditions. Aswad was told Anik suffered a broken arm defending Nazirah, and Yunus was badly beaten, possibly dying from a stab wound. Aswad looked up at Nazirah's window. As he did, one of the guards informed him there were two guards stationed outside Nazirah's door. Aswad journeyed up to Nazirah's room and saw the guards at her door. Aswad approached the armed men, and they immediately granted him entry to Nazirah's living space. The guard to the left informed that Nazirah was still asleep. Aswad stepped inside, the broken door easily swinging open. Only the moon provided light for the front room. Aswad could see the plants had been disturbed. Broken branches and leaves patterned the ground as if exploded from their stalks.

Aswad found and lit a lamp resting on a table. He searched the front room to see if Nazirah's book of formula was anywhere. He rushed into her room, the door broken as well, and saw Nazirah so peacefully at rest. She was cloaked with her bed's blankets and with her veil still around her face.

Aswad inspected the room for her book. He found nothing but a half empty cup of the remedy she concocted from her equation. He looked down at Nazirah and wondered if her own medicine kept her at rest. She was completely under slumber's influence, and she was undisturbed. Aswad put the lamp on the dresser. He removed the scabbard strapped around his shoulder and leaned it on the chair in the corner. Aswad knelt down in front of Nazirah and gently lifted her veil.

Nazirah was beautiful.

Aswad ran his fingers on her cheek and the woman smiled. He kissed her lips and she reacted immediately, not by waking, but with a smile. Aswad whispered a simple poetic phrase into Nazirah's ear. He told the woman that there was no better rhyme than the synchronicity of a kiss. He fixed her veil and took a seat in the chair. Aswad relaxed himself, staring at Nazirah's sleeping body. The dramatic ordeal of the day's and night's events lifted from him as he watched Nazirah. Slowly, he too drifted into slumber's embrace, dreaming that he was in Nazirah's arms.

Nazirah awoke. It was dawn. She sat up in bed and noticed Aswad sleeping in the corner chair. She was perturbed at his presence; he had disobeyed her orders. However, she did not confront him. She stood up and walked to the mirror. She was immediately disappointed without removing her veil. She noticed her light blue eyes peering at her. The sight chilled her. Her heart shattered, attacked by the failure of her work, equation, and her remaining disfigurement. Nazirah did not have to remove her veil. The color of her eyes was an indication absolute. But she did look, first making sure Aswad was asleep. Then she removed the cloth from around her face.

The illusion of her deformity remained.

Nazirah punched the water filling the basin under her mirror. It splashed and spilled everywhere. She screamed, wrenching Aswad from sleep. He jumped from the chair and rushed to the woman's aid. Nazirah backed away from Aswad and screamed, yelling for Aswad to leave her presence. Aswad ignored the order. He stood in front of Nazirah who backed up into the corner across from where Aswad approached. Nazirah felt trapped and threatened, Aswad standing in front of her, boxing her in.

"Leave, Aswad!" Nazirah demanded in an exploding voice.

Aswad put out his hands in protest. "Wait, *mora*. Listen to me. You are still beautiful. You suffer from a hallucination. Your attackers—"

Nazirah slapped Aswad. "How dare you speak of my tribulations as a façade," she slapped Aswad again. "How dare you!"

Aswad backed away, holding his face. "You believe it and therefore you see it, but it is not real, *mora*. You are beautiful as the day I saw you. You are as beautiful as the night I sensed your presence in the window. You are whole, not scarred."

Nazirah put her hand over her veil. She clenched her teeth to keep from crying. "The only facade is my life's work. The elixir does nothing."

Aswad approached cautiously. "No, Nazirah. It does nothing because you suffer from nothing."

"Get out, Aswad," Nazirah demanded. Her tearing eyes shifted to her nightstand. She saw her book was missing. "They came again?" She looked at Aswad. Nazirah looked around the room. She saw her door busted open. Nazirah hurried through it and saw her apartment in shambles. "There was another attack?"

Aswad followed Nazirah to the front room. "Your medicine put you to sleep, I believe." He stepped toward her carefully, an expression of guilt on his face. "I will find your book of formula, Nazirah."

"It will do them no good," Nazirah said making her way back to her room. She turned and said to Aswad sharply, "The formula does not work."

"It does work," Aswad insisted.

Nazirah removed her veil to the young guard's surprise. "Look at my appearance, Aswad," she yelled. "Look! I am still malformed, ugly. I am not presentable." She put her veil back around her. "I am not fit to be seen."

Aswad was becoming frustrated. "Nazirah, I would look at you for the rest of my life in any condition. The only thing wrong with your appearance is your perception of it."

Nazirah trembled. Her eyes overflowed with tears. "I will not cry in your presence. I refuse to."

Aswad continued his slow approach. He held out his arms to embrace the confused woman. But Nazirah struck him again, her nails biting into Aswad's cheek and leaving four, jagged, bloody scars. She entered her room and returned with the half empty cup in her hands. She pounded it against Aswad's chest.

"Take it!" Nazirah yelled. Aswad took the cup, his mouth agape. "May your scars, like mine, never heal!" she turned around, entered her room, and slammed the door. The door swayed open, broken as it was.

Aswad was hurt, cut. But the pain and sting came from his heart, not the marks left on his face. He sipped the elixir. His vision blurred as the medicine tried to pull him to sleep. But Aswad fought against the medicinal intoxication. He remained on his feet, wobbling. The side of his face became cool and then warmed as his flesh mended back together. He felt his cheek. Trickles of blood remained, but the scars did not.

Aswad was stunned. Nazirah was brilliant, but no longer had the confidence to know, he considered. Aswad walked to the door and heard Nazirah sobbing. He backed away and looked down at the cup. "Anik. Yunus." He said devising a plan. He turned around and ran from the apartment, down the stairs, out of the building, and toward the City Guards' barracks. Aswad walked carefully through the hordes of people. He did not want to spill a single drop of the formula as he made his way to the barracks.

On arriving, Aswad ran into Khushtar. He looked tired, as if he too was up the entire night chasing murderers and kidnappers. Khushtar was drained of all his usual jovial self. He barely smiled at Aswad's presence, which made Aswad nervous.

"Commander…?" Aswad asked.

"We've locked the city down," Khushtar informed Aswad. "All exits are blocked. A unit has been set up around the city perimeter." The Commander sighed. "I don't like doing this to the people. The Governor will have my head." He panned the sky. "All this because of three men," he looked at Aswad, making the young guard feel guilty.

"This is my fault," said Aswad.

Khushtar put a hand on Aswad's shoulder. "No. Don't worry. We have to protect Nazirah." He sighed again. "Anik tells me they took the woman's book. He told me what's in the book."

"No bother," said Aswad confidently. "I can track them down."

"I heard that you cut one down," Khushtar said trying to sound congratulatory.

"I had to," Aswad nodded. "I crossed blades with the leader—at least I suspect him to be the leader. But he ran off. And that's where we'll start tracking them down." He lifted the cup and stated, "But first, I need Anik and Yunus well."

"That's the woman's formula?" Khushtar asked in awe.

"And it works." Aswad smiled. "A simple sip, some rest, and Anik and Yunus will be as fine as they were before their scuffle. How is Yunus? I heard it was bad. He's not…because Bari—"

"No," assured Khusthar. "He's the toughest human being I know. He's barely hanging on. Refuses to sleep out of fear of death. Physicians have him patched up as much as possible."

"He'll sleep after this," Aswad said showing the contents of the cup. "Then we find our cultists."

"And you know where these criminals can be found," Khushtar asked.

"Yes, Commander," said Aswad.

Khushtar folded his arms and continued to ask questions. "How is that?"

"When the leader got away from me, we were near the Library of al-Idris," Aswad notifed.

Khushtar raised an eyebrow. "Are they hiding *in* the library?"

"Near it, I believe," Aswad suspected. "It's just a feeling I have." Aswad saw Khushtar's face contort. "Bari and I chased them far. Most likely the culprits were keeping close to home. We were led down a path they knew, especially in the dark."

Khushtar considered Aswad's statements. "I'll have all residences searched."

"Inns," Aswad recommended. "We should stick to the inns."

Khushtar nodded. He pointed to the barracks and commanded, "Get that stuff applied to Anik and Yunus."

"Yes, Commander," Aswad bowed. He ran into the barracks and winded through the hallways to find the infirmary. Inside, Anik and Yunus lay among several other ailing guards. Yunus' wounds were the worst in the entire infirmary. Anik's arm was in a sling. Aswad went to Yunus first. His wounds were patched, and he was medicated to ease the pain. His eyes were opened halfway, sluggish.

"Yunus," called Aswad. "Can you understand me?"

"Excuse me, sir," a nurse called from behind Aswad.

Aswad raised his hand. "I've been cleared to be here, take it up with Commander Khushtar." The nurse backed away. Aswad looked at his friend again and asked, "Can you understand me?" Yunus shook his head wearily. "I want you to sip this," Aswad instructed. "Okay?" He lifted the cup and presented it in front of Yunus' drooping eyes. He eased the cup to Yunus' lips. "Nurse," Aswad called. "Help lift his head."

The nurse came to Aswad's aid, lifting Yunus' head and pillow. Aswad placed the cup against Yunus' lips and poured half of what was left into the guard's mouth. Some of the elixir dribbled from between Yunus' lips. But even in his inebriated state, Yunus was able to ingest the elixir. He immediately fell back to sleep. The nurse lowered his head gently. Aswad walked over to Anik.

"Is that Nazirah's work," the aged guard asked. Aswad nodded, yes. "Do you think it can mend bone?"

"I felt it magically mend my flesh," Aswad said approaching. "And we are in haste to kill men. Doubt cannot fog us."

Anik took the drink with his good hand. He swallowed the rest of the cup's contents. He dropped the cup, the medicine's initial effect mummifying him with sleep as it mended his broken arm. Aswad picked up the cup and handed it to the nurse. He took a seat and kept watch as his friends slept.

Anik woke an hour later. Aswad stood up and walked to the guard's bed. Anik removed his arm from the sling and moved it around to check its functionality. He twisted his hand, twirled his fingers, and threw air punches with his mended arm. Anik put his other arm across his body to grab his shoulder and began rotating it. "I think it even got rid of a nasty bar in my rotator."

Aswad slapped Anik on the back. "Sword up," he commanded. "We have men to kill."

Anik jumped from the bed. "I take it this profound elixir did not heal Nazirah of her hallucinations."

"No," Aswad said in a defeated voice. "And when I tried to tell her what she suffered from she became hysterical. She even slapped me."

Anik continued to check his arm, holding and rubbing his wrist. "Welcome to a real relationship with a woman." He chuckled. He looked over at Yunus and asked, "Is he still healing."

Aswad nodded. "Yes. I don't believe we have time to wait. Khushtar is putting together a squad of guards to corner these men."

"I heard Bari was slain," Anik said sadly.

"Yes," acknowledged Aswad remorsefully. "But I took the life of his attacker."

"There are two left," computed Anik.

"In this outfit," said Anik. "Let's hope there's not more."

Aswad and Anik marched from the complex and met up with Khushtar outside. Khushtar addressed a squad of twenty-four guards. Aswad and Anik bowed respectfully toward their Commander. He motioned for both of them to join the others. He then singled out Aswad to lead the men to the Library of al-Idris. Among them was a designated Captain, al-Hakim, who would split them into smaller squads once they reached the vicinity. The guards were assigned horses, and Aswad took the lead with Captain al-Hakim.

The squad of guards traversed the main streets while on horseback. They looked intimidating to the citizens. Aswad pointed to the various alleyways the cultists led he and Bari through. Captain al-Hakim assigned two groups of four guards to follow the alleys into the connecting main streets and meet them at the library. "There are three inns near the library," said Captain al-Hakim. "We'll search them all." He sighed, much like Khushtar had done. "I hate doing this to the people."

"They'll understand," said Aswad. "These criminals can't be taken lightly."

The mass of guards merged with the other two groups that had earlier split from them. Their convergence came exactly as they flooded the street in front of the library. Captain al-Hakim again made squads of four. He kept Aswad by his side, which unnerved Aswad. He wanted to investigate with the other guards. Anik was sent with one of the four squads. They spread out. One group searched the alleys while the others searched the inns lining the street.

One of the search parties discovered the inn holding the gruesome sanguinary scene made by the cultists. The bloody body of Ahlam lay in the corner. Dried rivers of her blood snaked from the body and stained the floor. The room smelled like dead flesh and burning ash. The furniture was pushed to the wall. An altar lay in the middle of the floor. There was no sign of the cultists other than the massacre they left behind.

A guard screamed an alert cry!

"Over here," the cry sounded. "We've found something."

Aswad swiveled his horse in the direction of the announcement. He looked at al-Hakim. The Captain nodded his head in the direction of the cry. Aswad started forward on command. Suddenly, there was a rattling sound more percussive and reverberating than thunder. Aswad's horse instantly bucked and screamed. Aswad was thrown from his mount. Smoke and debris clouded the streets. The bodies of guardsmen were tossed onto the road, some missing limbs. It was as if the inn was bombarded by a cannon blast. Horses stampeded through the streets. Citizens ran for cover. The guards who remained on their feet tried to calm the hysteria in the streets. Al-Hakim shouted orders to the guards that were still conscious and standing.

Aswad ducked away from the stampede, his eyes looking for Farraj and his remaining accomplice. Anik came to his side, helping him off the ground. The two of them took cover in an alley as the streets became chaotic. Aswad continued to survey his surroundings. "I know he's around here somewhere," he said to Anik. "He has to be admiring the display."

It was then that Anik's eye spotted Dharr turning the corner at the end of the alley. The guard chased the cultist and signaled for Aswad to follow. "This way," he alerted.

Both men raced at top speed. They turned the corner, following Dharr. Their pursuit was surprisingly not too far ahead of them. Aswad sensed another trap. Dharr kept straight on a main street, turning left at the end.

Aswad unsheathed his sword.

Anik did the same.

Dharr jumped from out of nowhere as Anik and Aswad turned onto the next street. He crashed into Anik, the two of them rolled into the street. Anik lost the grip on his sword. He managed to get from under Dharr's attack and to his feet. The two fighters circled one another again. The citizens dispersed from the brawl.

Aswad lifted his sword toward Dharr and ordered, "You are under arrest! Cease your resistance."

Dharr grimaced at Aswad. The split second glance gave Anik the opportunity to strike the giant in the face. Anik's reach extended long, crossing Dharr's chin. "You heard him, you brute! You're under arrest."

Aswad caught sight of Farraj from the corner of his eye. He turned his sword away from Dharr and chased after the cultist leader. His pursuit led him down the street and into a wide opened lot. Farraj pulled his sword, smiled, and again engaged the young swordsman. Aswad's sword style was more relaxed than the previous night's quarrel. The removal of rage from Aswad's rhythm tempered his focus as sharp as his sword. Farraj's only strategy was to disturb Aswad's rhythm by taunting him with threats to Nazirah's person, and her present condition. This only focused Aswad's rhythm more. His style was flawless, and only matched by Farraj's experience. Aswad proved to be a more difficult opponent than in their previous night's skirmish.

The same could be said with Anik in his brawl with Dharr. He grappled the brute with ease, throwing and landing punches vehemently. But again, a fatal error occurred. This time Dharr made it. He gained an advantage in the fight when his fist landed across Anik, twisting the guard around. His mistake was not to finish him off, but to wrap his arm around Anik's neck. The guard tossed Dharr over his shoulder. Anik removed a dagger and jammed it into Dharr's chest, but this was part of the brute's plan. With the few critical seconds of his life fading away, Dharr removed the dagger from his chest, and then dropped it on the street. At the same moment, he took out a vial of Nazirah's elixir from his pocket. Anik snatched the vial from his hands before a drop could reach Dharr's lips. The guard picked up the dagger and slammed it into the giant's throat.

Dharr fell dead.

"Nice try," Anik grimaced as he corked the bottle and slipped the vial into his pocket.

Anik grabbed a citizen and instructed him to find Captain al-Hakim. He told the citizen that the Captain could be found near the Library of al-Idris. Anik ran to find Aswad. He came across the fight in the back lot. Anik's sudden presence distracted Farraj. Aswad twirled Farraj's blade from out of his grip and then stabbed him through the stomach. Farraj stepped back, the sword still through him. Aswad opened his hand, the sword's hilt lost as Farraj dropped to the ground.

Anik ran to Aswad's side. "I got the other one," he informed. "They concocted an elixir. The other cultist tried to use it. I stopped him."

"A pity," said Farraj.

Aswad and Anik looked over at the remaining cultist. Anik's body jerked as a throwing knife caught him between the collar and neck. Aswad backed away, but Farraj tossed another dagger. The blade ripped through Aswad's hand. Aswad stared in disbelief as Farraj raised from off the ground, sword still piercing his stomach.

"I've re-calculated the woman's equations," the cultist chuckled sadistically as he removed the sword from his stomach. He dropped the weapon on the ground, his wound started to mend itself together. "I can't be hurt at all. A little extra potency for the medicine I sipped. Too bad for my brethren. But, men like him are a dime-a-dozen."

"Halt!" al-Hakim yelled.

Farraj ran to his left. He jumped a fence at the far end of the lot and disappeared over it. Al-Hakim commanded three guards to pursue Farraj. Aswad dropped to his knees. He held his wrist to soothe the pain throbbing in his hand. Anik crawled to Aswad, his breath dying.

"P-p-pocket," Anik said spiting up blood. "M-m-my po-pocket…"

Aswad searched through Anik's pocket and came across the vial of elixir. He set the vial down and yelled to al-Hakim. "Come! He needs assistance." Al-Hakim ran to the two wounded guards. "Take the dagger out of his body," Aswad commanded.

Al-Hakim sighed. He looked at Anik. The guard was dying. His breath was slowing down. His eyes were half closed. Al-Hakim only had a few words and a prayer to offer. "He's dying, son," al-Hakim said sadly. He hated to say the words. He knew that Anik could still hear him.

"Take the dagger out of his body," commanded Aswad forcefully.

"That'll only make it worse," al-Hakim proclaimed.

Aswad cursed. He removed the dagger from his hand. He screamed loud but was then soothed by the urgency to save his friend. He removed the dagger from Anik's collar, the blood's egression increasing. Anik opened his mouth, blood dripping from the side of it. Aswad poured half of the vial's contents down into his friend. Anik choked, but managed to swallow the elixir. The medicine dragged him to sleep. Al-Hakim thought Anik dead, until magically, the guard's wound started to mend before his eyes.

Aswad drank the remaining medicine. His wound was too great for him to fight off the sensation of sleep. He fell unconscious. The medicine started regenerating the flesh in the center of Aswad's hand. The internal damage was composed new. Al-Hakim had Aswad and Anik transported back to the barracks.

Aswad did not dream when he slept, but there was peace. The dark fog dissipated into the images of Khushtar, Yunus, and al-Hakim standing over him as he woke from rest. Al-Hakim shook his head. "Truly amazing," said the captain.

"Anik?" Aswad asked. "How is he?"

"He's still at rest," Yunus informed.

"A woman is here to see you," said Khushtar.

Aswad quickly jumped from the bed, parting the three men standing over him. He rushed from the infirmary and into the barrack's lobby. Lamps were lit in the front room. Outside, the sun was setting. Aswad's eyes panned the room.

Nazirah was nowhere to be found.

There was, however, an elder Moorish woman. Her sight caused Aswad to jump. Though the woman's skin was lighter than Nazirah, Aswad believed that she might have been Nazirah, her ailment having taken an actual physical form. The woman walked up to Aswad, a smile on her face. It was this smile that indicated this was not Nazirah. The woman did not wear a veil, though she did have a shawl and head wrap. The woman was pretty, aged and distinguished by time. And she was proud of her features. In her hands was a small vial filled with a black substance. This again confused Aswad. He wondered again if it was Nazirah, and if the vial was filled with another concoction. The elder woman extended her hand, giving Aswad the vial.

"This is yours," she said warmly. Aswad took the vial. He was perplexed, and the expression showed clearly on his face. "My name is Dahia," the woman introduced herself. "My sister, Ahlam, a day before she disappeared, instructed me to give this to you."

"Your sister? She's disappeared too?" Aswad started to become worried.

"She was taken by the cultists," Dahia clarified. "She was missing for two weeks. They said her body was found today at an inn, the one that was destroyed."

Aswad nodded. "My apologies for your ordeal."

Dahia shook her head. "Accepted," Dahia bowed graciously.

"I have to say," began Aswad reluctantly, "I did not know your sister. I cannot accept this gift." He held his hand out, issuing the vial back to Dahia.

Dahia just smiled. It was a mother's smile. She closed Aswad's hand over the vial and told him, "She knew you. She had dreams that gave her insight." Dahia's eyes were like a mother looking at her child. "She said that you would need it. It is ink blessed by a prophet." Dahia put her arms around Aswad. "My sister said to tell you: *scribe vengeance with this ink, and breathe magic from your breath.*"

Dahia let Aswad go. Aswad continued to hold the woman's hand. He saw his mother in Dahia's eyes. Rather, a motherly trait he trusted and wanted to hold on to. But Dahia let him go, and disappeared through the front door. He looked at the vial in his hand. Aswad returned to the infirmary. Khushtar and Yunus were there to greet him, al-Hakim gone.

"What was that about?" Yunus asked. "Did you see the woman?"

"Yes, but I need my sword," Aswad demanded, brushing passed Yunus' inquiries. "And find me a long parchment."

Aswad sat at a desk in Khushtar's study. He scripted feverishly, his pen swiveled like sword strikes against the parchment. The rhythm and language of his poetry thundered with vengeance extracted. Nothing could defend against his sword, said his poem. There was no armor that would prevent piercing, nor layer of clothing that would cushion the blade's point. There would be no remedy for a fatal strike. Even immortals had to yield to the blade's power. Anyone who confronted Aswad, so said the poem he scribed, was resigning their life to his blade. No building or great distance would hide them. Aswad indicated the location of his prey would not elude him the moment the sword was in his hands.

Every word was scribbled in the blessed ink of a prophet. Farraj's fate was sealed. Aswad ended the poem with his signature attached to the parchment. He took his sword, which leaned against his chair, and wrapped the parchment around the blade. He stood up and took the sword from the study, out into the hall, and then outside into the night.

Aswad laid the sword on the street, and then set the parchment ablaze. The magical ink melted onto the sword. It created a purple smoke that swiveled into the night sky. The fire blazed the same color. Guards watched from the barrack windows. Aswad stood outside alone. The fire burned itself out in a flash, and the sword magically cooled. Aswad lifted the weapon and started off down the road. As he walked, he remembered the cold words of his father. *Never fall in love, because the woman will own you. And when she is taken away, whatever captured her life will own you as well.* Aswad felt it was time to reclaim this beautiful, black, Moorish woman. She was Africa to him, with all the secrets of the ancients wrapped up inside her physical form.

He knew where the cultist would be. His mind could see Farraj sneaking through the night, hiding in corners and shadows to escape detection. But there was no escaping Aswad's vision. He could see Farraj heading toward Nazirah's apartment. Aswad did not know the cultist's intentions, and he did not care. The woman who stole his heart was in danger.

Aswad followed his vision to Farraj. He too used the night to his advantage, cloaked in shadows as he moved about the city streets. He snuck up behind the cultist, though Farraj was alerted to his presence, hearing his footsteps. "I really hope you're not here to kill me," Farraj snickered.

"You won't escape this time, cultist," Aswad warned him. Farraj faced Aswad and unsheathed his sword. "You are careful to keep your sword on you," said Aswad.

Farraj twirled his blade with a fancy rhythm. He then aimed the tip at Aswad, taking a fighter's stance. "I'll kill the woman. Then I'll find her father and kill him." He looked Aswad up and down. "What I'll do to her mother, not even your words can describe." He grinned. "I will then take the remaining manuscript of formula that I know her father has—her version lost in the explosion at the inn, as was my plan, having memorized the greater formulas in the book. I will have unstoppable soldiers marching this earth. Even my backers will be forced to their knees. My superiors will bow to me."

"You still have me as an obstacle," Aswad said with determination.

"I don't even register your existence," Farraj sneered. "I'll kill you so quick."

"You will try!" Aswad screamed as he lunged forward.

Aswad flipped in the air, landing in front of Farraj. The cultist was waiting for him, sword at the ready. The two clashed again, their blades sparking like flint rocks. Farraj was again taken aback by Aswad's skill, ferocity, and focus. He stumbled back, every blow made on his sword like a giant wave crashing onto him. The cultist tried not to lose focus. He matched Aswad's speed, trying to gain the offensive. He twisted, parried, and thrust with a well-trained, classical style of swordplay that would leave the greatest fencer in awe. Aswad was raw energy. He stepped in the rhythm of the poem he composed. He struck as he recited the lines of poetry in his head, twisted as he accented a word. His sword crossed the air in the pattern of a spider's web. It was blinding. Aswad's long, locked hair, though bound by a strap, flailed like a whip.

Just as inspiring was Farraj's ability to counter Aswad's assault, but the cultist was clearly on the defensive. However, his confidence and focus started to rise as he marveled at his own ability to keep in step with Aswad. His confidence was short lived. Aswad, strong, and with immovable conviction, slapped Farraj's sword away, turned and swiped his blade across Farraj's stomach. The cultist stumbled back. The cut was deep. The pain stung much like Farraj's pride. He was cut twice. His legs went numb. His own weight pulled him backwards. Farraj used his sword like a cane, balancing his wobbling weight.

Nevertheless, Farraj kept a smile. He looked down at his wound and waited for it to heal. Even Aswad's attention was fixed on his opponent's injury. Blood continued to waterfall from the deep gash across the cultist stomach. The opened flesh showed no signs of mending back together. Farraj's smile faded, set like the sun, and bent into a frown. Frustration jumped onto his face. He grit his teeth and cursed.

The smile that left Farraj found a new home on Aswad's face. Aswad winked at him. "You have your magic, I have mine."

"I'll...kill you..."

Aswad cocked his head. "Care to wager your life on that remark," he asked.

Farraj regained his stance. He held his wound, trying to dam the blood with his hand. He charged Aswad, who stepped aside and ran his sword along Farraj's back. The cultist turned, tried for another swing of his sword, but it was knocked aside when Aswad parried the strike. The young Moor twirled around, and then shoved his sword through Farraj. In a swift motion, Aswad removed his sword.

Farraj slumped to the street, dying. The look of disbelief was the last expression he held on his face before he died. Aswad sheathed his sword. He continued to watch Farraj's body until he was convinced the cultist was truly dead. He looked up the street in the direction of the city square. He remembered the words of Dahia's sister, Ahlam. She instructed him to breathe magic from his breath. Nazirah's words also re-visited him. She told him there was magic in his poetry. Nazirah said that she could be reborn from his words.

Aswad started walking toward Nazirah's apartment. He alerted two city guards about the last cultist. The guards ran to attend to Farraj's body. Aswad stopped and watched the men journey down the street. He saw them stop at Farraj's body and pick it up. Aswad sighed. He was still nervous that the cultist would heal. But, Farraj was dead.

Aswad resumed his pace to Nazirah's apartment. He wondered what he would say. The poet felt unarmed. He was more nervous facing Nazirah and her troubles than facing Farraj and his blade. He whispered possible phrases and stanzas that he would speak up into her window. None of them seemed right. There were no words that expressed his feelings.

Aswad arrived at Nazirah's window to find it closed. He entered her building and walked up the stairs to the second floor and came to her door. He dismissed the guards, assuring them the threat against the woman was handled. He stepped inside Nazirah's apartment. It was dark, but comforting. The shadows were like a blanket, unlit motherly arms. Aswad could hear Nazirah's low sobs. She was still suffering. It was then that words started to flow from Aswad. He felt that if he could slay immortality, he could dissipate illusions. He removed the scabbard from around his shoulder and laid it gently on the ground.

Aswad opened Nazirah's bedroom door. He spoke in wild rhythms about Nazirah being dragged three steps below the path of her heart. Aswad rhymed that Nazirah was cooled of her fiery desire and intent to love him. He spoke sensual sentiments about the fruit he would eat from her body, giving him sustenance that was taken away in all its abundance. Aswad talked of his hunger pangs, describing his hunger as gluttonous. He told Nazirah that she was under a mystical ruse to believe her fruit was bruised. Aswad whispered to the woman, kneeling before her bed, that she was the core caretaker, ultimate Earth cultivator whose garden he would keep from danger, her g(u)ardener. Aswad then likened Nazirah to Persephone, held in the Underworld against her will. He spoke of the journey he made to find her and bring her three steps above the path of her heart, to be married with Aswad, crowned as his wife.

Aswad loosened the veil around Nazirah's face. She was relaxed. A smile was underneath the cloth. His words permeated Nazirah's ears and resonated in a harmony that dropped the illusionary veil her eyes suffered to see. Nazirah did not jump to check the mirror. She saw her reflection in Aswad's eyes, even through the darkness of the room. Aswad's smile kissed her before his lips met hers. He dived into Nazirah, and she welcomed Aswad like the earth welcomes rain to nurture and cleanse it. This Moorish adventurer moistened the Moorish woman, their clothes loose and tossed to the floor. They became waves flowing over each other as they made love through the night.

The large boat moved away from the dock. Nazirah and Aswad walked away from the ship's side, they waved goodbye to their friends gathered to see them off. Their adventures together were just beginning. Their first stop would be Nazirah's parents' home. The woman had to consult with her father about the book, and hopefully stop any more members of The Brotherhood of White Light from obtaining their research. Nazirah also wanted to introduce Aswad to her family. Nazirah kissed Aswad at the thought of one day being his wife.

Aswad looked at her and smiled as if he was sighing. He had been through a lot for this woman. She was the greatest adventure he had ever…been on. He rubbed her cheek with his finger and said with his teeth grit, "If I ever tell you that you're beautiful, will you please take my word for it?" Nazirah laughed at his sarcastically frustrated comment. "Really, all I ask is for an appreciative smile, not resistance from my compliments."

Nazirah struck Aswad's shoulder playfully. "I was *drugged*," she argued.

"Yes, by your feminine hormones," Aswad joked as he rolled his eyes.

"Excuse me," Nazirah put her hands to her hips. Her tone was playful, yet threatening.

Aswad winked at her. "I almost drew my sword at you, I was so frustrated."

Nazirah now rolled her eyes. "You would've done nothing."

"I know. You're too beautiful."

Nazirah raised her eyebrows. "And I'm an expert at throwing knives," she laughed. "My brother taught me. *And*, I always keep some stashed around my apartment."

"A whole hell-of-a-lot-of-good they did," said Aswad watching Nazirah walk past him. "You're lucky you had *me* stashed at your apartment. A *real* swordsman."

"Yes, I am." Nazirah said stopping and waiting for Aswad. She took his arm and continued walking. The two of them journeyed to the other side of the ship and watched the stretch of sea before them. Over the horizon was a long life filled with excitement, adventures, and love.

Together.

I WISH, SERVITUDE

The holes in the ship did not look like cannon strikes according to the short, Moorish dwarf named Arihman. He had seen his share of battle in his day, by land and sea. The metal brace used to stabilize his leg from an injury received over twenty-five years ago, and the scars that scratched the right side of his face, attested to those days of battle. So, with his knowledge of war, cannon fire, and its progression since he had last seen battle, he calculated that the blast points, tears, and holes in the ship were like nothing he had ever seen. The damage was like none any weapon he knew of could ever make. There was something bigger that struck this large vessel that was now docked in his shipyard. The ship was barely a skeleton of its former self.

The damaged ship was either built to look like a War Galleon, or an actual War Galleon stolen and modified for the very pirates who had sailed into his shipyard for repairs. It was most likely stolen, considering its pirate crew and leader. And because they were pirates, Arihman decided not to question the origin of the damage. However, his facial expression could not hide his curiosity. His eyes were opened wide, in awe at the damage displayed in front of him. He knew he could fix the vessel, to be sure. And he felt the urge to assure its pirate captain. Arihman did so want to know what had actually damaged the ship, but he felt it safer to stay out of piratical affairs.

The leader of the Turkish pirates looked down at the Moorish dwarf. The leader's name was Pelin. He considered himself an adventurer, not a pirate. But his ruthless way of extracting loot and artifacts branded him the latter. He did so resent the title, especially since he considered himself a gentleman. But that was an adjective far from the truth. Pelin was a brutal man. His name was uttered in whispers that trickled off quivering lips. Arihman knew Pelin by name and reputation. However, the brutality of war and battle, and all the vicious imagery he had seen in his life, made him too numb to be frightened. Arihman was cautious because of his own crew, especially his niece Sesen. So, Arihman spoke carefully to these particular customers.

"You can repair it, can't you," Pelin asked. The pirate smiled at Arihman's expression. He looked back at his ship. "We barely made it out," Pelin said. "But trust me, we survived. The one who damaged us did not."

Arihman's eyes slowly turned to Pelin. He straightened his face and then said in a voice that sounded like a grunt, "I'm a man of war. I was in several battles, by land and sea. I served in the Moorish army that held Granada, and even faced Santiago himself the day it fell. But I've never seen damage like this, neither to palace nor to ship."

"But you can repair it," Pelin repeated.

Arihman limped forward to inspect the damage. "This ain't gonna be repairing. This is gonna be rebuilding." Arhiman let out a haughty laugh. He looked into a hole, bending down and peering straight through the hull. "You're lucky you made it here." Arihman stood up and looked back at Pelin. "This ship is between life and death."

"Make it breathe again," said Pelin with a sinister undertone. His voice suggested that he would stop Arihman's breath if the deed were not accomplished. Arihman was not threatened, and Pelin could see that. The pirate added, to sweeten the deal, "I have gold to pay you. It's a considerable amount."

Arihman chuckled, "I know it will be." He saw the look in Pelin's eyes become murderous. Arihman did not budge. "You're also gonna have to spend time as well as money."

"How long," Pelin asked.

Arihman looked back at the ship. He inspected the damage again and then estimated aloud, "Three weeks."

"That's more than reasonable," Pelin said, his temper subsiding. "Especially for damage such as this."

Arihman faced the pirate again. He limped toward Pelin with his arms crossed. He took a deep breath and then addressed, "I know who you are, Captain Pelin. I know your crew, the *Water Dogs*. I know your career."

Pelin could not hide his smile. "You have nothing to fear," he assured. "The talks surrounding me are just rumors from enemies."

"I'm not afraid of you," Arihman boasted, returning the smile. "Remember, I'm a man of war. I just don't want any trouble tracking you to end up at my shipyard, whether they have a legal marque for your head, or are just out for revenge."

Pelin bowed his head, doing his best to imitate the behaviors of a gentleman. "You have nothing to worry about. The adversary that engaged us was defeated, though he left his mark." Both men watched the pirate crew unload provisions. "Most of my crew will hold up in this port city. The others, along with myself, are going to Tunis."

"It's not too far east," Arihman informed him.

"Thank you," the pirate countered. There was a hint of sarcasm in his voice. "But I'm well aware of my location. Again, though, I thank you for all your services."

Pelin then walked over to his crew and handed out instructions. He commanded most of his crew to take money and rent a caravan to haul the goods into the city. He wanted them to set up at an inn. Pelin then commanded five of his lieutenants, to journey with him to Tunis. Arihman noticed Pelin take from one of his lieutenants a vial filled with a purple liquid. It was a long, slender vial with its liquid contents filled to its corked brim. Pelin cupped the container quickly and stuffed it into his pocket.

Arihman thought nothing of the transaction. He pivoted and then limped his way toward a group of seven boys. He commanded for them to begin to steer the ship into the yard for repairs. The youngest of the boys was nineteen, of a normal build, and a blackamoor like the others surrounding him. His name was Naku Ani, and today was his birthday. Arihman caught the young man by the arm before he passed. Naku looked at his employer with a blank stare. "Not you, Naku," Arihman said.

Naku froze. His heart raced. He hoped that he had done nothing to anger his boss, getting fired before his apprenticeship was up. He had two years left as a ship-builder. Naku's eyes widened, frightened by the possibility of being dismissed from his job. Arihman took him aside and instructed two more young men to take his place. "All *is* well with me, sir?" Naku asked, his words breaking with uncertainty.

Arihman chuckled. "More than well. You have three days off."

"Sir," Naku questioned.

"It's your birthday present," the dwarf smiled. Naku was still stunned, unsure. Arihman could see the anxiety in the young man's face, so he assured him, "You're my hardest, and damn-near my best worker. You've earned it. Go home."

"Home, sir," Naku continued to inquire.

"Yes," Arihman pressed. "These men are heading to Tunis. You can ride with them."

Naku's eyes inspected Captain Pelin and his crew. Naku and the other young men had been speaking about the Turkish pirates. They speculated the pirates were the infamous *Water Dogs*. Naku had to wonder why Arihman wanted him to ride with a dangerous crew all the way to Tunis. "They're pirates, sir," Naku said in a very low voice.

"They won't do anything to you," Arihman responded matter-of-factly.

"And you're sure of this because...?" The usually introverted Naku made a subtle hint of a playful smile.

Arihman inspected the pirates as Pelin sorted his crew. "They're trying to keep a low profile, that's for starters. They're looking to stay way out of trouble, at least for the time it takes to repair their ship. You'll be fine. It's a free ride, and a little less than an hour's travel. Your family will want to see you for a change."

Naku conceded, and surprisingly with a smile. He bowed at the neck. "Thank you, sir."

Arihman signaled for the young man to follow him as he walked up behind Pelin and called the pirate's name. Pelin turned around with a smile. Arihman immediately spoke, "I would like you to take this young man to Tunis. It's his birthday, and I'm giving him three days off to visit his parents and friends."

Pelin kept his smile and gave a gracious bow of the head. "The young man is welcomed." The Turkish pirate looked at Naku and asked for his name. Naku replied with the information, and Pelin had a quick follow up question. "Do you know of any tattoo artists in Tunis?"

"Yes," Naku answered, forgetting the company he was keeping. "A good friend of mine named Wu Jing. His parents hail from China, originally. But he's lived in Tunis since birth."

"Good," congratulated Pelin. "Good. I'd like to meet him." Pelin's tone was contemplative. "I'll need him to hold something for me. A liquid. Ink. Nothing special." Pelin quickly added, "And I'll need him to use it to give me a tattoo. The job pays very well."

"He'll do it," Naku said with a smile.

Arihman broke up the conversation by inserting the command, "Get your stuff and pack up, Naku."

Naku turned to his employer and acknowledged the command. "Yes, sir," he stated darting away to his quarters.

Arihman stepped to Pelin, hands on his hips. He looked downward and then slowly arched his head up to look at the pirate. "Don't get this boy in any trouble, Captain"

"I wouldn't imagine it," the pirate said with a smile on his face, though a slight sneer in his voice. "You have my word. There's no harm in receiving a tattoo. I'm in the most danger," he joked, "putting myself in the path of a drilling needle."

At the moment, Naku rushed to bag his clothes. Slowly, almost with each piece of clothing bagged, he began to think of the consequences of employing his friend's services to a pirate. He rationalized that it was just for artistry. There was no harm in helping Wu take on a client, not even one as dangerous as Captain Pelin. Besides, Wu dealt with ruffians of all kinds. He was no stranger to pirates, robbers, assassins, cutpurses, or brigands. They were his usual customers, receiving brands with the emblem of their crew or gang. They were flag bearers for their kind. Naku also eased his thought by convincing himself that his friend would thank him for bringing a well paying job.

"Happy Birthday, mister," a melodic, feminine voice sweetened the air.

Naku's head looked over his shoulder and caught Arihman's niece, Sesen, standing in the doorway. She was not the average Moorish woman, working with her hands in a shipyard filled with raucous men and their conversations, but she did not mind, loving the opportunity to work on ships. She wore white pants, cut long, and snug at the ankle. A tanned ruffled shirt covered her. Sesen still wore her working gloves, and her cheeks were adorably caked with soot. One eye on her spectacles was also blackened with the substance. Naku laughed while approaching her. He reached out and removed her eyewear.

"I can't see, Naku," Sesen argued.

Naku swiped a towel from the young girl's belt and wiped off the eye. He then gently placed the glasses back onto Sesen's face. "There," he said.

Sesen adjusted her spectacles. "I was doing fine."

Naku kissed her forehead, the only spot on her face without soot. "Thank you for saying 'Happy Birthday'."

Sesen blushed and then asked, "And where are you going?"

"Your uncle is kind enough to give me three days off," said Naku going back to packing. "He insists I go home to Tunis."

"Home," Sesen exclaimed. "What about us?"

"Us," Naku questioned as he continued to pack.

Sesen's heart skipped. "I wanted to take you out for your birthday tonight," she said sounding defeated.

Naku stood up straight, pivoted quickly, and rushed back to the young woman. "I'm sorry," he said folding his arms around her. "I actually would stay but your uncle wants me to travel with these new clients."

Naku's words were barely audible to Sesen. She was lost in the young man's embrace and the mental imagery of spending a romantic dinner with Naku. But then his words slowly registered, taking Sesen away from her imagination. She looked up and inquired, "Those pirates? The *Water Dogs*? Is my uncle insane? He wants you to go with the *Water Dogs*? They're cutthroats!"

Naku placed Sesen's head back against his chest, mostly to cease her rant. "I'll be fine, little sister."

The title bestowed upon Sesen by Naku was jarring. She did not want to be thought of as a *little sister*, especially since she was two years older than Naku, and more so, since she developed feelings for him. Sesen was willing to reveal those feelings at their dinner tonight. She had everything planned. She also wanted to show off a beautiful gown she saved money to buy. Naku had always seen her caked with soot and dressed like a man. Sesen believed it was time for Naku to see her as the woman she was underneath.

Naku let her go and went back to packing.

"Maybe your uncle will let you come," he suggested. "Your grandparents live in Tunis, don't they?"

Sesen let out a low, inaudible sigh. Her voice, however, echoed its defeated sentiment. "They moved to Morocco with my parents. I do still have an aunt there, though, but…"

"But what," Naku said lifting his shoulders. "Come on. I'll introduce you to my friend Wu. We'll hang out and celebrate my birthday."

Sesen leaned against the wall and quickly shuffled an excuse together. "I have to finish this ship. And I'm drawing up plans for something I want to build for me. You know how I'd like to be at sea for a living?" Sesen also knew the real excuse. Being with Naku and his friend would not be the same compared to what she had planned. Sesen decided to admit that aloud. "Besides, I wanted you to see me in my new dress. I look like a Company Boss' wife."

Naku snickered. "That would be a sight," he said sarcastically. "It would be hard to focus. Seeing you in a dress would be weird. You're like one of the boys."

Sesen's heart sank, but she retained confidence and countered, "Exactly. I wanted to be a woman for a change. It's what I naturally am."

Naku stopped packing and faced Sesen again. "You're a cute girl, little sister. In my opinion, very beautiful, even with soot caked on your face." Sesen laughed. "You have nothing to worry about when it comes to the idiots around here looking at you as a woman. The comments I hear about you." Naku smiled, trying to hide the guilt from his next comment. "Even the comments I make and the thoughts I have would make you blush…or slap me."

Those particular thoughts began to run through Naku's head as he watched Sesen lean against the wall. The masculine clothes she adorned herself with could not hide her feminine curves. It always amazed Naku how Sesen's femininity was able to be exposed at just the right moments. Sometimes she was completely unaware. It was exactly as she expressed. It was what she was naturally. She was a woman, and there was no doubt of that. It was the way she spoke, stood, and walked, even when hard at work on a ship, or mingling with the boys. The sight of Sesen's femininity broke the monotony of all the young men employed by Arihman. Naku liked Sesen. She was his best friend while living in this port city. She was the only one he could talk to without trying to prove something to her.

However, Naku's heart lay somewhere else, in the past, still dreaming of a woman who lived in a small sub-urban area of Tunis. Her name was Ona Ramu. She was the only reason he wished to return home. Maybe this time Naku would have the nerve to pursue her. Despite all his feelings for Ona, Naku promised Sesen, "We'll have that dinner when I return."

Sesen managed a halfhearted smile, though she was extremely excited inside. "You won't be disappointed, Naku," she said flirtatiously. Naku only thought it a jest. He returned to bagging his clothes and provisions. Sesen's smile faded. "I'm going to return to work."

"You'll see me off, little sister?" Naku asked.

The phrase struck her like an arrow, and not one sent by cupid. She said with a sigh, "Of course I will, Naku. Just stop calling me your little sister. I'm older than you." All she wished was for Naku to say her name. She scoffed and then disappeared from his quarters.

Naku finished packing shortly after. He strapped his bag around his shoulder, sauntered from the room, and back to the docks. Pelin and Arihman were still in conversation, light laughter shared between the Turkish pirate and the ex-soldier. Pelin and Arihman noticed Naku approaching. "There he is," the Moorish dwarf said, and then noticed a smile on the young man's face. He commented, "You've been speaking to Sesen."

Naku nodded his head and said, "Yes. She came to my room to wish me well on my travels."

Pelin teased, "A woman wishing you off, and coming to your room, no doubt."

Naku's emotions froze. He stiffened and became defensive. "She's just a friend," he said. "Besides, there's another woman."

The pirate smiled slyly. "Well, you know what we say at sea? Always have a backup treasure to go for in case the other just slips away."

"Not from me," Naku said with a confidence that surprised Arihman. His tone even struck Pelin who did not even know Naku, though the pirate understood the young man to be meek and mild.

Pelin smiled proudly, like a father seeing his boy maturing into a man. He reached out and scooped Naku into his arm. He shook the young man wildly. "And here I thought you were some mild mannered cub," he hollered. Pelin then tossed Naku aside and commanded to one of his crew, "Ready the caravan and take the kid's sack."

A man stripped Naku of his bag and hurried away. Sesen approached from Arihman's side. Pelin took quick notice of her and calculated she was the woman in question. She was beautiful to Pelin, though he felt she needed to remove herself from such masculine attire. He imagined her cleaned up and adorned with feminine clothes. The pirate smiled with desire.

"Is this your lovely catch?" Pelin teased Naku. The young man looked up and noticed Sesen's arrival. Pelin stepped away from Naku, approaching Sesen. He continued to imitate the mannerisms of a gentleman by kissing Sesen on the hand.

Sesen blushed, playful and exaggerated. She then stepped back and sided up to her uncle. "There's only one man for me," she said grabbing Arihman's arm. She leaned her head onto her uncle's shoulder and said playfully, "My uncle."

Pelin laughed at his own naivety. He aimed a surprised, yet sly smile toward Arihman. "Oh, she's your niece?"

"My brother's daughter," Arihman said patting his niece on the head, which was far extended above his own.

"Will her lovely hands be a part of the crew repairing my ship?" Pelin asked while looking back and forth between Arihman and Sesen.

"It'll take everyone here to fix your ship, Captain," Arihman explained. "We'll even slow down on our other ships because of the money you're promising."

Pelin caught Naku in another tight hold around the boy's shoulders. "Thanks for that sentiment. However, not everyone will be working on the ship. We're taking the birthday boy away from you."

It was then that Sesen let go of her uncle and snatched Naku away from Pelin. "Be safe in your travels," she said to him with a stern, commanding voice.

Pelin towered over both of them. He commented with a smile, "My dear, he's with the best crew and soldiers land and sea has to offer."

Sesen pointed toward the dock that contained Pelin's ship. "That is *your* ship we're repairing isn't it?"

Pelin laughed hard and loud. "Quick, quick, quick witted…for a woman." He kept his smile but gritted his teeth behind pressed lips. The pirate's nerves, connected to his pride, had been struck hard by Sesen's words. But he continued to play the gentleman. He took Naku away from Sesen and said, "We're off. Goodbyes are over."

Naku was whisked away too quickly to speak another word. All he could do was gesture with a wave of his hand. Arihman waved Naku off while holding Sesen who also waved goodbye to Naku. The pirate and the apprentice walked through the large company house, exited, and came to a dusty road where a caravan waited. The two of them stepped into a palanquin that was then hoisted onto a small, resting elephant.

"You're traveling in style," said the pirate to Naku.

Naku chuckled lightly. He looked at his clothes and added, "Maybe I should've washed and changed."

"No time," the pirate said matter-of-factly. "I'm used to being on the up and go. Besides, it's just an hour ride."

It was an hour ride that continued with minimal conversation. The most that was exchanged pertained to Naku leading Pelin to Wu Jing. Pelin continued to chip at Naku for more of a conversation, but got nothing. All this annoyed Naku. When his demeanor was more than obvious, Pelin then asked the young man why he had such a disposition. The pirate was surprised when Naku answered honestly. "When I open myself up to someone I end up at war with them."

"You don't need to be so defensive with me," Pelin assured.

Naku nodded. "I'm also thinking about someone back home."

"Who is she," interrogated the pirate, trying not to sound teasing.

Naku became tense. Slowly he relaxed long enough to let out a light chuckle, which sounded more like a sigh. "Why does it have to be a 'she'?"

"Well, you have a cute girl throwing herself at you back at the dock," Pelin stated. "And unless you're a sissy, your heart must belong to another." The pirate then lifted an eyebrow and re-worded his question, "Or maybe I should ask, if it is a man, who is *he* who stole said *she*? Besides, back at the docks you said there was another."

There was another surprising smile from Naku. He was becoming more relaxed. "Her name is Ona." He said the woman's name with both excitement and fear in his voice. It was like a whisper, a secret. "No one has stolen her, at the moment. I knew her since school. She's beautiful."

Pelin conjured up his own image of the woman. He simply imagined someone beautiful, someone a kid like Naku would be smitten for. The woman he saw in his mind was nothing like the women he ran through as a pirate, or rather, gentleman. But he smiled at the thought of love, just to continue his gentleman's grace. He slapped his hand on Naku's knee and said, "You have three days to win her over." He leaned close and said devilishly, "Try and get *somethin'* out of the lady in that time."

"It's not like that," Naku said as his defensive nature began to climb.

"It's gonna have to be, kid," Pelin sneered. "Happily every after is not true. Just get what makes you happy. And if you can't get the whole thing, reduce the prize to what will give you instant gratification."

Naku became silent again. Pelin did not mind. The last fifteen minutes of the trip were quiet, however, not awkward. Naku informed Captain Pelin where his friend Wu Jing's parlor was located. Once inside Tunis, Pelin and Naku exited the elephant and were given camels. Naku led Pelin's crew to his friend's place of business. He dismounted and walked to the front door. He looked over his shoulder and realized how intimidating the army looked. He hoped Wu Jing would not worry. Naku knocked on the door, and it was not long before his friend answered.

Wu Jing was the same height as Naku, muscular, and dressed in the traditional robes of Tunis rather than his Chinese culture. He never saw the army behind Naku, his concentration on his friend. Wu jumped at him, shaking Naku's hand and throwing the other around his back.

"Naku! Naku!" he expressed joyously. "My friend is home! My goodness! This is a surprise. How're you doing? I didn't think I was going to see you, birthday boy."

Naku patted his friend on the shoulder and said while beaming, "I got three days off."

"We're getting you in trouble tonight, birthday boy," Wu declared shaking a finger at Naku. "Have you been home?"

"Not yet," Naku stated. "This was my first stop." Naku could see the perplexed look in Wu's eyes. Then Naku's friend looked over his shoulder and saw the mass of twenty-five men mounted on camels. Pelin stepped down from his mount and Naku moved from Wu's line of vision to expose the pirate's approach. "I brought you a client," informed Naku.

Wu recognized Captain Pelin, and he was familiar with the rumors surrounding the pirate's exploits. This was not the first time the pirate made an appearance in Tunis. Wu stepped forward and met Pelin's approach. Wu reached out a hand and shook Pelin's. "Captain Pelin, a pleasure. I worked on a crewmember's insignia once before. His name was Rafan ibn Kazemi. I believe he was a high ranking lieutenant in your crew."

Pelin nodded his head, half a grin on his face. "He no longer sails with me," Pelin said to Wu. "He's retired." His voice hinted there was more to the story, perhaps Rafan ibn Kazemi's untimely demise by Pelin's hands or orders. Pelin then chuckled and grabbed Wu around the shoulder, shaking him. "Your friend Naku says you're the best. And if we've been here before, I'm sure its true, if I can remember Rafan's insignia. It's a shame Algier's government keeps him locked up."

The mystery was solved. Rafan was imprisoned. Pelin's half grin could now be interpreted as frustration at losing a valuable crewmember.

"My friend's word is as good as your aim, Captain," Wu commented. "You'd be paying me back for taking down some of my clientele. Captain Rubio, Captain Douglas."

"Rumors," Pelin said, his half grin resurfacing. "However, the seafaring world suffered no loss when they disappeared. But, if any real money was lost, I'm willing to make it up for two simple tasks—a gentleman as I am." He reached into his pocket and pulled out the vial of purple liquid. "Keep this hidden on you. I will return in several days. I want you to tattoo something on my back. It will be an ancient emblem. You will use this ink on me." He added in a subtly, threatening tone, "And no one else."

Wu accepted the vial and nodded his head. "What's the purse?"

"Five-hundred gold pieces," Pelin answered in a serious tone.

Wu slipped the vial into his pocket. "That's more than enough to makeup for my loss. This'll be my pleasure." He bowed honorably. "But I'll need to see the sketch first, so I may begin practicing on—"

"I'm manning a small crew to a Mediterranean Island," Pelin interrupted. "A fellow sea traveler holds a piece of parchment sketched with this ancient symbol. I'll return in a week's time, or so, to give it to you." Pelin looked over Wu's shoulder and spotted Naku. The young man kept his place away from the business at hand. "Will you be all right, Naku? My crew and I must be leaving. Business. You may keep the camel."

"Thank you…and I'll be fine," Naku assured. "My house is not too far from here."

Pelin nodded. "I'll get your sack, then be off." The pirate pivoted and then called for his man who had taken Naku's belongings. The man jumped from his mount, found the mules carrying the provisions, unhinged Naku's bag, and then walked it over to the young man. The crony rushed away quickly, leaving Naku to wonder if he heard his gratitude expressed. Pelin waved a hand at the two young men and then jumped back to his mount. Naku took the reins of the camel Pelin gave to him, and then walked it to Wu's building, hitching it to a post stationed next to another. Pelin saluted both young men, and then he traveled away with his crew.

Wu turned back to Naku. "What-the-hell," he exclaimed in Chinese.

Naku did not know Chinese, but he'd heard the expression before. Guilt crept onto Naku's face. "I hope you're not angry at me for involving you with—"

"Relax, Naku," Wu interjected. "You know half my clients are brigands and sea dogs. This is no different." Wu then added with great incentive, "And he's paying me five-hundred gold pieces. Crime-In-Rome! I wish you'd send more of those sea bastards my way." He slapped his friend on the shoulder. "After you touch base with your family, we're getting drunk. I'll close the shop early."

"Nothing too rough," Naku pleaded. "I don't want my second day to be spent recovering. I'm also here on a mission."

"Mission?" Wu questioned.

"I'll explain over drinks," Naku said to his friend.

Wu did not press any further. He changed the subject by saying, "Watch out for Ferran."

Naku became tense at the mention of his childhood nemesis. All the atrocities of the pirate whose company had just left him could not compare to Ferran. He was the son of an exotic dancer and a smuggler. Ferran's father taught his son everything there was to snatching and grabbing anything declared his. The most important lesson was the take could be done at any moment. Ferran's father was finally caught in Italian waters and sentenced to a long term in prison. That was four years ago. Naku's fingers balled into a fist. "He's still around?"

"It's worse than that," Wu continued.

"Worse?" The perplexity of Naku's tone insisted that Wu answer immediately. But there was hesitation, silence. Naku stepped closer to his friend. Wu dropped his head. Naku asked, "What are you not telling me?"

Wu's eyes met his friend's. Both of their gazes were stern. "He governs our area of the city." Naku was somewhat relieved to hear that was all there had been to the news. Wu continued, "Imagine that, an idiot being a politician."

Naku exhaled and then confessed to Wu, "I thought you were going to say he was married to Ona."

Wu laughed hard and slapped his friend on the shoulder. "Is that your mission? You gonna try and snatch her up?"

"It was a thought," Naku said.

Wu simmered his laughter and straightened his stance, folding his arms. "Well, she's available. She took over her father's business when he fell ill. He's doing better, though. She does cross paths with Ferran when he hires her business to cater events. She is a fine cook and caterer."

"Then I'll swing by her café tomorrow," Naku beamed.

Wu hit Naku playfully. "You better swing by your parents' place," he demanded. "They'll be surprised."

"Yes," Naku said in good spirits. But he was not thinking about his parents. Ona was available, unmarried. There was a chance to claim his prize. "I'll be back tonight. Be ready."

Naku waved to his friend, slung his bag over his shoulder, and departed down the street. His camel stayed behind, he would use the mount as a ride when he returned and Wu and he journeyed into the city. His family's quaint house lay just several blocks from Wu's parlor. Naku's trek to his childhood home was quick. His soaring spirits gave him a burst of renewed energy and confidence that quickened his steps. Naku spotted his younger brother playing in front of the house. A stick was in the eleven-year old child's hand, and he swung it around like a sword.

"Eno!" Naku called.

The child looked up and spotted his older brother. His face became overwhelmed with excitement. He rushed toward Naku who dodged out of the child's way so as to avoid being punctured by the stick. "Watch yourself, Eno."

"What're you doing here," Eno exclaimed.

"I got three days off," Naku explained. "Are mom and dad home?"

"Yes," Eno answered. He swung his stick around, leading his brother toward the front door. In his imagination he batted away enemies blocking their path. "I'm learning how to fight."

"Really," Naku said with a raised eyebrow. "Learn how to *not* fight. It'll keep you out of more trouble."

Naku opened the front door, stepping into the hallway of the quarters where he grew up. He and his brother journeyed forward until the hall opened up to a sitting area. Resting inside the room was Naku's mother and father. His father looked up and smiled through spectacles. There was a book on mathematics in his hands. Naku's mother jumped from her chair and reached out toward her son. Her embrace almost toppled Naku over. Naku's bag dropped from his grip.

"Naku! You're home!" His mother shouted. "My boy! Happy Birthday!"

"So, Arihman gave me my request," said Naku's father. He marked the page of the book he was reading, closed it and stood. He reached out and shook his son's hand while his wife continued to embrace him. "I sent a letter two days ago."

"Request, huh?" Naku said adding up all the events that transpired behind his back. "And here I thought Sir Dan-Jerus was being nice."

"Be kind," said Naku's mother, Deka. "If it wasn't for Arihman—"

"I know, I know," Naku interrupted. "We wouldn't be alive." He recapped the story to show his parents how much he had memorized the events they drilled into him since childhood. "He helped you escape Granada when it fell and moved you here among his family. You were already pregnant with Zahina."

Naku's father, Yao, lightly slapped the back of his son's head. "Don't be too smart. And how are you fairing over on his shipyard?"

"I'm one of his best workers," Naku stated tensing up with the question.

"And how is your interaction," Yao asked firmly.

Naku became quiet.

"I guess that's my answer," said his father.

Naku rolled his eyes. "The attitudes of some of those guys are damn near savage," he stated. "They're as beastly as the pirates we repair for, which, by the way, I had to ride with all the way here. I was with Captain Pelin."

"That sea dog?" Deka shouted.

"He's actually a gentleman," Naku reported. "Wu is going to make a tattoo for him."

Deka turned to Yao with frightened eyes. "He's hanging with pirates," she hissed.

Yao chuckled and told his wife, "He'll be fine, Deka."

The woman rolled her eyes and headed for the hall. "Well, I'll prepare a birthday meal."

Eno followed his mother but continued down the hall and out the door to battle more imaginary enemies. Deka made an immediate right into the kitchen. Naku looked back at his father and asked, "So where's my big sister?"

"Timbuktu, studying," his father answered.

"Oh, yes. Always studious," Naku commented. He did not like the silence that proceeded. He could see that his father wanted to bring back another subject. He moved very uneasily before his father even spoke.

"You have to open up more. Stop bottling up your feelings," Yao chided his son.

Naku shook his head. "Those guys remind me of the people I grew up with here. Bunch of jerks. My crew is Wu and El-Ras, and El-Ras is in Morocco. So it's just me and Wu."

"You don't give them the impression you think you're better, do you?" Yao asked worried.

Naku snickered. "I come from a humble background, father. Most of those kids are spoiled rich. Even Arihman will admit that. I keep my mouth shut and just do my work. I get along with some, but they try and play thug just because we repair the vessels of thugs. These guys are from Company Boss money. Besides," he began as he took a seat. "I flirt with Arihman's niece. She's the only person I need to talk to." There was a huge smile on Naku's face. He scooped up the book lying on the chair his father earlier occupied. He looked at the cover and then said to his father, "Kind of arrogant reading your own book."

Yao walked to his son and grabbed the book from him. He smacked Naku on the head with it. "Don't be too smart."

Naku brought the conversation back to its subject, and also a way for him to segue into another. "Speaking of people acting like an ass, how do bastards like Ferran become politicians?"

Yao shook his head and laughed. "Well Arihman is certainly teaching you how to curse."

Naku did not want to lose the subject matter. "Really, though," he pleaded with his father.

"Your friend—" Yao started.

"He's not a friend," Naku insisted.

"Either way, it's not a real political position," Yao clarified. "It's something he can do for both legal *and* illegal coin. It's a way for him to spend time with any woman looking for a powerful man to spend a night with. There's actually a more noble cause behind his political climb."

"And that is?" Naku asked incredulously.

"He's trying to get his father free from prison," Yao answered.

Naku did not find the cause so noble. Ferran's father was a criminal; he was said to be as vicious as Captain Pelin, and his acts weakened the Moorish community. Many people were relieved when he was caught. Imprisoning Captain Masun, Ferran's father, cut off a supply of illegal materials that poisoned its share of cities, and ended the career of a man responsible for some of the most vicious murders of innocent and pirate alike, and also saved future lives.

"A man like that can stay in prison," Naku commented with a stern voice.

"I agree," said Naku's father. "But, Ferran will give it a good try and use legal means to get his father free. He's already begun his campaign by ranting that his father is an innocent man and that he has proof of this. He feels his father was betrayed and framed by the Euro-political class."

Naku shook his head. "I feel his father was a bastard. And once his father is free then he'll use his son as cover to take to the seas." Naku contemplated. "Maybe I can get Pelin to take him out."

"Don't get involved," his father said with great authority. "Complete your apprenticeship and move on with your life. Don't even be bothered."

"He's as savage as those Christians who continue to burn Moors in Spain," Naku barked. The force of his voice released an anger that lay buried inside him for years. "How could a Moor be like that?"

"I guess he's part of the same bloodline, or rather, the same counterfeit spirits that taught the Europeans how to manufacture guns," Yao joked.

The topic ended with those words, then the conversation turned light. Yao explained his further research into mathematics and a new course he was teaching at one of the local schools. Yao also informed Naku that his mother had been hired to decorate the new Beylerbey's palace. The contract paid very well.

Candles and lamps were lit to provide light for the house as the day moved on. Eno was called in as dinner was served and conversation moved to the dining area. Naku talked about his last two years working at the shipyard. He spoke mostly on how he and Sesen designed ships that one day they promised to build together. Deka and Yao exchanged looks that spoke to each other as to how serious was the relationship between their son and Arihman's niece. Eno blurted out the question his parents were transmitting through inconspicuous glances. Naku blushed at the inquiry, though only made by his much younger brother. He figured his parents might have been thinking the same. He answered by stating Sesen and he were just friends, explaining Sesen was more like one of the boys. He then remembered her statements about being the woman she naturally was and he added, "Though, before I left, she wanted to take me out for my birthday." Naku began to dig into his meal with a fork, looking down and avoiding eye contact. "It was mostly for her though. She said she had a new dress. She wanted to feel like a natural woman." He scooped up a piece of meat and some vegetables and placed them into his mouth to chew.

Yao smiled at his son's naivety. He looked at his wife and shook his head. However, he was not aware of Naku's intentions toward Ona. But he was partially correct about his son's situation. Naku had no clue as to Sesen's true intentions. "Well, whatever will be, will be," Yao stated.

"Sure," Naku said chewing. He swallowed, wiped his mouth, and then pushed his chair out. "I have to get ready. Wu and I are hanging out in the city."

"Not too late," Deka warned. "There are criminals around."

Naku stood up from the table. "They mess with me and they'll have to deal with my friend Captain Pelin."

Yao laughed at his son's retort. Deka did not.

"Don't mention that sea dog's name again," she told her son.

Naku kissed his mother on the cheek and apologized. "I won't. Now let me get washed up."

Naku dismissed himself from the room, delved into a good wash, placed on scented oils, and then changed into dark pants, a long white shirt and black shoes. He grabbed a burnoose and wished his family well before departing for Wu's parlor. Naku took his time walking down the blocks separating his house from Wu's business. He looked over the familiar streets that he and his friends would duck in and out of when they were younger. Nothing changed. There was an addition to the sub-urban area making this part of town no longer the outskirts but almost the center. But his area was still the same.

Naku pounded the door when he arrived at Wu's place. Wu came from behind the building, exiting from the back of his business and residence. "Just locked up," he said. He walked over to Naku with a smile and declared, "Let's get drunk and find some women."

"Can't argue with that," Naku replied.

Wu started off down the street, leading the way. "And everything is on me. It's your birthday."

Naku repeated with a sly grin, "Can't argue with that." As the two of them unhinged and mounted camels Naku asked, "Have you heard from El-Ras?"

"I got a letter from him today, actually." Wu said. "He wrote that he was sending you a letter for your birthday."

"It probably arrived after I left the shipyard," Naku guessed aloud.

"He's doing fine. All is well in Morocco," Wu informed as he guided his camel into the streets. "He'll be back in a month to stay for a good while."

"I'll have to con some time off to visit," said Naku following behind Wu.

"Maybe we'll visit *you*," Wu proclaimed. "We'll finally see this Sesen woman you write about so much."

"She's very cute," Naku expressed. "Beautiful, even. She can hang with us. She's not bogged down in any form of faith that stops her from having fun. I wanted her to come."

"And still you pursue something in the past," Wu said jokingly.

Naku spoke very honestly when he confessed, "It's ego driving me. I didn't like how Ona's friends associated me with Ferran. He used me to rob those houses. She thinks I helped him."

"Her friends didn't like us anyway, regardless of Ferran," Wu reminded him. "That ordeal was an added incentive."

"They used her," Naku added, "the way Ferran used us."

Both reflected on past events, talking and commentating on contemporary times. The overview was simple. After the fall of the Moorish Empire many surviving families relocated along the northern coast of Africa. Wu's father had been doing business in al-Andalusia during the brutal roundup by Cardinal Xemenos of any non-European or non-Christian in al-Andalusia. His father sent a letter to his wife in China who decided to meet him in Tunis, to where he was escaping. Naku's family had escaped there as well.

In the aftermath, Moorish soldiers took to the waters of the Mediterranean and gave hell to the seafarers of France, al-Andalus, and Italy. Discord happened when Europeans settled among the refugee Moors of North Africa and the indigenous population. The Europeans claimed they were seeking asylum from persecution of all types. Many Moorish nationalists believed the Europeans were spies, meant to keep a close eye on ex-soldiers turned sea renegades. The European immigrants created sub-urban areas; these were small clusters of settlements around the Moorish refugee settlements. The children played out what was felt in the hearts of the adults. There were those who wanted to live in harmony. It was the Moors who mostly honored the harmony. Ona Ramu was a woman who came from a family who lived among the settled Europeans. Naku believed her European friends only feigned the spiritualism their parents claimed in order to live among the Moors.

There was a second group of Moors who worked strictly for their communities, strengthening Moorish power in what was considered corsair-states and cities. Naku, Wu, and El-Ras were part of such families. Wu's father instilled into his son that though they were Chinese, that they too had Moorish blood in them. Wu's father said he had seen atrocities committed like none the world had ever seen at the behest of the unification of Europe, and under the guise of Christianity. He insisted the troubles of the world were just beginning, and he stressed that civilization was over.

Finally, there were those who worked as soldiers and captains for Company Bosses. Ferran's father was such a man. However, the coin that usually fell into his hands came from the European settlers who asked for protection. No one knew where the European settlers' money came from, but they had large amounts of it, which was why they were suspected as being spies for European states. Their children were very privileged. The popular theory was that European settlements inside North Africa, along with illegal activity, was all to sabotage the Moorish communities. And though the adults played their games without too much violence, the children settled violent affairs for them. Naku and his friends never engaged in anything more than fisticuffs. Throughout the years, Wu and El-Ras were all he could trust as friends. When he met Ona, Naku thought he found another friend. And she being a woman, he thought he found something more. However, Ona's friends guarded her from Naku's attempt to get closer. Naku's presence and background intimidated them.

Naku's memory stopped on one particular scenario that made him smile. "Remember the party," he asked Wu.

Wu chuckled as he reflected, conjuring up the moment in time. "Furio thought you were going to kill him," he stated.

Naku nodded. "I remember his hands shaking when we were introduced. He almost dropped his drink every time he walked by me." Naku became silent as he remembered the event's detail. He rolled his eyes and huffed his words, "As if it was the first time we met."

"Well, the adults were trying to make it formal," Wu pointed out.

"We were sixteen," Naku blurted. He then did the math. "That was just three years ago. I should've beat his ass like an unruly farm animal, but Ona would've been disappointed in me sooner for hitting her friend. She knew there was tension between he and I. She dismissed him from the room every time I entered."

Wu added, "His pride surely didn't like that. That European had his eyes on Ona."

"Luckily she thought they were too good of friends to be anything more. And her father would've never allowed her to marry a European, even if he was from an aristocratic family." Naku became curious and asked, "So what happened to Furio?"

"He just turned twenty, actually," Wu answered not exactly addressing the question. "It was four months ago. His father is prepping him to inherit the politics. He works closely with Ferran, mostly as a lawyer. He will be working for a *Renegado*."

"And here I thought he was a spiritualist," Naku joked.

Those were the final words for the conversation. The two of them neared an old hangout. *Al-Raby Tavern*. The two of them dismounted and Wu paid a man to attend to their mounts. They straightened their clothes and headed into the first of many taverns they planned to enter for the night.

Inside was a quaint social scene. Wu had obviously chosen this tavern just to warm them up, get them started for what would be a long night. Naku always needed to lighten up and take it easy when entering a social atmosphere. The tavern was relaxing. There was a bar, a band playing lightly, and a lovely eatery and dining area. The two young men were more interested in the bar. Wu ordered them a round of drinks and made Naku promise that there would be no talk of people or events of the past. Naku opted to speak more about Arihman, his niece, and all the mishaps and happenings at the port-town where he worked. The mood then turned extremely light. There were jokes shared and stories that reminisced on women conquered and nights of lust. Naku said he was able to slip away on his own and find a few catches in the area where he worked.

The consumption of drinks lightened their heads. It also seemed to make the atmosphere go from light, to slow, then completely boring. It was time for a new place. The young men gathered themselves, exited the tavern, decided to leave their mounts, and drunkenly stumble to the next tavern. They mostly followed the noise and crowd. The next tavern was loud, a raucous choir reverberating all the way down the street. Through the door was a heavier carousing atmosphere than the previous tavern. There was wild play, dance, and game. There were drinks along the wall and a man standing on guard for pay to access one or more of the drinks. Wu pitched several coins the man's way and scooped up four large mugs, handing two over to Naku. There was no time for conversation. Naku—socially open because of the alcohol—and Wu were swept up into the song and dance of the friendly place.

Naku stopped the alcoholic momentum and spin of the room long enough to see a very attractive woman swoop him up and bring him into a circle of dancers. His eyes were able to catch that another pretty Moorish girl snagged Wu for dancing. Naku suddenly found himself lip-to-lip with the woman. Her arms were wrapped around him.

Naku loved his birthday.

He and Wu moved on to another tavern, the women following. The third tavern was filled with the pirates, the hustlers, and the smugglers. And the dregs of the sea knew how to ignite the night. Naku could only remember the consumption and dance as a continuous spin. The scene twirled around him, lightening his spirits and stumbling his walk and words. Images, feelings, and emotions became jumbled to Naku. There was an image inside of a backroom. There was heavy kissing of the same woman. Suddenly, she was absent. There was a sound of scrapping. Someone operated what sounded like a sewing wheel. Then there was pain. Naku felt as if lightning struck his back, spreading out to seize every nerve. He felt a cool, watery liquid spread through his flesh, pumping like blood.

Blood?

Naku passed out.

Sunlight forced Naku's eyes open. He felt as if small needles were stabbing his retinas. His head weighed three hundred pounds. He groaned. His blurry vision slowly focused, and he recognized that he was not in his bed at home. Naku lifted his body. His back surged with pain and he arched as if someone grabbed his shoulders and bent him back. His body trembled with pain, but his nerves began to shake off the disturbance. He took a breath and relaxed. Naku then realized he had no shirt on. He was dressed in only his black pants.

"Careful," said Wu as he walked into the room. "Your skin is still tender. You might still infect—"

Naku turned quickly and stood. "Infect what?"

"Your tattoo," Wu said with a smile. "I'm sort of proud of the work myself. Considering I was drunk out of my mind, I believe I did a helluva job."

Naku twisted his neck to look at his back. The tattoo looked like a giant, purple stain from his perspective. The pattern looked as if it had no rhyme or reason. "Tattoo? My goodness!"

Wu snatched two mirrors. One mirror was medium sized. The other was large. Wu handed the smaller one to Naku. He instructed Naku to hold it over his shoulder while Wu aimed the larger mirror at his back. Naku adjusted the mirror to glimpse at the image drawn on his back, reflected from Wu's mirror as the artist stood behind him.

Naku was in awe. Wu had done a wonderful job. The artistry crafted on him was amazing. On his back was etched the picture of a djinn that appeared to be amalgamated with a phoenix. His fiery tail swirled down and ended at the base of Naku's spine. His wings reached out and crossed over Naku's shoulders and spilled over to his slender biceps. The djinn's hair was in a ponytail but had tremendous detail to it. The hair was locked. His arms were aimed downward, fists balled. His eyes were golden and he blazed a wonderful purple aura.

"How the hell did you do this so fast," Naku asked.

"I'm good," Wu said with a cocky smile. "Best job I ever did drunk," he stated further, looking closer at his artwork. "A wonderful purple," he commented. "It blazes and jumps out."

Naku's hand began to shake. He threw the mirror on the bed so as not to drop it. Wu commented that placing a mirror on the bed was bad luck and Naku retorted, "Too late." He stepped over to Wu and asked. "How inebriated did we get last night?"

Wu backed up. He placed the mirror down and shook his head. "Not that drunk. Don't worry. I remember kissing women not each other."

"Not that," Naku hissed. "Where did you get the purple ink to use?"

Wu's jaw dropped.

They rushed from the room, down the upstairs hall, and then descended a flight of stairs. Wu ran into his office and checked the shelves filled with ink vials. He shook his head with frustration, he remembered he had not stored Pelin's vial among the others. He put it inside a special lockbox. He snatched a key from a drawing table and then bent down in front of the case. He opened it and pulled out the half empty bottle of purple liquid. He held it to his face and cursed. Defeated, he put the vial back into the lockbox and closed it.

"We're dead," Wu groaned.

Naku stood firm. "No," he said. "We can fill the bottle the rest of the way with another liquid. There was nothing special about that ink, I don't believe."

"I'd have to know where he got the liquid from," Wu said to Naku. "If I put something that doesn't mix right it may turn another color."

"Then concoct something that has the same tint and hue," Naku suggested. "That should hold him off until we can find out more about the liquid, why it's so special. We have one week before he returns here and two weeks before he even wants the tattoo made."

Wu agreed. "That'll buy us some time," he thought aloud. Naku turned and walked away, making his way back up to the room. "Where are you going?" Wu called.

"First I'm gonna check in at my house," Naku yelled back. "My family needs to know I'm all right. Then, I'm going to snatch up Ona. Just continue your business. I'll be back tonight. We'll plan something before I leave tomorrow."

Naku stood outside the café, frozen in his tracks. All that moved was the pain in his back, plucking at his nerves every time his shirt pressed too hard against his tattoo. The pain started to numb, but only because Naku's attention was on the anxiety he felt. He was too nervous to simply take several steps into the café and say 'hello' to a woman from the past. He took one step, and then another to even his stance. The steps felt good, and they raised his confidence. But only enough to secure the thought that sometime between now and tomorrow he would venture into the café.

Naku stayed put.

Behind him was a noise made from a gathering crowd. The crowd headed inside the café. Naku decided to be swept up by its flow and use them as a shield to make his way in. He took a seat and looked around for Ona. She was nowhere to be seen. Minutes after he entered the café, and a while after he settled into his seat, he heard her familiar voice behind him. Naku's heart raced. He took a breath, and then he peeked over his shoulder to catch a glimpse of Ona. She was draped in a wonderful red, blue, and gold trimmed dress. Her hair was black and reflective of the sunlight that peered inside the café windows. The way the sun kissed her flesh made it burn brown and gold. She was a wonderful treasure. Oddly enough, Naku suddenly thought about Sesen. He began to wonder what she was doing and how she looked doing it. He also wondered how Sesen would look in the very dress Ona was wearing. Naku was so engaged in his thoughts that he missed Ona pass by him. He did not see her, and she did not see him.

Naku realized he missed Ona. He watched her back move away from him as she headed into the café's rear. Naku stood up and followed her. He called her name several strides into his pursuit. Ona turned around. Her face was absent of any affection when she recognized who called her name. "Naku," she said. "I'm surprised to see you around here." Her tone was as absent of affection as her expression.

"Just visiting," he said. "My employer gave me time off. A birthday present."

"Happy birthday," Ona said with a smile.

Naku chuckled lightly. "So far, it is," he admitted. "Wu and I went out last night."

"You're still friends with him," she questioned. Ona turned around sharply and walked away.

Naku followed Ona, trying to keep up with her quick steps. "Last night he told me you were running this place, and—"

Ona made another sharp turn, this time to face Naku. "Why are you here?" she asked in a stern voice.

Naku straightened himself and answered, "I believe we ended on a confused note. I just wanted to see if you would like to go out—"

"To talk politics," she said rolling her eyes. "I don't think so. That's all that's stirring up nowadays. My café is for anyone who wants to reside in it. I give my business to all people."

Ona was speaking fast. She threw out excuses like an unclogged waterspout. Naku looked for a way to slice into her rant. When he found one he spoke just as quickly. "No, no," he pleaded. "There are no politics behind my asking you to a nice dinner except the fact that I still fancy you."

Ona exhaled, the tension deflated. She was flattered by Naku's honesty, but she was not completely moved to change her decision. "I'm busy," she told him.

Naku felt his back tingle. It stopped him from responding. It seemed like a gentle breeze flowed through his spine. The sensation became very warm, but never burned uncomfortably. The feeling turned heavy, and the vibration of his back made Naku believe it had nothing to do with his tattoo. And though his back faced the door he saw an image of it in front of his eyes. Naku blinked. The image became more vivid to him with his eyes closed. The café door swung open and Furio walked through, escorted by five other European men. Naku opened his eyes again and faced the door. There was no one. He began to turn back to Ona when just a few seconds later reality played out the very scenario previously displayed behind Naku's eyelids.

Furio walked through the door, escorted by five other European men.

Naku looked at Ona. She misinterpreted his perplexed look. Naku was just in wonder of what had transpired in his head rather than Furio's presence in her café. "They meet here for business only," Ona explained. "They have plans to push for harmony among everyone in our district. The Beylerbey has sanctioned it. And I don't think the kind of people with family backgrounds such as yours will fair well staying in my establishment."

"Ona…"

The woman folded her arms and shook her head. "You can't handle situations the way you use to, Naku. Some of us are growing up and trying to make this place better. The world is changing."

Naku had to laugh. "I just came here to ask you to dinner."

"I can't be seen with you," Ona told him. "Not with your kind."

"What kind," Naku protested. "We're the same kind. We're Moors. And if no love can exist between a-Moor, then what love is there?" Ona was not unfazed by the sentiment. But she stood firm. Her rattled emotions were unseen. Sadness and defeat gripped Naku. He sighed, "I thought politics was behind you."

Before Ona responded, there again was the sensation of a cool breeze rushing up Naku's spine. It transitioned into the hot and burdensome agitation he felt before Furio arrived. Another vision formed in front of Naku. He closed his eyes and concentrated for its image to sharpen. Captain Pelin entered the café with his crew of *Water Dogs*. The vision cleared. Naku turned around and saw reality catch up to his thoughts just seconds later. The corsair surprisingly shook Furio's hand and commented that he had just spoken to his father. Naku tried to shake the image away, to make it disperse like his extrasensory vision. But the scenery remained. It was now reality, and there was nothing he could do but watch.

Pelin and Furio made their way to Ona. Naku turned away, trying to hide his face from Pelin. It was too late. The corsair spotted him. "Naku," Pelin called.

Ona gave Naku a serious look. She shook her head and said with disappointment, "I though you didn't hang with pirates."

"He was just shaking hands with Furio," Naku scoffed. "What? It's okay for Furio to be seen with cutthroats but not for—"

Pelin grabbed Naku's shoulder before he could finish his response. The Captain dragged Naku back and wrapped a single arm around him, giving him a shake. "How'd your birthday go?"

"It went fine," Naku said in an undetectably uneasy voice. "My friend Wu and I hung out," Naku explained. "We scored with some women."

"That's my boy," Pelin said shaking Naku harder. He reached out to Furio and got the young politician's attention. "Furio, meet a friend of mine."

Naku and Furio locked eyes. Though Furio considered himself a pacifist and spiritualist, there was a hint of disdain in his gaze. Disdain was clearly on Naku's visage, however. Furio smiled at Pelin. "Naku and I grew up together," he informed the corsair. He reached an arm out toward Ona and pulled her close. "This beautiful woman was the link between us. This is Ona Ramu."

Pelin was speechless, his mouth hanging agape. He then began to laugh at the irony. He let go of Naku and greeted Ona with a kiss to the hand. "A great pleasure," he said to her.

"A pleasure to serve, Captain," Ona retorted in a lovely tone.

Furio whispered something in the woman's ear and the two of them dismissed themselves. Naku looked at Pelin with a look of disbelief. The Captain raised his shoulders and confessed, "I work where the coin takes me, Naku."

"You have *some* honor don't you?" Naku asked grimacing.

"I have a job," Pelin said, putting the situation in a simple perspective. "But just because I work for the European settlement here doesn't mean that you'll lose the woman you came here for."

"Don't take this job," Naku said with an authoritative voice. "Walk away."

"And then how will your friend and Arihman get paid," Pelin continued to show the bigger picture. "Not only will I make a killing when all is settled, but my mentor-turned-partner will return again. His name was Captain Masun, and he was unjustly jailed. With the help of his son and Furio, our campaign will set him free."

There were schemes that Pelin withheld from Naku, but the young Moor could somehow feel Pelin's clandestine intentions. Furio was just a pawn to help free Ferran's father. Pelin wanted war to break out in the corsair-state. He would quell the war with…a weapon. Pelin sought to be Beylerbey of the state. No one would challenge him. He would have power because of…his weapon. Naku ignored what he felt, not understanding why these feelings penetrated him.

Pelin reminded the young Moor, "If all goes wrong with your plans, Naku, always have a backup treasure to go for." He grinned and nodded toward Ona who spoke to Furio in the corner. "After all, the other just might slip away."

"Right," Naku said in a low voice.

Pelin slapped the young man's shoulder. "Good. Now go and tell Wu that I'll make my way toward the island tonight."

"Right," Naku repeated. He walked away and exited the café. Outside, his walk became quick strides and then evolved into a bolt toward Wu's business. Naku's speed increased, turning him into a blurry vision. The people's movement around him began to slow, and then suddenly they froze stiff. The scenery then blurred as if he was coming out of a dream. He felt as if he had only been running a short distance until he was able to translate the blur as the street with Wu's parlor. He stopped and turned around, noticing that he missed the parlor by several houses.

Naku believed he was still feeling the effects of the drinking he engaged in. He walked to the parlor entrance. It was then that he noticed his heart's beat was regular. There was no hastened pace. It was as if he had not been running at all. There was no sweat or feeling of exhaustion. He did not even have to catch his breath. Naku's body functioned normally. He opened the door to Wu's parlor and quickly realized things were about to get worse, if not more interesting. His brother Eno sat inside the parlor. Both he and Wu looked up at Naku who asked his brother, "Why are you here? What's wrong?"

Wu quickly approached Naku. "You have to leave."

Naku started worrying. He asked, "Why? Is everything all right with my family?"

"Ferran's looking for you," Eno blurted.

Wu answered Naku before he could ask why. "He wants to arrest you."

Naku thought the statement was ridiculous. He barked, "What? On what grounds? For old time's sake? A fight we had a couple years ago?"

"No," Wu drawled, shaking his head. "It's for harassing his mother, the Good Lady Lisha."

Naku was stunned. What was more disturbing was the guilty look on Wu's face. It was as if he had condemned his friend for the crime. "I haven't even seen his mother since I've been here," Naku protested.

Wu made an uncomfortable laugh. He raised a hand to stop Naku from speaking any further and explained. "Actually, you know, uh..." Wu searched for the words. "How can I say this?"

"Quickly," Naku answered the rhetorical question, "before I get angrier."

Wu snapped his fingers. "Right." He realized how to put everything into perspective. "You know how alcohol can make things look different than what they appear...if you consume too much of it? Such as—for example—a woman's age. You might actually believe you were dancing and kissing up to a woman your age when in fact—"

Naku covered his mouth. His eyes went wide, and he looked at the floor hoping to find a magical gateway that would take him back in time to change the events of last night. "My goodness," he gasped.

"There's really nothing to worry about," Wu said lightly. "Lady Lisha is still an exotic dancer, and has a wonderful physique for her age. She is still an attraction. She was always quite a looker. What's a twenty year difference in age?"

Naku's hand began to tremble. Ferran was going to kill him, he thought. Ferran was going to throw him in jail and then murder him under good context. "But...she approached me. She grabbed me and started to dance. She kissed me!" His tone was excited, as if he was pleading to an imaginary Ferran. He looked at Wu and asked. *"Did she tell him I was harassing her?"*

Wu shook his head and lifted his shoulders. "I don't know what she told her son. All I know is how he's handling it."

"We're in a lot of trouble," Naku pointed out.

Wu placed a hand on his chest. "I only have the potential threat of a pirate wanting to kill me," he then pointed to Naku, "which we both share. But you got that *and* the police after you."

Naku leaned against the wall. "Ferran and Furio work together," he told Wu.

"I know," Wu replied. "It's politics. They're probably using each other for gain."

Naku sighed. "Captain Pelin works for them," he explained. His eyes then looked over at Wu. "Ferran's father was his mentor. And Pelin wants him out of jail too."

Wu's heart sank. His legs almost gave out on him as he began to tremble. "We're in a lot of trouble."

Naku hit the wall with his fist. "Imagine what happens when Ferran's father finds out I was 'harassing' his wife."

"Oh, they were never married," Wu said as if it made the situation better.

"I'm sure that'll hold up in his form of court," Naku stated sarcastically.

Wu sat down next to Eno. "We'll think of something."

Naku headed for the door. "Eno, let's go home."

The young boy jumped to his feet and followed his brother. Naku opened the door and walked right into Ferran, a large muscular, black Moor. He wore a political suit and robe, and a scoundrel's sneer. Ferran's fist was the last thing Naku saw. When he woke up, he was lying on a wooden shelf-rest in a cell, clasped to chains. His head was absent of the usual concussive pain that followed a giant fist slamming into a face and knocking someone out. He felt his face and found no bruises, scars from a beating, or even a tender painful feeling to any areas he applied pressure to. He was fine. But he remembered being hit. Ferran had hit him, and hard too, real hard. Despite all that, he woke pleasantly…or rather without any aftershock from an unconscious beating given to him.

There was more strangeness. The prison was dark, but Naku's eyes were well adjusted and could see the scenery around him as if the sunlight peered into the room. Only a few torches lit the halls, and a single window exposed an almost full moon that was smothered by clouds. Naku saw the guard walk down a hall and heard him exit through a door. Moments later he returned with Ferran and three other guardsmen.

Instead of approaching the situation with the frustration he held, Naku took it easy and addressed, "There has been a terrible mistake."

"My mother does not make mistakes," the brute grumbled.

Naku tested the chains to see how far they could extend. He walked to the front of the cell. He was able to press himself against the steel rods with enough slack to move around comfortably.

"Ferran, I came home yesterday," Naku explained. "I'm visiting for my birthday. I went out with Wu and got drunk. I don't remember harassing anyone."

"Of course not, you were drunk," the brute yelled. He raised an eyebrow before he huffed, "And that's added to your charge. Disorderly, drunken conduct in a public—"

"Don't be so righteous," Naku hollered. "You're no Mohammedan, and the faith is only a cover for this state. And, I was in a tavern you id—"

"If you raise your voice at an official again," Ferran warned, "there won't even be a court held in your right and honor. I'll decide your fate right now."

Naku pulled on the bars as his frustration mounted. "Your mother was dancing and carrying on as usual," he barked. "I don't care what she said. Besides, it's not like I defiled her."

"You did all the damage you needed to," Ferran grumbled, tapping a foot. "Tomorrow, your court session is held." He turned sharply and walked away.

Naku blew up, his emotions running over. He screamed aloud, "Damnit, Ferran! You should be use to your mother's antics by now! After all your mother is a whore!" Naku quickly realized how offensive and degrading his comment was rather than argumentative to the situation at hand. His face froze in a position of disbelief. He knew he was going to die. All of his nineteen years that flashed before his eyes came down to regretting his last comment that most certainly guaranteed he would not see year twenty.

The large politician stopped dead in his tracks, pivoted slowly, and walked ominously back to the cell. "What. Did. You. Say?"

Naku was stiff. His eyes were all that moved as they focused on Ferran. "When? We've had such a long conversation."

Ferran wrapped his large hand around Naku's neck at lightning speed. He squeezed tight, lifting Naku off the ground. "Did you really think that comment was going to free you from this cell?" Ferran tossed Naku aside and slammed him into the wall adjacent the bars. Naku's body curled up on impact. Ferran walked away, leaving one guard behind.

Naku crawled to his feet, using the wall for support. He walked back to the shelf-rest and lay down. He realized being tossed by Ferran did not hurt him, nor did he feel pain lying down, even with the pressure against his back, freshly etched with the tattoo. Naku exhaled. Feeling no pain did not provide any comfort. Perhaps, considered Naku, it would not hurt when he was beheaded or hanged.

He rubbed the wall with his hands, winding the tip of his finger through the rocky patterns. It was then he noticed the pitch color of his arm. It was not smooth, and dark brown. It was completely black. The blackness covered his right hand, all the way to his forearm. Naku sat up on the bench-rest and looked at his other arm, rolling up the sleeve.

It was the same.

Naku started to worry that a disease was overcoming him, but he still had feeling on the blackened areas of his flesh. He ran his fingers along his arm, and he felt as though he was touching liquid. He applied pressure on his arm and his flesh stiffened. The texture changed, as did the feeling in his blackened skin. It felt like his arms were locked inside a cast. The urge to dig his nails into his arm overwhelmed him and he began to claw at his pitch skin as if it were a scab. He bore into the now delicate flesh with all his fingers and tore it away to reveal a forearm strangely glowing purple.

Was he dreaming?

"I need to get the hell out of here," Naku said to himself, face resonating with the glow of his forearm. He suddenly felt sick. He placed his back against the wall while looking down at his other blackened forearm. Flesh crumbled into dust, whittling away to the purple glowing flesh underneath. He made a fist with his right hand and slammed it against the iron clasps wrapped around his left wrist. The iron shackle shattered as if made of glass. His left arm was free. He punched the right clasp and shattered it as well.

Naku watched his glowing arms increase in size, his forearms bulging. His muscles bubbled and pulsated as they expanded. Naku stood up and tried to walk forward, but his legs were tightly bound together by an invisible force. He slammed face first into the ground. The tattoo on his back blazed with a golden energy. His legs burst into a long snaking tendril of smokeless fire. He could feel the heat from the waist down. It felt as if his real legs were wrapped tightly within the energy. His body had blackened and crumbled to reveal the body of a djinn underneath. It was the very djinn etched on his back. Naku had become the specter of myth and legend.

Naku was identical to the drawing tattooed on his back. However, he was absent of the pair of wings, and he differed in color. His glowing flesh resonated as a much darker purple than the liquid used to ink him. Naku's critique took him away from the reality of the situation. The guard outside his cell looked on in complete disbelief and terror. Naku-Djinn aimed an open palm toward the guard and sent a shockwave of energy into the guard's chest. The guard slammed against the iron bars of the empty cell lying opposite Naku-Djinn's. The back of the guard's head smacked against one of the bars, and he was rendered unconscious. Naku-Djinn glided over to his cell's bars and bent them open without struggle.

He hovered outside his cell. His large, golden eyes witnessed the other prisoners cowering in their cells, hiding their face from the creature he had become. At the end of the dreary hallway was the door to freedom. And although Naku-Djinn knew he had no wings, there was an unconscious understanding that he possessed the ability to fly. He balled his fists and then shot forward like a projected cannonball, his resonating flesh just a streak of blazing light. He crashed through the door with a scream and knocked down two guards on the other side. He turned his body and aimed for a wall, slamming through it and causing immeasurable damage to the room on the other side. Naku-Djinn flew upward, tearing through the ceiling. He continued straight up and out of the prison.

Naku-Djinn lifted into the night sky, a dazzling display of bright, smokeless fire. He could feel the cosmic backdrop of stars calling to him. He was an ascending shooting star. He shot out into space, passing the boundaries of Earth's atmosphere. He looked down as he continued to ascend. He saw the Earth become a distant memory, a tiny spot miniscule to all of creation. Naku-Djinn ceased his ascent. A hole in space opened near him, twirling with black energy and spewing forth beings no different than him. They were male and female djinn. They shimmered, black, with a gold lining. Naku-Djinn understood they were far from the virgin he was with his own power. And where Naku-Djinn had two glowing eyes, these spirits had a single eye centered in their foreheads, swirling with energy. They surrounded him and spoke what would be gibberish in any human language except two.

They spoke in music.

They spoke in mathematics.

Naku-Djinn's understanding of how they were using this language was infantile. Telepathically, he was able to translate some of the musical and numerical grammar. But even then it was senseless. Before Naku-Djinn could respond, making an attempt at speech, he was thrust back to Earth by the collective power of the black spirits surrounding him. His eyes widened as he approached Earth at top speeds. There was Africa. There was Tunisia.

Naku-Djinn blacked out.

He woke up screaming! He grabbed the blanket and crawled up into bed, pressing his back against the headboard. He looked around and noticed he was back in his room at the shipyard living quarters. Naku paced his breathing and tried to connect himself with the environment around him. His eyes panned the room in disbelief of his placement back at the shipyard. He was wearing his clothes from the night of his birthday. He still had not changed. He wondered how many days had passed since he became…

This was ridiculous.

He wondered how many days had passed since he had…turned into a djinn and journeyed into the heavens. Naku dismissed the possibility of everything being a dream. It was too real. Negating the events of his transformation would also negate the events of his birthday and his meeting with Ona, though he wished he could. Naku jumped from his bed and removed his shirt. He snatched a small mirror from the desk in his room and aimed it toward the mirror mounted on the wall. His back faced the mirror. He could see Wu's artwork crafted onto him in all its glory. Naku put the mirror down on the desk and smiled.

"I still wish I had the wings," he said to himself.

There was a light tap on the door. Naku looked over and then heard Sesen's voice ask, "May I come in?"

Naku put on his shirt and invited Sesen inside. She looked beautiful, still in her night robes. Naku had never seen her like this. Her black skin blazed like the backdrop of the heavens that he witnessed some time before. She was clean, and as naturally feminine as she wished him to behold. Naku had to take a deep breath. All the spectacular imagery he had seen a night or so ago, Dark Matter Spirits, the heavens, and openings to other worlds, did not compare to Sesen right now. This black woman was queen of all he knew at the moment. To break the silence he asked her, "How did you know I was here?"

Sesen closed the door behind her and answered, "I was on the dock last night and saw you sort of stumble inside. I was very surprised to see you home a day early." Then Sesen stated the obvious. "Plus, I…heard you screaming…at the top of your lungs."

Naku concentrated on Sesen's preceding words. She said he had come home a day early. He quickly contemplated that it had only been the next day. He realized that Ferran and his guards must have been dealing with both the damage he caused and his escape at this very moment. All of Tunis and its sub-urban areas would be crawling with police. And when they could not find him in Tunis they would interrogate his family and Wu, possibly threatening them with force. Once Ferran relayed all the events to Furio the storm would gain momentum. And if the news reached Pelin, he would decipher that Wu used the mysterious liquid on Naku. Pelin would drop his gentleman facade and brutalize Wu to death.

Naku's spine began to tingle, and his next thought made the sensation intensify. He believed the reasonable move for Pelin would be to come to the shipyard, and it would not be to check on the progress of his ship's repair.

Naku believed his very existence threatened the lives of anyone who knew him. But if everything happened according to what he remembered, his very existence as a djinn bestowed upon him the power to grant wishes. And since no one had him in his service, the way legend goes with djinn, he only served himself. His wishes were his command. His power was at his command. Anything he wanted could be his.

Ona...

He looked up at Sesen's beautiful figure and re-calculated his last thought. Her name came to mind.

"Why are you here so early," she asked, bringing Naku out of his deep thought.

Naku wondered if he could trust Sesen with the truth. After some consideration, he decided to speak and see where his words would lead him. "I'm in a little bit of trouble," he said to her.

Sesen raised an eyebrow and inquired, "In two days of returning home?"

"It's a record for me," Naku joked. "But it's nothing I can't get out of." He rubbed his neck and said with a heavy breath, "But the trouble may also involve Captain Pelin."

Sesen reached out toward Naku. "What happened?"

"Captain Pelin is involved with a lot of the politics in Tunis," he informed her. "Most of his plans are devious. He seeks to become the Governor-General by means of assassination and exploiting a lot of growing fervor in the city."

Sesen put her arms around Naku. He reciprocated. "I knew my uncle shouldn't have let you leave with those brigands," she said angrily.

"Trust me, Sesen," Naku retorted, "I'll be fine."

"Then why did you run," Sesen asked.

Naku was getting use to the woman's soft body against his. His grip became tighter and he felt Sesen react sensually. Her arms went around his waist and she laid her head against his chest. "I didn't run, Sesen," he began to correct her. "I flew."

Sesen looked up at him. She was perplexed. "What do you mean?"

Naku felt he had to tell the truth to at least two people. Sesen would be the first. He confessed, "Captain Pelin found something magical. It was accidentally applied to me."

Naku felt Sesen's hold loosen, but she never let go. He reached around and grabbed her hands and brought them in front of him, holding them tightly. "I told you I didn't run. I flew. I mean that literally. There's something magical about me now." He felt Sesen's hands flinch. She wanted to let go and draw away from him.

But something kept her hands in his grip, and that force had nothing to do with Naku. Although Sesen's instincts told her to run, she fought them. She stayed.

But she had to ask questions. She was not crazy to believe such stories without proof. "What do you mean," she inquired.

Naku let go of her and turned around coolly. "Let me start from the beginning."

"Please," Sesen insisted.

Naku folded his arms, leaned against the wall, and then put his hands in his pockets. "Captain Pelin asked my friend to hold a magical liquid for him. He wanted the liquid to be used as an ink, to give him a tattoo that would grant him magical powers." He stepped from off the wall and opened the palm of his hand. He stretched out his arm, and with a single thought, he conjured a brilliant aura that swirled like a small galaxy. Naku looked at Sesen's surprised expression, his eyes glowing gold.

Sesen's expression melted into a quick smile. She was not afraid, but in awe.

Naku ended the display of power. "My friend and I got drunk," he unbuttoned his shirt and removed it. "And he gave me this tattoo." Naku turned around for Sesen to behold the brilliance of Wu's artistry. "He used the ink given to him by Pelin, but not all of it."

Sesen moved forward. She held out her hand. She stopped Naku from placing his shirt back on. She outlined the tattoo with her finger. Her touch was warm to Naku. The tattoo started glowing the instant Sesen traced the drawing with her finger.

"I'm a djinn," Naku explained. "The magical ink turned me into a djinn."

"Then grant me a wish," Sesen said with a big smile.

Naku turned around, putting his shirt back on. "Your wish is my command," he said playfully.

"I wish to go to dinner with you," Sesen answered.

Unfortunately it was not a command Naku could attend to at the very moment. "I have some business to take care of first," he said to her. He then kissed Sesen's forehead. The simple kiss held enough power to keep Sesen's heart afloat. "I have to get back to Tunis and stop this before it spreads here." He ran a finger along her dark cheek. "I'll leave under the cover of night. That gives us the rest of the day." He took Sesen into his arms. "There are things I need to tell you. There are things that I saw."

"You have my ear, my Moorish djinn," the woman said to Naku. "And anything else if you wish." She backed away from him, heading toward the door. "I'll be back with some fruit and wine. I'll get a meal out of you yet. Don't fly off, African Zinn-Kibaru."

Naku smiled sheepishly. Sesen disappeared into the hall and closed the door. Naku's eyes went to the floor, his mind spinning with scenarios. An image of Sesen and Ona wrestling one another filled his head. A second scene appeared with

Pelin, atop a high tower. On either side of him were Ferran and Furio. Bound and gagged in Ferran's grip was Sesen, while Furio held Ona in the same fashion. Both women were pushed from the tower and Naku-Djinn charged forward, blazing with all his power and might. But he could only catch one.

Who would it be?

Naku sat on his bed and pondered the thought.

The prison was in shambles. The pattern of destruction was all too familiar for Captain Pelin. He traipsed through the rubble and debris casually, without any true emotion. But a murderous sensation stirred inside him as ravenous as the damage before his eyes. Flanking him was two of his five lieutenants. There was Ulucan, head of gunnery, and Sencer, weapons expert. His other three lieutenants had continued on to the Mediterranean Island holding the sketches he wanted tattooed to his back. Furio and Ferran called for Pelin the minute the damage to the prison, and the prison break, was reported.

The Italian, Furio, walked close behind Pelin. He was trying desperately to read Pelin's face for the slightest emotion. Pelin's expression was bare. Furio's heart quickened. "I've never seen damage like this," Furio commented to spark something from the corsair captain.

Pelin stopped and continued to inspect the scene. "I have," he said in a low, cold voice. He spoke over his shoulder, "Ferran said he held Naku prisoner here."

"Yes," Furio answered. "Now he's gone."

Pelin turned around and finally showed an emotion with a sly grin. "And what was the boy doing in prison?"

"He degraded Ferran's mother," Furio answered. "He harassed Lady Lisha."

Pelin snickered and asked for clarification, "The whore? He's a bit touchy of his mother's occupation, don't you believe?"

"Regardless," Furio said with an angry tone. "Inmates dare to report a spirit did all this. A djinn."

Pelin did not flinch. His men looked up at him with concern. The pirate turned around coolly and said, "Do they, now? How ridiculous." He sighed. "I will interrogate his friend, the Chinaman. In the meantime, I want you and Ferran to meet me at that wench's café. Understood?"

"Of course, Captain Pelin," Furio bowed.

Pelin walked away from Furio, his two lieutenants close behind. The corsair left the prison. He and his lieutenants felt it safe to talk once clear of the penitentiary. First, Pelin looked around, checking the environment for spies.

"Do you think the boy used all of the djinn's blood, Master?" Ulucan addressed Pelin.

"I'm sure he used enough," Pelin sneered. "We'll have to reshape our plans. As long as we have our choice of weapons between the spear and the bottle this boy won't be much of a threat." The three continued down the street. Pelin waved down a public coach. The men jumped inside. "I am not without my plans," Pelin told the two men. "Trust me." Pelin then instructed the driver to take them to the area of Wu's parlor.

The men were silent for the entire ride. Ulucan and Sencer felt that if their leader did not speak, there would be no conversation. Pelin was in deep thought, devising a plan to counteract the incurred setbacks. The greatest advantage Pelin possessed over Naku's new ability would be experience. Pelin killed a djinn at sea. The djinn was an ancient spirit. Pelin navigated the known waters of the world to find two special items to battle with the apparition. And though the scrimmage killed a good number of Pelin's crew, and left his ship crippled, the djinn was defeated, its blood preserved. Naku's naivety would make him an easier opponent. Pelin, however, was not planning to kill the boy. Instead, Pelin was going to make the boy's power serve him, granting the most diabolical of wishes. He was also eyeing a sample of Naku's blood, substituting for the loss of the original djinn's vital essence.

The coach stopped.

Pelin paid the driver and the three men ejected. They walked up to Wu's parlor and knocked on the door. Pelin was surprised to see the young Chinese boy open the door without any alarm to the danger he was in. Wu invited the three gentlemen inside and sat down at a table. He was unaware of the intentions of Pelin's visit, or the happenings to Naku other than his imprisonment the day before.

"Captain Pelin!" blurted Wu. "You've returned already? Do you have your sketch?" he asked.

Pelin hesitated to answer. He looked at Wu with a curious eye. He shook his head before he made the answer audible. "No," he said. "I've sent a crew of soldiers to complete the task." Wu remained calm.

"So to what do I owe the pleasure of your visit," Wu beamed.

Pelin's curious eye remained fixed on the tattoo artist. The pirate's tongue pushed out his cheek as he tried to figure what made the young man so calm. "Are you aware of Naku's imprisonment?" Pelin asked.

Wu leaned back in his chair and huffed, "Ferran's an ass." He looked up at Pelin with stern eyes and concluded, "And though he's your employer, you can deliver the message personally. I care not of the consequences. My father is working on freeing—"

"Your friend is already free," Pelin interrupted. "There was an unexplainable destruction to the prison, and his cell is empty. The bars were bent. It's believed he ran free."

"So are you here to interrogate me as to Naku's whereabouts," Wu expressed in a cynical tone. "He's not here."

Pelin looked at Ulucan and Sencer. They understood the look as a command. They surrounded Wu. The young man looked at the lieutenants flanking him. Sencer was the first to strike. He slammed a hard fist into Wu's face while Ulucan held Wu's arm down on the table. Sencer grabbed the other arm and bent it behind Wu's back. Wu struggled to no avail. Sencer was able to grab Wu's neck and hold a tight squeeze.

Pelin walked over, standing next to Ulucan. He looked down at Wu from his angle and said, "I'm not going to lie to you, Wu. I'm going to hurt you very badly so I can get your friend's attention." The pirate snapped his fingers and Ulucan flattened Wu's hand against the table. Pelin removed a dagger from a sheath attached to his belt. He aimed the blade downward and thrust it through Wu's hand. The blade passed through Wu's hand and into the wooden table, nailing Wu to the furniture. The young man bit down to keep from screaming. "You're a tough, *tough* young man," Pelin complimented. He looked over at Sencer and commanded, "Other hand."

Sencer laid out Wu's left hand. Wu struggled again, and again it was to no avail. Pelin removed a second dagger, the blade of which was thrust through Wu's second hand. This time the young man groaned, a muffled scream. Wu's head dropped to the table face first. Pelin signaled to Ulucan. The lieutenant grabbed Wu by the hair and lifted his head to face Pelin.

The corsair captain took a seat at the round table opposite Wu. "Naku will understand why all this has happened," he explained to Wu. "But there will be some confusion, which is to be expected. So, I'm going to use you to fill in the blanks for him." The pirate leaned over the table, close to Wu. "Have you ever heard of the Blood of Osiris?" Wu did not answer. He grit his teeth to keep from screaming. The inquiry was just rhetorical, however. Pelin continued to speak. "That is what you call the blood from a djinn. It's said to have magical properties; and if applied to human flesh, inked into the skin, that bearer of the blood will be granted all the powers of a djinn."

Wu breathed rapidly. His hands were becoming cold, pain throbbing through his entire body as a lake of blood expanded onto the table. But as his ears heard Pelin's words he smiled and began to laugh. Pelin did the same.

The pirate pointed toward Wu and said, "You're starting to get it, huh." Pelin leaned away from Wu. "I know you used the blood on Naku. Now I need to know where he is, so that I can extract it from him like I did the djinn at sea. You see, I've already killed one of his kind."

Wu continued to laugh. "My…pocket…" Wu struggled to express as he continued laughing. He was forced to repeat what he said for Pelin when the pirate put his ears close to Wu's lips. "My…pocket…"

Pelin commanded Sencer to check the pockets on Wu's pants and jacket. Sencer removed a vial of purple liquid from Wu's left pocket, filled to its corked brim. The lieutenant was completely perplexed. He showed the vial to his Captain. Pelin held out his hand and Sencer tossed the vial to him. Pelin opened the vial and sniffed the contents. The corsair broke out into another fit of laughter. He corked the vial again and placed it on the table.

"No wonder you were so calm, Wu," Pelin said in a congratulatory voice. "You might have been able to stall me with that for the next three weeks. I wouldn't have even questioned this liquid's fabrication if these circumstances hadn't come about." Pelin winked at Wu. "You're good." The Captain got to his feet and called Ulucan and Sencer to his side. He whispered, "Sencer, take Wu to the town port and drop him off. I know Naku is there. Afterward, I want you to gather the men stationed there and bring them here."

"Yes, Master," said the lieutenant.

"Ulucan," Pelin called, "come with me. We will commission a ship from these bumbling politicians, and we will all meet on Daath Island."

"Yes, Master," Ulucan addressed.

Pelin smiled at Wu and told him, "It's time for you to deliver a message."

Pelin walked inside the café with Ulucan at his side. His lieutenant carried a long, wooden case. The café was bare of customers, save Ferran and Furio. The two apprentice politicians sat at the center table, drinks in front of them. Ona was at the bar watching carefully. Pelin continued forward. His lieutenant slapped the case on the table, just missing the drinks placed in front of the two young men. Ulucan opened the case to reveal an elaborately designed spear. Furio knew immediately what he was looking at. His mouth dropped and his eyes looked up at Pelin.

"Is that…?"

"The Spear of Onuris," Pelin said closing the case. "And this is no replica. It is the actual ancient artifact." Pelin closed the case and took a seat. Ulucan stood watch beside him. The Captain spoke in a low voice. "It's been used appropriately."

Furio stiffened his excitement. He smiled and then laughed. "Oh, come on. You almost had me."

"What's going on here?" Ferran asked.

Furio leaned back and explained, "The Spear of Onuris is legendary for having the ability to slay spirits. Most of all, it has the ability to kill a djinn."

Ferran's interest rose, much like the eyebrow he aimed toward Pelin. "You've slain a spirit?"

"A djinn," Pelin specified. "A djinn that was no different than the one who ravaged your prison. The very djinn your friend Naku has transformed into."

"What?" Furio said with complete skepticism.

Pelin shook his head and sighed. "I knew you were a fraud, spiritualist," Pelin said keeping his voice low. "You don't know or believe true spirituality. You don't understand that which transcends what you define as reality. How very European of you." The pirate placed a hand on the wooden case. "You feign to be civil, Furio, much like the rest of your kind. Truthfully, what burns inside you is a tumultuous fire waiting to engulf everything the world has to offer."

"I am a civilized man," Furio protested.

Pelin smiled coolly. "Of course you are. You have been made civil through the taste of Moorish women and the most excellent ability to imitate the Moorish man." The Captain tapped the wooden case with his fingers. "I'm a Turk of mixed blood, mostly European myself. But, I fall somewhere between your kind and Ferran's. But because of what I have seen, I lean a little more toward Ferran's blood. I have studied all the occult knowledge left behind by the Moors," and he concluded while looking at Ferran, "and your father taught me more than any book could translate. He was a true Master."

Ferran's hand casually went to his hip, where his dagger lay. He readied his hand for Pelin's order to take Furio's life. His hand trembled with anticipation. But the order was never given.

"Imagine Tunis ruled by two men of distinct bloodlines, and a third who can sway those who fall in the middle," Pelin suggested. "We could settle old grievances that tend to tear the sub-urban areas apart. And once we capture this djinn, we would have the power to rule outside nations and states of the world."

"Capture the power...?" Furio questioned.

Pelin reached down and unhooked a pouch from his belt. He opened the pouch and removed an hourglass-shaped bottle. He placed it on top of the wooden case. "We capture the djinn in this bottle. Once it is blessed by the full moon and re-opened, the djinn will serve us and all our wishes."

Neither man resisted Pelin's offer, a promise too real to ignore or dismiss. Pelin had both young men far more than just intrigued. They were now a part of his new hunt for the djinn.

"How will we get Naku here?" Furio asked.

Pelin put the bottle back into his pouch, tied the end, and wrapped it back around his belt. "We will bait him to Daath Island."

"How," Furio continued to inquire.

Pelin beamed a devious smile. His eyes centered on Ona. "Naku doesn't much like the people of this area, but when he finds one he cares about, he cares so deeply. So why not let us take his favorite?"

Furio turned around and looked at Ona.

Ferran turned his head toward the woman.

Ona became extremely uncomfortable.

Sencer tossed Wu from the mount. The young man's body slapped against the dusty road hard. He used his shoulders to balance himself, trying to stand. Sencer turned his mount around and sneered at Wu, "Tell your friend that the woman he loves dies unless he meets Captain Pelin here." Sencer tossed down a parchment etched with directions to find Daath Island. "Good day artist." Sencer left swiftly, a trail of dust and sand kicked up behind him. He was off to gather the rest of Pelin's crew who were stationed in the town port.

Wu coughed and spit up blood. His face was lacerated with scars; his hands were poorly bandaged, and his clothes were torn. He managed to stand up and swipe the map from the ground. He surveyed his surroundings. He was at the front end of a dock. This was the shipyard where Naku worked, he thought. Wu spied a housing complex and stumbled forward. Several men surrounded him quickly, including a stocky, Moorish dwarf.

"You okay friend," the black dwarf asked with a grunt. "You need a physician?"

Wu looked at him and bent down, the pain in his hands suddenly attacked his stomach. He felt as if his body was on fire. "N-N-Naku…" Wu unintentionally spat blood as he spoke his friend's name.

"Naku ain't here, friend," the Moorish dwarf informed. "He left two days ago. He went home to Tunis. That should not be your concern, though. You need a physician to look at those wounds, get some proper bandaging."

"Tr-tr-trust me," Wu huffed, "he's here. I need to see him."

The dwarf looked at the others and commanded, "Go look for Naku in his quarters. Now!"

The men ran into the housing complex. They winded their way through the first corridor until they came across Naku's apartment. The door was closed, but there seemed to be conversation going on beyond the barrier. The men knocked. Sesen opened the door not too long after. She was still in her nightgown. Seeing Sesen in Naku's room intrigued the men, especially as she was clothed in her night robes.

"Naku," said one of the men. "You're back?"

Naku stood up. "Yes. Yes I am. I came in last night."

"A friend of yours, an Asian fellow, he's here," the man reported.

Naku moved Sesen aside and stood in the doorway. "Wu?"

"We don't know his name," the other admitted. "But he's been beaten, nearly to death. He's struggling—"

Naku raced past his fellow workers, charging out of the complex. Sesen was close behind him. Naku slammed through the doors and saw Arihman standing over his friend. Wu was slumped, bleeding. Naku skidded along the ground and bent down to help his friend. He saw Wu's bandaged hands caked with dried blood. "Wu, did Captain Pelin do this?"

"You better believe," Wu snickered. "The bastard knows how to use a knife."

"Captain Pelin did this?" Arihman interrogated angrily. He grit his teeth and a fiery rage began to bubble inside him.

"Sir, let's just get him to my room." Naku scooped Wu into a cradled embrace with ease. He turned to walk back toward the housing complex.

"My hero," Wu joked.

Naku ran into the complex, making his way to his room. Sesen and Arihman followed close. Naku carefully put his friend on the bed. He looked at Wu's hands again. They seemed damaged beyond repair.

"I'm going back to kill him," Naku said, tears watering his eyes.

"No," said Wu.

"Look what he's done to you!"

"I just mean it's not that easy," Wu said struggling with his words.

"Why?" Naku hollered.

"He has Ona," Wu informed in a drowsy manner. "He wants you to meet him." Wu wearily searched for the parchment. Every move made his entire body ache, but he needed that map. "Where's the map? Where's the parchment?"

Arihman presented the map to Naku. The young man took the parchment and looked it over. "Daath Island," he questioned.

"You're not going anywhere," Arihman commanded. "Especially not after a pirate."

"I can handle this, trust me," Naku said confidently. His confident tone was backed up by the look on his face. Arihman never saw the young man so firm.

"I can vouch for him, uncle," Sesen added much to Arihman's surprise.

The elder swept his eyes to each person in the room, a look of complete and utter disbelief scribbled onto his visage. "Have you all gone crazy? This is a bloodthirsty pirate! He's as deadly as Barbarosa!"

Naku just ignored Arihman and asked Wu, "How much time do I have?"

"They want you to come tonight," Wu groaned.

"That gives me little time to exercise," he said to himself. He looked at his hands and stated, "All this power. I wish I had more time to master it."

Wu groaned, "I just wish I had my hands back."

Naku immediately reached out his hand, as if his appendage had a life of its own. He grabbed Wu's hands and stated, "Your wish is my command." A brilliant light covered Wu's body. It mended his flesh and healed his scars. The blood on his face dissipated, his face became smooth again. Even the fabric of his clothes mended back together, stitched as fine as the day he bought them. Wu rubbed his hands, a sly smile popped onto his healed face.

"I wish I had a million gold coins," Wu said with a raised eyebrow.

Naku countered his friend's smile. "Don't push your luck," he told him. He turned around and looked at Arihman. "This is all very hard to explain, but—"

"It's not hard to explain," Wu interrupted. "I gave Naku a tattoo, inked with the blood of a djinn. This, of course, bestowed him with the power of the djinn spirit." Arihman's confusion was evident by his expression.

"Thank you," Naku said sarcastically to Wu. He turned to Arihman and concluded, "The problem was that Captain Pelin wanted himself to be sketched with the blood, to give himself power. A night of drunken mishaps put the tattoo on me."

"And now he wants to kill you?" Arihman deduced.

Naku snapped his fingers and exclaimed, "Exactly!"

"You've had quite a birthday," said the dwarf. The ex-soldier folded his arms. "I don't care what kind of power you have, you won't be going to face him alone."

"You can't come," Naku insisted. Arihman gave the young man a stern look. "Your leg." Naku pointed out.

"I can have my One-Twenty back you up," Arihman announced.

Ahriman was too persistent for Naku to resist. "Okay," he capitulated. "Have your crew stay off the shore. Let them be prepared to help Lady Ona. I don't want Pelin to hurt her because he feels overwhelmed and threatened by an army."

Wu stood up in the bed and suggested, "Have you even thought this a trap? Pelin killed one djinn already."

"Whatever happens, happens," Naku said. "My main concern is to get Ona out of there."

"And if he gets your blood and your power," Wu continued.

"You still have some of the djinn's blood left," asked Naku. "Give everyone in this room a tattoo, and take him down."

Wu pulled up his pant leg and revealed, strapped to his leg, the vial with the remaining contents of the djinn's blood. It was sheathed like a dagger. He tossed it up to Naku who handed it to Sesen. "Guard it well, Sesen," Naku commanded. Her name spoken from Naku's lips ran through her like a cool breeze. He kissed her forehead and then told her, "Stay far away from this situation. I don't want to choose who to catch."

"What," she asked confused.

"Just keep the vial safe," Naku said, deciding not to explain his thoughts and dreams. "I'm going to exercise."

Arihman followed Naku out of the room. "I'll go round up some friends."

Wu jumped from the bed and started after Naku. "I have to see this!"

Sesen stayed behind, waiting for the others to disappear from the complex. Her hand gripped the vial firmly. She had her own plans for the Blood of Osiris. She peeked outside the door and looked down the hall, both ways. The coast was clear. She quickly made her way back to her room where she took out the gown purchased for her dinner with Naku. It was long, sleek and green with golden embroidery. She uncorked the bottle and poured the contents over the gown.

A magical cloud of smoke billowed from the dress as the blood seeped into the seams. The fabric was redesigned in color and shape. The stomach of the gown broke away, making two separate pieces of clothing. The sleeves disintegrated to the shoulder. The fabric's color turned into the black, smoky background of the night sky. Colors dotted the new outfit to make it look like a constellation of stars resided in the skirt and top. Everyone had a back up plan to ensure Naku's safety. This was Sesen's.

At that same moment, Naku and Wu laughed about their circumstances while outside near the docks. "It's odd that you can keep such a sense of humor in the face of death," Naku said to Wu.

"El-Ras is wearing off on me," he replied rubbing his hands together, impressed with the mending of his wounds. "Besides, I was never that worried, even when my hands were being used as knife holders. By the way, thank you for healing me." He looked at his friend and asked, "What else can you do?"

"I can turn into the very creature you etched onto my back. But I don't have the wings," he whined. Naku pointed to the sky. "I've flown beyond the Earth and seen creatures like myself floating in the heavens."

"My goodness," said Wu.

Naku waved the comment away with a hand. "It's not that impressive. They spoke in mathematics and music. It was their language. I was beginning to understand it instinctively, when suddenly I was forced back to Earth."

"And you feel that's not impressive," Wu said narrowing his eyes at Naku.

Naku chuckled. "Well, I also have a danger sense like Anansi, the Spider Man."

"I always loved his adventures," said Wu. "Him swinging from village to village, tricking his enemies with speed and skill."

Naku thought about the sentiment. "That's what I'm gonna have to learn to do if I'm to get Ona to safety." He looked around. Arihman dismissed everyone home for the day to give Naku privacy. The sun was beginning to sink below the horizon. It had been quite a holiday. He looked at Wu with a smile, eyes blazing gold. "Watch this," he declared.

Naku's body ignited into the blazing, smokeless, purple fire of the djinn spirit. His legs wrapped together and became a tendril of energy as he launched himself into the air. He flew out over the sea, a fire trail of speed. He was a cosmic arrow shooting straight out into the horizon. He circled around, heading back to where he had left Wu. His eyes became like spyglasses as his vision focused on the distant scene of Sesen taking Wu's side. She was now dressed in her work clothes and spectacles. He stopped in front of his friends and announced, "I guess I can see far away." His voice echoed and boomed with the might of his newfound powers.

Naku-Djinn started flying circles around his two friends. He stopped and hovered next to Sesen who looked at him the way he always wished a woman would. He reached out a hand to her.

"May I have this dance," he asked her.

The woman smiled, biting her lower lip. "Certainly, showoff." Sesen reached her hand out and cupped Naku-Djinn's. It felt like she was touching warm water. He scooped her up and cradled her close, taking to the sky with a mild speed. Sesen looked down and then back to Naku-Djinn. "Do you think you can be spotted? It's still daylight."

"I think I'm pushing out an aura that keeps me from being seen," he informed. He lifted his shoulders and rolled his golden eyes. "But who knows." He slowly descended and let Sesen down gently. Arihman joined Wu's side. The Moorish dwarf was armed with a sword. What transpired next tested Naku-Djinn's danger sense. Arihman attacked with thrusts that came like lightning. Naku-Djinn was impressed with the old man's speed, considering his leg.

"How's your father?" Arihman asked to distract the specter in front of him.

It was to no avail. Not only did Naku-Djinn dodge the attack but he answered the question as well. "Both he and my mother are doing fine. My father is teaching math courses at a local school." He thrust Arihman to the ground, not too rough, with a blast of magic. He floated over to the dwarf and laid a hand on his leg to heal it.

Arihman dodged out of the way. "No need, Naku. No need." He got up limping, dusting himself off. "Need to keep my war scars. They're trophies."

"As you wish," Naku-Djinn replied transforming to his natural self.

Arihman limped over to Naku. "Come nightfall, you'll have backup. But there will be no sudden moves," Arihman assured. The ex-soldier backed away. "Let me form a tighter plan with these soldiers before they're off. Wu, I want you to draw a copy of the map."

"Yes, sir," Wu addressed politely. He and Arihman walked away, leaving Sesen and Naku to themselves.

Naku grabbed the woman's hand and brought her to the end of the dock. The two sat down and were silent for a while. Naku put his arm around Sesen's shoulder and drew her close. She leaned her head against him. "After all this is over, we'll have that dinner," he promised.

Sesen chuckled and kissed Naku on the cheek. He turned to her and reached for her lips with his. When their lips touched, Naku knew that all of his power could not contend with the power of Sesen's kiss. Naku wished he could freeze time and stay in the warmth of Sesen's power.

All three villains had their plans. Each one reveled in the sheer genius of double-crossing the other. The power to exclusively re-create reality from a simple wish was too tempting to remain loyal. Ferran's main objective was to betray Furio; Pelin had tempted him with the offer just an hour ago. He told the Moor the days of the 'civilized savages of Europe' would never come. Pelin renounced his *'mostly European blood'* and promised Ferran a reunion with his father. Ferran shook on the deal, making a silent oath to slay Pelin the minute his father was free. But Ferran was dealing with a professional brigand with plans of his own.

Pelin's deceptive, silk tongue also tickled Furio's ear. He told the young political apprentice that the days of the Moors were over. He informed him that the Portuguese, at the command of the Vatican, were enslaving the Moors and shipping them to the New World. The Arabs had already begun conquering Moorish clans and nations by stealing their noble women, impregnating them, which led to mixed-blood heirs. Small communities of other Africans were being cut off from their urban centers, which were already becoming overrun with foreign invaders. Fine and noble garments were being exchanged for chains. Temples were being raided, the contents shipped back to Rome. The systematic removal of the African was beginning.

The proposal hooked Furio, but not enough to trust Pelin. He quickly went to do his own reading on the subjects of djinn, their capture, and the ability to kill them. The occult book was fascinating to Furio. The passage that caught his eye centered on how to catch a djinn off guard. The section spoke of how to render djinn helpless. The book stated that djinn must witness a horrible act. Furio thought if there was anything worse than betrayal.

He realized there just might be.

Naku was gone. Arihman's One-Twenty was beginning to ship out, keeping a distance behind the Naku-Djinn. Arihman briefed the One-Twenty on their fight ahead. He described it as spiritual, which only excited the One-Twenty Moors. When Naku-Djinn disappeared over the horizon, many bragged they had seen a spirit like that before. This spiritual fight for the One-Twenty would be nothing new. They took the replica map drawn by Wu, and readied the ship for leave. The crew's ship of choice was much like Captain Pelin's. It was a modified War Galleon, built for speed.

Inside the housing complex, Sesen slipped into the clothes newly fashioned by the last of the djinn's blood. As soon as the last piece of her garment was thrown around her, a shimmering field of energy covered her. She felt the cosmic pattern swirling on her garments form into a liquid, and then bleed into her flesh. It fluxed through her like snakes, traveling to her heart and turning the color of her flesh to a galactic pitch. It seemed like her skin turned into the night sky itself as a moving scene of stars and galaxies flowed all around her body. Her eyes turned purple and her hair was a wide crown of black matter and smoke.

Sesen was now a djinniyeh, a feminine form of djinn. She stretched out her arms and hovered above the ground, head back and legs together. With a single thought she disappeared into a cloud of black matter. In an instant, she was standing on the roof of the housing complex. She bent to her knees, though she was as black as the night around her. Sesen stayed low and eyed the War Galleon moving quickly away from the docks and heading toward the horizon. Her purple eyes shimmered intensely. Equipped with a higher form of vision, Sesen peered through the wooden panels of the ship and straight through the hull. Sesen concentrated, and in another blink of an eye, she was gone from sight, leaving behind black matter dust clouds to settle magically on the roof, and then evaporate.

Sesen reappeared behind several boxes of cargo in the hold of the One-Twenty's ship. She exhaled and instantly turned back into her natural form. Her clothes were nothing like the ones she slipped on. She wore a purple skirt, flowing to her sandal dressed feet. The top matched the color of the bottom. She had long sleeves and her stomach showed. She ducked behind the boxes and placed herself in a lotus position, legs folded. She threw herself into deep concentration. The picture of the entire ship flashed into her mind. She could see everything, the crew and where they were heading.

This was how Sesen was going to keep her watch on the situation. And then, a feeling of closeness to Naku came to her. She could feel him, as if he was the blood in her veins. And then she understood. The same blood connected them. She and Naku were as one. The young woman bit her lip sensuously as she wondered what power would come from kissing Naku as his equal.

She wished to find out.

The palace built on Daath Island was a magnificent spectacle. It had not been occupied since the days of antiquity. Pelin stepped inside the throne room. He was disinterested in the make of the palace's main quarters. It was no different than any other throne room in all the palaces he had seen. What was impressive was that for the palace's age, it seemed remarkably contemporary to the modern make of a castle.

What managed to capture Pelin's interest was a large stone pedestal in the center of the room. Above the pedestal, carved into the ceiling, was an opening to the night sky. Slowly positioning itself above the pedestal was the full moon, its light creeping in from above. Pelin placed the magical hourglass-shaped bottle onto the round, stone stand. He backed away and smiled. Behind him entered Sencer and Ulucan. Pelin turned to meet them. The two men bowed.

"Where is the spear," the Captain asked.

"Hidden outside the room," Sencer answered.

"Good," Pelin complimented. "Be ready. We'll need it."

"Yes, sir," replied both his lieutenants.

Furio entered the room. He walked hand-in-hand with Ona. A large smile was on his face. He bowed toward Pelin and said in a proud manner, "I'd like for you to meet Ona Ramu."

"We've met," Pelin said, holding back his annoyance at Furio.

"But you didn't meet her as my fiancée," Furio announced.

Pelin let out a haughty laugh. He reached out toward Furio and kissed both his cheeks. He did the same to Ona's hand. "May your future be bright," he said to them. He lightened his excitement and took Furio aside. "Putting your seed in this ancient treasure."

Furio chuckled. "It took some convincing. But even if she reneges, I'll make it my first wish."

Ferran charged into the throne room, his sword drawn and an anxious look on his face. He was out of breath, but with a message. Furio and Pelin backed away from one another and waited for what Ferran had to say. "Ready yourselves," said the Moorish brute. "Something glimmers on the horizon."

"Sencer," Pelin called. "Ready the crew."

With that as his command, the lieutenant was off. Ferran closed the door behind him and barred it shut. He backed up to the others and they all just waited. Ona was oblivious to what was happening. Her heart quickened and she begged Furio to be set free. He held her arm, tightly, and kept her in place. "Stay here, little girl," Furio said, looking at her with a loving smile. "Tonight you will witness my power, and I will use it to make you the queen no one else can."

Ona froze with fear. The look in Furio's eyes was blank, gone of sense and understanding. His smile was ominous, child-like, and void of control. His lips quivered as he turned back to the door.

Everything was quiet.

Except...

Men screamed in the distance. Something slammed against the palace walls, and the interior shook and cracked. Someone was shouting the order to retreat, and there were screams like none except Pelin and his two lieutenants had heard before. Furio backed up behind Ona and removed a shortsword. Pelin unsheathed his longsword while Ulucan and Sencer did the same.

And then it became quiet again.

The pirates took a fighting stance, and no chances. The door blew open with the scream and billow of a magnificent wind. Everyone in the room almost lost their footing. Naku-Djinn stood before them as the wind died. Ona hid herself, turning around and wrapping her arms around Furio.

"Let her go," Naku-Djinn screamed in a voice that could deafen the thunders.

Pelin snickered, "How impressive, the boy has confidence."

"Ona, these men are dangerous," Naku-Djinn said to her in a softer voice.

Ona was lost inside her fear. She gripped Furio tighter, staying close to the corsairs and piratic politicians because they seemed to be the most human in the situation. Furio shielded her from the sight of the djinn.

Pelin stepped to the side. He aimed his sword forward. "My boy, you might have become God for a day, but I've been killing your kind for the last six years."

Naku-Djinn trembled as he hesitated. He wanted to strike Furio and Ferran most of all. But the sight of Ona clutching to Furio was overwhelming. She was terrified of Naku-Djinn, and he had no way of proving to her that she was in extreme danger, not from him, but from who she clung to. And then danger struck. With Ona's back turned to the djinn, Furio put his blade close to the back of her neck, his eyes on Naku-Djinn. He smiled as he made a gesture to end Ona's life if Naku-Djinn stepped further. Pelin saw Furio's gambit and smiled. The pirate looked back to the djinn and told him, "If you make one move toward us, we will end your world."

Naku-Djinn grimaced, his fists blazing with power.

"Show a hint of your power, Naku," Ferran added, "and the same will happen."

The name resonated a feeling inside Ona. It was another source of familiarity, a connection to her past. And Ferran had just called this monstrous spirit by the name of that particular childhood acquaintance. Pelin referred to the specter as a 'boy' who had become a god. He actually used the word 'god' and not 'demon' to describe the creature. She turned around and saw Naku's face somewhere behind the djinn's visage. Her fear dissipated into perplexity.

"N-N-Naku...?"

Furio reached around Ona and cupped her mouth. He pulled her back and slammed his short sword through her stomach. Naku-Djinn arched his back and screamed, gurgling up a blast of fire that shot through the opening of the ceiling and exploded into the air. The flare alarmed the One-Twenty pirates. The Moorish Captain ordered, "Tear that place apart!" The ship caught the winds and made a final approach to the island's shore.

Inside the throne room, Naku-Djinn was frozen in place. His mouth was agape, his golden eyes sparkling wide with horror. Pelin walked over to the hourglass-shaped bottle and opened the cork. Naku-Djinn's smokeless, fiery physique was caught by a vacuum and pulled inside the bottle's body. When all of Naku-Djinn's essence was trapped inside, Pelin sealed the top and placed the bottle back onto the stone pedestal.

The Turkish pirate looked over at Furio with a smile. "You are heartless."

"Don't be a fool," Furio said kneeling down and wiping a hand over Ona's dead body. "When we have the djinn in our service, I will wish her to life again."

Pelin winked. "A marvelous plan. Just make sure she forgets all that happened."

Furio bowed at the neck.

"How long do we have to wait?" Ferran huffed.

Pelin looked through the skylight and answered, "Thirty-three and a third seconds after the light of the full moon hits the bottle." He surveyed his crew. "The moon is almost in range." The captain walked over to Sencer and ordered, "We'll need to show the djinn the spear so that he knows who's in charge. He will serve us all," he told the other two. "Therefore he will not be able to make a wish that betrays the three of us."

But each of them had plans to get past that particular failsafe.

At that moment, a wide cylinder of the moon's light covered the hourglass bottle. The men in the room turned to gaze at the sight. They were in awe, captivated. Sencer was slowly backing out of the room when an unexpected cannon blast struck the palace exterior. Pelin looked around as perplexed as the others. A Turkish member of Pelin's crew rushed into the throne room and announced, "A ship attacks us. A War Galleon."

"Just hold them off," Pelin commanded with ease. He deduced that the vessel possessed reinforcements for Naku. "We'll wish them away in a moment."

The soldier turned to run but stopped abruptly. In his path was a beautiful Moorish woman draped in purple garments. The soldier took a step back. "Captain Pelin," he called.

The Captain turned around and recognized Sesen. "I didn't think you'd be leading this assault," the pirate quipped. "So very brave of you, princess. I don't know how you got here, but you'll regret your decision to come. Subdue her."

Sesen said not a word. She displayed her newfound powers and transformed into the djinniyeh, a swirl of black matter accompanying the marvelous transformation.

Captain Pelin's eyes widened at the sight of the magnificent, feminine form of Sesen-Djinniyeh. Her sight was stunning. She was the first djinniyeh spirit he had ever encountered. Up to now, he had only dealt with male djinn. Not only did Sesen-Djinniyeh temporarily remove the Captain of his breath, but he also figured there must have been blood unused by Naku.

Pelin quickly ordered his soldier to warn the others. The soldier proceeded forward but was caught by the djinniyeh, his neck in her hand. She flew up, a thin tail of smokeless fire trailing beneath her. She tossed the soldier into the wall, the impact breaking his neck and spine. Pelin backed up and slapped Sencer on the shoulder. The lieutenant took the moment to dart past Sesen-Djinniyeh and head out of the throne room to secure the Spear of Onuris as an advantage against the feminine spirit.

Sesen-Djinniyeh ignored Sencer's escape. She whipped her tail around and knocked the bottle from off the pedestal. Ulucan jumped back and caught the narrow mouthed jar before it shattered against the floor. Pelin cursed. He knew the ritual would have to be reset. He screamed for Ulucan to place the bottle back upon the pedestal to restart the entire event. Sesen-Djinniyeh flew down to stop Ulucan. She could feel Naku-Djinn's essence inside the bottle, and the urge to free her other half rushed through her like adrenaline. Pelin jumped up and caught Sesen-Djinniyeh. He dug his feet into the ground, bracing himself against the spirit's strength.

"I've swallowed a drop of your blood," the pirate sneered, losing breath as he battled Sesen-Djinniyeh's might. "I can match you with both speed and str-str-str-strength…"

Sesen-Djinniyeh disappeared, causing Pelin to slam against the floor, face first. She reappeared in front of Ferran and slammed her fist into the giant's jaw. Ferran was lifted off his feet. He crashed against the floor with a heavy thud. Pelin attacked her from behind. The Turkish corsair wrapped his arms around the female spirit and gripped her tight. Sesen-Djinniyeh reached over her shoulder and tossed Pelin's body onto Ferran. She readied herself to make a final charge that would crush both persons.

"This way," a voice called to her.

Sesen-Djinniyeh turned her head and noticed Furio waving his bloody short sword. She reached out a hand and lifted him by the use of a magical force. Through the invisible grip, Sesen-Djinniyeh could feel Furio's neck on the tip of her fingers. She wished to squeeze it and empty the breath and life of the young villain. Furio tried desperately to grab the invisible and intangible force that choked him. But his fingers fiddled around his neck without any impact, save his own skin.

"Pelin," another cried. It was Sencer. In his hands was the Spear of Onuris. He tossed it to his Master and Captain who jumped from the giant Moor to catch the spear in his grip.

Sesen-Djinniyeh loosened her magical grip on Furio as Pelin charged at her. She dodged quickly, the tip of the spear missing her by inches. Pelin planted one leg forward and swung around, slamming the butt of the spear into Sesen-Djinniyeh's stomach. Lightning erupted and cackled with the spear's impact on the djinniyeh. Sesen-Djinniyeh rolled onto the floor, her body shimmering between her human and spirit form. She reached out a hand and used her power to force the bottle from off the pedestal. Sencer dove to the floor and cradled the bottle before impact.

Sesen-Djinniyeh took a peek behind her, her danger sense warning her of Pelin's attack. She wrapped her tendril around his legs and swept him up and off his feet. The pirate lost his grip on the spear. The weapon soared through the air and lodged itself into Furio's shoulder. He dropped his sword and screamed!

Pelin, lying on his back, kicked up and landed back on his feet. He turned quickly and removed the spear from Furio's shoulder, kicking the young man from off the end of the weapon. Pelin turned around and ordered, "Restart the ritual, Sencer!"

Sencer got to his feet and ran toward the pedestal. Sesen-Djinniyeh hovered upright and fired a dark force at the stone base and shattered it. She fired another blast into Sencer's stomach, knocking the pirate over. The bottle dropped from his hands and shattered. A gust of wind escaped the opened bottle, dust and debris kicking up from nowhere.

Pelin cursed! He charged the female specter. Sesen-Djinniyeh turned at the last moment and caught the spear with her hands, the tip just inches away from her stomach. The weapon seemed to increase Pelin's strength. He edged her back toward the wall. Sesen-Djinniyeh transformed her tail back into her legs, and balanced herself on the stable floor. But Pelin kept pushing until she could go no further, the wall at her back. The spear began to slip through her grip, and Pelin's strength increased. He was determined to slip the weapon through her stomach.

Sesen-Djinniyeh stepped to the side and allowed the spear to pierce the wall behind her. She spun around and slammed her fist into Pelin's face. He buckled but recovered quickly, retaliating with a fist into Sesen-Djinniyeh's jaw. She toppled to the floor. Pelin laughed, the wind around the room dying. He removed the spear from the wall and said, "I told you I have enough strength to handle the likes of you."

It was then that a hand gripped his neck and squeezed, popping the final breaths from Pelin's throat. The last image his eyes gazed upon was the smokeless, black and purple fiery sight of Naku-Djinn. The pirate fell dead. With lightning speed, Naku-Djinn gripped the spear and tossed it swiftly into Ferran's chest. The impact lifted the giant from off his feet and nailed him to the wall behind him. Caught in the same motion, Naku-Djinn transformed back to his human form and charged at Furio. He balled his right fist to strike, his eyes narrowed on Furio's charge. The tip of Furio's short sword glimmered like a star.

Though sloppy with his aim, because of his pierced and busted shoulder, Furio made a marvelous attempt to attack Naku with a fatal strike. But his thrust was aimed too high, and it passed just above Naku's shoulder. Naku winded his arm around and slammed his fist into Furio's windpipe with all his natural might. The blow cracked the young man's throat and killed him instantly. Furio dropped to the floor completely lifeless. Naku stood above him, panting, wide-eyed and filled with ten long years of rage. Sesen-Djinniyeh stood up and rushed to Naku's aid. She tossed her arms around him and held him close. A calming green aura washed over both of them. Naku's anger subsided.

Sencer and Ulucan jumped to thier feet and rushed from the throne room. Neither Naku nor Sesen-Djinniyeh cared. The pirates would meet their fate with the One-Twenty. The fight was over for them. Naku felt he could stay in Sesen-Djinniyeh's embrace forever. His eyes looked over at Ona's lifeless body and they began to water. Sesen-Djinniyeh spotted the woman as well.

Sesen-Djinniyeh loosened her embrace and flew over to Ona's body. She placed an open palm over her and swept it through the air. Ona revived. She remained unconscious, and her body disappeared in a brilliant blue light, returning to her bedroom in Tunis. "This will just be a dream to her," said Sesen-Djinniyeh. She then took to the air and flew out of the skylight. It was then that a thought occurred to Naku. He looked at Sesen-Djinniyeh's flight path and then voiced as he transformed into his djinn counter-flesh, "Waitaminute! Sesen, what the hell are you doing here?" Naku-Djinn soared through the skylight and followed Sesen-Djinniyeh back to the War Galleon. "And you're a djinniyeh."

The woman stopped her flight and hovered in the moonlight. Naku floated next to her. Their tails wrapped around one another and Sesen-Djinniyeh caressed the handsome, black djinn's face. As she touched him, the events that transpired without him swirled through his head. He saw it all. He saw Sesen take the blood and pour it over her gown. He saw her slip her newly fashioned garments on and the blood drain into her skin, turning her into the specter of soulful femininity that hovered before him now. He was completely excited. He touched his forehead to hers and sent, **There is so much to show you,** his voice echoed inside her head. **There are beings like us and places beyond this world that we can see, together.**

Naku-Djinn passed from his mind to Sesen-Djinniyeh's the image of the dark spirits, and the opening of space the spirits passed through. Sesen-Djinniyeh saw the Earth become miniscule and distant, and the universe awaiting their venturing spirits.

That's beautiful, she said back to him. **And I want to see the universe with you, and no one else.** She smiled slyly and added, "But for now, I just want to share a nice dinner with you."

Naku-Djinn laughed. He straightened his head and took the woman's arm. Together they flew back to the One-Twenty's ship. The corsairs were finished with Pelin's crew. It was time to return home and enjoy the Earth through new eyes, before carrying on beyond its atmosphere. They landed gently onto the deck of the War Galleon, transforming back into their human appearances. The Captain patted Naku on the shoulder and expressed, "I see you found the girl."

Naku nodded and replied, "I sure did." He kissed Sesen. A wondrous feeling ran through both of them. It was as if they had taken flight with their powers. As the kiss ended Naku stated, "I wish to travel the stars with you."

"And I wish for a nice, simple dinner," Sesen replied.

The two of them simultaneously sent, exchanging thoughts, **_Your wish, is my command._**

3 Cigs United

His eyes were glued to the extinguished cigarettes in the ashtray. The sight of the two snuffed cigarettes reminded Jackson that he liked to smoke. He reached into his suit jacket and pulled out a pack of cigarettes. It was almost empty, down to two smokes. Jackson removed one, placed it between his lips and, with his lighter, lit the tip of his addiction. Taking a drag he looked around the bedroom. He removed his black fedora and set it next to the ashtray. To the right of the ashtray was a rose. Jackson purchased the flower for the Queen of the Castle. He was waiting for her to return home.

Jackson removed the cigarette from his lips and then lifted the flower. He inhaled, holding the rose extremely close to his nose. His eyes were shut and he reveled in the simple thought of the deed following the Queen's return.

He smiled.

Jackson inhaled the rose's aroma as if taking a drag from a cigarette. He set the flower back down, this time on the brim of his fedora. He looked in the mirror and fixed his tie. He put his cigarette in the ashtray and used both hands to straighten his suit. He pulled the collar of his suit jacket forward then stomped his right foot, impressed with himself. To him, he looked good. He was tall, black, and handsome.

Jackson's eyes caught the burning cigarette in the ashtray. He then had a thought. He smelled his coat. It was drenched in the fragrance of cigarettes. He paid it no mind. He still looked good. He reached inside his jacket and felt the real package he had for the Queen. It was there, intact. He was about to get his money's worth when the Queen returned.

Jackson's eyes went back to his burning cigarette. He then focused on the two smoked, shriveled butts sitting to either side. His cigarette, the third in the ashtray, burning, penetrated and separated the union the two butts shared before Jackson set his between them. He put his hands in his pockets and stood straight, staring at the ashtray. It reminded him of Virginia Patterson Hensley's song *Three Cigarettes in an Ashtray*. The song was written by Eddie Miller and W.S. Stevenson and sung by Hensley under the name she used as a performer. Patsy Cline. Cline was her first husband's last name. Gerald Cline. The song was released August 12th, 1957. Jackson was a music buff. He was a walking library of musical knowledge, from Classical to Hip Hop.

The song was sad, about betrayed love, and had a crescendo that matched a wail of tears. *That white woman sang her heart out,* Jackson thought to himself. It was at that moment that he heard the locks to the front door coming undone. *Speaking of white women, here's the Queen of the Castle.* Jackson took one last drag of his cigarette and then picked up the rose. He took his hat, and then sat on a chair facing the doorway.

At the front door was the 'Queen' herself. Her name was Kristen. She was dishwater-blonde, tall and slender; her physique was fit, not skinny. Like Jackson, she was dressed for business and returning from a hard day's work. She rushed into her house and shut the door. She was out of breath. She put her back against the door and slumped to the floor. She was exhausted from work and other mishaps of the day. Kristen reached into her purse and pulled free her comfort devices, a cigarette and a black lighter. She took a quick drag and exhaled smoke and words. "What a day," she groaned as she rubbed her forehead.

"Hello," she heard Jackson's voice.

"It's just me, baby," Kristen answered. She took another drag and then said through exhalation, "I didn't think you'd be here."

From the bedroom she heard Jackson say, "Well, I decided to leave the office early." His voice was higher in tone, trying to speak in a whimsical voice that soothed the woman who lay at the other end of the ranch-style house. He could tell she was tired. "I needed to get some work done with some quiet. My own house is a place for peace." He sat back in the chair fondling the rose between his fingers. He kept the flower at his nose.

Kristen wanted to stand, but she was frustrated, overwhelmed, and angry about her day's events. "Well, I have had a helluva day," she said while continuing to smoke. Finally, she stood up and stated, "I could've quit my job today." She took another drag. "Three of the departments are at war because of financial reports that came back." She took another drag and screamed, "I mean, it's nothing that devastating. We're too big of a company to have something drag us down, but we're responsible for the reports. We're the messenger. We get killed. People want to continue to be fucking drama queens. This is fucking usual for this time of year, goddmanit! But do people accept this fact and keep moving? No. They want to know why, and get all bent-the-fuck out of shape. But no one wants to figure anything out. No, of course not. They want to blame people. So, three departments are pointing their fingers at each other like guns." Kristen began jabbing her cigarette in three directions, *"It's your fault! It's your fault! It's your fault!"*

Back in the bedroom, Jackson just smiled. He chuckled lightly, imagining Kristen's antics exactly as they played out.

"And who's the middle-*woman* left to do all the detective work for three departments that don't want to cooperate worth shit?" She took a drag of her cigarette and then said each word as a sentence, "You. Fucking. Guessed. It. Me." Kristen shook her head. "And these assholes don't want to cooperate with me or each other. Each fucking department is trying to manipulate me to blame the other."

Kristen removed her shoes. Her feet exhaled. She reached down and rubbed them. "Oh, it feels good to be out of those fuckers," she said to herself. She stood up again and continued, "And you know what? Michael—who usually has my back—he's not doing shit! Oh, he's trying to be 'understanding'. More like pretending. That prick." Kristen went back to smoking.

"Is that right," Jackson questioned in a calm manner.

Kristen then said in a very low voice, "And to think I'm fucking this guy behind your back." She took another hard drag. Kristen started toward the bedroom so that she could meet her husband.

Jackson could hear her approach. Kristen continued to rant.

"But that's not the worst part of my day, baby," Kristen stated. "I almost got into a fucking accident."

"Are you hurt," Jackson asked.

"No. I avoided it," Kristen answered. "And to confess, I was in the wrong." She then explained, "My head was back at work. I was frustrated. I wasn't concentrating at all. But, this guy was going far too fast. And he was driving erratically. Definitely woke me up. I got a good look at him in his car. Sonavabitch! I just wasn't expecting him." She stepped closer to the bedroom. "I mean, out of no where some goddamned, *black-fucking-nigger* cuts me off in traffic!" Kristen stepped in her bedroom's doorway and spotted Jackson sitting in the chair.

He was a total stranger.

He was in her house.

He was a black man.

He was holding a rose.

A cigarette burned in an ashtray on her dresser.

This was not her husband. She was not surprised, frustration with the day's events keeping her calm. She stepped inside her room and yelled, "Who-the-fuck-are-you?"

Jackson answered. He removed the gun tucked inside a shoulder holster underneath his jacket. Kristen's arms dropped to her side; the cigarette left her fingers. It fell and fell and fell, hitting the ground the minute the first bullet hit her chest. The next three bullets threw Kristen back against the wall adjacent to the door.

Jackson holstered his gun. He stood and placed his hat atop his head. He took his cigarette and walked over to Kristen's lifeless body. He knelt down and spoke in his natural, deep voice, "Truth is, sweetheart, I'm the guy your husband hired to kill you for fucking another man behind his back." He took a drag of his cigarette and blew the smoke into her face. Kristen was wide eyed, an expression frozen in time. Jackson put the cigarette out on her cheek, placed the rose next to her body, and stood. Jackson put his hands in his pocket and added, "And I'm sorry about cutting you off in traffic. I was just trying to get here before you did, sweetheart."

The hitman stepped over Kristen's body. She stared, wide eyed but lifeless. Jackson's footsteps disappeared in the distance. The front door opened. The front door closed. Jackson was going to get his money from Kristen's husband. And then he would be off to the next job.

The Monk & The Moor

Jahiz, The Moor

Exhaustion weighed heavy on Jahiz. It teamed with all fifty years of his old life. He lay slumped over the neck of his mount, the horse continuing to trot through the forest unburdened by Jahiz's slouched condition, and without his hand to guide. The creature sauntered through the thick wooded area carrying its tired rider to a destination far off into the tree-clustered horizon. Fatigue added the weight of the world onto Jahiz. It dried his mouth and made him long for water.

His fever added hallucination.

When Jahiz possessed enough strength to open his eyes, he saw the trees as demons reaching for him with multiple, skinny arms. The sun became a dragon making ready a breath of fire to incinerate the weary Moor. His delirium was even worse when he shut his eyes to the environment.

His mind showed him the reality he had been through.

Cannon fire echoed in his head. The darkness swirling behind his eyelids gave way to the scene of a fortified city. Moorish soldiers, with swords drawn and at the ready, waited at the gates of the last Moorish stronghold. Granada. Soldiers scattered frantically to find something to bar the gates. Their efforts produced a secured wall, unable to be open or penetrated by outside forces. He could see himself, just seven months younger, speaking to a fellow Commander named Musa. Commander Musa was a brave and gallant knight. Of all the Commanders gathered, he was the oldest and most vocal. He was sixty. For ten years he held the boarders under Moorish rule and from the hands of the Europeans. His armor was the finest and almost as tough as his nerve and courage.

Commander Musa was so tough, so compacted of sterner-stuff, that just four hours after the barricade had been made to fortify the gate, he called for its removal. The Commander reminded the knights in his service of their duty, which was not to defend the city, but to hold off the invading army until much of its citizens made an escape. Once the barricade was removed, Commander Musa walked to the front of the army. Jahiz was centered with his commanding unit, four rows back from the front. He swore that if he were going to die it would be extremely fun. Commander Musa shouted an order for every soldier to be at the ready with sword, shield, and pistol. His next set of words raised the morale of his soldiers so high that he more than doubled the might of the army.

"It is time for us to prove that we are true to our ancestors and never despair as longs as we have strong arms and fleet horses wherewith to foray!" Jahiz and the other soldiers lifted their swords high and hollered into the air. *"Our bodies will bar the gates! Our swords will scratch the enemy! We have nothing to fight for but the ground we stand on. Without that, we are without home and country. If it be so written, may the Heavens be our next homeland!"*

The roar of the crowd seemed to push open the gate, and though the barricade dammed the soldiers like water, their spirits were not damned at all. The floodgate was opened! Moorish cavalry and Moorish infantry rushed forward like strong waves of water. Their battle cries sounded like songs to God. The Christian troops stood ready in the distance. They were first overwhelmed by the might of the black soldiers rushing them. Jahiz was there. He remembered that day. The sounds of popping fire-sticks, and the clanking of swords onto shields, armor, and against the wrath of another blade, polluted the ears of those far and wide. The smell of blood and the sound of screams flooded the senses.

With the setting of the sun came the setting of the story of the Moors Kingdom of Spain, al-Andalusia. Rallied though the original knights may have been, but the fervor and savage shield of the cross was forged for conquest. And it was not defeat that was written in blood, but the spreading of The Faith.

It was no less written with black, Moorish blood.

Explosions and cheers from the army of King Ferdinand and Queen Isabella rocked the Moorish city of Granada. Cries of retreat escaped from Moorish lips, as the innocent fled and the swarthy, black soldiers stood their ground to allow the others a chance to leave from the destruction. Cannons pounded and overwhelmed the Moorish soldiers. Christian Knights marched in, swinging and cutting. Buildings crumbled, their foundation rocked by heavy artillery fire. Jahiz and his fellow Moorish Knights gave valiant efforts against what they saw as Euro-Christian pirates.

But the sun was setting.

The last stand turned into surrender on the day and the year of the Christian calendar of November twenty-fifth, one thousand four-hundred and ninety-one. It was on that day that Moorish magistrates and King Boabdil, otherwise known as Abu Abdi-Llah, handed over Granada in writing to the Christian army. They signed a treaty for their lives in recognition of King Ferdinand and Queen Isabella as the rulers of Granada and all of Spain.

The word spread as far as Italy where the Pope declared November twenty-fifth to forever be a day of Thanksgiving for the defeat of the Black Kingdoms of Spain. But ever more devastating would be King Ferdinand and Queen Isabella's next discovery. Jahiz's mind tossed him back into the Spanish prison where he was held captive with other Moorish soldiers. When his mind envisioned the cold air of the cell, his body felt it. His mind also tapped the rhythms of voices into his ear. There were whispers of the discovery made by knights sent from the Vatican. They desecrated the libraries and found volumes of literature and maps on a land west of

Europe and Africa. It was across the great ocean. Any ship with sail could catch an air current off the coast of West Africa and find this land as a prize.

Though it would be hundreds of years before Milton penned his epic of *Paradise Lost*, it just might have been this moment in time, and not the Holy Bible, that was his inspiration. For a snake, in the most diabolical sense of the image, was about to enter the last known Edens on the Earth, and she would never be the same again.

Some of the volumes of literature were incomplete. They continued in volumes that were stored in the library of Timbuktu. But it was all the new rulers of the kingdom needed. What interested the European knights, called the Crown Knights, was the fable of the Seven Cities of Gold that resided in the new land. The Moors called the land Amexem, Amenta, and Antilia. It was there where the seven cities of gold resided with all their wealth. As the legend told, in 1150, after the Moors conquered Merida, Spain, a single Christian Bishop escaped. The story of the legend was re-invented, saying that seven Bishops escaped with either the knowledge of the seven cities of gold, or actually finding them. But the volumes of literature contained evidence that the Bishops did not exist, and that the single Bishop who fled Merida was taught the knowledge by an all-too trusting Moor.

Jahiz's mind rekindled the low conversations with the man in the cell next to his. He was a fellow Moor named Azamor. He was crafty, cunning, and had the will to survive and escape. *"They're all wrong in their calculations, these Vatican Crown Knights,"* he would laugh. *"If they wanted to know where the Seven Cities of Gold were located, they would have to consult with the descendant of the great Bodhidharma."* Azamor formed a plan to escape. He would need the help of Jahiz and a good deal of the imprisoned Moors. His plan included handing over the Seven Cities of Gold to the Crown Knights.

This was only to the belief of his captors.

Jahiz remembered being exhausted then, lying in that prison cell. He was malnourished and frustrated that he would die an imprisoned death rather than in the quick flash of battle. That was the preferred death for such a warrior. If Jahiz had to die outside of battle, he wanted it to happen in a bed while his wife and seventeen-year old son watched over him. He was old enough to die in battle; he was too young for a fate like prison. This was how Azamor's offer for freedom became his sustenance. Azamor needed a warrior for his plan. He needed someone who could find a family in a small urban center in Africa named Mbala. Jahiz was to search for the daughter of a blacksmith. Her name was Quyionah, a lovely songbird. Her family was waiting for a Moor who would come for her.

While Azamor concocted his scheme, many imprisoned Moorish families were put to the blade and the bullet. The Crown Knights searched for anyone who would navigate them to the new land and translate ancient coordinates to the Seven Cities of Gold. When the Moorish men refused to comply, their families' lives were used as leverage for them to speak. The men, their wives, and children all decided to die. It seemed like an insane commitment to an oath of silence.

It was then that Azamor spoke up, telling the guards he knew the location to the Seven Cities of Gold. The Crown Knights made haste to speak with him, and Azamor proposed to lead them to the Cities of Gold with a team of thirteen Moors. This team included Jahiz, who Azamor advised to act like a rebellious youth. It was hard for Jahiz, who was fifty years of age and a very disciplined soldier. Azamor told Jahiz he needed to look like a reluctant player. Azamor and Jahiz, along with twelve other Moors, were released from their cells. They were nourished and equipped. Sailors were summoned from around Europe so that one might be chosen to lead the expedition to what was being dubbed *The New World.*

The scenes of memory went black. From the dark waters of memory stepped forth the Italian Crown Knight General Jacopo Achille. He wore purple armor engraved with a black crown on the chest. A black cape flowed menacingly behind him, his brown hair caught in a gust of wind. His green eyes turned fiery red as he drew his sword from his sheath and stabbed the black floor of Jahiz's mind. Jahiz's body jerked on the horse, blood seeped from between his lips. Jacopo grimaced at Jahiz and eventually erupted into laughter. Jahiz was twenty years Jacopo's senior. The Italian Knight was young, cunning, and ruthless. It was this very ruthless energy that allowed Jacopo to surpass many elder knights in the ranks.

Beside Jacopo glided such an elder of the Crown Knights. His name was Damiano Cosmo the Lesser. He had a blonde mustache and beard. Short blonde hair was cropped atop his head. His brown eyes also burst into flames. Horses appeared underneath the two men. They charged forward, an army behind them, and suddenly they were on the sandy dunes of Africa. They charged toward the small city where Azamor had commanded Jahiz to flee. All the battles Jahiz had been through could not ready him for this mission. Even the last stand at Granada had not the same significance. The world and all that existed naturally was at stake.

Jahiz escaped one night with the help of Azamor. He took a small sloop, manned by four other Moors sprung from the prison. Jahiz and his small crew disappeared over the horizon. They landed in Africa a day later. They were quick to commission camels for the ride south. It was only three days travel, southeast. The five riders came upon a dusty old city with a scarce population. When Jahiz asked for the urban center's blacksmith, he was quickly taken to a man named Gebre. The African was not surprised to see the Moorsish troupe. In fact, he had been waiting for the moment for the last nineteen years of his daughter's life.

From the back of the smith's workshop came the melodic tone from the most perfect singing voice. Gebre closed the door, muffling the songstress in practice. Jahiz remembered the man's sad eyes. Gebre's voice sounded like the smith's hammer crashing against molten steel. He was rough, a tough breed. He reminded Jahiz of the soldiers he fought alongside. But the man was sad. Gebre confessed that his wife was gone, dead.

Jahiz swore he saw the woman's ghost fly by in his memory.

Gebre was a powerful looking man. He was massive. But all his strength was sapped with the death of his beloved. Jahiz knew what little strength he held onto was needed to hold him up for his daughter's departure. It all began when an old woman named Lerato trained Gebre's daughter. Lerato focused the younger woman's vocal skills to pull off the most intricate notes music, sound, and voice had to offer. She bestowed onto Gebre's daughter a song that when translated through an ancient language, and the character scripts were placed side-by-side on a particular sheet of paper, would draw a map to the descendant of Bodhidarhma. The only people who were said to possess the ancient script lived in China. The family was part of a lineage that prepared for this day for many generations. Their son or daughter was prepared for their duty as much as Gebre's daughter had been.

Jahiz saw himself float from the front room of the workshop and through the door to the backroom. There sat the blacksmith's daughter, Quyionah. She was the night sky wrapped and folded into the picture of perfected femininity. She sat, legs crossed, wearing a beautiful blue dress while setting her locked hair up into a wrap. Her voice resonated with the sounds of all that was natural, making her voice supernatural. Jahiz glided toward her, caught in her siren's call. Jahiz thought of his wife at the sight of Quyionah. He had not seen her in what seemed like forever. His wife escaped from al-Andalusia months before the fall of Granada. Quyionah reminded him of his wife in her youth. Jahiz promised Gebre he would protect his daughter as if she were his own.

Quyionah looked over at him, large amber eyes blazing. Jahiz pulled closer, drawn by her voice. It was then that a giant blade broke from the ground and separated Jahiz from Quyionah. The warrior jumped back and reached out with his hands. Quyionah stood up. Her melodic voice turned into a chilling scream! Jahiz reached around the giant blade to retrieve the woman, but a magical bolt of lightning jumped from off the sword and scratched him. Jahiz pulled his arm back, which in reality jerked and trembled. The reaction did not wake him from his fever-induced dream. He stayed inside his head, locked down. He could see and feel the foundation of the house rock and the roof start to crumble inward. Quyionah's voice hit a pitch so high it shattered the sword's blade. Jahiz grabbed the woman's arm and rushed her from the house. The two escaped on camel.

From the ground came the giant form of Jacopo laughing maniacally. Behind him was the army of Crown Knights. They charged toward Jahiz with a wide wave of fire trailing behind them. The wave's height was ominous. The fiery wave reached up and covered the sky. It crashed down onto the small city, incinerating every one of its inhabitants. Jahiz pushed his mount to top speed, Quyionah clutching his waist tightly. She turned her head and sang again to raise the sands as a counter wave to the fire. The sand storm dispersed the flames covering the city and even blinded the giant Jacopo. Quyionah sang again, this time into the sky where clouds formed and rained down arrows onto the attacking army. The giant Jacopo sank beneath the sands, angry and thwacked with arrows. His army fell, cut down. The songbird released another musical breath and a glowing black hole opened up in front of their path. When the camel went through, Jahiz and Quyionah were suddenly transported onto a boat that was crossing the Indian Ocean.

Truthfully, their escape was less dramatic than what the Moor's mind recalled. Jahiz and Quyionah left in the middle of the night when Mbalian spies spotted a faction of Crown Knights approaching on the horizon. Jahiz's guards decided to stay behind. It then became apparent to Jahiz as to the composition of the small city's population. Warriors. The event also revealed Gebre's job as a smith. He made weapons. The small city was ready to hold off the knights long enough for Jahiz and Quyionah to make their escape. It was no different than the last battle of Granada. Jahiz just switched roles from defender to fleer.

The warrior's mind then remembered the next weeks of travel being peaceful, without pursuit or threat. All that was ahead of him and Quyionah was their quest's end. Jahiz took comfort in the variations of the black and brown shades of people he saw in his travels. They reminded him of the finer days of al-Andalusia. However, most were angry at his Moorish garb, and many accused him of being a part of a people that put the world on a course of destruction. Jahiz met with disdain almost everywhere they went. Despite the jeers, it was far more peaceful than where he had come from.

Jahiz thought of Quyionah so much as the daughter he never had. They grew close, she seeing Jahiz as a second father. Jahiz talked to Quyionah about his son. He told the young woman that his son was around her age. He and Jahiz's wife fled al-Andalusia several months before its fall. Jahiz believed his family was in Mauritania. He hoped that wherever his son was he was pursuing his dream to study medicine. Jahiz told Quyionah that he did not want his son to become a soldier in any army, but his son insisted on learning to use a blade, coupled with minor skills of hand-to-hand combat. Jahiz said his son was a sportsman, and he was as much a participant as he was an observer.

Once in China, Jahiz learned that Quyionah spoke the language fluently. She became a guide and managed to commission a caravan to take them north. Once again, he was met with disdain. But he paid it no mind. When asked where they were en route to, Quyionah would answer cryptically. They searched for the *sun's way*, she said.

The caravan traveled for three days northeast when Crown Knights led by Jacopo and Damiano attacked them. Quyionah formulated a plan quickly. She needed Jahiz to escape. He fought the knights valiantly but was commanded to flee and search for the monk named Rah-Mun-Do.

Jahiz's scimitar fell several Crown Knights before finally clashing with Jacopo's broadsword. The two warriors swung their weapons effortlessly. Their heavy swords felt lighter than air. Their weapons were ethereal, gleaming and reflecting the sun's light off their blades. Jahiz's body was fluid, though his old bones creaked. The warriors surrounding him might have been young, but Jahiz outnumbered them with experience, might, and heart. When Jahiz was blade-to-blade with Jacopo he could feel the battle was between youth and experience. Wisdom and age held its ground firmly over the wild, fiery youth.

Damiano took hold of Quyionah, screaming for Jahiz to surrender. Jahiz fought his way to a horse and made his escape. Two bowmen, blessed with aim and sight, struck Jahiz as he fled. One arrow caught the side of his abdomen. The other arrow struck his back just under his left shoulder. The projectiles pierced him deep. Jahiz would later remove the arrows from his body when he was far enough away from the army to take rest. The wounds were the worst kind, not instantly fatal.

Jahiz made makeshift bandages from his clothes, tearing his garment's fabrics and wrapping his wounds with his inventive yet crude engineering. The fabric did not keep long. The torn cloth became overwhelmed with blood as Jahiz moved. The aged Moor's only hope was to find Rah-Mun-Do, or he would die. The blood loss ignited fever and hallucination, but there was no infection. He hoped the foreign land that he ate from was not poisonous to his physical body. Either way, the land, coupled with his exhaustion, did not offer much sustenance in the two days of continued travel. Jahiz became just as weak as when he was in the Spanish prison cell. Jahiz believed this could have made for a more appropriate death, on duty, in the field of battle. But he would have failed in his mission.

This would be a stupid death, he reconsidered.

Memories and hallucinations shook him. Jahiz's body convulsed so wildly he woke up, standing his body tall like a king striding through his kingdom. He was cold, beginning to shiver. The trees were no longer demons reaching to attack him. The sun was not a fireball ready to be tossed from a dragon's throat. All was normal, save his fever and cold induced trembling. Jahiz relaxed. His body slumped forward against the horse's neck. He realized the horse stopped. He looked up by only moving his eyes. Jahiz's wife and seventeen-year old son stood before him. He was so overwhelmed by their sight that his body slid from the horse and onto the ground with a hard thud.

Jahiz's wife rushed over to him. His vision began to blur, but he noticed that his wife's dark flesh magically turned desert colored yellow. Her eyes, much like her physique, became slender. Their shape was like a butterfly's wings. They flapped just the same, in awe at the sight of Jahiz. Her hair became slender, black strands that flowed in the light wind. Jahiz realized he had been hallucinating again. This woman was not his wife, and the image of his son simply disappeared.

Jahiz passed out.

Overwhelmed.

"Rah-Mun!" The young Chinese woman called. "Rah-Mun!"

The old monk answered his pregnant wife's call. He ran from his quaint house and stood over the body of Jahiz the Moor.

Rah-Mun-Do, The Monk

The Moor was beaten, drained, and dying. His impenetrable, warrior physique seemed to be crumbling from inside out. His face was soaked with sweat, and his body trembled while short breaths escaped from his nose. He was bald, save one long, thick graying dreadlock that spiraled and twisted out of the back of his head. His face was dark and smooth but imprinted with aging lines scratched onto his visage through war. Rah-Mun-Do knelt down beside the Moor. He looked closely. He figured all forty years of his training came to this moment. It was forty years ago at the age of fifteen when his training began. He too was old. But he was ready to complete his assigned task.

Now.

It was time.

"San Li," Rah-Mun-Do called his wife. "Prepare a bed and some medicine. I'll carry him to the house."

Rah-Mun-Do knelt down and scooped up the aged warrior with a surprising ease, especially for his age. He carried Jahiz back to his retreat, the quaint house sitting in the center of the manmade clearing. The area of the forest was specifically cleared for the retreat's plot. San Li rushed ahead of him and entered the house. She rushed to the guestroom and prepared the soft bed. Rah-Mun-Do entered and rested Jahiz's body down moments later. San Li removed herself from the room to fetch medicine. She re-entered minutes later with a tray of particular remedies. She took a wet cloth that was soaked with water and a medicinal herb, applying it to Jahiz's head. The Moor's trembling eased as the medicinally enhanced water seeped into his pores. His body relaxed and his breathing was regular.

"Let him be," said San Li. "I'll look after him."

"You're four months with child, my wife," declared Rah-Mun-Do. "This is no place for you."

"When I'm fatigued I'll call you," said the woman. "You have your duties. I have mine."

Rah-Mun-Do took a breath. "Yes, dear," he yielded. "If he wakes, get me." Rah-Mun-Do insisted.

"My fatigue or his recovery, whichever comes first," San-Li replied.

Rah-Mun-Do made a reluctant exit. He returned outside to gather the Moor's horse and scimitar. He walked back to where his wife found the Moor. He snatched up the sword and grabbed the horse by the reins. He looked around the forest and then listened closely for anyone else's arrival. There was nothing. This made Rah-Mun-Do uneasy. Since he was twenty, five years into his training, he was told that one day a black warrior would bring to this spot an Afra woman. She would be a songstress. And then, bestowed onto him, would be the duty to translate a song she would sing. He would use an ancient script taught to him by his masters and reconfigure the characters into a map, verse-by-verse. Today appeared a black warrior, but there was no sign of the black woman. And worse, the Moor was beaten, near death. Rah-Mun-Do even spotted patched wounds, possibly made by bullet or arrow. The Moor had been attacked. Rah-Mun-Do could only hope that the woman was okay, or even the slight possibility this just happened to be a black, Moorish warrior…passing…through China. *It was more often a circumstance than not,* Rah-Mun-Do tried to convince himself of the notion.

He remained uneasy.

For the first time, darkness was calm. There was no disturbance, and Jahiz felt light and euphoric. The darkness was peaceful. Jahiz first felt as if he was floating, then he felt like he was rising from a body of water. His face cooled as air hit him and interacted with the water on his face. He felt his mouth open and he took a deep breath. His ears heard a woman's voice call a name that was not his. Jahiz opened his eyes and noticed he was in a candlelit room lying down with his back against a soft cushion.

Sitting over Jahiz was a young Chinese woman. Jahiz noticed she was several months pregnant. The woman offered him a drink. Jahiz accepted the cup and thanked the woman. The drink was cool and flavored with herbs. It calmed Jahiz. The Moor could feel his wounds were properly bandaged. The pain that throbbed from them had subsided, cooled by an ointment. He saw that he was re-dressed in dark purple pants, black boots, and a red sash tied across his waist. Cool air wiped his bare chest.

An aged Chinese man walked into the room wearing warrior robes. He was bald, clean-shaven, save white, bushy eyebrows resting above brown eyes. He stood next to the woman and observed Jahiz. Rah-Mun-Do introduced himself.

"Hello. I am Jahiz," Jahiz replied. They nodded heads, and then Jahiz asked, "What sort of name is Rah-Mun-Do for a Chinese man? It sounds more Japanese."

Rah-Mun chuckled. "It sounds the way it sounds," was the only way he explained it. "It's more title than name. It's not my birth name."

"Still sounds Japanese," Jahiz remarked.

Rah-Mun chuckled again, and then he asked the Moor, "Where are you from?"

"Al-Andalusia," Jahiz answered.

Rah-Mun became silent and grave. When he spoke he said, "I'm sorry about its fall."

Jahiz bowed his head and said a prayer in his head. "Well, let's not become too grave," he said brightening up with a smile. "Let me say, I'm impressed. You speak my language."

Rah-Mun-Do smiled lightly. "I speak many languages," he informed.

"The rumor is you know an ancient one," Jahiz retorted.

"I do," Rah-Mun-Do nodded. "But I've been trained to hear the lovely voice of an Afra woman and translate an ancient song for her."

Jahiz could not help but chuckle. Life brought him to a strange place, a secret world. He remembered his events, his thoughts focusing on Quyionah's capture. His demeanor shifted. He turned serious and informed the monk, "We were attacked. The girl was taken. I don't believe she's dead."

"You were traveling here," San Li asked in her native Chinese. Rah-Mun-Do translated her words for Jahiz. San Li could understand his words, but not speak them.

"Yes," the Moor answered. "I have no idea where she could be leading them."

"Most likely in circles," Rah-Mun-Do presumed. "She's probably waiting for you to find me."

Jahiz sat up in bed. There was still stiffness to his old bones, though he was well rested and recovering. This was a sensation that could not be mended. He was just getting old, or rather, already arrived there. He gave a quick glance to Rah-Mun-Do from the corner of his eye. "You're a lot older than I expected," he said to the monk. "What're you, my age? Fifties?"

"Something like that," the monk smiled. "But age won't slow me down."

"Especially living here, peacefully, among the trees," Jahiz commented as he groaned. "You haven't seen much combat have you? I don't know if word reached China, but al-Andalusia has fallen. But, I'm sure you have guessed that considering my arrival, which heralds the Afra woman—your family, generation after generation, has been told to expect." Rah-Mun-Do remained silent. Jahiz narrowed his vision on San Li's pregnant belly and asked, "Sister or wife?"

"Wife," the monk answered.

The Moor's eyes were wide, and he questioned aloud, "For a monk?" He rolled his eyes away from Rah-Mun-Do. "The surprises keep coming."

Rah-Mun-Do laid a hand on San Li's shoulder. "I'm granted an heir," the monk explained. "But now, my child will not have to endure this duty. It ends with me. I thought I was going to hand this burden over to my child. But, even with my age, it's still up to me." He then asked Jahiz, "Is the Voice young or old?"

Jahiz considered the monk was inquiring about Quyionah. "She's young," he answered. "She's around the age of my son. Seventeen, eighteen or so."

Rah-Mun-Do hummed in contemplation. "Our line of monks and priestesses dedicated to this task, passed on from heir-to-heir, we've died prematurely from being sidetracked from duty. Wars, missions, and other tasks have re-routed our duties."

"I was just thrown into this," Jahiz proclaimed with a warm smile. "I'm a soldier. Taking command is no foreign concept to me. Duty is duty. But, I just want to see my family, not a lost city of gold."

"We find the descendant of Bodhidharma," stated Rah-Mun-Do, "and he will stop whatever threatens the lost cities and Amexem."

"How's that," Jahiz probed.

Rah-Mun-Do shook his head and said in a stern voice, "That is not my concern."

Jahiz expressed through clenched teeth, "Neither was all this to me days ago—following imprisonment and a string of luck and skill keeping me from being killed in a grand fight." He took a breath and concluded with a question, "What if it does involves us?"

Rah-Mun-Do conceded, returning Jahiz's words to him. "Then duty is duty," he said respectfully.

Jahiz shook his head. "Our first line of strategy must focus on finding the Voice, as you call her. Quyionah."

Rah-Mun-Do did not respond to Jahiz. His eyes focused on his wife. She smiled up at him, her eyes gleaming with tears. "You have to leave," Rah-Mun-Do told her. She shook her head with an understanding nod, but her face contorted with sadness and several tears streaked down the side of her face. Rah-Mun-Do returned his gaze to Jahiz. "I'll send a signal up for escorts to take my wife away. The flare should also alert our enemies."

"I need two things," Jahiz said in a low demanding voice.

"And what's that," Rah-Mun-Do asked.

"A shirt, and my weapon," the Moor answered.

"You'll find both in my weapons room," Rah-Mun-Do told him. The monk helped his wife to her feet and then led her from the room. "Excuse us," he said back to Jahiz. The two disappeared from the room.

Jahiz lay back and closed his eyes. Good sleep was had, and the morning came. Jahiz awoke and noticed a tray of food left for him. He placed the tray onto his lap and reveled in the meal. When he was finished, he placed the tray upon a stand, got up, and slipped on a white robe and into soft, comfortable shoes. He walked to the door and exited the room. In the corridors of the house he spotted San Li. She smiled at him and then pointed to another room far off. Jahiz figured she was directing him to where Rah-Mun-Do resided. The Moor bowed at the neck, acknowledging the woman's direction. He then followed her aim. He walked inside another room and encountered a large display of weapons. Rah-Mun-Do observed the mounted weaponry, calculating which he would need. Jahiz stepped up beside him.

"Your scimitar is next to the door," the monk told the Moor. "A shirt is draped over it."

"Thank you," said Jahiz. He turned around and saw his sword with a golden-brown silk shirt draped over it. He walked to the items, removed his robe, and slipped on the shirt, buttoning the garment all the way to his collar. He then slipped the robe back on. Jahiz took the handle of his sword and walked back to Rah-Mun-Do's side. He inspected the weapons lining the walls, his eye catching a pair of claws strapped to the wall. He pointed to the weapons and said, "I want them."

Rah-Mun-Do smiled, "Always a favorite. But if these knights are armored, you'll have to go for the face or the neck when using that weapon."

"Not a problem." Jahiz expressed matter-of-factly. "When do we light the flare?"

"Now," Rah-Mun-Do answered with a sad tone. The minute he ignited the signal tower he would have little time left with San Li. And if he died on this mission, he would never see his child born into the world. Rah-Mun-Do spent the night speaking to his child, his lips close to his wife's belly. He sang an old Chinese song to his wife, and they conversed until sunrise. Rah-Mun-Do had little sleep. But his body was well prepared for a fight of any magnitude. Forty years of training, along with countless side missions and grueling tasks, helped Rah-Mun-Do stand better than his own two legs. The monk pivoted with an elegantly balanced and trained motion to his body. He snapped his fingers and commanded when he saw Jahiz, "To the signal tower."

Jahiz followed him. The monk and the Moor exited the house and Rah-Mun-Do led them deeper into the forest down a small pathway. The path lay opposite the site where Jahiz was found. They came to an object that resembled a cannon, it was silver, and it was aimed upward. It was four feet tall, heavy looking. Next to it was a wooden crate. Jahiz raised an eyebrow and asked, "Is this the signal tower?"

Rah-Mun-Do's lip curled into a sly smile. "Well, maybe tower isn't the appropriate word to describe such a thing," he admitted. "But we will use it to fire a signal into the sky."

"Why not call it Signal Cannon?" Jahiz suggested, noticing the tower's ability to swivel and be aimed in any direction.

Rah-Mun-Do's face contorted and he shook his head in disagreement. "Too war like."

"What do you think we're preparing for," spoke the Moor.

Rah-Mun-Do relaxed back into his smile when he answered, "Yes, my friend. But we should carry peace with us at all times."

"I guess so, Rah-Mun," the Moor agreed. "It's been kind of difficult with all I've been through. The thought of my son keeps me at peace. He won't be involved with the things I've come across."

"I hope the best for my child too," the monk nodded. He then looked up at the sky through a carved out area just above the signal tower's shooting range. It was cleared of foliage; no obstruction of branch from the surrounding trees blocked its firing path. Rah-Mun-Do took a deep breath and then walked to the wooden crate. He opened it to reveal the contents to load the tower and fire up through the trees. He removed two jars of gray powder and a sphere that looked like it was made from a blue grainy substance.

Jahiz figured that the ball was going to be fired into the sky from the tower. He then asked the monk, "How long before your people arrive?"

"Hours," Rah-Mun-Do said placing the material for the signal tower into its muzzle.

"Hours," Jahiz repeated monk. "Specifically…"

"Hours," Rah-Mun-Do reiterated forcefully.

Jahiz considered that 'hours' was quite some time. He could only hope Jacopo's army would not arrive before. "Do you think they could stay and give fight to—"

Something exploded inside Rah-Mun-Do. He erupted into a flurry of sentiments he believed the Moor needed to hear and understand. The monk stood quickly and stepped close to Jahiz's face. The Moorish warrior backed up just as quickly as Rah-Mun-Do jumped at him. The Moor could see frustration and hurt in the monk's eyes. "The duty I am heir to," began Rah-Mun-Do, "was passed down from generation-to-generation and originates with black travelers fleeing their ancient kingdoms to disperse the secret knowledge of the world. They fled as their civilizations collapsed, passing off knowledge and forming covenants to those they deemed worthy. No one but my specific lineage respects what we're about to attempt." Rah-Mun-Do paused for effect and then emphasized, "No one cares. They figure all the troubles of the world are because of the blacks' attempts to push the powers of knowledge and creation. We don't like you very much. And if the storm that is about to hit does not subside, then your people will be looked on as fools in the future. And though other races with color, those here and those yet born, may become oblivious as to the origin of their disdain for your people, make no mistake, it will remain. And it will be used to someone else's advantage."

Rah-Mun-Do returned to his duties at the signal tower.

Jahiz lifted his shoulders and said with a humble voice, "I just want to see my son."

"I want to see my child too," the monk said over his shoulder. "Be happy that you had a good seventeen years with him. I may not have any at all."

There was silence.

Jahiz stared off in the distance, lost in contemplation of the seventeen years he had spent with his son. The monk was right. Knowing he raised his son into a good man, and the years he spent watching him grow, made Jahiz comfortable with death. Though the warrior preferred specific deaths, noble and in the midst of battle, he was comfortable with the transition no matter how it came. He had fifty years of happiness. He had fifty years of friends. He had seventeen years with a wife and son. There were hard times, yes. But there was nothing that negated the qualities of any moments of peace.

Rah-Mun-Do finished with the signal tower and ignited it to fire. He rushed Jahiz away from the instrument, the two standing at a distance as the tower fired a brilliant blue comet into the sky. It exploded above the trees in a wide, dazzling display. Rah-Mun-Do grabbed the Moor's arm and led him back to the house. "I have little time left with my wife. I will attend to her."

Jahiz nodded.

"Keep watch," Rah-Mun-Do commanded. "Knock once for the army following you. Knock twice for the escorts."

Jahiz nodded again.

"Take a break every hour," the monk suggested. "There will be food for you in your room."

Rah-Mun-Do walked inside his house and into his bedroom, taking rest with his wife. Jahiz stood firm and on guard outside the house. He leaned on his scimitar, the blade planted firmly into the ground. He turned his back to the house and kept his eyes on the surrounding area. Inside, the old monk cuddled up to his pregnant wife. He repeated the previous night's events by singing into his wife's belly. San Li settled back, amused at the vibration of her husband's voice against her stomach. She laughed as he strained himself to sing the old song, but Rah-Mun-Do was not embarrassed. The two of them fell asleep in each other's arms.

Jahiz kept his place outside. His mind wandered to Quyionah. He hoped the woman was well and unharmed. She was, though locked into the coach of a caravan, miles away. At the very moment, and for the past several days, she was able to keep back the lewd advances of her attackers by expressing to Jacopo that her voice would change if penetrated and her virginity lost, negating the greatest of the two tasks she was to perform to find the descendant of Bodhidharma. Her voice had to hit a particular pitch and sound. Jacopo ordered no knight to ravage her or they would be put to his sword. Quyionah was treated well.

However, time was running short for the monk and the Moor. The Crown Knights witnessed the flare's faint burst far in the distance. Quyionah remarked under breath that Jahiz must have found 'it'. Jacopo interrogated her as to what 'it' was. Quyionah confessed that it must have been the site of the descendant's tower. Quyionah hoped it was really an army, found by Jahiz, and at the command of the monk she was to meet. The troops began to move in the direction of the flare. It would require a good deal of travel to find its origin. Jacopo's troops were already weary from the travel Quyionah had brought them through. They would probably require rest halfway there. Quyionah rested comfortably, the coach's movement rocking her to sleep.

And so came the night. The moon beamed a spotlight down on the retreat and provided illumination for Jahiz. He sat on the stairs, eating. He brought his food outside and feasted while he kept watch. The door opened behind him. The Moor looked up and saw Rah-Mun-Do exit from the house. The monk took a seat next to him. "I apologize for my behavior earlier," Rah-Mun-Do atoned.

Jahiz put his plate down. "I understand," he expressed. "Maybe I should apologize. I'm not aware of the pressure your life has called for."

Rah-Mun-Do shook his head. "True," the monk replied. "But, you were just recently thrust into this. The Voice and I were born into these duties, as were many before us. I just had high hopes that...well," and then the monk changed his words. He became honest when he said. "Maybe I should say *selfish* hopes. I thought my duties were over. I thought my child would take up the right. I thought I could rest. I thought I earned the right to rest." Rah-Mun-Do exhaled. "I'm just tired. An old, tired man. I was looking forward to raising my child. That was going to be a short, new life before I passed from this old one."

Jahiz considered the thought. "All this for the descendant of…Bohd…" Jahiz paused. "Who exactly are we looking for?"

"The descendant of Bodhidarhma," Rah-Mun-Do answered as if it was obvious.

"Who is Bodhidarhma," asked the Moor.

Rah-Mun-Do looked at Jahiz with surprise. "You don't know? I thought all Moors carried with them great knowledge."

Jahiz laughed. "I'm just a soldier."

"Well," Rah-Mun-Do began. "Bodhidarhma was a black, Dravidian man who traveled to China a thousand years ago. He came from India. He brought with him the foundation for meditation and the deadly martial arts."

Jahiz exclaimed, "Oh! I've heard of him. The Moors call him Indigo-Eyed Traveler."

Rah-Mun-Do smiled warmly. "Yes," he said as he tapped the center of his forehead. "His third eye glowed bright with its indigo flame. They say he could bore a hole through solid rock—"

"—When in deep stare," Jahiz finished. He chuckled. "I always loved hearing his travels. My father would tell his stories as adventures. They say he was a very passionate and—"

"—Ill-tempered man," the monk laughed. The laughter subsided quickly and he added in a sincere voice, "He is the link between you and I, *A-Sir*."

The Moor was surprised at the monk's knowledge on how to address his knighthood. But Jahiz waved the comment away modestly. "There's no need to be so formal toward me, Rah-Mun."

"I wouldn't be," Rah-Mun-Do started to confess. "It's just that I don't know your name."

Jahiz then recalled the fact that he had never told Rah-Mun-Do his name. He laughed at the thought. All this time had passed, and the most simple of information had not been granted to the kind monk. The Moor extended his hand and greeted, "My name is al-Jahiz ibn al-Raby."

Rah-Mun-Do accepted the Moor's hand and shook it. "A fine, powerful name. *Al-Jahiz, the Hero*."

"Shit," Jahiz cursed. "My old tired self? I just got lucky."

"In my book there's no such thing as luck," the monk expressed.

Jahiz raised an eyebrow and slapped the monk on the shoulder. "Not good luck, at least. Look at the hand you were dealt by fate."

The monk and the Moor erupted into heavy laughter.

"Well, I have *some* good luck," stated Rah-Mun-Do, his words jumbling through his hearty laugh. "I'll be asleep in a nice bed tonight with a fine woman. You have guard duty."

Their laughter continued!

Jahiz felt at home. It was as if he was back in an al-Andalusian town square, gathered with a fellow guard and soldier, the two of them intoxicated and euphoric with joy. The Moor and the monk began to share small adventures from their pasts. Jahiz was amazed at the amount of time the monk spent traveling. Most of Rah-Mun-Do's stories were about being a message carrier. He always seemed to find himself at the end of a hot tempered lord willing to take his anger out on the very messenger delivering the usually bad news. Rah-Mun-Do's skills were also serviced for guard duty. The monk spoke of how he evaded death when a city was raided. He was among rioters, soldiers, and revolutionaries. The Governor, an honest man who was caught between politics and his devotion to the people, commissioned Rah-Mun-Do to save his daughter and help her flee. Her name was San Li.

"That was five years ago," he told Jahiz. "I was fifty. She was twenty-two. I hadn't found a woman to conceive with yet. I was getting old. I couldn't keep getting caught up in near death adventures." He chuckled a bit and then said with a sigh of relief, "And, she wanted to stay by my side." Rah-Mun-Do reflected a bit. His wife filled his senses and he remembered his great love for her. She was as devoted to his duty as he was. He then asked Jahiz, "How did you meet your wife?"

Jahiz picked at his plate of food. "She had a rough and mean suitor. He had been courting her for an abusive two months. I had to show him I was twice as fierce. I killed him."

"Short and to the point," Rah-Mun-Do snickered.

"Yeah," grumbled Jahiz. "That point being at the end of my sword." He looked over at his scimitar that was now balanced against the stairs. "That's the very sword I did it with. I call it *Suitor's Blood*." His head turned to Rah-Mun-Do. "And as morbid as it sounds, she thinks it's romantic." His eyes spotted the heavens. His imagination blossomed bright, focusing his eyes on a set of stars that formed a constellation of his wife. She reached down to him and blew a shooting star as a kiss. "She was twenty-four at the time. I was thirty-three." Jahiz released a long sigh. He put his head down and then thought of something. "What happens if the Crown Knights get here first?"

"There's a tunnel with an escape path for my wife," Rah-Mun-Do stood. He kept his eye on the aged warrior. "There will be a second path for us to follow with the Voice." The monk stood up and started up the stairs. "When the Crown Knights attack, we'll have to concentrate on getting the Voice from them, and then quickly get into the house. How many do you think there are?"

Jahiz tried to remember. There seemed to be an endless swarm of knights when he and Quyionah were attacked. He fell at least four, maybe five. But they were substituted quickly. The Moor recalled that their caravan escorts were hit first.

Afterward, the forest was overcome with knights, dropping from the trees like falling leaves in autumn. "They have an army, compared to us two. There could be fifty soldiers, or just thirty. But I'm sure you and I together outnumber them."

"I hope so," Rah-Mun-Do exhaled. "I am getting old after all." He bid Jahiz goodnight, and then the monk entered his house. Jahiz clutched his sword and closed his eyes. The sounds of the forest amplified. Jahiz relaxed his mind. He was at peace. From the darkness walked the image of his wife. She was beautiful, voluptuous. She always complained that with age came weight; but Jahiz was appreciative of her figure. She was more desirable to him, even more so when she pouted about both age and weight. His wife approached and kissed him. He felt the sensation everywhere on him. His arms went around his wife. She felt real inside his meditative state. She leaned her lips to his ear and spoke. Her voice sounded like a twig snapping and trees parting. Light smothered his wife's image and Jahiz's eyes opened. In front of him, coming from the path he and Rah-Mun-Do followed to the signal tower, were seven horsemen. Four of the horsemen wore blue robes and held long pikes. Between them was a large carriage manned by three men wearing purple robes and hoods.

Jahiz stood up slowly, cautious not to make any sudden moves. He would rather face the entire army of Crown Knights than these determined men. He walked up the stairs, keeping an eye on the approaching men. He backed up to the door and gave it two hard knocks. The escorts ceased their approach. They did not move or say anything to Jahiz. The next movement and sound came from the front door as Rah-Mun-Do escorted San Li outside. He tapped on Jahiz's shoulder and pointed to a trunk filled with clothes. Jahiz placed his sword against the railing and then helped the monk carry the trunk to the carriage. San Li followed close behind. The trunk was slipped into a cart attached to the carriage. Jahiz backed away to respect the last moments between Rah-Mun-Do and San Li. When the Moor passed the woman she grabbed his arm and gave him a kiss on the cheek. She said 'thank you' to the Moor with her eyes, smile, and her heart. Jahiz bowed in respect, and then he backed away.

Rah-Mun-Do ran a single finger along his wife's face. He closed her eyes as they began to water; she put her hands on her belly. Rah-Mun-Do knelt down and spoke to his child again. Jokingly, he promised he would not sing. San Li laughed, choking back her sadness, but forcing her tears to streak down her face. Rah-Mun-Do spoke as any gentle father would to their child. "I will see you, my child. I will watch you grow. And you will know me as your father." He kissed San Li's belly, stood and kissed her forehead. Rah-Mun-Do helped the woman into the carriage and then backed away, standing next to Jahiz. Both he and the Moor watched the entourage circle around and travel back down the path from which they arrived. The sky was beginning to lighten as the sun was coming up.

...And Broke Their Crowns...

Forest brush and leaves crumbled, flattened, and were stomped away as the army of Crown Knights stampeded into the clearing where Rah-Mun-Do's house lay. Jacopo jumped from his horse and made his way to the carriage holding Quyionah. He opened the door, grabbed the woman by her arm, and dragged her from the vehicle. He tossed Quyionah to the ground only to grab her by the neck and force her to stand. He aimed her sight toward the house and shook her. He asked in her native tongue, "What is this place?"

Quyionah knew the place from story and instruction. *The House in the Center of Trees* is what was taught to her. She knew she was at the residence of a monk named Rah-Mun-Do. A name, like a title, passed down from generation-to-generation. Quyionah looked at Jacopo out of the corner of her eye. "Are you going to choke me?" She gasped. "You'll ruin my voice, you idiot."

Jacopo relaxed his hold on the young woman.

Quyionah caught her breath. She eased and reposed herself. She began to sing in a musical voice that even touched the soldiers around her. When she ended her song, the front door of the house opened wide. Rah-Mun-Do stepped outside. The monk was robed, hands behind his back. The entire army, including Quyionah, was expecting a younger man. Rah-Mun-Do stood stiff, straight. Everything and everyone was still, save Jacopo's mouth. "We've brought this woman for you," Jacopo said in Chinese. "We seek the descendant of Bodhidharma. Is that you?"

Rah-Mun-Do walked forward. He said in Italian, "You do not look like a Moor." The monk joked. "I was trained to expect a Moor."

Everything and everyone remained still, including Jacopo's lips. From their left came a hissing sound. It became louder, disturbing, as if a giant snake slithered its way from down the winding path next to the house. Quyionah's attuned ear alerted her to the exact location of the sound. Jacopo looked at the songstress. He aimed his head in the direction of Quyionah's gaze. The hiss was overwhelming. The horses bucked and screamed. Their riders worked hard to restrain them.

And then there was an explosion!

A purple comet soared from down the path and slammed into the carriage earlier occupied by Quyionah. The vehicle flipped over, ablaze! Quyionah ducked away from Jacopo. The army was in disarray, horses bucking wildly, soldiers running for cover. Another colorful comet soared down the path and slammed against the ground. Crown Knights were tossed into the air. Quyionah lost her footing. Jacopo reached for her but was knocked aside by the monk. Rah-Mun-Do grabbed Quyionah and quickly led her inside the house. Another blast was fired and slammed into the ground, tossing up debris. Jacopo got to his feet and screamed, "Charge the house!" His knights jumped at his command.

Rah-Mun-Do led Quyionah down a long corridor and into a room packed with crates, baskets, and loose items. He moved one crate aside and then flipped over the carpet underneath. He stomped on the ground, and a passage slid open. He pointed to the opening and Quyionah noticed a ladder. She made her descent, her ears picking up the stampede of soldiers flooding the house. She hurried quickly down the ladder, making room for the monk to follow. He reached for the carpet and drew it back to cover the opening as he made his way into the secret passage. Completely beneath the floor, Rah-Mun-Do smacked the floorboards with his fist and the trap door covered again.

Quyionah and the monk descended into a long corridor, carved out from the earth. There were two lit lamps at the base of the ladder. Quyionah lifted one, Rah-Mun-Do the other. The monk took lead down the open path. The two of them crept carefully as they made their way through the underground corridor. "Are you well, Quyionah?" asked the monk in his native tongue.

"Yes," she answered in Chinese. "I made the knights fear hurting me. They needed me whole in order to find what they seek. What we all seek."

"Good, my child," Rah-Mun-Do complimented. "You do need to be well for this task."

At the end of the corridor was an opening to another room. Inside the room was a drawing board. It was in pieces, cut out and stacked atop one another on a table. A lamp was also on the table. Jahiz sat at the table. Quyionah ran to him, set her lamp down on the table, and threw her arms around the old warrior. He held her tightly. Quyionah held Jahiz like he was the father she left behind. They exchanged no words, but plenty of feelings and emotions were bartered between them.

"He was manning the cannon outside," said Rah-Mun-Do in an African language shared between Quyionah and Jahiz.

"It's a signal tower, actually," Jahiz said throwing a wink and a smile at the monk. He looked at Quyionah and added, "But I fled into another underground passage that connects through there." He pointed to a closed door to Quyionah's left.

"We have our tricks," said Rah-Mun-Do as he slid a metal sheet downward, blocking the path he and Quyionah had come from.

Quyionah looked around the room and noticed there were three exits. She also noticed there were buckets of paint and large brushes leaning against the wall holding the drawing board. "How safe is this place?" Quyionah asked.

"Extremely," Rah-Mun-Do answered sternly. "Now, I have a song to interpret." He pointed to Jahiz and asked, "Could you move the table?"

Jahiz pushed the wooden table to the wall, making a clear space. Rah-Mun-Do removed the stacked pieces of the board from the table. He placed the pieces on the floor side-by-side in rows of four, four pieces per row. He picked up the brush and dipped it into a bucket of paint. Rah-Mun-Do looked over at the songstress and nodded his head as a cue. Quyionah began to sing. The song flowed about seven kingdoms touched by seven angels and turning into the Seven Cities of Gold. Rah-

Mun-Do translated the lyrics into the ancient language in which he was trained. He scribed the characters on the drawing tiles. His strokes were calculated to fit an appropriate amount of words onto each tile. The monk was able to fit all four verses onto the drawing board pieces. Rah-Mun-Do marked each piece with a number, to know the chronological order of the tiles. He stood up as he finished. Quyionah and Jahiz walked over to him and inspected the translated lyrics.

"Jahiz," called Rah-Mun-Do. "Take the board from the wall and put it onto the table."

Jahiz stepped away and completed the instructions. He took the board from the wall and laid it flat onto the table. "There," he said backing up to Quyionah.

Rah-Mun-Do gathered the tile pieces. The paint already dry, making the inscription undisturbed by the monk's piling of the tiles. He placed the tiles on the single chair in the room. "Now, there were cardinal directions in the song and numbers inside the verses," Rah-Mun-Do said to the others. "The numbers, except for seven, only go from one to four. Each number is accompanied by a direction. They are inseparable."

"What could it all mean," asked Quyionah.

"It's how we're suppose to arrange the verse to create the map," Rah-Mun-Do answered. "Line-by-line. Verse-by-verse."

Quyionah recited the lyrics of the song in her natural voice. Jahiz watched as Rah-Mun-Do shuffled the tiles appropriately. He lined them up on the drawing board to create a map. All three of them examined the map. Rah-Mun-Do recognized it as the surrounding area. The descendant of Bodhidharma was located ten miles to the north. Rah-Mun-Do scooped up a piece of rolled parchment from the corner of the room. He unraveled it and started to scribe a smaller version of the map on the paper.

Jahiz took Quyionah through the third door that revealed a large room with three beds. There was a lamp burning next to each bed, providing light. On each bed was a plate of fruit, bread, and cheese. Two bottles rested next to the plate of food. One was a small bottle of wine. The other was a bottle of water. Quyionah charged the bed to the far left and began to feast. She apologized for her overindulgence, but she was hungry. Jahiz assured her that he understood. He took the middle bed, apologizing for his overindulgence in sleep. He was tired. Quyionah eased away from the food. She thought of her father. Her sigh pried opened Jahiz's eyes. He stood up from the bed and asked, "What's wrong, Quyionah?"

Her voice was sad, but very melodic. She answered, "I know my father is dead. But I don't know what I'll do once this is over. I have no family. My mother passed away years ago."

Jahiz bent to one knee and looked up at the young girl. "I thought this was all obvious," he said to her. "You will come home with me and marry my son."

"Marry?" Quyionah blurted.

Jahiz returned to his bed and lay down. "Yes," he said in a fatherly tone. "I've found the perfect wife for him. What a gift to bring back on my travels."

"Good Moor, I am not a gift," Quyionah protested.

"Indeed you are, fine woman," Jahiz corrected. "And in this coming storm, you would do well to hold onto my son like the rare object men like him will become."

"Rare?" Quyionah questioned.

"Yes," the Moor's stern parental voice erupted. Jahiz concluded, "A good, stable, honest, black man."

Jahiz rolled over and went to sleep.

The knights extinguished the flames of the carriage while their two lead commanders, Jacopo and Damiano, looked on. Damiano asked what their next move was to be. Jacopo answered that the men should make camp, using the house for rest.

"What about the monk, the Moor, and the Af-Ra girl?" Damiano continued.

Jacopo waved his hand and said, "Of no bother." He eyed Damiano and smiled. "We're also here to propagate a lie."

"A lie," Damiano questioned.

"Yes, Damiano," Jacopo answered. "The Italian brother hired for Spain is promoting an easier and safer route to Asia. We're here as scouts to investigate a possible safe passage." Jacopo laughed. "Ultimately there will be one found, down and around Africa."

Damiano snickered, "Who would believe that?" He then elaborated, "Around Africa is longer, more expensive. It's not an economical venture. Goods would spoil before you arrived at your destination, or before you got those you were retrieving back to Europe. And then you would have to take over seaports to have rest areas for your crew along the way. You would need—"

"My dear Damiano, people will believe what the authority dictates as the truth," Jacopo reminded. "Most people will believe the authority regardless of plausibility." He swept his hand out toward the other knights. "They're lucky to be a part of this secret unit. But they'll never be leaders, not a single one." With the same hand he slapped Damiano on the chest plate. "Besides, my old friend, the Vatican is promoting that this man is trying to prove the world to be round." He burst into laughter. "The masses are still preaching it's flat. They speak on heavenly spheres of influence. People are still caught on old myths. They're ripe for the picking. This place is a garden. These people are our food!"

"I never saw Atlas holding up a flat land," Damiano joked.

Jacopo's eyebrows rose with sarcastic sorrow. "Some people haven't seen a statue of Atlas at all." His laughter bombarded the air with a second volley.

Damiano waited for Jacopo's laugh to recede before he asked, "Do you think this merchant can be trusted to navigate to the New World? He's not even a Christian. How can we trust such a man?"

Again Jacopo waved the comment away. "Bah!" he barked. "So he studies Maimonides and Rashi philosophy and calls himself a Jew. Bah, I say again. He's one of us. He's Italian. Other labels mean nothing." He crossed his arms and snickered again. "This will be a fun world we get to live in."

It was noon the next day when the monk, the Moor, and the songbird rose from out of the ground, following a tunnel that opened up at the edge of the forest. Three horses, tied to forest trees, and left behind by the same people that escorted San Li away, awaited them. They quickly mounted up and headed north. The forest became thin and was soon left behind for a wide-open field. In the distance stood a mountain. Though its formation was ominous, its physical presence never drew closer despite the hard travel on horseback. The ten miles to the north to reach the descendant of Bodhidharma ended in the field. Just on the horizon was the beginning of the mountain pass. In the wide-open field there stood an elegant tree. It was tall with one branch shaped like a horn. The end of the branch was hollowed out to resemble a horn's bell. Quyionah and Rah-Mun-Do dismounted and walked over to the tree. The monk knocked on the tall, natural monument and could feel that it was hollow. Rah-Mun-Do turned his head to Quyionah. She walked over to the horn-shaped branch and began to sing into the bell.

Quyionah's voice echoed through the hollow monument with a pitch that reverberated deep underground and stirred ancient gears and pipes. The ground began to rumble and split. From the earth rose a black tower. It was in the shape of an ancient Egyptian obelisk. The tower was tall, four-sided, and ending with a pyramidal top. At the base of the tower was an iron door that fell open. The monk, the Moor, and the songstress stood in awe. The tip of the tower was touched by the sun in such a way that it reflected strong, purple beams of light that stretched out for miles in every direction. The drawback to the awesome sight was that the Crown Knights became alerted. The purple beams hovered over Rah-Mun-Do's house. Jacopo rounded his soldiers to follow the purple beams to their source.

At that very moment, Jahiz, Quyionah, and Rah-Mun-Do continued their search for the descendant of Bodhidharma. They entered the tower, which quickly led to a set of stairs that winded its way up to six other levels. The ground level they left behind was a simple cooking room. The second area was for dining. The third level was a room for exercise and practice for combat. The fourth area was a bedroom. When the group entered the fifth room, a black Dravidian man descended from the stairs connected to the sixth room. His skin was pitch black and he had long, thick tendrils of locked hair that fell below his waist. He wore a brown robe, and looked to be in his early forties. His locks had speckles of grey, dusty hair strands woven into them. He stopped and allowed Jahiz, Quyionah, and Rah-Mun-

Do to spread out inside the fifth room. He followed them once they parted from the stairs and his path.

The fifth room was for council. There was a round table with eight chairs at its perimeter. The black Dravidian moved to the table but did not take seat. He faced the other three and bowed politely at the neck. Jahiz and the others did the same.

"I am Om'Radho," the man introduced himself. "I am the descendant of Bodhidarhma." He witnessed each of his guests smile and give a low sigh of relief. "My bloodline is cousin to his family's bloodline. This duty was bestowed upon on us long ago. As was yours, I am sure."

Jahiz remained silent on the matter, not wishing to tell Om'Radho that he was a newcomer to all this. Instead he stated, "Then you must know why we're here."

Om'Radho nodded, yes. "Amexem is threatened," he said with a heavy sigh. "More secrets have to be dispersed and hidden."

Rah-Mun-Do stepped forward. He said in a quick breath, "We're here regarding the Seven Cities of Gold."

"And what would you like to know about them?" Om'Radho asked in a voice oblivious to the urgency.

"An army pursues us," said Rah-Mun-Do. "They call themselves the Crown Knights. Our duty was to find you and protect the Seven Cities of Gold."

Om'Radho shook his head, disagreeing with Rah-Mun-Do's last statement. "Your duty was to find me, so that I may alert others and make sure ancient secrets are never secured by the wrong hands," he corrected. "The story of the Seven Cities of Gold was used to motivate you to find me."

Jahiz smiled softly. He figured Azamor might have known this all along. Wherever the Moor was going to lead the Spanish Crown across the ocean, it would be to their death, if of course, he was not dead already.

"So the Seven Cities don't exist?" Quyionah asked. Her life flashed before her eyes. Her dedication to her voice, all the training with the specific notion of finding one man, fluttered through her memory. Quyionah always wondered how one man was going to hide seven cities—made of gold no less.

Rah-Mun-Do had other feelings. His duty was simply to lead Quyionah to this man. What would transpire after their meeting was never discussed. His duty was done. His old life was over. He just wanted to see his wife give birth to their child.

"Oh, the cities exist," Om'Radho stated lifting a single finger. "But not as this Western Man would know it, or ever understand it." He turned his back to the others and reached around to point at his spine. "The Seven Cities of Gold are a story about activating the seven energy points, or chakras, in the body; the seven major chakras on the spine." He faced his guests. "Mankind will begin to literalize the various mythologies about the body, mind, soul, and spirit. They will become histories that never happened. They will become people who never existed. They will be objects that were never forged." He took one step and then continued, "The physical science decoded from the stories will be separated into a distinct field of study. Mankind will then label the spirit as existing on the outside; they will cast thousands of definitions to various objects, lands, and people that do not exist. This has already happened. These states of consciousness concerning the technology of the soul, and the body, and the mind, and the spirit will be cast to something strictly physical, and it will be anything other than the self that is labeled. It will have to be held or seen in order for it to exist. Science will explain only what the eyes can see." There was a slight smile on the Dravidian's face. "And the miracles of the self will be regarded as superstition." He raised an eyebrow. "But let it happen, because it can't be stopped. Let whatever that wants to tear this planet apart do so, all the miracles and legendary items of mythology exist inside you. I'm ready for the next world."

Om'Radho walked over to the wall and pulled a lever up. The fire in the lamps increased, other lamps became lit. With more light provided, Jahiz, Quyionah, and Rah-Mun-Do noticed the etchings on the wall. Men and women were being carted away in chains, taken to a boat. Homes were burning. Men on horses whipped men and women in fields. Some etchings showed men and women being tossed from boats, eaten by sharks. Some of the hieroglyphs portrayed men and women hanging from trees. The scenes were grotesque.

Om'Radho pointed to the mural. "Take this very literally," he told them. "These are re-drawn from a hidden city in India. They are of future events."

Quyionah and Jahiz looked at one another. The songbird's eyes were sad, watery.

"So what's your next task?" Rah-Mun-Do asked.

"I will be traveling the world," said Om'Radho. "I will be finding other Wisdom Keepers."

"There's a bit of a problem with that," voiced Jahiz. "An army of Crown Knights is after us. They're heading this way." He looked around the room, then back to Om'Radho. "Does this tower have any defenses?"

"None," said Om'Radho.

"Alternate exits?" Rah-Mun-Do asked.

Om'Radho shook his head, no. "I've lived here for the past five years. All I know is an alternate way to make the tower rise and sink." The Dravidian walked to the winding stairs and ascended. He called for the others, and they followed him to the sixth room. It was dark, but their journey did not end there. Om'Radho took them to the seventh room, which glowed with hovering, moving images of the environment outside the tower. Quyionah, Jahiz, and Rah-Mun-Do were in complete awe. Om'Radho explained, "The light of the sun is reflected off of mirrors, and then reconfigured into the images around the tower. That is what the purple beams are for."

Jahiz spotted the image of the forest they had come from. Jacopo's army scurried through the wooded area like ants through a field. Jahiz pointed to the image. "They're still a good way off," he informed.

"We should sink the tower and just wait," suggested Rah-Mun-Do.

"They'd see the horses," said Jahiz. "And they'd figure out the tree was hollow."

"They wouldn't be able to sing into it, though," Quyionah reminded.

Jahiz raised an eyebrow at her. "They're determined and intelligent. They'll figure something out."

"So what do you suggest?" Rah-Mun-Do asked.

The Moorish warrior answered through gritted teeth, "We sink the tower, get to the horses, and take down as many knights as possible."

"We hit their leader, and the rest will retreat," Rah-Mun-Do continued.

"His name is Jacopo," Jahiz clarified. "Soldiers are extremely dependent upon their leaders. We kill him, and the other named Damiano. It will be over. They'll scatter." He looked at Quyionah. "You stay here, songbird. We'll be back for you." He hugged Quyionah and then gave the young woman his sword. "If I don't return, you deliver this to my wife." He leaned close and whispered. "And get to know my son."

"You'll be back, Jahiz," said Quyionah.

The Moor just smiled. He spotted Om'Radho and commanded, "Raise the tower in twenty-four hours. See what the field looks like."

Om'Radho nodded.

Rah-Mun-Do pointed at the hovering, light images. His finger was aimed at an area twenty miles to the southwest. "Past this area is where they took my wife," he told Quyionah. "If there is any trouble, head there. They'll take you in. My wife will command them to help you get out of the country."

Jahiz looked back at the image of the Crown Knight army. The army was approaching rapidly. They had little time left. He and Rah-Mun-Do descended the stairs. They winded their way down to the base of the tower and charged outside. Jahiz jumped to his horse while Rah-Mun-Do ran to his mount as it trotted around the hollow tree. Jahiz looked up at the tower as it started to shake. The ground rumbled! The tower lowered into the earth. The beams of light died one-by-one as the tower descended, a wide patch of dirt covering it.

Rah-Mun-Do and Jahiz raced with incredible speed toward the forest, and as they neared the wooded area, Jacopo and his army of Crown Knights poured from the shadows of the trees. An arrow whizzed by Rah-Mun-Do's head. The monk turned his horse and charged the army, Jahiz following close by. Rah-Mun-Do put a gentle, praying hand on his mount's neck. He saw Jahiz pass him.

The Moor slipped on his claws while pressing forward. He cocked back one arm while holding the reins of his horse with the other. He jumped up, planted the back of his feet on his ride's saddle, and then vaulted forward, claws extended. Jahiz swiped and slashed the face of a Crown Knight. He wrapped his arms around him and brought the soldier off his horse. The two crashed against the grassy field, barely escaping being trampled by the rest of the charging army. The aged warrior slammed his claws into the knight's neck. He jumped up and pounced on another passing rider.

Rah-Mun-Do tugged at the reins of his mount and the creature dropped onto its side. The monk rolled out of the way as the horse became an obstacle for several incoming riders. The fall had a domino effect, oncoming riders trampled over one another. The confusion was devastating to the army of Crown Knights. Jacopo screamed, "Halt! Halt!" His army came to a stop.

The remaining knights, forty in number, stood in front of Rah-Mun-Do. The monk had just confiscated a dead knight's short sword. Jahiz stood next to him. Damiano smiled at the two, old warriors. "Do you think you can kill us all?" the knight asked in a surprisingly pleasant manner as he drew his sword.

Jahiz's fists tightened, gripping the handle of the claws. Rah-Mun-Do swung his sword around, elegantly taking pose in a fighting stance. Jacopo looked past the two aged warriors, out into the great field. His eyes came back to the monk and the Moor. "Where is the girl," he demanded.

"She's with the descendant of Bodhidharma," said Jahiz, his energy ready for battle, ready to jump the entire army. "And even if you find them you'll never find the Seven Cities of Gold."

"We have our ways," said Damiano.

Rah-Mun-Do shook his head. "I don't think so," declared the monk. "Because even if you find the Seven Cities of Gold—"

"—You'll still never *find* the Seven Cities of Gold," Jahiz finished with a sly smile.

Jacopo yelled for his men to dismount and arrest the two men. The Crown Knights followed their leader's orders. Jacopo and Damiano stayed atop their steeds. "I have come too far for riddles," said the Crown Knight General. "I will enjoy watching the two of you great old ones die."

"You personally will have to come down off your high horse to secure that notion," Jahiz advised.

Jacopo only justified the remark with a call to his soldiers. His orders changed. The monk and the Moor were ordered to die. The knights charged, screaming. Jahiz took quick, fatal swipes at soldiers, and he ducked sword swings aimed at him. The knights' armor was too tough for his claws. Jahiz had to aim for his attackers' faces and throats, scratching like a lion. Rah-Mun-Do moved as swift as the wind, quicker than any of the younger knights who dared an attack. The two experienced warriors fell younger foes plenty. Before the army could surround and overwhelm them, they charged into the forest. The knights followed. Jacopo and Damiano galloped after the army.

The knights fanned out cautiously, searching for their prey. Their hunt eluded them. Rah-Mun-Do used the shadows as cover. Jahiz escaped to the treetops. The Moorish warrior, nimble, even with the weight of his age, passed from tree to tree with a single jump. He targeted the only two mounted men in the army. Jacopo and Damiano. Below, the two men stood waiting, overseeing their army spread itself into the forest.

Jahiz noticed Rah-Mun-Do jump from the shadows in the distance. The monk attacked four men. His body movements were like a dance, swift and elegant. The monk's attacks fell several men, but more knights charged him. Rah-Mun-Do's graceful movements were able to fend off the incoming knights. More attacked him. Rah-Mun-Do became overwhelmed, but the monk fought back strong with fists, foot, and sword. The monk even caught an arrow fired at him. He tossed the projectile aside and continued his defense.

Two other bowmen stood next to Jacopo and Damiano. Jacopo leaned down and commanded the men to move forward. They did so, firing barrages of arrows at Rah-Mun-Do. The monk dodged, twisted, and contorted his way around the wave of arrow fire. But two arrows found their mark. Their impact tossed Rah-Mun-Do off balance and allowed a knight to run his blade down Rah-Mun-Do's back. Jahiz could see his friend was in trouble. The Moor needed to act quickly. Jacopo and Damiano needed to be cut down. Their deaths would trigger confusion in their soldiers. It would be enough time to buy Rah-Mun-Do the chance to dive back into the shadows. But Jahiz needed to kill the archers attacking Rah-Mun-Do first. Jahiz would kill the bowmen quickly, and then he would kill their leaders.

Jahiz angled himself, ready to pounce on the unsuspecting archers. The two bowmen moved forward to take another shot at Rah-Mun-Do. Jahiz saw his moment. The Moor dived. His legs were bent back in his descent, and his arms were cocked back to strike. In his fall he heard Jacopo scream a command to the archers. The knight yelled, "Now!"

The two archers turned and aimed their bows up at Jahiz. They fired. Four arrows soared toward the descending Moor. One arrow went wild and thwacked against a tree. A second arrow slammed the lower right of Jahiz's body. The third caught his chest. The fourth arrow passed through his shoulder. The projectiles knocked Jahiz off balance. The Moor landed on his right arm. The bone snapped. The archers locked in another set of arrows and moved forward. Jacopo laughed. He slid from off his horse and approached Jahiz.

"Old, old, old fool," Jacopo shook his head. He stood over Jahiz. He put a hand on the hilt of his sheathed sword and continued to shake his head. "You almost had me."

Jahiz inhaled large gulps of air. He rolled over and balanced himself with his left palm flattened against the ground. "I still got you, little boy," the Moor wheezed. "You ready for the next world?"

"I'm just here to conquer this one," retorted Jacopo.

Jahiz attacked, slamming his claws through Jacopo's jaw. His arm was broken, but the warrior still had strength in him. The claws ripped up through Jacopo's jaw, mouth, and up into his skull. The Moor's grim, teeth-clenched gaze was the last thing imprinted in Jacopo's vision. His eyes were wide with surprise, and then they slowly rolled back into his head. The Crown Knight's body twitched as life, breath, and blood leaked from him. The archers fired their arrows. Jahiz, their mark, shielded himself with their leader's body. The arrows bounced off Jacopo's armor and fell to the ground. Jahiz slipped his hand from the claw's grip, and Jacopo fell back dead.

Before the archers could lock another arrow, the Moor was upon them. Jahiz swiped the first archer's face; the knight buckled to his right. Jahiz turned and slammed his left set of claws through the second archer's throat. The Moor ripped his claws free and finished the first archer with a swipe across the neck. He turned around to aim a heated gaze at Damiano. The knight was missing from his mount.

A sword broke through Jahiz's stomach. The Moor's body jumped forward. With life and fight still in him, Jahiz swung his left hand behind him ferociously. Damiano was surprised at the Moor's continuing strength. He let go of his sword and backed away from Jahiz's attack. The Moor turned to attack, but his vision began to warp. He took a step forward and collapsed on one knee. Blood poured from his mouth. He took a breath, and he managed to smile. His vision tangled and blurred, but one image was clear. It was his wife. She was there in front of him. She helped Jahiz stand, and then she folded her arms around him.

"I love you," she said to her warrior-husband. She kissed him.

"Farisa," Jahiz exhaled her name.

The Moor's body died, slumping down on the earth floor. His spirit lifted. This was a fine death for a warrior, even if it was from a sucker-punch delivered by a man too much a coward to fight him.

Damiano posed over Jahiz's body. "And here you will lay, you wicked Blackamoor—"

Something smacked against Damiano's spine. His armor rattled as if hit by a cannonball. His body trembled, overpowered by waves of vibrations. The plates of his armor cracked, and the reverberating waves of energy shattered the knight's spine. Damiano's legs gave way. He dropped dead. Rah-Mun-Do stood above him, his fist out. All the focused energy and years of training passed through his extended fist. He turned around and stared at the army of knights. They were in awe at the death of their leaders. Their eyes were fixed on the bodies of Jacopo and Damiano. The army of knights backed away from Rah-Mun-Do. The monk was down to his final breaths of life. Five arrows lined his body, deep and fatal. His clothes were torn to reveal deep, bloody slashes. He was no longer a threat.

A knight hollered for retreat. The remaining Crown Knights fled.

A fleeing knight took notice of the entire scenario. His name was Aaron Casimiro. He could not believe the remaining soldiers would not stay to defeat the monk or complete their mission to find the woman. Their leaders were dead. The army was broken. Every soldier was as shattered as Damiano's spine. Aaron admired the monk and the Moor. They turned an entire army by only killing two men. This had to be reported. This had to be seen as a lesson learned and not as a failure. Aaron knew his superiors would appreciate the news only told in a way he could deliver. He would tell them, *"If we could make an entire people depend on one man, and then take away that man, and with him, the people's hopes, we could rule the people."* The young ambitious knight knew he would receive a higher rank.

Rah-Mun-Do watched as the army fled. The monk dropped to his knees. He turned and saw Jahiz standing in front of him. The Moor shimmered in an ethereal form. The monk smiled. "We got them," he told his Moorish friend. Jahiz's spirit disappeared. It was then that life flashed before Rah-Mun-Do's eyes. But it was not his. It was the life of his unborn son. He saw his child's birth, and his son's years flowed by until adulthood. His son became an importer, controlling shipping. His son raised a fine family of his own. And he knew his father. He knew the man named Rah-Mun-Do. San Li never let him forget. She told him the stories of his father at night. When his son was old enough, she would give him his father's journals. Rah-Mun-Do's family was going to be fine.

The monk fell against the forest floor, his life passed.

With the setting of the sun came the setting of the story of the monk and the Moor. The black tower rose from the earth in the distance when the sun rose again and reached its zenith. Quyionah and Om'Radho walked from the tower and took Quyionah's horse that was left behind. They already knew the fate of Rah-Mun-Do and Jahiz. Before they exited the tower, they went to the seventh room and saw the bodies lining the forest floor. Om'Radho was able to reflect the light to produce a larger picture that showed Jahiz and Rah-Mun-Do's bodies.

Quyionah decided to take the news to Rah-Mun-Do's wife. The monk called her San Li. And then she decided to find Jahiz's family and return his sword to his wife. The Moor called her Farisa. Quyionah smiled. She would also get to know Jahiz's son. Om'Radho would protect her all the way to Africa, before he would tend to his next tasks. He had time. And if not, he had an heir.

Quyionah sang into the bell of the hollow tree. She sang the song backwards, and the tower sunk into the earth. She and Om'Radho mounted the abandoned horses. She told him that she did not want to see the bodies. "Let nature take them," she said. Quyionah commanded Om'Radho to head southwest, and then she was off to complete her new quests.

Freezing Reign In Summer

Oklahoma, 1880

Two In Town

Oiled gears pumped as the machine exhaled steam, screaming like a haunting banshee. Black ink filtered through pipes that poured into plates. Lettered stamps were dipped into the plates, and then pressed against flat sheets of paper that were rolled out and separated by black workers. Each man had cotton stuffed inside his ears to soften the noise blaring from the machine. The noise was deafening, echoing up from the basement of the *Our Times Press.*

Gary Evan's ears were use to the noise. It was like music to him. It assured him his business was running properly. His eyes were accustomed to the monstrous machine as it print page after page. His nose became fond of the smell of ink, oil, and steam mixed together. He welcomed the vibration of the machine like the sensuous movement of his wife pressed against him. The machine was like an oven. Day after day he printed up food for thought, each week there was a special issue, and every two months a giant sized paper was peppered with the spice of Black History.

All of Gary's senses absorbed the sight of the printing press in action. He was use to the entire scene inside the basement. But today was different. Today his sight was bombarded and disturbed by the presence of two men. Both of them were his friends. However, Gary suspected they had died violently four months ago in April. His paper reported that a posse was sent out to hunt them down for their crime against the town. These two men were part of a ring that helped steal the town's gold reserve, and most of its coin and paper treasury. Lawmen found them. There was a brutal shootout. The outlaws were killed.

But here they were, four months later, staring at Gary with conviction and murderous determination in their eyes. Gary could sense the men were not here for him, at least not to kill him.

The black man at the bottom of the stairs was named Logan Stanford, a twenty-four year old, educated young man. Logan tried to appear rough even though he was clean-shaven. He tried to wash away his proper upbringing. His lean and stance was that of a gunslinger. He stood against the wall, right leg bent up, and the sole of his boot was just as flat as his back against the cement. His attitude did little to age the boy underneath. He was dressed in brown pants, boots to match, and a white button shirt that was tucked in and covered by a jacket a shade darker than his pants and boots. A brown bandana was tied around his neck. A derby of the same color sat comfortably on his head. Holstered in front of him, not at his hips, were two .45, single action Colt Revolvers.

The second man, sitting on the stairs, was named Timothy Clark. He was like a mythological Golem come to life. He was a tall, muscular black man. They called him 'Knokem' for his ability to knock a man out—even dead—in one swing of his mighty fists. Knokem wore a disheveled beard over a wide, dark face. He was dressed in black pants, boots to match, and an officer's Civil War jacket, unbuttoned and opened to reveal a bare chest lacerated with tribal scars. The designs were intricate, spelling an adjective in an indigenous language. *THUNDER*, was the translation of the scars' design. Despite his might, Knokem did not mind flaunting a holstered Peacemaker and a Winchester rifle in his hands. Atop his head was a black, wide brim hat.

None of the workers noticed their arrival. Gary's employees remained loyal and focused to the job at hand. Gary took a cautious step toward the two men, ghosts, as far as Gary was concerned. He looked to his left and signaled a supervisor that he was going upstairs. He looked back at Logan and Knokem and made the same signal. Logan nodded, and then he and Knokem made their way upstairs to the front office, Gary catching up to them and following behind. He shut the door leading to the basement to smother the noise echoing from below. He walked to a desk and spun around, staring at the two men. He wanted to speak, but he just continued to stare. There was no relief when Logan smiled. The smile was self-assured. Something was going to happen. To whom and why, Gary had no idea.

Logan stepped over to the front door. His smile and eyes remained fixed on Gary. The clanking of Logan's boots mixed with the sound of a black man ranting and screaming outside across the street, preaching to a captive audience. Logan stepped to the side of the door, took his eyes off of Gary, and observed the preaching man.

"We should start with the obvious," Logan finally voiced. "Why are we alive?" He snickered and looked back at Gary with a raised eyebrow. "Is that the first question?"

"It's a good start," Gary said wishing he had a bottle of whiskey.

"The answer itself is obvious," Knokem said moving to the middle of the room. "We never died."

"Larry and Noble are alive too," Logan added. "And we know where former Mayor Wilson Bailey is located."

Gary looked as if all reality had been ripped away from him. He felt as if he did not know where he was, or where he even belonged. Larry Templeman and Doctor Jackson Noble were also considered as dead as the two men in front of him. And the former Mayor was a criminal on the run, taking with him a good deal of the town's gold reserve.

"Frank said his squad killed all of you," Gary stated.

Logan returned his gaze outside, again observing the screaming man. "How is Frank these days," he asked.

Gary walked up beside Logan and peered through the window. He eyed the man standing on the stool and preaching to an audience of twenty citizens. Frank Hydes. He wore a black tailored suit with a black top hat to match. His eyes were adorned with circular spectacles. His hands were dressed with black gloves. He was a short man with a scruffy voice. Frank was barely educated, but he was able to survive in business by way of a cunning and cutthroat personality. Making a perimeter around Frank were five black men wearing custom designed, black military outfits. They stood firm, arms at their side. Their foreboding presence kept the crowd at bay, though the soldiers were unarmed at the moment.

The noise from the printing press stopped. This caused Frank's rant to become louder, though he was across the street. Gary sighed at the sight of the howling man. "Frank is keeping the town together. Barely," Gary finally said. "He focused his wealth into the city when Mayor Bailey skipped town with the reserves."

Logan's hand went to the handle of one of his guns. His thumb lay firmly on the hammer, at the ready, to cock back while his whole hand pulled the weapon free in the same swift motion. But there was no such action. Logan just voiced, "Wilson didn't steal that money." He looked at Gary with an intense look. "You don't believe he would work hard to build this town just to rob it, do you?"

Gary answered, "No."

"And ain't it funny," Knokem continued the sentiment as he cocked his Winchester, "that the town becomes broke while Frank is suddenly wealthy enough to get it back on its feet?" He moved closer to Gary. He asked, "Has Frank been acting mayor since Wilson's been gone?"

Gary shook his head, no. He turned his back to the window and addressed the giant, "He's been a part of a committee that includes some of Wilson's trusted assistants."

Logan's stare became angry as he retorted, "They weren't that trusting. They set him up. They helped steal the town's reserved gold and frame Wilson for the deed."

"You have proof of that," Gary asked.

"We'll get it from Frank," Logan snarled, his eyes focusing on his target outside. "He'll crack when we bust him."

Gary informed, "Wilson's 'friend', Sheriff Reed, is now a professor. He's a scholar on politics. He's trying to do his best to become Mayor of Black Manor. Everybody is seeking the title, all of Wilson's old associates."

"That fucking idiot," grumbled Knokem. "He screams about how corrupt politics are, and how much of a web and trap it is, only to whittle his way *back* into it?"

Gary lifted his shoulders. He was not agreeing with Professor Reed's actions, but he believed he needed to explain them. "Terrence thinks he can change the way politics are handled."

"That's a whole lotta change," Logan sneered as he took his eyes off the scenario outside and looked at Gary. "He sold out his friend to have an opportunity at his job. How's that change? I guess his knowledge on how corrupt politics can be is being put to good use."

Gary sat on the edge of his desk. "Deputy Adams took on the Sheriff position," he continued to brief Logan and Knokem. "He's also part of the committee, with Claremont as Deputy, ready to be Sheriff if Adams wins *his* bid for Mayor."

"Claremont," Logan questioned. "He's being mentored by Douglas Adams? I thought Douglas hated the little kid?"

"He did," Gary said. "But Douglas had a quick change of heart when Claremont denounced everything Ronald Clemens had to say about Reverend Valley." Gary reflected on the man named Ronald Clemens. He was an up-and-coming black scholar with a passionate voice for truth. But Gary had to admit aloud, "If it wasn't for Ronald's accusations against Reverend Valley—"

"Then the plans to fuck up this town would've been set for a later date," Logan ended with a raised eyebrow. "Make no mistake, Gary. These bastards used that to split the town against Wilson and push their plans forward to usurp the Mayor's power."

"So what are you here to do," Gary said looking to either man. "You gonna put the King back on his throne?"

Logan's expression became sad. "Wilson ain't comin' back," he told Gary. "He's heading east with Mia. He's gone. He actually told Larry, Noble, Knokem, and me not to get involved. Those were wishes we couldn't honor." His eyes, once again filled with determination, fueled by anger, caught sight of Frank Hydes preaching atop his stool. "We're going to kill 'em all," Logan announced in a gritty voice. "Frank, Adams, Claremont, Reed, and Reverend Valley." Logan then looked to Gary. "And you—" Gary tensed up and froze in anticipation of Logan's next words. "—You're gonna be Black Manor's next mayor. It needs an honest man that can be a strong foundation for its future."

Gary shook his head. "I appreciate the gesture," he replied. "But my one attempt at political business was kind of shot." He stood up and walked back to the window. He gazed outside, staring mostly at a memory instead of the scene in front of him. "It happened a month ago. Bad trade venture. I was in charge of shipping goods. They went bad. It gave our town a bad reputation for a month before—"

"Frank restored the reputation," Logan finished accusingly.

Gary looked over at the young man. His eyes blinked rapidly as revelation impregnated his mind with thoughts of double-cross and a deal scripted against his favor. "Do you believe I was setup to look bad," he asked.

"It puts you out of the running for mayor," said Knokem matter-of-factly.

"Makes you know your place as just a paper printer," Logan concluded. He had a question. "Who watched your shipment?"

"Deputy Claremont and…" Gary was suddenly gripped with rage. He clenched his teeth and finished, "Sheriff Adams." He rolled his eyes and cursed, "Shit! I never trusted these bastards to begin with. I can't believe I didn't see it."

There was a sudden burst of applause from outside as Frank Hydes ended his speech. All three men looked out the window. Frank was stepping down from his stool, the crowd slowly dispersing from the scene. The candidate for mayor shook the citizens' hands as they gathered to greet him. A phony smile worked the crowd.

"We're gonna kill Frank tonight," Logan admitted. "We're gonna pry him for information, and then take him back to a cabin where Larry and Noble will want a piece of him. Then we go for the rest."

"Frank always has his five guards," Gary warned. "The Black Cats."

"What's their routine so we can work around them," asked Knokem.

Gary did not respond immediately. Things were going to be different once he spoke. He took a moment to hold onto an old, simple life as the owner and Editor-In-Chief of a local paper in a struggling black town. Blood was going to be on his hands after he spoke. Logan stood at the corner of his vision. Here was a young man determined to spill blood. Revenge was a hell of a drug. Gary decided to take a drag of its smoke, inhale its fumes, and exhale into a new reality.

"When the crowd dies down," Gary started, trying to put as many words as possible between the border of one reality and another. "They're going over to the warehouse at the other end of town," he finished, crossing over. "They play a private game of poker in a backroom. No one is there but them."

"Where's Adams and Claremont?" Logan asked.

"On leave with Reed," said Gary. "They went south. The Black Cats are acting as law."

Logan signaled Knokem, and the two men headed for the door. "When we return they'll be dead," he said in a darkly assuring voice. "We'll get back the town's reserves. You'll be mayor."

"And what will you do when this is all said and done?" Gary asked.

"I dunno," said Logan. "Let's just get this done first."

Gary was not convinced that the young man could pull all this off, despite the conviction on Logan's face. Gary believed Logan did not know what he was in for. He was a student, a promising scholar with a big heart that longed to help his people post-slavery. He was naïve to politics, but so was the former Mayor. Gary could let Wilson Bailey run, but he did not want to see Logan walk any further down a path of violence and revenge. "You ain't a killer, kid," Gary expressed in a calm but desperate plea. "If you want to become one, expect a rough transition."

Logan stopped and gave Gary a tough look. "I ain't a kid," he scoffed.

"And I'm killin' these men not because I want to, but because I have to."

"You're making another man's fight yours," Gary warned. "Wilson ain't even got gut enough to settle it himself."

Logan faced Gary and said forcefully, "These bastards ain't got good intentions toward this town and you know that." He jabbed Gary with his finger, and then pointed it toward Frank. "The more of these bastards I dust, the more this town stands a chance. The less chance I take on Black Manor, its poor future is gonna make you raise an eyebrow…and then you'll really see who's done the killin'."

Gary exhaled. Logan relaxed and stepped back toward the door. "You got balls, Logan," Gary called out.

Logan tipped his hat. "That and my guns is all I'll need," he said.

Gary took another look outside at Frank's farce. His eyes went back to Logan and he said, "Go on, get."

Logan pointed to Gary and said to him, "You're a good man, Gary."

"I'll make a better mayor, I guess," he replied in a voice that accepted his fate.

Logan and Knokem exited. Gary watched the two men walk down the street, inconspicuous to the crowd gathered around Frank Hydes and his men. They made their way to the warehouse at the end of town. Gary turned around and made his way back downstairs just as Frank Hydes made his last round of handshakes. The political candidate then carried off in the same direction as Logan and Knokem, minutes behind their departure. Frank's hidden adversaries had already tucked themselves away into the warehouse's backroom.

Frank's smile quickly dissolved as he left the crowd of potential voters. It became a sneer, and he grunted like a wild animal. "Goddamn, black people. They don't know—and don't want to know—what it takes to run this place. Goddamn niggers." His voice sounded like a non-oiled, rumbling machine. It was a raspy, irritating, cough-like sound.

Frank's men formed tightly around him as he continued to rant.

"I can't wait for the day you boys can carry guns properly," Frank grumbled. "Then these niggers will definitely know who's in charge. That's my first line of business."

"You don't think these people are too stupid to vote for Adams or Reed," asked one of his guards.

"They can vote all they goddamn want to!" Frank's rough voice cut the air, sounding like tumbling rocks. "It's already been decided that it's going to be in my favor, according to that no-good charlatan Reverend Valley."

The posse slipped inside the warehouse, Frank suggesting their usual card game to cool them down. Frank and his crew headed to the back, and Frank informed his men their guns were in the backroom.

Knokem lay waiting, high on the rafters, his Winchester angled at the six men below him. The rifle was already cocked, ready to fire. Frank opened the door, and Knokem let off the first shot. The bullet tore through one of the Black Cat's neck. Blood and chunks of flesh spattered on the wall adjacent the door. The man's body slammed against the wall, sliding down lifelessly. Knokem quickly cocked his gun. The men tried to rush through the door.

Knokem fired once, cocked his gun, and fired again.

One bullet crashed through the back of another Black Cat's skull, dropping him quickly. The third man was wounded in the leg, left for dead while Frank and his two remaining guards jumped inside the room. The wounded Black Cat crawled toward the door. There was another shot fired. Fire and ice attacked the Black Cat's hand. He looked at his right hand. Three fingers were missing, and his palm was punctured and bleeding. The Black Cat put his back against the door. He looked around for his attacker. He never looked up. Knokem fired two final rounds that landed in the Black Cat's chest. The giant pulled back his rifle and waited.

The room. It was dark. No light. Perfect for killing. Frank and his remaining two guards huddled inside, trying to catch a breath. One of the men felt his way around the room, his hands searching for one of the lamps he knew lay on the table. If he found the lamp, if he made light, he could find his weapons. He and the other Black Cat could fight back.

He walked around cautiously, slamming his knee into the table. Ignoring the jarring pain throbbing in his knee, the Black Cat began feeling over the table's top, finding one of the lamps. His hands touched a book of matches lying next to the lamp. He fiddled with the matchbook, opening it, and digging into the small box wildly. His nervous hands spilled matches everywhere. He managed to hold onto one. He struck the match and lit the lamp that rested on the table. It was then that the Black Cat saw the young man occupying one of the chairs. His derby was angled low over his brow. The Black Cat could only see the young man's cocky grin. Logan. He aimed both his pistols at the frantic Black Cat.

Logan thumbed back the hammers and fired into the Black Cat's surprised expression. The man was tossed back by the bullets' impact. He crashed against the floor hard. Logan cocked his guns again and killed the last of Frank's men, bullets drilling the Black Cat's chest. Frank's eyes were wide as he cowered in the corner next to the door. He sat, trembling. His hands reached for the door's knob, his watering eyes fixed on the man sitting at the table.

Logan aimed his guns at Frank. "Don't move, you sonava bitch," Logan hollered. Frank froze, save his trembling body. The young gunman lifted his head, revealing his face to Frank. Frank almost regurgitated his own heart when he realized his attacker was young Logan Stanford. The young man's brown skin glistened, reflecting the lamp's fiery light. Logan eased one of his gun's hammers from its cocked position. He holstered it. He stood up from the table, his second gun aimed at Frank. His smile melted into a determined expression. "You believe in ghost stories, Frank," Logan asked. Frank said nothing. "You surprised to see a ghost haunting you? There are several ghosts looking for you, Frank."

"You goddamned coward," Frank yelled, his voice trembling as much as his body.

"I beg to differ, Frank," Logan responded quickly, putting the muzzle of his gun on Frank's forehead. "I wasn't the one goin' around taken credit for a deed never done. Talkin' about a victorious battle never fought."

"My fight was to get Wilson out of here," Frank said as a desperate plea. "I'm tryin' to keep the white man out of our town. That no-good sonava bitch Wilson was rollin' out a fine carpet for those bastards."

"Is that what Reverend Valley told you?" Logan asked in a calm demeanor.

"Yeah," Frank said, believing his words were getting through to Logan. "Wilson got away from me, though. He ran off with most of the town's reserve. It's him you want, not me. Reverend Valley came into some family money and reimbursed the town. He put me on this new committee, and I've been——."

Logan lifted his hand. Frank shut up. Logan feigned contemplation, free hand on his chin. He looked at Frank with mean eyes. "You tell me where Reverend Valley is and I'll let you go. I'll see if your story checks with him."

"He's heading to Texas," Frank revealed. "He's involved in a deal that will replenish the town's gold. It's a Government thing, money for the black towns. He'll be back soon. You know where he lives. Five miles north of town."

Logan's eyes narrowed. He told the man, "You really are stupid, Frank." He motioned toward the door with his gun. "Go," he ordered. Frank stood up, turned around quickly, and opened the door. Knokem stood on the other side of the doorway. He was tall and ominous. Logan walked passed both of them. Frank tried to move around Knokem, but the giant slid to each side that Frank tried moving to. Frank looked around Knokem and yelled to Logan, "You lettin' me go, right?"

Logan nodded his head. "I am," he said. "But Knokem, Larry, and Noble, they ain't lettin' you go anywhere." He turned around and added, "Except to hell."

Frank's eyes widened, possessed by fright.

Knokem hit him hard. Frank's head twisted. Several of his teeth loosened, some were swallowed. Blood flooded his mouth in a violent gush. Frank dropped, unconscious. The blood in Frank's mouth flowed from his parted lips. Knokem reached down and scooped up the body. He and Logan walked out of the warehouse and tied Frank to the back of a horse. Knokem mounted the horse as Logan jumped to another. The two gunmen rode from town, dragging Frank behind them.

All Of Them

The shadowy outline of horses came over the horizon in exchange for the sinking sun that cast a bloody-red background in the sky. Larry Templeman leaned his light skinned, stocky physique against the outside of a lone cabin that stood in the middle of a grassy field. He drank from a bottle of liquor that he had been nursing for the last fifteen minutes. He watched the riders approach. His eyes narrowed on something bobbling and dragging behind one horseman. He grinned, and then knocked on the cabin door and called, "Noble."

The door opened. Jackson Noble stepped out, strapping on his spectacles to get a clear view of what the horizon had to offer. He too was stocky, but bearded, rather than clean-shaven like Larry. He was the same complexion as Larry, as if the two were brothers. He had a fresh, bushy head of hair, wild and chaotic. Larry covered a close shaved head with a wide brim hat, which he removed the minute Knokem and Logan approached closer, the straps of the hat latched against his neck, making the hat hang behind him. He handed his bottle of liquor to Noble and stepped toward the incoming horsemen. He spotted Frank Hydes' dragging body and unsheathed a hunting knife. Logan and Knokem stopped their horses. Larry cut the rope from the horse, and then from around Frank's feet and arms. Knokem dismounted saying, "I've been riding slow. He should be okay."

Logan dismounted and walked toward Noble. "He's all yours, boys," he said.

Larry lifted Frank by the collar and then slammed him roughly to the ground. Frank coughed. Larry was glad to see he was alive, though Frank was clearly in pain. Larry bent down and jammed his hunting knife in Frank's shoulder. The man's screams were silenced by Knokem's boot smashing against his face, not once, not twice, but several times over. Larry kicked Frank in the stomach. Frank vomited blood. Noble stared at the scene, eyes wide with curiosity. "Go on, get him." Noble heard Logan say.

Jackson removed his suit jacket, switching the liquor bottle into the appropriate hand to swing his jacket from off him. He held the tank of the bottle up high and approached the beating cautiously. His grip became tighter on the bottle and his teeth clenched harder and harder against one another. He remembered a time when he witnessed Frank spit on an elderly black woman for not understanding the politics to *'keep her town alive'*, as he put it. Jackson was arrested for grabbing Frank in defense of the woman. He was let free, and Frank covered up the incident.

His grip tightened.

Noble remembered hearing about Frank beating down a mulatto boy in the street, though the young man clearly acknowledged his white father's rape of his mother when she was in service to him. The young man even said he turned his back on his 'white blood' and wished to know and understand his black history. But

Frank beat him anyway.

Noble's grip tightened.

He'd heard of another incident where Frank slapped a woman when she accused him of attempting to ruin her husband's reputation as a scholar. He then ordered his men to take her to an alley and finish her off.

Noble's grip tightened.

When Paschal Beverley Randolf, the leading spiritualist and interpreter of ancient black culture, visited the town, Frank called him a mulatto coward. He invited the scholar to town only to run him from it with rants of war against white people. The irony was that Frank only made war with his own kind. He treated visiting whites with the utmost respect and kindness. In fact, most of his displays against his own people were at the entertainment of high government officials that came to see how the town was prospering. The only man who stood up to the prying eyes of the government officials was Mayor Wilson. A man Frank helped run from town, all for Reverend Valley's promise of power. The Reverend was a man Noble always insisted was a snake. Noble had seen the outcome of trying to work with these characters, but Mayor Wilson was blinded by an optimistic view of unity among every black person. Noble understood that some blacks were still slaves, the chains on their minds. Mayor Wilson shrugged off Noble's warnings.

Look at the predicament they were in now, Noble thought.

Noble broke the bottle against Frank's head with a wide swing. His vision blurred in yellow and red as blood and liquor spattered against his spectacles. Frank dropped to his side from being on his knees, held up by Larry. Frank's body trembled. Logan parted the three men, stopping them from beating Frank any further. He removed one of his guns and fired into Frank's leg. He commanded the men to continue. He walked inside the cabin to retrieve two bottles of liquor and some matches. Larry took a heavy swing that broke Frank's jaw and loosened several more teeth. He removed the knife from Frank's right shoulder and slashed his face twice. Noble tossed the broken bottle aside and used his fists to pummel Frank. Knokem kicked him in the back with enough pressure to loose several spinal discs.

Logan parted the men again. In his left hand were two bottles of liquor, his fingers configured tightly around their necks. Pressed inside Logan's teeth was a single match. He removed his gun again and fired into Frank's left shoulder. The body jerked and a soft scream came from the bloody disfigured face. Logan tossed one bottle to Larry who uncorked it and began pouring its contents onto Frank. Logan did the same with the remaining bottle. He dropped the bottle behind him when the contents were emptied. He removed the match from his teeth and lit it swiftly on his pants leg.

"You should've actually killed us, Frank," Logan said. "Instead, as usual, you just talked a good game."

Logan dropped the match. The body ignited instantly! Frank writhed and bucked, blanketed with flames. The four men stepped back as the body pounced wildly. They watched until there was no life left in Frank, or at least no life left to fight for. Logan leaned against the cabin and shook his head.

"Frank Hydes, boys," Logan declared. "A black man who hated racist white men so much he became one." Logan turned around and walked inside the cabin. "We kill the rest of these bastards tomorrow. Let's rest up."

"I'm gonna watch the fire," said Larry. "Make sure it dies down."

"Me too," voiced Knokem.

Noble followed Logan, snatching up his suit jacket and putting it back on after wiping it clean. Logan took a seat at a round table. Noble sat across from him. He removed his pocket kerchief and wiped the blood and liquor from his spectacles. He placed them back on and stated, "You know there's going to be some white folks at the end of all this." He breathed heavy, his eyes wide as if a prophetic vision was playing out in front of him. His eyes calmed and he looked up at Logan. "Government took down that Free Town over in North Dakota, near that ancient copper mine. That was them." Noble shook his head. "There's gonna be trouble."

"I believe it, Doc," Logan said. He then spoke with an educated tone. "But the way the government undermines black towns, they're too slick. The real culprits will never show their faces. It all just comes down to Reverend Valley's megalomaniacal behavior. It will only be a rumor as to who he was really working for."

"And if their face does appear?" Noble asked.

Logan's educated tone disappeared. Only anger remained. "I'll fucking kill them too." He reflected on the day's earlier events, slaying Frank's two guards. He then thought about Frank's brutal beating. Logan took a deep breath. "They say killin' a man is a hard thing, especially your first." Logan shook his head. "But takin' the life of a man who deserves it ain't hard at all."

Noble declared, "I'm still more at ease with saving lives than taking them."

"Then take this to heart," Logan started. "By killin' these sons of bitches we are saving the lives of many folk in Black Manor. We are amputating them from the body, Doctor."

Fire stirred inside Logan.

There was a dying fire outside.

All of them pulled out the next morning on horseback. It was dawn. In front of the cabin was left a burnt pile of bones and dripping flesh that was once Frank Hydes. The men traveled north, passed Black Manor. Within twenty minutes they came upon an L-shaped ranch house. It was the home of Reverend Nicholas Valley. The four men stared at the house. Logan figured Douglas Adams might be inside, possibly with several deputies, including Claremont. There was going to be a bloodbath. Hopefully it would fall in the favor of the four gunmen on horseback.

Lost in their thoughts, they missed the activity of someone staring at them from the window. The figure darted from the opening and made their way to the front door. Suddenly the four gunmen were taken from their inactive state as they heard the door beginning to open. Each man removed and cocked a gun. But out stepped the lovely form of Tabitha Valley, the Reverend's wife. Each man holstered his weapon quickly as she walked up.

Tabitha wore a yellow dress, with brown flowers patterned all over it. She was a refined woman, well mannered, with café au lait skin and dark brown, almond shaped eyes that captivated every man. Tabitha had the allure of a siren without the deadly consequence. Her long, braided, jet-black hair hinted at the mixed indigenous blood that ran through her. She was the same age as Larry, forty-three, but Tabitha retained her youth. Every man thought she was ten years younger when guessing her age. Even still, she was fifteen years younger than her husband. People considered Reverend Valley had robbed the cradle. He did, but nowhere near the extent of the rumors.

"Reverend Valley is not here," she said to the men forcefully. "Sheriff Adams, Deputy Claremont, and Professor Reed just returned to town. You just missed them." Tabitha knew the men in front of her, and she understood why they traveled to her ranch. "Reverend Valley is gone, though. For good. I'm here alone."

Each of the men was stunned to hear the news. She spoke as if Reverend Valley had moved on without her. Logan could hear disdain in the woman's voice. At first he considered the disdain was for him and the men accompanying him. Logan was wrong. This good woman had also been betrayed. Heat bubbled inside Logan as if he were a furnace. He inspected Tabitha's feminine frame and then tilted his head back toward the others to whisper, "You boys go deal with those bastards. I'll meet you back at the cabin."

Larry chuckled. "Goddamn, Logan," he said leaning close, continuing with a devious eye. "When you get revenge you leave no stone unturned. Seems like you're shooting at everyone, sorta speak."

"Just get to those bastards before they start askin' questions about Frank's disappearance," Logan said with a stern voice. "They"ll discover those Black Cat bodies sooner or later." He added with a smile, "Besides, that bastard of a Reverend shouldn't have left a fine woman here." Logan dismounted and stepped toward Lady Tabitha, the reins of his horse in hand. "Do you have any more information, Tabitha?" It was the first time Logan had ever addressed the woman by her first name.

"Inside," she said to him. It came as a command. Logan was right behind her, stopping only to hitch his horse. The two of them entered the house and Larry laughed as the door closed. He turned his horse around and signaled for the others. "Let's go kill those boys." Inside the house Logan and Tabitha were passionately locked.

They were fucking, as Larry would call it.

Three Minus One

It was night. Sheriff Adams decided to turn in, heading upstairs and leaving his friend Professor Terrence Reed behind. The two of them spent the evening speaking on the politics of the town. Sheriff Adams spent most of the conversation talking of Reverend Valley at length; he reflected on the man's intellect and esteem. He let it be known that he would follow the Reverend into hell if he had to. He then retired upstairs. The Professor stayed behind, reading and researching. He was dragged into his own world so intensely, he never saw the front door open and the three men slip inside.

"Hey Terrence," a voice pulled him away from reading. "Is that a book on how to fuck your friends and make enemies?"

The Professor looked up. His eyes barely caught Larry, who had addressed him, and Noble who stood beside him. Knokem's fist was at the forefront of his vision. It collided with his cheek, shattering his face's bone structure. Four of his teeth, followed by comets of blood, trickled onto the table. His head thumped against the wooden table shortly after the blow. Larry lifted Reed's head and slit his throat. Blood coated the tabletop, spreading ominously, until it dripped from the table edges. Larry wiped the blood from his knife then sheathed the weapon.

The three assassins heard moans coming from upstairs accompanied by heavy thumping sounds. Larry shook his head with a sly smile. "Goddamn," he said. "Somebody's fuckin'. That sounds like some heavy humpin'."

"I ain't killin' a woman," Knokem voiced.

"That includes me," said Noble. "I'd feel like I was killin' my wife."

Larry suggested, "We mask up, dismiss the woman, and shoot Adams."

"We need to interrogate him first," said Knokem. "We have to find Claremont, and even more importantly Reverend Valley's whereabouts."

Noble lifted his bandana around his face. "If Claremont is at the saloon across the way, he'll hear the shots," he notified.

"He'll bring a posse with him," Larry said shimmying his bandana over his face.

"I'll take the horses 'round back," Knokem suggested. "If Claremont comes out the joint, fire at him from the room window. If the two ain't fuckin' in a room facing the street, I'll plug Claremont when he runs out. You two go through the backdoor and meet me. Then we'll ride out."

Noble cocked his Winchester. The doctor-turned-gunman said, "Sounds like a plan."

Knokem went to his duties, leaving the building, finding their horses, and taking the mounts around to the back. Noble and Larry headed upstairs. The moans became muffled, as if the two people in the act were trying to keep their activity from being detected. The two gunmen had to listen close to decipher from which door the sounds were coming. They walked softly, the floor threatening to creak and expose Noble and Larry's approach. Larry stopped at the third doorway on the left. He placed his ear close and heard the noises of muffled lust coming through the door. He looked at Noble and raised a single thumb. Noble put his hand on the knob, turning it slowly. Larry removed a Schofield Revolver and cocked back the hammer. When the knob of the door was brought back as far as it could go, the two gunmen rushed the room.

Adams was undisturbed, continuing his activity on top of his lover. "Get off the woman," Larry ordered. "We got business with you, Adams."

Adams slowed his thrusts, and then he stopped completely. He moved himself away from his lover and turned to sit on the bed, his body littered with sweat. Noble loosened his grip on the rifle. The weapon jumbled in his hands, but it was his jaw that fell instead. He and Larry were still, surprise dripping on their faces. The two realized the woman lying on her stomach was no woman at all, but a man. Larry and Noble gasped. Larry stepped inside to investigate, hoping he was wrong and his eyes were playing tricks on him. Not only was Sheriff Adams with a man, this man was also the young twenty-two year old Deputy Claremont.

Adams reached for the gun lying on the nightstand, believing his attackers distracted. Noble fired. The doctor's actions were independent of his thoughts, almost accidental. The bullet pierced the Sheriff's throat. He gurgled on his blood and slumped dead. Claremont remained on his stomach, too scared to move. His only movement was through his bowels. Larry fired three shots into the Deputy's back. He walked over to the dying man and placed the muzzle of the gun to the back of his head and fired again. Blood covered Larry's gun and forearm. Chunks of meat thwacked against the headboard. Larry holstered his weapon.

The two gunmen exited the room and made their way down the stairs. A crowd of people exited the saloon, hearing the shots. From the side of the building Knokem waited, crouched in a shadow with his rifle aimed outward. He saw no sign of Claremont. The backdoor opened behind him and Noble and Larry jumped to their horses. Larry waved him on.

"I don't see Claremont," Knokem told them in a forceful whisper.

"We got him," said Larry. "That goat-faced pansy was bein' humped by Adams."

Knokem holstered his rifle in a sheath on the side of his horse. He mounted, face contorted in disbelief. "Get out of here."

"I'd like to." Noble shook his head, aiming his horse away from the building. "I never thought I'd see that sight."

The three men spurred their horses and bolted away from the town.

One Plus Three

Logan woke up. He immediately became aware that he was alone in the bed. He sat up and spotted Tabitha playing with his gun while sitting at her vanity. She sat facing Logan, her legs crossed. She wore her robe but nothing underneath. She looked heavenly, the morning sun brightening her already sunny, warm skin. She stroked the muzzle of the gun. Logan found her actions sensual. Tabitha spotted Logan rise in bed and she confessed, "I never believed Frank and his men killed you. The way my husband told me, the story just didn't add up." She smiled. "I thought you all just ran off. I thought you helped Wilson leave, and then went your separate ways."

Logan watched the woman closely as she handled his gun. He asked, "Did you ever believe the accusations against Wilson?"

"No," Tabitha answered honestly. "But what could I do?" She became quiet, still stroking the gun. Tabitha then asked Logan, "Have you killed anyone with this gun?"

"Yes, I have," he answered honestly. He put his back against the headboard.

Tabitha placed the gun on the vanity and slid her way next to Logan. He noticed the fading bruise on her eye. Her lip had a small split. It was healing, but still soiled with dried blood. He reached for her scars and said, "I didn't see these."

Tabitha smiled, taking Logan's hand and nurturing it with both of hers. "You were a little busy with other parts of my body," she laughed lovingly as she leaned close. "Are you going to kill him," she asked. "My husband?"

"Don't see why I would turn around now," Logan said to her, looking away. "You forgot to tell me where he was, or other information." He looked at her and accused, "Or was that your plan?"

Tabitha slapped Logan hard. "I didn't fuck you to change your mind."

Logan felt the sting of his cheek, rubbing it to soothe the pain. He just smiled. "Well, I fucked you cuz I always wanted to." Tabitha slapped Logan again. Logan laughed. "I'm beginning to think you started most fights between you and your husband."

The woman huffed. She then asked, "What are you going to do after you kill him?"

Logan kept his smile and replied, "I'm gonna come back here, Miss, and fuck you again."

Tabitha slapped him a third time. She pointed a stern finger at Logan and yelled at him, "Stop trying to be a man! You're just a boy."

Logan felt his cheek again, keeping his glowing grin. "You can't deny my manhood after last night," he said slyly. "I bet the only time you called for God with the Reverend was in his congregation." Tabitha backed away. Her face became sad and her eyes watered. Logan reached for her and asked, "What ain'tchu tellin' me?

Where do you think he could be?"

"There's a lodge," she admitted. "Two hours south of town."

"A lodge?" Logan questioned. "You mean a Masonic Lodge? Prince Hall?"

Tabitha's eyes met Logan's. She informed him, "It's a Mason Lodge, but not Prince Hall. They're called the Knights of The Morning Star."

Logan jumped from the bed and quickly dressed. "That's a white lodge," he blurted.

"I went with my husband there once," Tabitha continued. "He was talking to three white men."

"When was this?" Logan asked as he strapped on his gun belt.

"A week ago," Tabitha admitted. "He should be there. I heard Sheriff Adams talking about it with the other two. They were supposed to meet him in two days."

Logan finished dressing. He snatched his gun from the table, twirled and holstered it. He knelt at the bedside, looking up at Tabitha. "When you were there with your husband, what were his conversations about?"

"I wasn't allowed inside the lodge," Tabitha explained. "I was made to wait outside."

Logan kissed the woman's forehead, promised a return, and then left the room. Tabitha stood up and walked to the window where she waved Logan off. The young man waved back, a charismatic, boyish grin on his face. He turned his horse and started off toward the horizon.

A gunshot from outside the cabin woke the three men. Larry jumped to the window, his gun in hand. He unhinged the hammer when he spotted Logan atop a horse, hand raised and gun aimed up. Larry laughed and holstered his gun. Logan screamed for Noble. The man came from his room and exited the cabin, strapping up his suspenders and putting on his glasses.

"What's going on," the doctor asked.

"You were right," Logan told him. "Reverend Valley is at a Masonic lodge two hours south of town. It belongs to The Knights of The Morning Star. White boys run that lodge."

Noble shook his head. "This sumbitch," he cursed.

Logan ordered, "Get your guns boys. We got one last mark to hit."

Larry stood in the doorway. "Can we take some time to wash up? We ain't savages."

"Yeah, take your time," Logan said dismounting. "We hittin' these boys at night." He walked his horse over to a rail and tied the mount down. "So, tell me how your raid was?"

Larry leaned close and teased Logan, "Tell me how yours was."

Logan beamed a coy smile. "I'll be going back after all this is done, that's all I'll say." He gave a stern look and asked, "You got all three of those bastards?"

Larry nodded, yes. "And get this, Logan. Claremont and Adams were pansies—sissies for each other."

"What," Logan said with a perplexed look.

"We caught 'em humpin' each other," Noble clarified.

"Whoa," Logan expressed. "That's enough of that. What about Reed?"

"We got him first," informed Larry. "Knokem broke his face. I slit his throat."

"Good," Logan congratulated in a serious tone. "Tonight we shoot up a lodge."

Knokem walked from the cabin, making his way around back to the water pump to wash. Logan walked inside and took a seat at the table. Noble and Larry joined him. Noble looked away, lost in a stare aimed at the floor, as if another prophetic revelation was coming to him. "I think that lodge is where the gold is kept," he said, his eyes coming back to normal and looking toward Logan as if for approval.

"You haven't been wrong yet, Doc," Logan stated. "We'll keep an eye out." He put his guns on the table and asked Larry for more bullets. "Let's make sure our inventory is full."

Four shadows glided like ghosts over the night's horizon. Their presence crept in and out of dark spots, swiftly making their way toward a lone lodge in the distance. The Masonic Hall's windows glowed with a golden hue, lights shimmering on the inside. It was just a mile from another town, and two hours from Black Manor. The lodge was far enough outside a populated area for gunshots to occur without being heard. No one would hear the screams. They would carry away in the summer breeze. The screams would be cold and haunting, eventually muffled by time and forgotten like the crime that caused them. Of course, there might not be screams at all. The four gunmen, riding up to the lodge, were hell bent on killing slowly, but making sure no screams escaped.

Logan's eyes noticed four horses stationed outside the lodge. If there were one man per horse, his enemies would still be outnumbered. This was not a meeting, a conversation, or a negotiation. This was a surprise attack. The riders stopped their horses near a group of trees that was the beginning of a wooded area. They dismounted and wrapped the reins of their horses around several trunks. Knokem and Noble were the riflemen. Larry and Logan depended on their revolvers. The four-man gang walked up to the lodge and knelt near a window. Each of them peeked inside.

The lodge looked like a throne room. There were massive pillars, painted gold and engraved with black stars. They flanked a chest that was also painted black and gold. There was a purple sheet draping the altar, and a red carpet lined with purple and gold that rolled down to the front door. Behind the altar, away from view of the gunmen outside, was a door leading to a backroom filled with white robes and long, pointed white masks. In front of the altar was a table where four men stood. One was a tall, brown skinned black man sporting a beard. He wore a contemporary suit, shoes to match, and he possessed a low patch of hair that was wavy, black, and slick. This was Reverend Nicholas Valley. He was the target of the four black men outside.

Reverend Valley conversed with three white men. They each wore a contemporary suit. Their names were Ike Davis, Guy Steeles, and Anthony MacArthur. The four gunmen were unfamiliar with them. But, as it was, they hired the Reverend to make sure the town of Black Manor would eventually fall into complete control of the American Government. Their promise to Reverend Valley was a claim to the land. It was the same thing they always promised him. He had only seen some money. He never claimed or was granted land.

Each man wore a gun belt. Two rifles and a revolver lay on the table. But it was clear they were not expecting to use them, not out here. They were smart enough to hold firearms for safety's sake. None of the white men had a badge of any kind. It was also noticed that the Reverend was becoming a little nervous. He fidgeted with his pocket watch, waiting for Adams, Claremont, and Reed. He looked over at the door, trying his best to keep a smile. On his third look toward the front of the lodge, the door opened to everyone's surprise.

Logan, Knokem, and Larry looked over to see Noble bust in shooting. Five shots from his Winchester, cocked and fired at an unbelievable speed, smacked into Reverend Valley. His body tipped backwards, dusty clouds of blood spurting from his wounds. None of the hits killed him. The other three men scattered for their guns. Logan and the others barged inward, firing. The man named Ike Davis caught a bullet in the jaw, the shoulder, and stomach. He dropped, weak and bleeding to death.

Logan charged Guy Steeles, the only man quick enough to draw his gun. Guy fired on Logan, missing him, and hitting the wall behind him. Logan pushed his gun aside and slammed into the man. He jammed his gun under Guy's chin and fired up into his brain. The bullet ripped through every layer in his head and caused chunks of flesh and blood to land on Logan's face.

Larry tossed his knife into Anthony MacArthur's hand while Knokem shot him in the thigh. MacArthur buckled. He twisted left as Larry's gunshot entered his shoulder. Logan and Noble finished him off by firing two rounds, both hitting MacArthur. He dropped dead. Logan walked over to Noble and took the rifle from him. He stepped over Reverend Valley's body, cocked the Winchester, and slowly aimed it to the Reverend's face. "Where's the gold," he demanded.

Reverend Valley laughed while spitting up blood. "Is that what you came here for? The gold?" He continued to laugh. "Damn, boy. It's in storage under this floor, if that's all you want."

Logan shook his head at the dying Reverend. "That ain't what I came for. I came to kill you and your three friends here. I came because you're a bad man."

"Hold up," the Reverend screamed, angry. "Hold up! I was tryin' to save that town from a slaughter. You think you got problems now? You wait. I was easing that town into a place where it would maintain life. They're going to kill it now. You'll need an army to stop what's coming."

"We got one," Logan said placing the rifle's muzzle against the Reverend's face.

The Reverend's last breaths sounded like an explosion. *"Kill me and your soul will be as cursed as mine!"*

The hammer on the rifle dropped. The Reverend's face became a disgusting mess, exploding into flesh and blood. Logan tossed the rifle back to Noble and asked, "What the hell were you doing goin' in guns blazing like that, and all?"

"What were we going to do?" the doctor responded, "watch 'em through the window all night?"

"I expected something like that from Larry, not you." Logan retorted.

Larry snickered. "Look at the kid tryin' to be a man." He patted Logan on the shoulder. Logan managed to laugh, expressed more as a sigh of relief. It was over. They all looked at the mess of murdered bodies. They breathed easy, their eyes ingesting the scene. It was calm but bloody. The mess would hopefully make things clean.

"Let's open up this place and get the gold out," commanded Logan, breaking the tension.

"Then let's burn the place," Larry added.

"Right," they all agreed.

Underneath a hatch inside the floor the four gunmen found an underground room holding seven medium sized chests of gold and paper monies. Three of the chests belonged to Black Manor. They suspected the other chests belonged to other undermined black towns. Near the lodge, Knokem found a cart with enough might to hold the chests. He attached two of the horses to the cart, and it was loaded with all seven chests. The lodge was set ablaze and the four men made a long travel to Black Manor, two hours north.

It was a month later and there was no sign of war declared on Black Manor. There was a smooth transition for Gary Evans to become mayor. His wife continued to run the paper alongside Tabitha Valley, who now went by her maiden name of Tabitha Irulan. The town was as rich with culture as it was with its reserve. Knokem returned to California helping his father and mother work a ranch. Doctor Jackson Noble headed east, landing in Virginia with his wife, setting up a prosperous practice, and settling down to have children. Larry Templeman headed south to New Orleans.

Logan Stanford stayed around just to see the town prosper. At present, he stood in an audience, wearing a thick beard and an expensive gray suit with a derby to match. He was unrecognizable with his beard and trimmed hair. He introduced himself as Benjamin Capp. He watched as Mayor Gary Evans presented an inspiring speech to Black Manor's citizens, and then he left as the speech ended. He walked to the edge of town and came across Tabitha Irulan.

"I think this will be the last time I see this town," he said to her with a smile. "I'm beginning to hate this beard." He began to stroke the subject of his discontent.

"And where will you go?" Tabitha asked him.

Logan did not hear her. His mind was distracted by all the images of the events he had been through. Each gunshot and blood spatter racked his inner vision. He did not remember if any of the men actually screamed when they died, but he heard loud cries of anguish. Suddenly, the cries were silenced. They were replaced with dying moans that echoed as if in a tunnel. The moans became a clot of air that clogged Logan's throat, choking him. It squeezed him until his eyes began to water and then he exhaled tears for release. His arms wrapped around Tabitha. She held the young man close as he cried.

"It's okay, Logan." Tabitha comforted him. "It's over." Logan was not mourning the life he had taken, and he explained that to Tabitha. The weight of the event had just simply taken its toll. "It's over, good man," the woman continued to console. "You're a good man."

Logan backed away from Tabitha, straightening himself. "I'm—I'm not weak…?"

Tabitha caressed the side of Logan's face and kissed his forehead. "No, no," she assured him in a loving voice. "You're as strong as can be, good man. So where next will you take this strong, brave spirit of yours?"

Logan contemplated. He reflected on the little gold he was rewarded. He and the other three divided a sum of money that Mayor Evans called a reward for the recovery and discovery of the gold. It was also pay for putting down bad men. No citizen knew the real story. No paper reported it. But the corruption of Reverend Valley and the politicians was exposed. Other government officials came to clean up the mess and help Black Manor. Everyone was cautious of the government officials, but so far, all was well.

It all came down to Logan's reward.

He earned it. The world was now at his fingertips.

The world, he considered.

Logan had Tabitha's answer.

"Let's see what we look like around the globe."

Waiting For What?

You're black. You know too much. You've dared to study outside the box that has been built for you to understand, its walls sprayed with the graffiti of African-American symbols of slavery and struggle. The Matrix was not a movie for you. It's real, because everything is a lie. As cliché as it might be, you're angry because the lie cannot be exposed, and you'll be seen as unruly and militant even if you try and teach the truth in a calm and collective manner, which you've tried. Unfortunately, you got emotional and looked like the bad guy. White folks stayed calm and looked like the good guys. You could kick yourself for those incidences.

You're watching your people now, not really grasping the concept of the first black President. They're happy because they believe they've made it in a land that has kept them down far too long. Maybe times are better. But you know that's not true. The first black President should be seen as a symbol. He should be seen as inspiration to find out where else in Black History that occurred before. Black people would be surprised to see it happened for hundreds of thousands of years, and it happened everywhere on the planet.

They'll never know. Why? Because everyone, everywhere, went to the same high school, *Western View High*. Every Black person that crosses your path reeks with the stench of its graduate, miseducation program. They all look like the walking dead, no matter how beautiful, handsome, young, or old. They are zombies locked in a routine of religion and nine-to-die jobs. And they make you sick. Each of them married to a Eurocentric concept of reality from which they need to quickly divorce themselves. You would easily volunteer your services to act as the Divorce Lawyer. You have a great case to make. Their 'spouse' is cheating on them. Their spouse is dysfunctional. Their spouse is abusive. Their spouse is robbing them of freedom and culture, passing these concepts off as illusions and designs now perverted and counterfeited with time. Their spouse is not a gold digger, but a soul digger, mining for the spice of life to imitate being alive. All of this while black people, and people of color the world over, die.

None of these black people are aware of the fact the world has been twisted to keep them from knowing who they really are, and the potential of what they could become. History is now used to justify stories, to provide a valid historicity, wrapped up in religious writings, scrolls, and characters to justify the brutal treatment of black people. There was no such thing as Separation of Church and State. Plus, a black man is in charge. There's an actual HNIC in the White House.

God bless him, but there's still more to be done. You know that. There's history to reclaim as well as continue to make. There's mythology to decode. The rabbit hole goes deeper.

You've studied. You've been to the black history lectures. You've read the books. You know the conspiracy is no theory. Black people, in and outside of Africa, founded great civilizations and decoded the universe, creating sciences that govern the world to this day. Egypt. Nubia. Black Arabia. Black Asia. Black America. Black Europe, even before the Moors. And then there was the science, wrapped up in mythology. You know each ancient story might have started off as a black, ancestral concept of exact science, spirituality, psychology, biology, or astronomy, but all that has died. It's become a twisted lie prostituted to keep confused the very descendants of the people who decoded all the sciences. Black People. The Original People of the Earth. The Parent Race. You don't think this is a declaration for supremacy, but a declaration for a necessity to know reality and its history. In the beginning was Black, and Black created everything. You even know the astrophysical equation to life, how it started. Its foundation is simple, it depended on the family. The trinity. There is the Father, The Mother, and the Redeeming Son. These principles are symbolic of the universe and the physical reality.

Dark Energy. That's what scientists call it. The Father, protruding like a phallus. Then there's Dark Matter. The Mother. Her black halos like wombs, penetrated by the essence of the cosmic dark father. The two invisible dark forces, when combined, unleash a vacuum energy of creation in all of its magnificent power. The cosmic orgasm was The Big Bang. Creation. Dark Matter's womb exhaled dust clouds. The pieces collected, grew, compressed. There was force, inward, gravity. There came the dense sphere coupled with compression, collapse, reaction, and explosion. The first star. The first sun. Son. Out of this dense black material, life was formed.

This is sexuality between the Black Man and the Black Woman on a higher, cosmic plane. The residual carbon then became solid planets, life, ultimately the Black Man and the Black Woman in the physical. Melanin. They were the light, meaning innocent. They were free, until the light of the physical reality blinded them from their spiritual selves. Now, the light must redeem itself through darkness. It is not the other way around. The process must reverse itself. The fourth principal, the villain, the cultivator, must agitate the fallen light that is the physical Black Man and the physical Black Woman, to come back together again. Sexually. Mentally. Spiritually. Harmoniously.

The agitator is your mind. Militant. Angry. You repeat to yourself, *"You're black. You know too much. You've dared to study outside the box that has been built for you to understand, its walls sprayed with the graffiti of African-American symbols of slavery and struggle. The Matrix was not a movie for you. It's real, because everything is a lie. As cliché as it might be, you're angry because the lie cannot be exposed, and you'll be seen as unruly and militant even if you try and teach the truth in a calm and collective manner."*

Now your conscious eyes watch helplessly as the descendants of civilization become scattered and scatterbrained. We are equal, not because of any manmade law. And if so, some men are not honoring the law. You believe that black people have been duped. You consider that it's taken three-thousand years of a perpetual state of war and trickery, coupled with three-hundred years of slavery and colonization, one hundred years of violent segregation, and forty-years of a lock-out of *anything* black-owned, strong-armed into the gutter and ghetto.

It sure has taken a long time to subdue us, you think.

But it was done.

Damn, you think, *These white folks is persistent.* You wonder if black people freed themselves during the Civil Rights movement, or did black people sign up for residency on a new, cleaner plantation. *Willie Lynch did a helluva job,* you ponder as you recall the vicious slave owner who was paid and brought to North America to help North American slave owners keep their slaves subdued. *Put the fear of God into them,* he said. *Put the woman against the man. Put the child against the parent. Favor the light and not the dark. Breed mistrust among the niggers.* People argue whether or not Willie Lynch existed. It doesn't matter, you understand, someone did something, whether it was one person, or an entire body of slave owners. Someone devised a plan to divide black people. No need to argue anymore. Willie Lynch Syndrome is real, regardless, you conclude. White folks always want to get us wasting energy on an argument. It doesn't matter. The effect is still the same. The plan was infallible, but only made to last for three hundred years, guaranteed.

Three hundred years, you think. Three hundred. *Hmm,* you wonder. Willie Lynch's speech was supposedly delivered in the year 1712. Three hundred years after would mark the end of slave mentality among black people.

2012.

A prophetic date among many cultures, not just the Mayans. The black Olmecs of South America marked the date, a culture that predates the Mayans. Even the Nubian, Abyssinian, and Kemites mark the year as prophetic, all calculated within their time scheme.

Hmm, you continue pondering. It's a longshot, would take a whole lot of spiritual work, but you decide to decode that later, hold a cipher with some cats and discuss it.

But anyway, you think, *we signed a pact,* you continue on in your original thought. A treaty. The greatest weapon at the disposal of White Supremacy was the treaty. It worked every time. You begin to think about how more people of color have been killed through a treaty than by any disease. Black people and people of color always honored a treaty. *Civilized people don't want a war,* you think as you continue to watch the black passersby in the street. But Western rulers would use the treaty to stop the might of the Original Warriors from consuming them in a physical battle. Your mind wanders to the prevailing myth that Europeans conquered the world through physical strength. Truthfully, no European army ever physically subdued a people of color.

You lean back and think harder on the notion. Alexander the Greek made wise decisions on whom to attack and whom not to attack. He never even touched Nubia. He would only lay waste to lands that had already crumbled at its original foundation, in political upheaval, coming through as a mediator. Queen Isabella and King Ferdinand would consolidate all the armies of Europe, but would mostly exploit the discrepancies between the Arabs and the Black Moors, pushing both factions from Europe. Napoleon tried, but his biggest mistake would be Haiti. The battles in Haiti would take the lives of his greatest Generals and Commanders, leaving him ill prepared for Russia. And Hitler and Mussolini's mistake would be Africa.

According to a Japanese author, whose name, at this moment, escapes you, Western rule came with the treaty. You curse yourself for not remembering the name of the book or author. *Damnit!* But the book stated that as the people of color honored the treaty, the European would weasel hostile takeovers by setting up borders, boundaries, and colonies as police states. This was how lands were conquered. The gun or the sword did not conquer people of color. Those weapons were reserved for people of color to fight one another, after being duped into thinking brothers and sisters were the enemy. You remember the Japanese brother stating people of color were conquered by the word. Weapons have only been used to maintain control. The treaty has always been the greatest subduer.

Words on paper.

And to this day black people still hail like Shylock, *"My word is bond."* Of *course*, you think. We *invented the word.* The word is nothing more than the background harmonics of the Universe. The word is rhythm. Of course black people are bonded to the rhythm of the word.

The word is the tie that binds.

In the beginning was the word.

You smile at your calculation.

But, truthfully, as you look at the streets of downtown Brooklyn rushing along, you expect nothing less from White Supremacy. How could they be bound to the word? This was a society that was historically illiterate and without a language until its black parents introduced them to one. So, how could they honor a treaty? How could they honor the word? It's not in their nature.

You think about all the lectures and panel discussions you've engaged in with grassroots black people, militant black people, and even the so-called educated talented tenth. You were humble with the information you possessed, even when you addressed someone in a debate. Today the spirit of wisdom possessed you to become nauseous at the sight of your own people, vomiting your humility. This spirit of wisdom possessed all black people at one time or another. It even possessed those without the knowledge locked into your understanding. You recall referring to this phenomenon as *Tourette's Consciousness* or *Tourette's Awareness*. It was when a black person's neurological restraints, conditionings, and mental slave chains, broke for a small period of time and they had to speak out on reality.

You summed up black people's present dysfunction in an anecdote. You can remember the faces on the people you spoke to once you were finished. You told the audience, *"Since most of us are Christian, let's take the famous character Jesus."* That was the first time cynicism crept into your tone. You were hurt, a little, because you felt as if you were crumbling under the pressure of knowledge, wisdom, and understanding. That was the first sign of Black Conscious Depression. Then came the hate for life and earth. It ended with a declaration about death as the only release.

"Let's say He was on His way back," you continued. *"The Great Return was on its way. Tired of just warming the bench, Jesus removed the strap of linen around His eyes and decided Justice would no longer be blind. The Judgment was on! Building inside Jesus was a two thousand year anger nourished through the fast food of Western History that called for His Image to be distorted to enslave, declare war upon, confuse, steal, re-invent, assimilate, miseducate, and deconstruct the very people who had birthed His existence. These were the very people who He resembled racially. Black folks. Two thousand years of anger blossomed by watching His murderers—the Romans, the very people that put Him to the cross—re-structure His Image in their likeness. His murderers would be the custodians of His life and Image. His murderers would declare ecclesiastical powers in His name."*

You pause in your moment of recollection and think, *Didn't that happen with Martin too?* You can hear King in your head declaring, *"Somebody told a lie one day."*

In this sign they conquered. Your recollection continues.

"And so, Jesus did so much resent the world that He returned to it with a flaming sword, a white horse, and the wrath of War, Famine, and Pestilence strengthening Him. However, so strong was His intent, that as He descended at an incalculable speed through the dark seas of Heaven, the atmosphere, and the clouds of our world, He crashed against the Earth with a might that lifted the seas into tidal waves, typhoons, tsunamis, and earthquakes. When the shock of Jesus' descent passed, awake did the Lord of the Heavens without memory of who He was."

You can still hear the crowd gasp from your 'Biblically' poetic words.

"The first man He would come across was a Priest. This was a sinner hiding behind a costume of religion and spirituality. Quickly, walking up to the Priest was a Businessman, a sinner hiding behind a costume of commerce and economics. A third man would arrive, a Politician. This was a sinner hiding behind policy and management. Each one of these men knew who was before them. Jesus glowed brighter than the sun itself. The magnitude of His power dulled because of the death of His memory and task.

But the five fingers of fear still clutched at the hearts of these three men. Jesus stood before them, towering. But although he looked perplexed, these three men saw intent. All they could see was a man determined. In their eyes, He was a juggernaut, a warrior standing for battle. Reality wasn't clear to any of them because clearly, Jesus was actually staggering, reaching for something sturdy for support. He was weary, exhausted. His head spun the scenery around Him." You remember clarifying to your audience, wildly declaring as the energy of your story even captures you, *"But you have to imagine that the three sinners are terrified. They know exactly who this is. And they believe the Judgment has come. Jesus approaches, stumbling. Fear glues the three men, holding them in their place. Slowly they prepare themselves. Each goes through his sins and crimes and realizes it's time for them to die. Jesus opens his mouth, and to their surprise utters, "Who am I?"*

Fear lets go of their hearts.

"Oh," says the Priest. "You don't know?"

Jesus just shakes his head, no.

Each of the three men declared that Jesus worked for them. And so, He entered the world, ready to defeat its evils, only to sign a treaty and become defeated, even before He tried. So here's the irony. Jesus, in a Church, lost of Knowledge of Self, singing and praising the Second Coming of…Himself…who's… already here. He's just forgotten.

So, if everyone is waiting, singing and praising for the Second Coming, and that's Jesus…who's already here…lost of memory… then what is Jesus waiting, singing, and praising for in this Church?

You never waited for an answer. You remember just expressing, *"Right. That's the same dilemma Black people are in. Spike said, wake-the-fuck up!"* Your audience loved the story, but you never believed they really understood it. The black people walking by, looking like zombies, looked like the same people in the audience.

You scoff and think to yourself, *Everyone, everywhere, went to the same High School,* Western View High. Every Black person that crosses your path reeks with the stench of its graduate, miseducation program. They all look like the walking dead, no matter how beautiful, handsome, young, or old. They are zombies locked in a routine of religion and nine-to-die jobs. And, they make you sick. Each of them married to a Eurocentric concept of reality from which they need to quickly divorce themselves. You would easily volunteer your services to act as the Divorce Lawyer.

You have a great case to make.

The Curse of Cain-An*

Day One

The long and wide, white hallway shimmered brightly with humming florescent lights. It was blinding. Any drugged induced inhabitant would have believed they were off to Heaven. If Heaven was a bright hallway, and if the six, armed men walking in rows of three did not make them believe they were heading somewhere south of Heaven. Another sobering sight within the long, wide, bright hallway was the soldiers lining each wall at the end of the corridor where the marching, six soldiers approached. At the end of the passageway there lay a single door. The soldiers' approach was cautious. Each man was dressed in fatigues and a helmet, visors drawn down over their eyes. They were fitted with knives and guns, sheathed and holstered over their attire. In their hands they carried MP5KA4 submachine guns. Each soldier, in both rows, had this particular weapon raised and aimed at a lone, shackled subject: a young, black man calling himself Cain.

There was no record of Cain's actual identity. He was twenty-five years old, and he had spent the last two years of his life incarcerated. Cain's skin was dark brown, a wild Afro raged like a firestorm atop his head. A small patch of hair decorated his chin. The color of his eyes was an odd shade of violet. He was six feet tall, but carried himself as if he was taller. He walked down the hallway confident and cool as if the guards behind him were a part of an entourage. A devious and arrogant grin was painted on his face. Cain was a celebrity, if only for the security cameras that lined the ceiling in the hallway. His hands were cuffed in a bizarre fashion, incased in heavy gloves made of iron. Cain was not weighed down by the hulking constraints. A chain dangled at each wrist and locked to ankle restraints.

Cain kept his composure, even with the submachine guns aimed at him. He found the situation flattering. The best soldiers the United States had to offer were selected to guard him. Him. One man. The weapons aimed at him were often used to slaughter multiple opponents in a single pull of the trigger. The muzzles were not eyeing an opposing army, just a single man. Him. Cain. He could not help but feel important.

---

* Inspired by the series <u>Blood Omen: The Legacy of Kain</u> and <u>The Legacy of Kain: Soul Reaver</u>

The guards lining the hall lifted their weapons as Cain passed. This was his Paparazzi. Cain stopped at the end of the hall. A loud buzzing noise sounded, echoing through the hallway. The door in front of Cain opened. He stepped inside and the door closed immediately, locking with an electronic hiss. The soldiers relaxed their weapons, pivoted in a military fashion, and turned around to face the other end of the hall.

Cain took a seat at a table inside the room. There was a dull light that illuminated the even duller, gray interrogation room. There was no two-way mirror, but a camera, mounted on the wall directly in front of Cain, which allowed his captors to view him from another room. There was an intercom positioned next to the camera, and there were no windows. There was an unoccupied seat on the other side of the table.

The intercom cackled with static, which was quickly interrupted by the clear sound of a voice commanding Cain, "Look into the camera and state your name for the record."

Cain cleared his throat, his ego carved as a smile. Every move he made seemed self-important. "My name is Cain," he said in a raspy voice. He sounded as if he was introducing himself as a newscaster. He then expressed his entire name, "Ham-Horus Cain. I'm your conscience, muthafucka!" Cain rested his hands on the table and waited for another command. There was none. He continued to look into the camera, keeping his smile.

Cain's image beamed clear through a monitor stationed in a United States Government Security Operation Center. Technicians and agents scurried around the room, facilitating other important data and cases. Two agents were the only people watching Cain, his smile eerily eyeing them. One of the agent's was a man named Victor Terrence. The second was the Chief Director of the facility holding Cain. His name was Nicholas Holt.

Victor was thirty-three years old, African-American, and clean cut. He was dressed in a gray suit with matching tie. Victor stood with his arms folded, his eyes narrowing on Cain with hawk-like perception. Victor was anxious. Several minutes from now he was going to interrogate Cain face-to-face. Victor was a Criminal Psychologist. Today was his first case. For five years he had been a field agent for the Federal Bureau of Investigation. With his uncanny ability to understand the criminal mind, and the practice of his knowledge to predict high profile criminals' movements, Victor was urged by his superiors to continue his education, concentrating on Criminal Psychology. He picked up a doctoral degree. The Bureau paid for his education. The money was not a loan. They would recoup their loses by hiring Victor to aid them in understanding criminals they marked as *special projects*.

Nicholas Holt, chief facilitator of the operations, had been Victor's mentor for the past five years. Nicholas was in his late forties, Caucasian, had a receding hairline, and needle thin lips that looked as if he was tucking them in when he spoke. He was tall and heavy, the physical build of a cop who was just a little past his prime. But there were still some good fighting years left in the Director. Nicholas was dressed in a brown suit and tie. His eyes went from Cain's image on the screen to Victor standing next to him. He was waiting for the doctor to give a quick analysis of Cain.

Victor remained silent. His only words to the Director, after shaking his head and taking a breath, were, "When can I go in there and speak to him?"

"When you're ready," the other grunted in a low, tough voice. Nicholas' eyes went back to the monitor. Cain was so still that it looked as if his video image had been paused. His smile remained. Cain's image burned at Nicholas. The Director looked at Victor and stated, "You know I'd rather have every criminal, and every psychotic in this world's history—including dictators—released on the world all at once, than this young man walking our streets, or even existing."

Victor reacted to the comment immediately. He looked up from the monitor at Nicholas with a perplexed expression. After a moment he turned his eyes back to Cain. "What makes this guy so deadly?"

"Don't worry about him," Nicholas said to Victor. "He's no real threat now. Just talk to him."

Victor shook his head up and down. "I'm ready," he said confidently, though he was not necessarily sure what type of information he was supposed to be pulling from Cain. "Let me go in," he exhaled.

Nicholas handed Victor a folder. Victor peeked inside. It was Cain's case file. Victor had been reviewing Cain's file for the past two weeks. He was told Cain should not be taken lightly, and Cain's dangerous behavior was constantly reiterated. Even after reading Cain's file he never quite understood why. Cain was accused of the murder of a serial rapist. Though, even in the file it was said the rapist, David Reily, killed himself. There was nothing more. There was nothing at all that gave merit to Cain's incarceration inside a secret, underground, Government prison. Furthermore, Cain was deemed a threat to national security. Victor again saw no reason as to why. Cain was not a militant, grassroots lecturer. Cain did not adhere to conspiracy theories, or have any ties with African-American parties classified as 'terrorists' or on the 'watch list'. Victor felt as much a test subject as Cain.

It was time to find out what made Cain high-risk.

Victor left the room. Three soldiers, dressed identically to the guards who earlier escorted Cain, flanked Victor immediately as he entered the hall. Victor stiffened with their presence. The soldiers saluted. Victor relaxed and saluted them back. The soldiers pivoted and escorted Victor to an open elevator. The group stepped inside. Victor followed. He pushed a button for the elevator to descend two floors. The doors closed and the elevator hummed in its descent. When the doors opened, Victor found himself in the long, wide hallway Cain had passed through earlier. At the end of the hall were the soldiers posted outside the interrogation room. The line of soldiers that had earlier escorted Cain, were on one knee, their guns aimed at Victor. The soldiers surrounding Victor signaled with their hands.

The six soldiers stood up, three of them lined the left wall. The other three lined the right wall. The three soldiers accompanying Victor walked side-by-side ahead of him.

The soldiers in front of Victor broke away. One guard walked up to the door and then moved aside to allow Victor to step up. The buzzing sound echoed through the hall and the door opened. Victor walked inside coolly. He looked at Cain and greeted him with a pleasant smile. Cain, however, viewed Victor's entrance with curiosity, like a king viewing the entrance of a stranger into his kingdom. At first there was a puzzling surprise on Cain's visage. His mouth hung open. He inspected the African-American Criminal Psychologist, lost in awe and wonder, his head slightly turned, viewing Victor more closely with his left eye. But then Cain regained his composure. He chuckled a bit, and to no surprise, with intense arrogance. Victor perceived that Cain considered him some sort of joke. Victor was impressed with Cain's stature, not physically, but Cain, though he was sitting down, stood taller than any man standing before him. He leaned back in his chair as if it were a throne. He asked Victor, "And what wonderful deed did you perform that bestowed upon you the honor to grace my presence?"

Victor's smile faded. He became serious when he answered Cain. "I've performed many deeds that led to this moment, Cain. I'm a Criminal Psychologist."

Cain raised both his eyebrows, looking as if his interests elevated. Whether his emotions were sarcastic or not, could not be determined, even when he retorted, "Really? Is there a criminal present?"

"You, Cain," Victor said in a stern voice. He stood next to the table and dropped the manila folder onto its surface. "You're the criminal in question."

Cain snorted. "*Hmph!* I question the accusation of being a criminal," he replied. His eyes narrowed on the folder. His smile reappeared. "Exactly what is said in that folder that blasphemes me with such a title?"

Victor opened the folder. His eyes perused the first page and came across the name *David Reilly*. He felt the need to remind Cain of this man. "What can you tell me about David Reilly? What happened to him?" He took the seat opposite Cain on the other side of the table.

The mention of David Reilly only caused Cain to laugh. His head fell back, aiming his laughter to the ceiling. He relaxed and shook his head, arrogant smile drawn sharply. "Alas, poor Reilly, I knew him well," He partially quoted. His lip curled into a sneer, and he added, "Well, not really." He leaned forward, forearms resting on the side of the table. "But if you must know anything, that rapist took his own life." Cain began to ponder aloud. "How ironic, he gave the most, when he took himself away. His last heinous act, a great gift to the world." He looked up from his contemplative state and addressed Victor, "Wouldn't you agree Doctor Victor Terrence?"

Victor's heart skipped a beat. He questioned how Cain knew his name when he never introduced himself. Nicholas, from two floors up, viewed the two men on the monitor. He wiped his brow and hoped that Cain's antics were not getting to Victor. Victor remained calm. Cain narrowed his eyes on the psychologist. He cocked his head and lessened his smile.

"You hide it very well, Doctor Terrence," Cain taunted Victor. "But, you know, I don't have these eyes for nothing." The very violet eyes Cain possessed held Victor in their sight, their color twirling supernaturally. "I can see it swirling in you now, the feeling of wonder." Cain looked closer at Victor, as if he was peering straight into the doctor's thoughts. "I can see your emotions in a scuffle. There's a soporific task force of chemicals trying to put down the rebellious need to ask the restless question," and Cain leaned forward, mocking a concerned expression as he concluded, "*How does he know who I am?*" Cain chuckled sinisterly as he leaned back.

Victor did not move, though his insides were just as Cain described. He fought hard to keep his composure, but he slipped in the simple skip of his heartbeat when Cain mentioned his name. But it was unnoticeable, wasn't it, thought Victor. Cain could not have heard his heart skip, could he? But what eased Victor's nerves was the thought that Cain was simply stating the obvious. Who would not wonder how a complete stranger would know their name? Victor could not think of a possible reason for Cain's knowledge of him. Though Victor was aware of this facility in Washington D.C., he never once had clearance to enter it until now. And he was never assigned to Cain's case as a Federal Agent. Victor remained calm on the surface. His eyes inspected Cain's restraints.

"Those are some odd handcuffs," Victor said casually. "What's with the need to cover your hands?"

Cain lifted his shoulders. "Perhaps they believe I'll scratch," he exhaled, his face contorting in disgust. It was not too long before his arrogant smile resurfaced. "But I'm sure an assassin such as you could handle a simpleton like me," he spoke, eyes again searching for Victor's reaction.

Victor was still.

Cain continued to prod. "So many titles you go by, Victor," he said. "Doctor, Federal Agent." He raised an eyebrow and said, "I'm sure profiling was a lot easier when your mark wasn't sitting in front of you. And, especially when there was much more inside their file for you to go by."

Victor became noticeably angry. He turned his head and looked directly into the camera behind him. He looked back at Cain. "I'll admit, Cain, I don't know what they're looking for. And my superiors seem to know more about you than I do. They seem to know more than what's in this folder." He gave another frustrated look into the camera and then faced Cain again.

Nicholas watched the two men closely, and with all intensity. He cupped his hand over his mouth, his eyes twitched in anticipation of Victor's next move. But Victor did not move at all. Instead, Cain moved. He adjusted the heavy iron gloves and started to grimace. His hands were becoming uncomfortable. His forearms shook. Victor noticed Cain beginning to squirm.

"Nervous?" Victor asked.

Cain straightened himself, exhaling. "Under no circumstance, Doctor," Cain assured Victor. He leaned back in his chair, his arms resting on the table. "For two years I waited for this day. And I expected you no sooner or later. This is where fate has decided we should meet." Cain's devious smile returned. He stated, "Such an ineluctable bitch, fate. She's far different than her sister destiny. Destiny can be avoided. It's simply a destination in life. We've all veered from her path at one time or another. Fate, however, is a relentless whore. She *will* fuck you."

Cain's babble was far from impressive and did not offer Victor any answers. Victor rolled his eyes. "Are you saying you can predict the future," he inquired with a tone of sarcasm in his voice. "If that's the case, you're in the wrong facility. This is not for the criminally insane. I'll have you transferred immediately."

Cain shook his head, no. "I cannot predict the future, Doctor," retorted Cain, his tone a sigh. "I can only calculate events. I can see cause and all the trouble it creates. It's simple mathematics."

"Maybe you are criminally insane," said Victor with a raised eye.

It was Cain who rolled his eyes now. "*Amla leugim,*" he said the phrase as if it were a curse. The phrase was in a language unfamiliar to Victor. Cain noticed Victor go for a pen in his pocket.

Though the word was foreign to Victor he reacted to it as if he had heard it before. He stood up straight, back against the chair. He inquired, "What language is that, Cain?"

"Spanish," Cain joked, his smile wide.

Victor turned his head and gave Cain a curious eye. "I'm fluent in Spanish, French, Italian, and German. That's no word I've ever heard." He placed the pen onto a sheet of paper he pulled from the folder. His eyes never left Cain, as he demanded sternly, "Spell it."

"Phonetically?" asked Cain.

"Whatever," Victor said impatiently.

"There's a gut instinct in you isn't there," Cain teased. "There's a clue. There's something about this word. You have to know. So, dear friend, I will tell you. *Amla leugim,*" Cain repeated. He then proceeded to spell the words. His eyes watched every stroke of the pen as Victor finished spelling the foreign phrase. His arrogant smile returned. "This, Victor, is where they say the game begins, and you will be so surprised to find out who 'they' are."

Victor chuckled, "On the contrary, Cain. This is where our first meeting ends. I have what I want, but you know that. I'll research what you've given me. This conversation need not go any further." He stood up and shuffled his papers back into the folder. He swiped up the manila folder and knocked on the desk. "I'll see you here tomorrow." He turned to leave.

A buzzer sounded. The door opened.

"No you won't," alerted Cain sternly.

Victor turned. "Excuse me?"

"We won't be meeting here tomorrow, Doctor," Cain said in a sorrowful voice.

Victor exhaled a playful breath, a smile on his face. "Is there something I should know, Cain? Are we going to be in a different room? What's your calculated prediction?"

Cain did not smile, and the absence of his playful behavior made Victor's heart skip again. Cain stated confidently, "I'll be escaping from here tonight." He looked away from Victor. His eyes looked directly into the camera. "And two of the guards outside this room will be found hanging in my cell," he lifted his hands, "by these restraints." He lowered the heavy, iron gloves. "They will have hung themselves, and you can dust for prints if you find my claims unbelievable."

Victor rolled his eyes again. He reiterated to his subject, "I'll see you tomorrow, Cain. This was actually more fun than I expected."

The doctor walked from the room. The three soldiers who escorted Victor through the hall took their stances around him again. They made their way back to the elevator at the end of the hall. The elevator doors slid open. All four men stepped inside. Victor pushed a button to raise the elevator two floors. The ascent did not take long. The doors opened, and Victor found himself back in the hallway leading to the Security Operations Center. Victor walked inside, his escorts remaining by the door. He returned to Nicholas' side. He slapped the manila folder into the Director's chest.

"Don't get too comfortable with that," said Victor. "I have some notes."

The Director opened the folder. "I only saw you write down that odd phrase," he said shuffling through papers as if there might be more.

"That'll be enough," said Victor raising his eyebrows. He looked at the monitor, Cain staring up at both of them. "He's so confident, so sure that he's in control. Though, he just might be. He talks a good game." Victor then gave Nicholas an uneasy look. "I don't know what I'm looking for, Director," he said, his voice straddling the line of sounding frustrated and humble.

Nicholas ignored Victor. The Director's eyes locked onto Cain's image. "Tomorrow, mention the name A.J. Dyack. See how he reacts."

Victor became frustrated, expressed through the tone in his words when he spoke. "What about how I react."

Nicholas turned back to Victor. He felt Victor needed an explanation. "We suspect Cain to be responsible for other heinous crimes," he explained.

Victor felt the Director was not being honest, only presenting information he believed would quell his inquiries. Victor put his hands on his hips. "We really can't prove the one we have him locked up for."

"We don't have him locked up for the suicide of David Reilly," Nicholas corrected. The comment surprised Victor. Nicholas noted Victor's reaction. "We're holding Cain for other reasons. That's obvious. Those reasons point to why he's a threat to national security. The death of David Reilly helped us apprehend him. It was something to give to the civilians."

Victor moved uncomfortably, trying to regain composure.

Nicholas swayed to get into Victor's line of vision. "Listen to me, Victor," the Director pleaded. "You are slowly being initiated into this program. Several years ago you never knew this place existed. Six months ago you had clearance to enter this facility. Slowly, but surely, we will give you all the information you need." He returned the manila folder to Victor. He reached around and grabbed another folder. He shook it in front of Victor. "A.J. Dyack."

Victor took the second folder. He opened it and flipped through the pages. "What about Cain's prediction," he asked. "He might try an escape."

Nicholas assured, "Try he might, but he won't succeed. I'll have five guards stationed outside his compartment. Let's see him even attempt an escape." He slapped Victor on the shoulder. "Now get out of here. You're still on the clock, just take the work home."

Victor nodded. He shook the folders triumphantly and then walked to his briefcase that was located on a counter. Victor opened the case and neatly put the folders inside. He saw, out of the corner of his eye, Nicholas walk up to him. "IIow does he know about me? Name? Titles?" Victor asked Nicholas, never looking at him. He then thought of something. He faced Nicholas, and before the Director answered, Victor asked, "Is this some kind of initiation prank?" He pulled the briefcase from the counter forcefully.

"No. Not at all," Nicholas answered quickly. "This all seems strange, I know. But if we threw you into the reality of who Cain is…" Nicholas' voice trailed away. "Let's just say, ignorance will allow you to keep courage."

"That makes me feel better," Victor said jokingly.

It felt good for Nicholas to see Victor joke. The Director put an arm around Victor's shoulder. He led him back to the door and out into the hallway. "Trust me," he said. "With this as your first case, it'll be like losing your virginity to a porn star. You will learn a lot about this program. This is an excellent case to get more than your feet wet. We need you on this."

The two of them stopped at the elevator. The door opened. Victor stepped inside. He put his arm on the side of the door to block the metal panels from closing. He said to Nicholas, "I'm going to regret taking this job, aren't I?"

"Not when you see the benefits," Nicholas saluted Victor with two fingers. The Director then turned away to deal with transferring Cain back to his compartment.

Victor backed up into the elevator. The doors closed and he inserted a small card into a slot underneath the console of buttons. He then hit the button marked LEVEL ONE. Victor removed the card as the elevator ascended thirty stories into the first floor of an office building in Washington, D.C. Half of the buttons were suddenly sealed off by a metal panel. Only anyone with a security card, such as the one Victor possessed, could access the lower levels. To everyone else in the building, the underground floors did not exist. The *legitimate* tenth floor contained Victor's office, as well as other psychologists'. Victor decided not to bother with returning to his office. He was on his way home.

Victor stepped from the elevator and into the lobby. He kept his eye on the front door and swiveled his way to the outside. He took a right, and walked down the sidewalk until he came to the parking lot. He removed his keys from his pocket and unlocked his car by pushing a button located on the remote chained to his keys. He opened the door and put his briefcase on the passenger's side before slipping in. He started the car and backed out onto the street. Taking a left, Victor made the proper directions and path out of Washington and into the Maryland suburban neighborhood where he lived. He parked his car in the garage and exited, taking his briefcase with him.

Victor lowered the garage door with the single push of a button. He unlocked the garage entrance to his house and then opened the door. He walked into his kitchen and set his briefcase on the kitchen table. "Honey, I'm home," Victor joked. He was not married. The house was empty. He took off his suit jacket, sat down, and opened the case. Victor removed his tie and unbuttoned the first couple buttons on his shirt. He stretched and relaxed. He took out the file on A.J. Dyack and sifted through it. "Let's see what kind of reading we've got for tonight."

Victor's eyes skimmed A.J.'s profile. His full name was Andrew Johnson Dyack. He was a forty-five year old African-American male with light skin. In the picture provided he had a graying, low cut Afro atop a thin, oval face. He had the physique of a basketball player, tall, thin, but muscular. His profile read that he taught a literature course at Howard University. His class focused on mythology, and he only taught one semester out of the year. According to the file, Andrew had a degree in History with a concentration on ancient culture and mythology. He was a national lecturer who spoke on subjects including legends, the occult, and mythological objects. Andrew's file also noted that he had just recently married. His spouse was named Amy Hennig. She recently gave birth to twins. The file also revealed that Andrew had another child, grown. The young man was named Charles. He was twenty-two years old.

Victor closed the file wondering how a teacher and lecturer fit into the equation. He also wondered if Andrew was being dubbed just as dangerous as Cain. He put the folder back inside the briefcase and figured he would find more on the connection between Andrew Johnson Dyack and Cain tomorrow in the interrogation. He substituted Andrew's file for Cain's. He thumbed through the papers until he came across the phrase *amla leugim* scribbled in his handwriting. He took out a pen and twirled it in his fingers. His eyes cased the word continuously. Each time he read the phrase his thoughts plucked a potential meaning.

Victor got up from his seat and walked from the kitchen to his study where a laptop lay. He grabbed the device, unhooking it from its recharge cord, and returned to the kitchen. He moved his briefcase aside and made room for his laptop and flipped it open. He turned the machine on and went to the refrigerator to prepare a sandwich. Afterward, he took his seat back at the table. He put the plate on his briefcase and his drink next to the right of the laptop. Victor entered his password and the computer loaded its main screen. Victor punched up the Internet and typed *amla leugim* into a search engine.

The search yielded nothing.

Victor tried three more search engines. There was nothing. He looked back at the word. A thought came to him. He remembered that Cain remarked, jokingly, that the phrase was Spanish. "Amla leugim," he said aloud. He spoke the word slowly, hoping it would expose its meaning. He tried another pronunciation. "Am-*la le*-ugim." Victor raised an inquisitive eyebrow. "French? Le Ugim?" And then he came up with an answer, gazing long at the word. His mind rearranged the letters. Perhaps it was an anagram, he considered.

Victor flipped his pen to its point and started to spell the phrase backwards. He slowly spelled the Spanish word *Alma* out of *amla*. The word meant *soul* in Spanish. Victor worked on the second word and came up with the name *Miguel*. Victor smiled. *Miguel Alma*. It was a name. Spanish. Victor took a bite of his sandwich and chips. He swallowed and followed his bite with juice. His fingers went to his laptop's keyboard and typed the name Miguel Alma followed by Andrew Johnson Dyack. He hesitated to hit the ENTER key. There was a tingling sensation on the back of his neck. Despite the sensation coming from his neck, Victor had a gut feeling. He deleted Andrew Johnson's name and substituted it with David Reilly.

Hundreds of links loaded up, twenty of them displayed on the first page. Victor looked close and inspected the first link, reading the synopsis. Written there were the words: *The brother of Reilly's last victim speaks out about rapist's suicide. "It's over," says Miguel Alma, brother to Eva Alma who was David Reilly's final rape victim. "May that monster burn in hell!"*

"Why the hell didn't they give me David Reilly's file," Victor murmured. He deleted Miguel Alma's name from the search box and hit ENTER. Thousands of websites profiling David Reilly appeared. The sites did not give Victor any more information on the sex offender than he already knew. It was a case he was never assigned to but heard much about. David Reilly was a rapist that preyed on Latino women. He was a forty-eight year old white male with silver hair. David was of average build. It was speculated that his career as a serial rapist spanned ten years. There were fifteen known rapes, but he was suspected of more. He died from a self-inflicted gunshot wound two years ago while Victor was attending school for his doctoral degree.

Victor exited the online program and leaned back in his chair. He was excited. He cracked Cain's code and now possessed two names he could use to slap the young man's arrogance. Victor reached into his pocket and pulled out his cell phone. He punched up Nicholas' number but hesitated to hit SEND. Instead, he flipped his cell phone shut.

No.

Victor did not want to waste his energy speaking to Nicholas. He wanted both Nicholas and Cain to be overwhelmed by his discoveries. Cain was going to fold tomorrow. And, to add insult to injury, when Victor spoke to Cain, he was also going to point out the fact that he was still incarcerated.

Victor put his hands behind his head and smiled. The situation was all under his control. He closed his laptop and finished his meal. He wiped his mouth with a napkin and stood up with the empty plate and cup in hand. He dumped the two items into the sink and went into his family room to relax. He flipped on his television with the remote and turned it to the channel zero-zero. The screen was black with the words *Unusable Signal* scrawled across it. Victor bent down and flipped on the switch to his videogame console. He relaxed into the chair behind him. He used another remote to turn on a stereo and activate a Miles Davis CD. It was time for him to cool down with a simple fantasy game and the relaxing sounds of jazz. A shower and bed were next on the list.

Day Two

In the morning. At work. Victor passed his office building, making his way to the parking area. He saw a group of soldiers stationed outside. A police tape marked off the door, and Nicholas Holt engaged in conversation with another suited man. Victor turned into the parking lot, showed his badge, parked, and quickly jumped from his car. He left his briefcase and rushed to the front of the building. A soldier walked up to Victor and blocked his path. The soldier lightly shoved Victor away, pointing and ordering him across the street.

Nicholas quickly made his way to the guard and cleared Victor to pass. Victor still flashed his badge and clearance I.D. in his wallet. The soldier apologized. Victor accepted the soldier's apology, smiled, and saluted him. Nicholas led him into the building and toward the elevator. Inside, Nicholas used his card to open the panel to expose the buttons to the lower floors. The elevator coasted downward.

"Cain's gone," Nicholas revealed. "He escaped last night."

Victor turned his head, perplexed. "What?"

Nicholas explained, frustrated, "Two guards were found hanging in Cain's compartment. They were hanging from Cain's shackles. One was dressed in Cain's jumpsuit. Cain must've disguised himself with the guard's uniform and got out. Both guards were missing their gloves."

"But there were five guards," Victor said with a contemplative tone. "That's just two. What about the three other guards stationed at his cell?"

"They blacked out," answered Nicholas, frustration rising. "They don't remember a thing."

"Cameras," Victor questioned.

"All video goes black at midnight," Nicholas said releasing a heavy sigh. "It gets worse."

Victor blurted, "Worse?"

There came another sigh from the Director as he said, "Forensics of the scene revealed that only the guards' prints are on Cain's shackles." Nicholas was afraid to look at Victor. "They hung themselves," he clarified.

Victor hit a button that brought the elevator to a halt. He put his hands on his hips and jumped into the Director's face. "What the hell is going on here, Nick," he demanded. "Who is this guy? What makes him so dangerous?"

Nicholas raised an eyebrow and halfheartedly joked, "Other than the fact that he escaped from a secret, underground, heavily guarded, Government facility?"

"We'll add that to the list," said Victor, stepping away and putting his back to the wall. "This is my first case, huh? I guess it's down hill from here." He looked back to Nicholas. "How the hell does an unarmed man coax two highly trained, armed guards into hanging themselves? How does the same man get out of his shackles? How does he leave three other guards unconscious? And how does he do it without being seen?"

Nicholas was silent. He contemplated the proper answer. He decided to give out what little he could. Victor anticipated Nicholas' move. The Director believed Victor was not ready to receive the full answer. "You ever hear of a Codebreaker, Doctor?" Nicholas asked.

"Excuse me," Victor said with a perplexed expression.

"It's what the Government calls people like Cain," Nicholas elaborated. "Codebreakers."

"So what are you saying," asked Victor. "Cain can break into computers?" He tried to piece together the current events with his knowledge of Cain and Nicholas' vague revelation. "So, what did he do? Did he break into Government files and find something he shouldn't have? That might explain his incarceration but it doesn't explain his escape."

Nicholas shook his head, no. "He doesn't deal with codebreaking computers, or hacking of any kind. People like Cain have the unique ability to codebreak reality." His eyes went to the floor. "I'd say, with his strategic ability, Cain's been planning this since we apprehended him two years ago." His eyes then met Victor and he said, "If being apprehended wasn't part of his plan as well."

"His plan to what?" Victor asked in a low voice.

Nicholas took a breath. He confessed, "From what I gathered yesterday, it's all been to meet you?"

Victor did not understand. His perplexed look remained. He asked, "Meet me? Why?"

"That's what you're going to find out," Nicholas sighed again. "This case is taking you back into the field. Be careful."

Victor huffed. He pushed the button for the elevator to start again. "At least I know where to start."

"A.J. Dyack," Nicholas concluded prematurely.

"No," Victor said quickly. "*Amla leugim*. Turns out *it is* Spanish."

"For what," Nicholas asked as he leaned against the wall and folded his arms.

"It's *Miguel Alma* backwards," Victor revealed. He noticed Nicholas' perplexed expression. The pleasure of revealing the information had been taken away by the day's events. Victor clarified, "He's Eva Alma's brother. She was David Reilly's last victim. When we get downstairs, I want you to get me his address."

"You think that's where Cain may have gone," Nicholas wanted to know.

Victor lifted his shoulders. "I don't know," he admitted. "But I don't want to go there with a squad of people armed to the teeth. Let me go solo."

Nicholas quickly disagreed, "Hell no. Besides, you don't know what you're up against."

"Then tell me," Victor pleaded.

Nicholas went silent. He took a moment to think about the situation. "Maybe you're right," he conceded. "We don't want to cause frenzy. Up there, we got people thinking there's a bomb threat made on the office building. Terrorists. That's easy in this day and age. We already have a man we're going to arrest. He's an Agent. Arab-American. We'll reassign him. The usual protocol."

The elevator door opened to the familiar hall Victor occupied the day before, two floors above the interrogation room. Soldiers lined the hall, along with other agents. Victor signaled with his head for Nicholas to take lead. The Director stepped into the hall and the two men walked back to the computer room. Inside there was business as usual. Victor guessed, however, that the fiddling around with computers and consoles was to make sure everything was secure, or that possibly one camera was able to have at least a partial recording of last night's incident. This was confirmed when Nicholas informed him as he led Victor to a twenty-nine year old computer specialist named Harrison Burke. Harrison saw the two men approach from their reflection in the computer screen. "And what do you guys need," he asked as Victor and Nicholas flanked him.

Nicholas gave the young man a sharp eye. "We need you to address us properly," he said in a stern voice.

"Sorry, Sir," Harrison apologized.

"That's better," Nicholas stated. "Now, find the address of a-one Miguel Alma," ordered Victor.

"Will do," Harrison said casually as he punched the name into his computer. Immediately there appeared an address and profile. Victor leaned over Harrison's shoulder to get a closer look. "Seems like he's right over in Alexandria. He owns a convenience store there."

"How convenient," Victor joked. "Print the address for the store as well as his place of residence," demanded Victor.

"Will do," Harrison repeated his casual reply. He moved the pointer with the mouse and applied the command for print. "It'll be across the room. I'll get it." Harrison lifted himself from his seat and walked away to retrieve the pages.

"You heading over there today," Nicholas asked.

"What else am I going to do," Victor said annoyed. "Just sit around here?"

Harrison returned. He held the papers with Miguel's addresses and directions in his hand. Victor took the papers from him and folded them. He patted Nicholas on the shoulder and walked away. "You forgetting something, Victor," Nicholas shouted.

Victor spun around to face him. "What?"

Nicholas walked up to Victor slowly. "You have your piece on you?"

"And badge," Victor stated. "Always in my wallet," he shook a finger, "Always an agent."

Nicholas put a hand on Victor's shoulder. "Just investigate," he instructed Victor. "If you start coming into heavy leads, you call for backup. I'm allowing you to go in alone because Cain won't hurt you. Whatever he's after, he needs you alive for it."

Victor considered his Director's points. He responded, "If I discover enough clues to track Cain down, then we'll add up everything we both know and solve this puzzle."

"That's a deal," Nicholas said as he saluted. Victor walked away, heading through the door to the elevator in the hall. "Burke," Nicholas called.

Harrison stepped to the Director's side. "Yessir?"

"Take five men and tail him," Nicholas ordered.

"Yessir," Harrison repeated. He was not just a computer specialist. He was as much a trained field agent as Victor.

"Keep a good distance from him while he tracks down this guy Miguel Alma," Nicholas commanded. "He's ultimately going to seek out A.J. Dyack. That's when you keep an extremely close eye on him."

"What about Cain?" Harrison asked.

"Be cautious of him," Nicholas warned. "He needs Victor alive. I tell you now: Victor is expendable. It might come down to that, whatever Cain is planning. You're ordered to neutralize Cain and Victor if you have to."

"Yessir," the agent repeated.

Nicholas assigned another computer specialist to replace Harrison at his desk. Harrison walked away to prepare himself and gather a crew. At the same moment, Victor had already gone through the lobby and out the door. He flashed his clearance I.D. and badge at several of the officers stationed outside as he made his way to the parking lot. He opened the front door and leaned inside to pop open the trunk. He removed his coat and left it on the front seat, leaving the front door open as he made his way toward the rear of the car. He removed his holster from the trunk and strapped it on. He opened another briefcase and found his gun. He put the weapon into its sheath. He closed the trunk and returned to the driver's side, put his coat back on, slid inside, and started his car. He backed out of the lot and onto the street, getting clearance from another guard.

At a red light he removed and unfolded the paper with Miguel Alma's information. He took a second to adjust the rearview mirror and take a glance at the environment behind him. He then looked back at the paper. The directions printed on it started from the office building. The first set of directions was to Miguel Alma's store. Victor punched the address into his GPS and followed the computerized voice out of D.C. and into Virginia. He entered the city of Alexandria, Virginia and arrived at Miguel's store shortly after. He parked directly in front of the store, checked his rearview again, and then stepped outside. He walked inside the store and saw a young Latino man working the cash register. Victor walked up to the young man and flashed his badge.

"Miguel Alma," Victor stated.

The boy trembled at the sight of the badge. It was as if Victor put the muzzle of a gun to the teenager's head. "M-m-my father's in the backroom," the boy said, his words jumping off his quivering lips. The other customers seemed to freeze and part away from Victor. The Special Agent lowered the badge but kept his wallet in his hands. He nodded his head to the left and commanded in a cordial yet authoritative voice, "Can you bring him out here, please?"

"Yes, sir," the boy said turning his body, but keeping his eyes on Victor. "Dad," he called, finally making a complete turn and walking toward the door on his far right. "Dad," he called again.

Victor watched Miguel's son slip behind an aisle. He witnessed the top of a door swing open. The door remained ajar. The other customers waiting for checkout were still and silent. This allowed Victor to overhear the conversation between Miguel and his son in the backroom. It consisted of no more than Miguel's son alerting his father that an officer was here to see him. Miguel came from the backroom shortly after, his son following.

Miguel was a tall man with light-brown skin. He had broad shoulders, and well groomed jet-black hair. He wore navy-blue slacks and a short-sleeved dress shirt accommodated by a black tie. He walked up to the counter and suspected Victor to be the man in question. They greeted one another with a polite handshake.

"Hello...?" Miguel stated in an unsure voice.

Victor flashed his badge as he let go of Miguel's hand. "Yes. Hello. I'm Federal Agent Victor Terrence," he introduced. "I'd just like to ask you some questions about your sister's case, and her attacker, David Reilly." Victor felt the need to state as much information as possible. It was not just to assure Miguel that there was no trouble, but also to calm his attentive customers.

Miguel sighed. "Yes, indeed." Victor could tell that Miguel believed the incident was far behind him. He was barely over it, if at all. But he felt he had no choice in the matter. "Tino, ring up the rest of the customers and stay on duty," Miguel commanded his son in Spanish.

Victor smiled at the teenager and said in Spanish "Listen to your father."

Miguel chuckled, embarrassed. "I guess nothing gets by you."

"No," Victor said keeping his smile.

Miguel waved Victor toward the backroom. "Please, some privacy."

Victor followed Miguel into the office. Another door led into a dark room with monitors displaying images of particular areas of the store. Inside was Pedro, Miguel's oldest son. Miguel dismissed him to the front of the store and the young man headed out, closing the door as he left. Miguel took a seat at his desk and motioned toward the other seat for Victor. Victor sat down and explained, "Truthfully, it's not your sister's case I'm here for. I'm here regarding an acquaintance you made during your sister's run-in with David Reilly."

"Oh," Miguel said, his eyes squinting with contemplation. "Who?"

"A young man who calls himself Cain," Victor answered.

Miguel leaned back in his chair. He took a deep breath. He looked everywhere but at Victor. He cleared his throat. Victor deduced that Miguel was not trying to hide anything. The man was searching for the right words to speak. Victor waited patiently. Miguel, looking at Victor, finally stated, "I would like to go on record by stating Cain is a great man. What he did for my sister—"

"He escaped from prison last night," Victor interrupted.

"He hasn't come here," said Miguel, "if that's what brought you here."

Victor shook his head, no. "I was profiling him, yesterday. We had a conversation. It was my first session with him. He mentioned your name." Victor smiled and recounted, "He said your name backwards, taunting me with a hint as to who you are. I've been kept in the dark about Cain. I thought maybe you could fill me in."

Miguel exhaled. He fixed himself and cleared his throat. "Your superiors haven't said anything about what Cain can do?"

"No," Victor stated. He became attentive.

"I'm surprised you don't have a partner backing you up," Miguel said with a smile, trying to break the tension.

It worked. Victor chuckled and revealed, "I have six, unofficial partners following me, actually." He was referring to Harrison Burke and his team of five men. He had been aware of them following him since he left Washington D.C. "They're not aware that I know they're following me, however. But they're tailing me. They're parked around the corner in a blue van."

"They don't trust you," Miguel asked.

"It's the Government," Victor answered firmly. "They don't trust anyone." He shifted himself in his chair and added, "And, truthfully, I'd like to know why a twenty-five year old kid is deemed a national threat. I'm hoping you could give me the insight they refuse to. How did he help your sister? And how did he make David Reilly kill himself?"

Miguel did not want to explore every memory of his sister's rape. He shifted uncomfortably in his chair and raced through thoughts on where he could begin in his explanation, a place where he could feel comfortable. Miguel guessed he should simply start when Cain walked into the lives of he and his sister. "Cain approached me one day," Miguel started, "outside my house. I was crying. My sister was in shock and pain from her attack. It had been four days since the incident. I was angry. I wanted revenge."

"Cain offered you a chance for revenge," Victor interrupted.

Miguel said sternly, "This conversation, Agent Terrence, will take us away from what you believe is reality. I mean no disrespect, Agent Terrence, but it's best you remain silent for this. No interruptions."

Victor agreed.

Miguel went back to his story. He smiled as his eyes watered, remembering the events of the day he met Cain. "Cain showed up at my house," he continued. "He drove up, got out of his car, and sat down next to me on my porch. He took my hand, like a mother takes the hand of a child. I don't know why I let him. Imagine a strange kid coming up to you and holding your hand. Your first instinct is to pull back and hit him. But, I immediately trusted Cain. The minute I saw him, I knew he could be trusted." His recollection stirred up images in his head. "He was dressed like a street thug. Cain had baggy jeans, Timberland boots, and a purple sweatshirt—the kind with a hood. But I trusted him. And when he took my hand, everything I was feeling, the emotions that ailed me were magically alleviated. I felt this cool air surround me, and a calm rushed over me. Cain let my hand go when I relaxed. He just smiled, never looking at me. He said he had David Reilly, tied and gagged, in the trunk of his car." Miguel started to laugh. "I'll never forget that raspy, arrogant sounding voice."

"Forgive me for interjecting, but, was your sister friends with Cain, or even more," Victor questioned.

"No," answered Miguel, searching himself for some form of reasoning. He thought he was use to the event by now, it being passed and done with. But, he never shared the story with anyone, not even his wife or children. Only his sister knew. "Cain simply showed up," Miguel stated. "He asked to see my sister. And without any proof of David Reilly being in his trunk, just a genuine feeling to trust Cain, I led him upstairs to where my sister was trying to recover. I can see her now, jumping up from the bed. Cain held out his hand and simply told my sister to relax. She did. She lay flat on the bed. She remained calm, even as Cain removed the covers from off her. I can remember being so amazed at my sister's trust in Cain. Even as her brother, she was afraid to touch me after she was attacked. She became afraid of all men, even her fiancé—who, by the way, you resemble. And of course, is now her husband. He's Dominican."

Victor nodded like he was trying to dodge the comment. "So, what did Cain do next," he asked, prompting Miguel to continue.

Miguel blinked his eyes and put himself back into the story to continue. "He laid his hand flat against my sister's forehead. It was his right hand. His left hand hovered just below her stomach, and…and…" Miguel shook his head, ending his story. "This is going to sound crazy."

"Just continue," Victor prodded.

Miguel felt unsure to continue. But, the amazement he felt while being in the event resurfaced as he told the story. "Strands of red light jumped from my sister's body and into the palm of Cain's hands." He looked at Victor to see his reaction. The Federal Agent was leaning closer, completely enticed by the story. "Then she was alleviated from all her misery. She fell asleep. She was smiling. Then I followed Cain back to his car. He opened the trunk. There was David Reilly, bound and gagged. Cain put both his hands on David Reilly's forehead." Miguel mimicked the movements in his narrative. He held out his hands out as if he was putting them on someone's forehead. "And, he put all the misery he extracted from my sister into the very man who caused her pain. Cain also said, as David Reilly started to scream, and his body began to buck as if struck by electricity…Cain said that he took all the pleasure David Reilly felt from all his victims and reversed it into their misery."

Victor remained still. He wanted to speak. His lips did not move.

Miguel finished his story. "Cain got into his car and left. He returned three days later and told me and my sister that David Reilly, in order to alleviate the collective misery of ten years of victimized women eating his mind, blew his brains out. And I'll say again, may that monster burn in hell. And for the record, Cain is a great man."

Miguel's hand trembled as he placed a cigarette into his mouth. He lit it and took a long drag. Victor too felt overwhelmed. He asked politely, "You got another?"

Miguel chuckled a bit. He slid Victor the pack of cigarettes and the lighter. Victor removed a cigarette and lit it. He began smoking. Miguel held his cigarette between his fingers as he admitted, "You're the only person I told that story to. Never even told my wife." He took a hit of the cigarette and then added, "Forget the badge you wear, Agent Terrence. I'll forget my straighter hair, my lighter skin. But even as I continue to acknowledge my Venezuelan and Puerto Rican background, I know we both niggas. You and I. As the joke goes, I'm just a bilingual nigger. Shit, my sister's husband looks like you, as I said. Hell, we're connected by way of the Olmecs—if you've ever heard of them. So let's be honest," he shook the cigarette in Victor's direction and asked, "What do you think this Government has to fear from a black man endowed with that kind of power? And I ask without any militant bone in my body. I ask with just a sense of reasoning that I like to call common sense." Miguel took another drag.

That question had been repeating itself in Victor's mind ever since Miguel revealed his story. The scenario was out of the realms of possibility, but it made complete sense. Victor thought about Cain's shackles, the iron gloves. He thought about the need to incarcerate Cain in such a facility, and declare him a threat to national security. Victor's senses had no choice but to accept Miguel's words as the truth. Victor then wondered about the next move. Not his, but Cain's.

It was one-twenty in the afternoon. Andrew Johnson Dyack's day of teaching was at its break. He walked the halls of the English Department, returning to his office, books under his arm. He was ready to spend the next two hours enjoying a lunch and doing research for his second book, a compilation of his latest lectures. He would then return to teach a three o'clock class. He was anxious to go home to his wife and newborn twins, however. He wanted no distractions at home for at least the next six months, even if that distraction was his second book. Andrew was even cutting down on his lectures across the country. He wanted to devote his time to his wife and newborns.

Cain sat in Andrew's office, in the chair across from his desk. He was dressed in baggy jeans, Timberland boots, and a green, hooded sweatshirt. Andrew did not react to Cain's presence. He turned his back and shut the door. Cain raised an eyebrow at the lack of enthusiasm displayed by the professor and lecturer. There was no acknowledgment at all. Andrew set his books down and then looked at Cain with a smile. "Boy, do you think I'd jump up and down with civilians out there," Andrew said with a low laugh.

Cain lifted from the seat and put out his hand. "My man, Andrew," he said with excitement.

Andrew looked down cautiously at Cain's outstretched hand. He put up both of his hands and shook his head. "How 'bout a hug instead. I guess it's safe to show you some love, even with the threat of your powers throwin' something into my head."

"Nothing but reality, my friend," Cain retorted confidently. "Come here, you bastard." Cain grabbed Andrew's arm and gave him a hug.

Andrew let go of Cain and the two took seats at Andrew's desk. "So, whachu doing here, boy," the professor scoffed playfully. "I know you weren't sentenced for just two years for murder."

Cain joked, "The advantages of having a black President. The energy I felt on that day. I saw it all." He folded his legs, left foot atop his right knee. "They had me in an underground facility, located here in Washington D.C. I escaped last night." He aimed his finger at Andrew. "And let me tell you something, those two years were everything Emmett Streamer predicted."

"How so," Andrew asked, leaning forward over his desk so as not to miss a single word of the answer.

Cain paused for effect. His arrogant smile crept onto his face. "I met, as of yesterday, Victor Terrence," he revealed. "He was a Federal Agent turned Criminal Psychologist. He was sent to profile me." Cain started to laugh.

The name resonated eerily through Andrew. He felt the need to express his thoughts aloud. "You be careful, boy. He's supposed to kill you." Andrew became worried and spoke in a hurried voice. "Don't you think it was safer to be locked inside that prison with this guy profiling you rather than hunting you as an escapee?"

Cain furrowed his brow. "Absolutely not," he protested. "Let the games begin, Andrew."

"Cain," Andrew hollered in a fatherly manner.

"Andrew," Cain said sarcastically imitating the professor's pleading tone. He waved a hand and grimaced. "Emmett said that Victor Terrence would be the one to *hunt* me down. He never used the word 'kill'."

"We ain't got time to argue words and specifics, li'l negro," Andrew said forcefully.

"Yes, we do," retorted Cain. "For all that sniveling bastards rituals, and occult objects he professes to claim, he can't see reality in the same light that I can calculate it." Cain cocked his shoulders as if victorious. "Besides, the only time he used the word 'kill' was to describe his own fate when next we met."

"I'm sure he's banking Victor gets you before then," said Andrew.

"Impossible," replied Cain. "It's not a destiny. His death is fated."

"And you'll make sure of that, won't you?" Andrew said shaking his head. "But what about the fate you suffer at the hands of Victor Terrence?"

"Victor is an unwilling participant," Cain said rolling his eyes. "He is very unaware of the reality he's stepping into."

"I'm sure you're just waiting to initiate him," Andrew fired.

"And the moment I do," Cain started, "his superiors are standing ready to kill him. Trust me with that notion."

Andrew thought for a moment. "This all seems very ominous and dooming."

"Two words synonymous with fun," Cain joked. "Now, business. How do we solve this entire dilemma?" He looked around the room as if the office was saturated with all his problems. He put his violet eyes back on Andrew. "I know I haven't sought you out for nothing."

"Is that what you calculate, Cain?" Andrew quipped. He opened a drawer and removed a tattered book. He flung it at Cain who caught it with ease. "The page is marked," informed the professor.

Cain opened the book to the marked page. There he came across an article on an occult item named the Skeptic Stone. It was a magical item forged in France in the year fifteen-twelve. Cain read the Skeptic Stone was forged in the bloodiest of fashions. The stone was carved from the black stone of Cybele, after the stone was transferred from Pessinus to Rome. When a piece of the black stone was taken, it was delivered to France where it soaked in the blood of occult madmen. These madmen were seduced and murdered by women who passed the Skeptic Stone down through their secret society. The stone was said to possess the ability to negate any mystical power and wipe the mind of any known person. Knowledge of self would be lost. The stone's holder could then reshape the reality surrounding their victim. The victim would forever be trapped in an illusion.

The article continued with comments from debunkers and believers. A photo of a gray stone with red spatters patterned onto it was in the upper right hand corner of the page. Cain guessed the photo was just a possible likeness to the stone in which the article referred. Cain flipped the page and continued to read. The article concluded that the stone could be broken and destroyed by the rage of a dark woman whose bloodline reached far back into antiquity. Cain found the article interesting, but of no real use. In fact, Cain was hoping Andrew had more knowledge of the item he sought after. Cain was looking for Aesop's Diary.

Aesop, the black storyteller of ancient times, did not necessarily own the diary. The book was magical, blessed by ancient priests from Abyssinia. Aesop was actually a word that meant *Ethiop*, or *Ethiopian*. Many scholars believed that there never was an actual man named Aesop, but that moralists of all races and creeds carried with them the profound folk tales that originated in Ethiopia, the land of the Ethiops, or Aesops. Aesop's Diary had the ability to create the reality scribed within its pages. It was also known as *Djhuti's Tablet*, a reference to the supposed Emerald Tablets of Thoth, a Kemetic or Egyptian god.

"What am I looking at, Andrew," Cain asked the professor, slightly acrimonious. He placed the book on the desk in front of him.

"The Skeptic Stone has the ability to negate your powers, Cain," Andrew explained to him. "It can also negate the power of Aesop's Diary."

Cain lifted his shoulders, unfettered by the news. "I find one and don't worry about the other." Then Cain saw the hesitation in Andrew to speak. He knew what he was going to say. But again, unfettered, Cain just smiled and rolled his eyes. "Let me guess, Emmett Streamer possess both of these items."

"Nothing gets by you, boy," Andrew said in a low, defeated voice.

"Relax, Andrew," Cain drawled. "Every move these bastards make, bring them closer to a fate they are trying to avoid. They would fair better standing still. But, as it stands, they are all moving targets." Cain huffed again. "Look at the good side, Emmett has done all the research, searching, and finding of these objects. It saves us time. After all, I've just escaped from an underground, Government prison. I'm a little tired."

"Funny," Andrew commented. "The most important information in that article is how the Skeptic Stone can be broken and destroyed."

Cain leaned over the desk and fingered through the last page of the article. *"By the rage of a dark woman with ancestral bloodlines,"* he read aloud. "Sounds like a Black woman to me. And I'm in need of one. I have been locked up for two years, y'know? I may hold great power in the palm of my hand, but they don't hold *that* much power."

Andrew ignored Cain's joke. "You still have to find Emmett," said Andrew implying that he knew where to look. "You might want to start with our old friend Edius Clarke. He's a Pastor at a church in Virginia."

Cain snickered, "An occultist disguised as a church head? He's following in the footsteps of every church head in the world." Cain looked over at the opened window. "Well, it's time for me to leave the way I came in."

"Wait, Cain," Andrew petitioned. Cain relaxed back into his chair. "I may not have your abilities, but I know trouble when I see it coming."

Cain became curious. He remained silent, unable to pick up on the meaning behind the professor's urgency. He waited for Andrew to continue.

"Tomorrow, a rapper by the name of Black Mouth is performing a concert," Andrew stated. "He's affiliated with the Atherini Gang. Now that Black Mouth is big, the community anticipates their presence at the concert, and with it, trouble. Their activity has been on the rise following his success. They're rivals with the Gatos street gang. Black Mouth is staying at the Addison Hotel."

Cain felt something more from Andrew's attitude. He did not question it, or use his powers to pry. He stood up and bowed at the neck toward his friend. "I will not disappoint you." He straightened, and then his body dissipated into a cloud of black matter. The cloud then shifted into thin, lucid strands that waved like heat patterns as they slipped through the opened window. The thin strands of energy rippled through the college campus, passing through the air onto a street leading away from the University.

Cain wished to stay in his ghostly, ethereal form, gliding through the day whimsically, absorbing the sun's rays. But, something caught Cain's sight. He passed into an alley and solidified into his physical form. He walked around the corner and spotted, coming toward him on the sidewalk, a couple walking hand-in-hand. They looked to be in their mid-thirties. The man was white. The woman was black. Cain looked at the palm of his hand. His thoughts became devious. He observed the black woman. She had brown skin and straight, black hair. She was pretty but looked tired, despite her smile. Cain felt something coming from her. There was a strange ambience of sadness and defeat that emanated from her dull aura. Cain rubbed his hands. He kept his eyes on the black woman. She passed Cain, and left an impression with a smile.

Cain snapped his fingers and said toward the woman, "Montauk."

The woman stopped abruptly. She let go of her boyfriend. Cain noticed the engagement ring on her finger. "Excuse me," she asked as she faced Cain.

Cain stepped up to her, bouncing off the wall he leaned against. He noticed her fiancé become nervous. Cain snapped his fingers again. He pointed toward the woman and explained, "I know where I've seen you before. Montauk, Long Island."

The woman smiled, intrigued. She considered that Cain mistook her for someone else, but she was drawn to him. Cain never met her, truthfully. A film entitled *Eternal Sunshine of the Spotless Mind* inspired Cain's dialogue. The black woman backed away, despite Cain's radiating magnetism. She felt embarrassed for him, he believing she was someone else. She told him, "No. You must be thinking of someone else. I'm sorry."

"Then why did you stop?" Cain asked her with a flirtatious smile. He glanced over at her fiancé. The man was becoming furious. Cain's eyes went back to the black woman. "We *have* met before. Somewhere, deep in your memory, you know me. You just forgot."

The black woman's feelings of intrigued mixed with nervousness. But her uneasiness never overwhelmed her. She was more uncomfortable with her fiancé hovering over the event between she and Cain.

Cain put a quick eye on the black woman's fiancé with his trademark arrogant smile branded across his face. The man took a deep breath. Cain looked back at her and his smile faded. He was serious when he spoke, "Someone has taken the memories we have of one another, and is trying to substitute my image for theirs. I'm the original image."

The woman's fiancé stepped to Cain aggressively. The man gripped his hand around his fiancé's arm and said, "That's nice. We have to go. You're making my fiancée very nervous. Come, honey."

Cain put a hand on the man's chest. Immediately, on contact, the man's name jumped into Cain's mind.

Christian Lyons.

"Relax," Cain said taking his hand from Christian's chest. "The situation is under control."

"Excuse me," said Christian forcefully. He wondered what possessed him to stay his hand when Cain touched him.

Cain's arrogant smile returned. "Please, just some parting words." Cain cupped the black woman's hands with his. He whispered to her, *"Meet me in Montauk."*

With her hand cupped inside Cain's grip, and with the fluttering of Cain's raspy voice, the scenery around the black woman faded. Cain's image disappeared, but her fiancé remained. The woman's clothes changed into a tattered, long draping skirt and a dirty torn white blouse. Her fiancé's attire transformed into brown slacks and no shirt. Surrounding him was five of his close friends. The black woman recognized each of them. Mathew. Robert. Edward. Jeremy. Duncan. They were all gathered inside a cabin. A lamp flickered on the table providing little light.

The look in Christian's eyes was murderous, but it was not blood he lusted for. The black woman's heart started to race. She took a step back. Fear opened her eyes wide. Mathew grabbed her. The man wrapped his arm around her neck. Christian stepped close and hit her with his fist. He started screaming obscenities at her. She tried to speak back to him, pleading, but her words did not flow as English. Her fiancé hit her again and Mathew tossed her to the ground where she felt someone kick her. Christian commanded for Mathew, the largest of his friends, to hold her down. Mathew got to his knees and pressed his hands hard down onto her arms. Her body was flat against the floor. She could feel the floorboards against her back, the back of her shirt completely ripped. Jarring, pinching stings scratched at her back. She realized her back had been lacerated with cuts made by a whip. Streams of blood leaked from her.

Christian tore her dress and she screamed, kicking her legs. Christian slapped her, and Duncan kicked the side of her face. Edward knelt down and cupped her mouth with his hand. Christian removed his pants and mounted her, penetrating the black woman with a tearing force—harder and harder. The men switched positions after a time. The helpless black woman started crying. Her eyes, glistening with tears, spotted the figure of a black man staring at her. He sat on the floor, back against the wall. His mouth was agape as he watched in amazement as the men raped her. The black woman wanted to scream to him for help, but she was gagged by one of her attacker's penis. She reached out with her mind, trying to connect to the black man sitting in the shadows. She hoped that her tears alerted the black man to her plight. But, he just stared at her in amazement, doing nothing to stop the white men. The black woman's body eased, accepting her attackers' assault on her. She shifted her anger from the white men raping her and directed it toward the black man staring at her. She hated him for his refusal to help her. All he did was stare. But, she never noticed the gunshot in the center of the black man's forehead. She mistook the spatter of blood and flesh on the wall as a shadow, as it was covered by another patch of darkness.

The scenery changed.

The black woman was running through a wooded area. It was night, just the same. There were shouts and screams coming from behind her. The white men were chasing her, pursuing her close. Her attire was now a flower dress and a shrug. From out of the shadows leapt her fiancé, Christian Lyons. He slammed his body into her, knocking her to the ground.

"I got that nigger-bitch, boys," he screamed.

This time the black woman understood his words. She looked up and saw Mathew, Robert, Edward, Jeremy, and Duncan surround her. Mathew reprised his role of holding her down. Christian kicked her as she bucked wildly to escape. Duncan knelt down and knocked the black woman with his fist. Her nose began to bleed, her lips split. Exhaustion also attacked her. Christian repeated the ritual of raping her. The gray fedora atop his head was tossed aside. There was a wide, sinister, victorious grin on his face as he continued raping her. It was another place, another time. But it continued just the same.

There too watched another black man, just as submissive and useless as the first, she thought. This time he was staring down at her. He stood behind Mathew. And there again came the black woman's anger at the passive black man. She cried. Anger. She wanted to yell up at him all the obscenities shouted at her. She wanted to know why he again refused to help her. She wanted to know why he was not fighting back.

But, the black man was not staring down at her, despite his wide, opened eyes. He was hanging from a tree, noose around his neck. Before the imagery drowned her, the reality of the present day unfolded back into its proper place. The black woman saw Cain standing in front of her, holding her hand. Only seconds had passed. Cain turned to leave. The black woman tightened her grip on Cain's hand, but it was only for a second. She let him go.

Cain walked up the street, his back to the couple. Christian put his arm around his fiancée. She whittled out of his embrace, uncomfortable and shaken. She commented that she felt lightheaded. Christian looked up the street for Cain. He was gone, having already taken the form of his ghostly, ethereal self. He glided through the city environment until he came to another alley. He configured back into his physical form and stepped from the alley into a convenience store. He walked to an aisle with office supplies and pulled an architectural compass and a measuring square. Cain purchased the items and walked back outside. Across the street was a flower vendor. Cain purchased a single rose, inhaling its scent. He walked back across the street and into the alley. He hid the items under the dumpster and then reverted back to his ethereal, ghostly form.

His next destination was the Addison Hotel where the rapper Black Mouth resided. Arriving there, Cain circulated through the crowd of screaming fans gathered outside of the hotel. His mist filtered into the lobby, rippling unnoticed as he hovered near the ceiling. He floated over two teenage black girls employed at the hotel. Black Mouth's whereabouts were quickly divulged as the two young women conversed about his stay at the hotel. Cain slipped into the elevator as several of Black Mouth's entourage entered. His ethereal essence hovered above them, waving like lines of heat. The four black men below him used a card to access the top floors. The elevator ascended and the doors opened to a small hall that quickly led to another elevator. There were no hotel room doors lining the hall, and one of the four men used the card again to open the doors to the second elevator. They entered, Cain followed. The second elevator ascended one flight. The doors opened directly into Black Mouth's suite.

"Niggas," Black Mouth screamed as he lifted from a plush sofa in the front room of the well-designed suite. "Look how they hook a nigga up!" He waved a hand at the lavish room. Gang signs were exchanged along with handshakes and brotherly hugs. These men were Atherini Gang members.

Cain examined Black Mouth. He was light skinned, had cornrows, and held an amazing likeness to his friend A. J. Dyack, however a younger version of his friend, as he sported a light patch of hair around his mouth and chin. Cain used his power to find Black Mouth's age. The young man was twenty-two. The affirming information tingled Cain's senses. This was A.J.'s son from another woman, long ago. Cain's feelings were definite.

One Atherini lightly punched Black Mouth in the shoulder while laughing. "Last stop on your tour, nigga," he said in a congratulatory tone.

"Yeah, and I'm H-O-M-E in this muthafucka." Black Mouth slapped the man's hands forcefully. "And I know my entire crew gonna be fuckin' around wit' me tonight! Gimme dat, niggas! Gimme dat!"

"Why this place so empty?" an Atherini asked with a contorted look on his face. "I was expectin' bitches and all sorts of shit poppin' off."

Black Mouth shook his head. "Don't work like that. They got decoys perpetratin' me for rowdy muhfuckas to follow, and shit. Entourage is arrivin' at seven tonight. I'm sent ahead, alone. I just got in this muthafucka," Black Mouth explained. "This place is gonna be heavy bumpin' before the show. Get a nigga hype."

"So, you can slip away for awhile?" another gang member asked. "Cuz Li'l Mike wanna see yo' ass."

"Yeah," said another. "He wants to talk to you about gettin' a contract, nigga. Get these muthafuckas off you so we can do security for you. This shit ain't safe. You walkin' by y'self and all."

Black Mouth's nervousness was barely visible. He explained hurriedly, "Nah, man. I'm cool. Can't nobody get up here 'less they issued that card I gots my security to give y'all." He slowed his speech, relaxed. "But I hear you, my niggas. No doubt, no doubt."

Yes, Cain figured. It was no doubt that Black Mouth was caught between Atherini gang-loyalty and the loyalty of his new street gang—his record company. It was time for Cain to introduce Black Mouth to a third option. The ghostly waves solidified between the four gang members and Black Mouth. The Atherinis pulled guns as they jumped back with Cain's sudden appearance. Cain remained calm.

"Who the fuck is this," a gang member shouted.

"A new form of security," Cain sneered over his shoulder. He looked at Black Mouth and revealed, "Your father sent me."

Cain saw Black Mouth flinch.

"I'ma blast this muthafucka," an Atherini yelled behind him. "Nigga, get the fuck off my man!"

Cain turned his upper body, slightly facing the four gunmen behind him. "*Get off of your man?*" He mocked the phrase. "Sorry, I don't swing that way."

"Nigga, you lucky I don't blast you for that smart mouth shit, muthafuckah! Hands up," the Atherini declared.

Cain turned and faced the young black men completely. Their weapons did not rattle him, nor did their willingness to use them. Cain's arrogant grin lit up his face. His smile was his most visible weapon. "Just the same, could you please lower your dicks from my face?" Cain may have been smiling, sinister as it was arrogant, but his words were filled with derision.

"Who the fuck you think you commandin', nigga," an Atherini screamed, cocking his gun. "*We* this nigga's security!"

Cain cleared his throat and rolled his eyes. His stated casually, "Security, yet extremely insecure." He made a step in the gang members' direction. They backed up from Cain's approach. "What's the matter, Caucasian have your manhood? Was it taken from you over a—" he jiggled his hand as he estimated, "—let's say, a five-hundred year process?" Cain started to chuckle, deep and sinister.

"Don't…take another step, nigga," an Atherini warned, his hand and voice trembling. "We'll blast you."

Cain continued his approach, ignoring the Atherini's threat. "And in order for you to reclaim your manhood," he continued to speak, "you believe you need to act out the very savage nature of where your oppressor originates." He stepped closer. "And so, you take the most degenerated title in his history. You are now a 'thug'."

Cain used his power to increase the weight of the guns aimed at him. Each Atherini let go of their weapons, unable to hold their weight. Cain raised a hand and lifted one member from off the ground. The Atherini felt something grabbing at his neck, an invisible hand strangling him. Cain lowered his arm and the young gang member crashed hard against the floor. Before the others could run, Cain swiped his arm across the room and an invisible force rendered each Atherini gang member unconscious.

Black Mouth ran into the bedroom suite and locked the door. Seconds later Cain's image ghosted through the locked barrier. Black Mouth jumped to the bed and removed a gun from underneath the pillow. He bounced off the bed and aimed the gun in Cain's direction. Cain knocked the gun from Black Mouth's grip and grabbed his neck. He put the palm of his other hand on Black Mouth's forehead. He calmed the anger trapped inside the young man. The anger was mostly directed toward his father.

Cain did not probe the young black man's mind. He simply used his power to transform the anger into a desire for Black Mouth to seek out his father. Cain did not want to witness the point-of-view the child held of his father's leave and absence. That was for the father and son to work out. Cain did not know what Andrew used to be, how he carried himself twenty-two years ago when this child was born to him. But Cain understood the man Andrew was now. And this young man did so need his father at this crucial time. He also unlocked an opening inside Black Mouth's mind that would act as an amenable space to receive all the knowledge Andrew would give to his son, and the ability to forgive. Black Mouth would not even be bitter when he saw his father had another family.

Black Mouth relaxed. Cain knew his name. "Charles," he spoke the young man's name as if he were his older brother. "Your father is waiting for you at the University where he teaches."

Charles sat on the bed, catching his breath from all that transpired. He looked up at Cain. "He wants to see me?"

"Very much so," said Cain.

"Whatchu gon' do," Charles asked.

Cain motioned toward the door with his head. "I'm going to take your four friends and visit this *Li'l Mike* you were all talkin' about."

"Yo," stated Charles, "what the fuck *is* you, nigga?"

"Your father will explain all that," Cain answered. He then changed the subject. "Right now I need your address book."

"What? Why?" he asked.

"Because, there are going to be extreme changes to your life," Cain retorted in a strict voice. "And I'm going to make sure your manager and producer are going to back you with all the money they're making off you."

"Oh," said Charles. "F'sho, nigga. It's in my travel case."

Cain walked over to the small case pointed out by Charles. He unzipped it and removed the address book engraved with a golden *A* and a snake wrapped around it. "Let's go wake up your friends."

Charles stood up and led the way to the front room. Cain then walked quickly, passing Charles and attending to the unconscious Atherini. He woke them, one-by-one. He opened their minds to past lifetimes. They were warriors from antiquity. Their bloodline was revealed to them. The four men saw themselves as Abyssinian spearmen, Nuba warriors, traveling monks of the 6th century B.C., the Carthaginians, Moorish swordsmen, and Zulu warriors. When the Atherini stood they were tall, not slumped. Proud. Blackmen.

Cain rubbed his hands and announced, "Now, we get to work." He looked at the four Atherini and said, "Take me to see Li'l Mike."

"Cool," said the largest of the crew. His name was Leroy. "We can drive you over there."

"Fine," Cain acknowledged. "On the way we'll stop at the University." He turned and pointed to Charles. "You will meet your father. Tell him Cain sent you."

"Yeah," Charles said nervously.

Cain noticed the look on Charles' face. Cain could feel the young man's increasing heart rate. Before he dealt with the situation, another Atherini spoke, "How do we present you to Li'l Mike? He waitin' for Black Mouth."

"Truthfully, he wants business to be done," Cain stated casually. "We'll simply say that I'm there to negotiate the security contract."

"That's good," complimented an Atherini.

"So is starting the car," Cain stated. "Grab your guns and let's go."

The Atherini re-equipped their weapons, their firearms restored to normal weight. Everyone exited the suite. They took the elevators down to the lobby and left through the hotel's rear entrance, dodging the cluster of fans. Black Mouth phoned his official security and informed them of his departure. Seconds later, Black Mouth's official security swarmed around him to protest his actions. Cain convinced the security members otherwise, shaking their hand and insuring their comfort and ease of the artist's leave. The four Atherini members scooped up the SUV they arrived in while Black Mouth and Cain waited for them at the rear of the hotel. Once they were picked up, they headed to their first stop, Howard University. The college was not too far from the hotel. They arrived within minutes to drop Black Mouth off. He jumped from the car, turned around, and shook Cain's hands.

"Thank you, Cain," he said.

Cain nodded. He reached out and slapped Black Mouth's shoulder. "You're welcome," he said in a humble voice. "Get moving. Tell your father I'm on my duty. He's in that building right across the street."

Black Mouth closed the door. The van departed from the campus. He was now Charles. He turned around and walked toward the English Department building. People swarmed him, but he merely stated he just looked like the rapper 'Black Mouth'. He entered the building and asked a student where he could find Professor Dyack. It took time for him to continue forward, making his way to his father's office. Charles had seen gang fights, shoot outs, and tough arguments and negotiations in the gang and music worlds, and of course the rush of performing and recording. Nothing was more stressful than what he was readying himself to do. He stood outside his father's office for a long minute. He took a breath. He knocked. The door opened. Then the most important set of eyes inspected him. There stood his father, Andrew Dyack. Andrew reached out for his son and hugged him tightly.

Charles did the same.

Cain and his entourage completed their drive to a rundown building that held a gathering of Atherini soldiers. Gang members swarmed in and outside the building. They were anxious for their friend Black Mouth's arrival. Armed Atherini cased the perimeter of the building. Leroy parked the SUV near the entrance, and everyone ejected from the vehicle. Leroy and Cain entered the dilapidated residence while the other Atherini kept guard near the SUV.

Through the doors was a crumbling and decaying lobby. The two main doors leading into the ballroom were missing. There was a crowd of Atherini gang members swirling inside the ballroom area. Their ages were ranged from middle aged to teenagers. Leroy and Cain stepped into the room, Leroy shaking hands and throwing gang signs to fellow members. No one knew what to make of Cain. His attire was no different than theirs, but there was something about his walk, his demeanor. He was not slouched, his head was high, and he was confident to the point where he was making everyone around him, save the Atherini who escorted him, uncertain; their insecurities rattled inside them. Some felt the need to back away from him. Cain observed that females were among the gang. He liked their presence because he believed there could be progress once he 'changed people's mentality', but he understood the hardships the black females must have been through before and during their membership in the Atherini. He could feel the false sense of security wrapped up in the gang's mentality. His people were holding their heads high while their spirits were slumped over, dragging. Cain removed his hands from the pockets on his hooded sweatshirt. He drew out his hands like a gunman brandishing firearms.

In front of him and Leroy stepped Li'l Mike. He was short and muscular, with dark skin, braids, and a goatee. There were tattoos on either of his arms that were barely visible because of his dark color. The tattoos were the Atherini insignia, an *A* with a snake winding around it. He wore a black tank top and green pants. He stepped to Leroy and shook his hand.

"Wassup, my nigga," he greeted. "Where the fuck's our boy? What, he couldn't get away?"

"Yeah. Business, y'know," Leroy retorted, his voice rattling in the presence of his leader. He pointed at Cain. "But he sent a man who wants to discuss a contract. His name is Cain."

"F'sho, nigga. That's cool," Li'l Mike said, relieving Leroy of any tension. He shook Cain's hand without any effect. Cain held back his power for now. "I wish I coulda seen my nigga, though," Li'l Mike stated. "But, I guess we'll catch up with him tomorrow. Wassup, nigga? Cain, right?"

"Glad to be here," replied Cain with little emotion on his face. "There's nothing goin' on but business."

"I can respect that," Li'l Mike commented.

"Can you respect that business be done in private," Cain asked in his raspy, snooty manner.

Li'l Mike flinched, surprised by how sharp and authoritative Cain spoke to him. He stiffened, putting out his chest to display his Alpha Male status. Cain was unfazed, which continued to rattle the gang leader. Li'l Mike conceded. There was business to be done, and then he would deal with Cain's attitude. There was no time to cross egos for the moment. Not only would this bring in money and good hardware in terms of firearms, but he believed his friend's life was at stake. There was a hit being made on Black Mouth by the rival Gatos faction. Li'l Mike guided Leroy and Cain into an empty room. Cain entered. Leroy stayed outside.

Li'l Mike quickly dived into business. "We need some heavy hardware to keep some niggas busy," he told Cain. "There's another gang called the Gatos, some Spanish niggas. They got it in for Black Mouth. We know they gon' hit him. They think we hit them a week ago. I told them niggas it wun't us. I've been peaceful and shit, but we still got tension and beef."

"My, my, my," Cain said shaking his head, admiring the larger picture. "They certainly have us all at each other's throats."

Li'l Mike pushed the comment aside. "Look, them I-talian niggas is used in our area of the music industry to take out an artist's competition, make it look gang related. But, they never protect the artist." Li'l Mike stomped his foot. "Them Mafioso cats is used to protect white money and just they neighborhood. What about our shit? I figure I can speak to you, nigga-to-nigga."

Cain feigned contemplation. He raised his eyebrows and hummed. He looked at Li'l Mike and extended his hand. "We can seal all this with a handshake," he proposed.

Cain put his hand in Li'l Mike's, infusing him with the same knowledge as the four Atherini gang members. However, Michael August, a.k.a. Li'l Mike, saw himself in a leader's position through various ages and epochs. Emotions of guilt overwhelmed Michael when he realized his new life took the lives of others in search of destiny and fate. He was drowned by empathetic feelings for lives taken by his own hands or through his orders. Cain fluxed the spirits of the slain to wrack Michael's mind. Michael was spared from being torn apart mentally. The slain spirits conversed with him, shouting forgiveness and granting pardon if Michael's way of life changed. Michael's eyes cried backwards and he choked on his tears. His body convulsed and he gritted his teeth. Michael agreed with the spirits around him to redeem his life.

The images shifted into the Atherini's history. It was a history that surprised both Michael and Cain. The gang was formed in the mid-70s. Its founders were black men who turned their life around and wanted to give back to the community by helping to organize and teach the black and Latino youth.

The Atherini snake was chosen as a symbol to signify knowledge and wisdom, traits anciently associated with snakes. The African Atherini was the deadliest breed of snake, the most venomous. It was believed that knowledge and wisdom would be the venom used to slay the forces intruding on the black community in Washington D.C. The group's elders hoped to make the Atherini a national movement, with contacts in Chicago, Detroit, and New York. The F.B.I., in its efforts to continue dismantling black movements, made sure the elders' past caught up with them. The elders were arrested, leaving the Atherini youth to fend for themselves. When harder drugs were introduced into the neighborhood, in order to survive, the Atherini youth turned to the very life from which the elders were trying to save them.

Cain let go of Michael's hand. The young man backed away from Cain, blinking his eyes. He shook his hand as if it had received a shock of electricity. Michael stared silently at Cain, waiting for him to provide sense to what he just witnessed.

"First," began Cain, his voice raspy and stern. "Don't suffer the same fate as your father, and try being one to your child." He addressed other matters he found deep inside Michael's mind.

"Oh, I'm there for mine," Michael said humbly.

"Good," Cain sneered. "Also, the mother of your child has your back. Don't stab hers."

"Cool," Michael replied.

"Also, befriend your sister's husband," Cain instructed. "He's a good man, though a rival Gatos. You two will finally meet eye-to-eye." Cain leaned against the wall. "Now, business. The Atherini will return to their original game plan. You police our streets, clean them up."

"Gotchu," Michael nodded.

"I will make sure you have money backing you," Cain reached into the front pocket of his hooded sweatshirt and felt Black Mouth's address book neatly tucked inside. "It will just be startup money. It will be up to you, your sister, and her husband, to generate an economy for the neighborhood."

"What about the Gatos situation," Michael asked.

Cain stepped toward the door. "I will handle our Latino brothers and sisters much the same as I handled this situation," he informed. "It's in the palm of my hand. Trust me."

"Them niggas may not be as inviting," warned Michael.

"They will be," Cain said confidently. "They too have been led astray. I will show them where our histories coincide in antiquity, far before they coincided in shootouts in an inner city. We will again be united allies."

"You got so much knowledge," Michael barked, "but whatchu know about the streets?"

Cain turned to Michael. He answered coolly, "I know that streets are nothing more than pathways stretched out in every direction that *you* choose to walk."

Michael chuckled. "Anybody ever tell you, you a wiseass?"

"My mother and father, one brother, three cousins, two girlfriends, and every teacher I've ever had," Cain reported nonchalantly. "And to note, I have more enemies than some countries have people." He raised an eyebrow and then contemplated. "Truthfully, some countries are my enemies. That's a long story."

Michael laughed. "You a funny nigga, Cain."

Cain turned back to the door and opened it. "Let's go," he ordered.

They walked from the room. Michael took the lead, Cain close behind. He clapped his hands and got the attention of his soldiers and Atherini followers. "We got a deal," he announced. There was light applause from the crowd. Michael silenced them. "Now, this may take some time. But I want every nigga in this muthafucka to shake the hand of this man who got us the deal. His name is Cain."

Cain extended his hand to the audience.

It was night. Cain sat by himself in a bar in Virginia. Placed on the table in front of him were the rose he purchased earlier and a box containing the compass and square he stashed under the dumpster. Cain watched the television. The image on the screen was of Black Mouth, his producer DJ Phly, and manager Leonard Hurtz. Though the bar was noisy, Cain needed no audio to understand what the news was reporting. He was the cause of it. Black Mouth, whose real name was Charles Morning—having his mother's last name—called for a truce between the Atherini and the Gatos street gangs. The screen then showcased images of Michael August shaking hands with Lorenzo Tejada, the Gatos gang leader. Next to them was Leonard Hurtz.

Cain, while grinning, watched the image of Leonard Hurtz closely. He started to reflect on meeting the manager at his hotel, catching Leonard with a prostitute. Cain used his power to knock the hooker unconscious. He then rushed the room and tore into Leonard's mind. Cain assaulted Leonard with all the grief of the lives the manager destroyed, the careers he manipulated, and the song choices he forced young black artists like Black Mouth to breathe life into. Cain lacerated Leonard's psyche with the agony of the young girls he seduced with empty promises of stardom and fame. Cain also discovered the order Leonard gave to have a Gatos member killed, the Atherini blamed for the crime. The hit was for marketing purposes. The paroxysm Leonard's mind suffered almost threw him into a coma. But Cain needed him alive. Unfortunately, some people needed to see Leonard's image to legitimize the new direction of Black Mouth's career.

Cain chuckled to himself as he watched the television. His ears focused on a conversation at the bar, his power amplifying the voices of the men, and the bartender himself. Cain heard the comment, "You hear about that," a man asked. "Them gangbangers callin' for a truce?"

Another man shook his head. "That's just some propaganda," he spat. "Them niggers and spicks will be at it again once that rapper—what's his name? Loud Mouth—once he leaves town. It's all marketing."

The bartender leaned over to the second man and warned, "Watch your mouth, Kevin. There's a black guy at the table behind you."

Kevin rolled his eyes, seemingly unfazed by the news. Cain heard the flinch in Kevin's heart. He did not bother looking over his shoulder at Cain. "He can't hear me, but I got you." Kevin was in his early thirties. He had a long face, beard, and a receding, curly hairline. He wore a light blue dress-shirt and tan casual pants. "Just turn to something else," Kevin requested. The bartender obliged.

The next channel brought up another news broadcast that concentrated on the President. Images of war, Wall Street stocks, and houses with foreclosure signs were spliced together with press conferences and congressional meetings. Cain watched the television, looking close at the black President. The President remained calm and collected in his responses toward hecklers that posed as professional reporters, and some that did not. America's black President was too cool, and too confident, which Cain admired. And, because of his collected demeanor, the President was considered to be an 'uppity nigger'.

Cain, having kept his 'eye' on the world while being incarcerated, saw conspiracy theories rise among the population when America was faced with a black President. Cain scoffed and thought, *Oh, now they want to believe the conspiracies.* He remembered something his father told him when he was growing up. *"When white folks are in trouble they put a black man in charge,"* he said. *"If he solves the problem, good. If not, they got someone they can blame and take out all their heartache on."* Muhammad Ali said much the same in an old television interview. Even black conspiracy theorists scratched at America's first black President more than they had earlier, more diabolical Presidents, Cain observed. He 'listened' while incarcerated to all the news. The President was called every thing un-American in his attempt to fix problems he inherited, and that had been growing in America before he or his critics were even born. Socialist. Nazi. Hitler. Liar. Terrorist. He was shouted at and disrespected by members of Congress in ways no past President had ever been. Despite all the words used to describe America's first black President, Cain only heard the translation.

Nigger.

That's what they meant.

And this black President was a symbol of what black people went through day in a day out at their jobs. Constantly facing opposition to the point where it was hard to get anything accomplished. But despite that, much was achieved.

Cain's ear perked up. Kevin scoffed, "I can't believe I voted for this guy. I knew I should've gone with my instinct. I got caught up in the hype, like a good preview to a bad movie. This guy is oily and slimy, and only out for himself. He's dividing America up and handing it to the Arabs and the Chinese. He's giving away my hard earned rights and dollar as an American. He hasn't done anything for the economy but sit comfortably while the rest of us starve. He's got a 'let 'em eat cake' attitude. Or, he's taking my money and giving it to lazy, unemployed people."

The bartender laughed. "Why did you vote for him," he asked.

Kevin took a gulp of his beer. "Truthfully," he said laying his beer on the bar. "So all my black friends could shut up about racism." The bartender chuckled. He gave a quick, uneasy glance at Cain, his smile wavering. "I was so hopin' he'd win so I wouldn't have to hear all these sob stories about 'racist' America," Kevin continued. "Can't fuckin' complain now, if ever. Slavery's over. You can go to our schools. Hello. Don't you know your own history? Martin Luther King, Jr., look it up. He made things right for you. Hello."

Cain took this as his cue to approach the bar, abandoning the package and the rose on the table. Approaching, Cain put his hands on the bar, standing next to Kevin. He stared up at the screen in amazement at the image of the President. "I have to admire him," said Cain.

Everyone quieted down when Cain spoke. Kevin smirked, "Really? I find him very Hollywood. He's all look." Kevin added in a condescending tone, "And before you say anything, I voted for him. So it's not about race."

"I still admire him," Cain replied. "He has to deal with the scrutiny from the press, pressure of oversea affairs, theorists of all kind, comedians, enemies, the politics of his party as well as another, the politics of his race, and homeland issues that include economics *and* race. He has to keep secret certain affairs," Cain paused playfully and then slyly added, "of our country, offices and officials—both domestic and foreign, policies just the same, and threats at every corner." Cain slapped the bar. "And through all this his composure is kept cool, at least in front of the camera. I'm sure he's cursing up a storm behind the scenes. But, he deserves to."

Kevin patted Cain on the back. The hit was hard and knocked Cain forwards a bit. "I guess things are no different no matter who is in charge," spoke Kevin. "Black or white, right?"

Cain fought hard to keep his smile from twisting into a sneer. "Well, like I said, I admire him." Cain hiked his shoulders. "I would do anything just to shake his hand." A sincere, arrogant smile crept onto Cain's visage.

Kevin extended his hand. "Well, how will mine do?" he asked politely.

It was then that a thirty-eight year old brunette woman came between Cain and Kevin. Cain retracted his hand. He sneered at the woman's presence. The woman pointed a finger toward the television and ordered the bartender, "Turn it back to Black Mouth. I want to hear about the concert tomorrow night. Someone said it was postponed."

Kevin pushed the woman aside. "That propaganda shit is gone off, Alyson."

"What did they say about the concert," Alyson pleaded.

"Who cares," Kevin shouted at her.

Cain then asked, "Why do you call it propaganda?"

Kevin huffed, "I don't know if you heard, but supposedly there's a treaty between two gangs, one of them associated with that rapper. No offense, you being black and all, but these guys will be killing each other over nothing soon. It's an act. These rap guys are all the same. So are these street thugs." He waved his hand at the television as if dismissing Black Mouth's image, though it no longer played on the screen. "If they can memorize all those nonsensical lyrics why don't they get an education?" He flapped his lips. "I remember one of them said in a song, something about the justice system, and it being against black people. I'm like, how can a so-called thug that brags about killin' people in one song, be mad at the justice system in the next song. I mean, just become a lawyer. Stop complaining. Do something. Then you have the ones braggin' about how much they got, bitches, hoes, and money. It's pathetic. These guys are criminals, most of 'em. They're savage, and most of all actors. That's why half of them give up on rapping and go into acting— cuz that's all they are."

"It's the American dream, isn't it," Cain questioned. "Their savagery is a reaction to conditions inflicted upon them." He inspected Kevin. Hidden behind the aggressive mannerisms was not a businessman. No. Kevin seemed to dwell on the law, and take offense to a particular rapper's lyrics about the justice system. "Are you studying law," Cain asked.

"I majored in Criminal Justice, yes. But, as of now I'm—"

Cain cut Kevin off with a simple raise of the hand. "If I may correct, you studied on being a criminal by way of the justice system." He chuckled.

Kevin had no retort. He was silent, anger stirring inside him from Cain's cutting comment. Alyson jumped in the middle once again. She laughed and pointed out that Kevin was 'burned' by Cain's quip. She turned to Cain. "Y'wanna dance, honey?" The woman grabbed Cain by the arm. "I'm sure a young fellow like you could dance with me all night."

Cain escaped her grip and kept his eyes on Kevin. "No," he told her. "I have no interest in you." Cain's reply did nothing to deter Alyson's efforts. She continued to hold her smile. Cain calculated the woman. Alyson was trying desperately to retain a youth long withered away. She did not look old, and in fact, was even pretty. However, Cain could see a desperate attempt to be twenty rather than thirty-eight.

"C'mon," Alyson pleaded. She leaned close to Cain and whispered. "Even your *friend* can come and play as well."

Friend? Cain thought. *What friend?* He finally looked in the woman's direction. He calculated Alyson's reply, her tone, movements, and her intentions. He raised an eyebrow.

Black Mouth's image appeared on the television again. Alyson wiped her brow. She leaned against Cain. "I love him."

"He's a great kid," Cain replied.

"Don't you think he's cute? Why wouldn't you love him? Who couldn't?"

Cain laughed a bit. Alyson thought he was gay. But before Cain could speak, Kevin interfered. "What're you going to do? Are you going to start talking to me about how the system is so racist? If you wanna play the *race card* I know a good deal of white men who have suffered at the hands of the justice system. It's not a perfect system. It has nothing to do with race. Those days are over. Look, America has a black President. How did that happen? Because people voted for him. Everyone, including white people. That's proof racism doesn't exist."

Cain shook his head. He waved Alyson aside to look directly at Kevin. "No, my friend," he stated casually. "We live in the residual effect of those days. The present day circumstances are secured to make sure that the scenery has changed around black people, but the conditions have remained the same. And, the greater issues have yet to be discussed. There is still pain locked inside black people. It gets worse when others deny it."

"Is that my fault," Kevin shouted back. "That's all you people scream about. We this. We that. Poor we. What about 'us' as the American public?"

"When we say 'we' it is in the spirit of defense," Cain's voice was relaxed, though anger built inside him. "It is an inward power to fight off an oppressive aggressor."

Kevin laughed cynically. "I've heard the Klan say the same thing," he retorted. "There's no difference between someone screaming White Power and someone screaming Black Power. It's the same. It's racism on both sides. Something like the Nation of Islam is just as evil as the KKK. I've heard both speak."

The bartender and several patrons became nervous. There were some that clapped at Kevin's statements and pressed him to continue. *"You tell 'em!"* said one man.

Cain ignored the jeers. "That really is an erroneous conclusion since Klan mentality does not constitute the same attitudinal frame of reference or axiology." Cain noticed Kevin become stiff. "Oh, I'm sorry. Does it surprise you that I use such big words, looking like a young thug?" Cain snickered sinisterly. "Regardless, a black program—often deemed militant—of affirming and returning black originality and wholeness is not Black Supremacy, for it has no intent of domination, violation, control, or elimination of other ethnic groups. Rather, it is an axiology of separation, reclamation, and a reunion of people who were interfered with on every level of life by White supremacists, going all the way back to slavery, where the very conditions we find ourselves in, started." Cain hiked his shoulders again. "Those are the words of a white woman that I quote. Dorothy Blake Fardan. She has common sense, why don't you? Electing a black man President does not solve the problems of America."

Kevin scoffed, "Don't I know it."

Cain leaned against the bar and said, "It's easier to be cynical about a problem rather than find its solution." Cain sighed and extended his hand. "But, I am a gentleman. Let's agree to disagree."

Kevin took Cain's hand. Horrific scenes of conquest instantly bombarded the man. The bar around Kevin disappeared and was substituted with horror beyond the capacity of his mind's threshold. Invasion! Capture! Those who survived the sanguinary brutality were carted off in shackles that were clamped at the neck, the wrist, and the ankle. Kevin witnessed black men, women, and children stacked into boats that were already possessed with the foul odor of bodies long dead. The teeth of the sharks, that tore at the blacks thrown overboard, bit into Kevin's brain. He felt every terrifying rape that black women and black men were routinely subjugated to on the boat ride. The stench of waste, mixed with death, stabbed his nostrils and wrapped around his neck tightly like a noose. Hunger dissolved his stomach and whiplashes scraped his back. His mind scrambled with the decision to kill his baby, so the child would never know slavery. Families split. Kevin felt everything. He saw everything.

And then it got worse.

Kevin's mind arrived at a place known as the Breaker Islands. It was a place where captured Africans were brought before their destination to a plantation in North or South America. He witnessed immeasurable, and more disgustingly, systematic torture. He saw black men and black women disfigured, boiled, ripped apart, and children cut from their mother's belly, all for the purpose of instilling fear of disobedience—the indoctrination to obey without question. The disfigurements and tortures were put on display for the arrival of captured Africans. There was no age limit spared for torture, nor gender overlooked. He felt the helplessness of the black woman raped in front of her husband. He felt the helplessness of the black man, a warrior, unable to fight back. The scene of torture consumed the child. He saw the twisted, kaleidoscopic amalgam of slave master become Savior through sacrilegious lessons instilled in the African mind. Kevin saw the building blocks of America.

Cain then substituted these feelings with the simple emotions felt when a white woman suddenly clutched her purse at the presence of a black male. He injected the humiliation felt at the hands of a harassing officer, being hunted and targeted as a criminal, being followed in a store, the thousandth rejection from a job, the inability to provide for a family. Kevin experienced the humility of seeking illegal and alternative jobs to keep bread on the table. He felt the struggle, not as failure but as a conditioning. And this feeling penetrated the richest down to the poorest.

Cain then added the mistrust between black men and black women, brewed into disrespect. All this spilled over between the relationship of brother and brother, sister and sister, lighter and darker. He displayed the origins of the mistrust in times of slavery with the Slave Master purposely favoring the lighter slaves to turn light skin against dark skin. He felt the black man's use as a breeder to the point where his image sickened the black woman. He felt the abandonment of a father long dead, the anger toward a snitch that helped the slave master put down a rebellion or escape. He felt all the misguided anger and self-hate born out of physical features, skin color, and hairstyle. And he felt it from past to present. He was overwhelmed by the desire to know a rich, ancient, and civilized culture that was separated from him, smothered by a recent, violent moment in history called *SLAVERY* and *STRUGGLE*.

Kevin learned that the law changed but loopholes existed in the mentality that continued to govern the country called America. Kevin served Jim Crow while being molested by his Uncle Sam. He felt the undermined movements of blacks to better themselves. He felt the heat of the incinerated bodies left behind by burned black towns that were once prosperous. He inhaled the smoke of drugs pushed into communities that crumbled into ghettoes.

There was more.

But Cain was merciful.

He let go of Kevin's hand and tapped the man's neck four times. Kevin started to tremble. Before he opened his mouth to scream, Cain raised a finger.

"No, no, no. You cannot scream," Cain directed in a calm voice sounding like a hypnotist. "You must feel everything, but ignore the overwhelming want to scream. You cannot express yourself, because I dictate to you that everything is much better now. You are free to do whatever I tell you."

No one knew what to make of the moment that transpired. Alyson went from Cain's side to comforting Kevin. The bartender looked uneasy. Kevin began to tremble, his hands quivering over the counter. He became pale. Sweat lined his brow. He tried to speak, but his voice only came out in short, low breaths. He was afraid to scream, though he wanted to. Kevin wanted to yell. He wanted to shout obscenities to the world. But Cain's law forced him to remain silent. It was not a right to remain silent. It was an order. It was a command Kevin had to obey.

Kevin continued to tremble.

Cain looked at the bartender and got his attention. He pointed to the table where he sat and said, "There is a package and a rose on that table. I left it for Federal Agent Victor Terrence. See to it that it gets to him. Tell him it's from Cain."

Alyson looked Cain up and down while she rubbed Kevin's back. "A rose and a gift for a man," she questioned with a grimace. "I knew you were a fag!"

Cain laughed. "My dear, I am far from—" Before Cain could finish his words Kevin's trembling hands pounded against the counter.

The bartender turned to him and asked, "You need a drink, Kev?"

Kevin shook his head, yes. The bartender removed a bottle of beer.

"He probably needs a drug to take away all the pain, the hurt." Cain's tone was sarcastically sympathetic.

Kevin swiped the bottle from the bartender. The bartender looked at Cain and said aggressively, "Buddy, I don't know who-the-fuck you are, but there's been nothin' but trouble since you've been in here. You can go get your package, and get the fu—"

Kevin slammed the bottle against the bar. It shattered! He started exhaling hard, his eyes wide, looking into nowhere. He ran the jagged edges of the bottle along his neck, hoping to cut out his voice, to scream through flowing blood if he could not echo his sentiments through his mouth, but there were no screams. There was only a flow of blood bubbling from Kevin's neck. His attempt to scream only choked the life out of him more quickly.

Everyone jumped back in horror!

Cain shook his head, watching Kevin's body die as it hit the floor. "And I just gave him the Cliffsnotes," he spoke with a disappointed sneer on his face.

Someone pulled a gun and fired!

The bullet ricocheted back and tagged the gunmen in the shoulder. Cain looked to his left, disgusted. He watched the man writhe on the floor from the bullet wound.

Alyson tried to run. Cain grabbed her arm.

"Don't. You. Move," he growled. Cain looked back at the bartender. "You will obey my order, or you will suffer a fate far worst than this man's death." He swept the room with his eyes. "I know where all of you live." He looked back to the bartender. "2356 Hill Flower Lane. You have a wife named Marie and two children. Samuel and Christine." And if that was not proof enough, Cain added, "Your mistress lives three blocks away." He looked toward a young man who stood next to the pool table. "Jimmy, you live at 1825 Westview Avenue." He pulled Alyson close. "You may have been channeling Jimmy's thoughts, dear woman." Cain then emphasized, "Because, his *boyfriend* lives over in Maryland, 22-1 Central, Apartment Three-D." He looked at the young man standing next to Jimmy. "Isn't that correct, Paul?" Both Paul and Jimmy looked embarrassed and uncomfortable. Cain eyed the bartender again. "Federal Agent Victor Terrence," Cain reminded. "The package and the rose."

The bartender nodded, affirmatively.

Cain injected the images of Alyson's past lives into her, and then he let her go. She saw herself as an old-time Plantation Madame, prostituting black women and the indigenous women in America. She saw herself as a part of a group of women who attacked the bond between the black woman and the black man under the guise of independence for women. Alyson dropped to her knees in tears.

Cain walked toward the door. The patrons remained still. He opened his hand and the door magically opened. He walked out. The door closed.

Victor pulled up to the bar. The flashing lights of an ambulance and several police cars blinded his eyes. Federal vehicles were parked alongside the local police cars. A crowd gathered outside the bar, including the bar's owner and the bartender. The men were focused on two disturbing acts. The first, someone was being carted away on a stretcher. The body was bagged. The second act was of a thirty-eight year old brunette woman. She was being hauled away in handcuffs. Even from the car, Victor could make out the obscenities she screamed at the bar patrons, the owner, and the bartender.

Victor parked his car and got out. Nicholas was on the scene standing next to the blue van carrying Harrison Burke and his team. Nicholas held a package and rose in one hand. He and Victor approached one another.

"So, you came after all," Victor shook Nicholas' hand. "I figured your crew would be here," he pointed to Harrison who sat in the opened van door. "But I thought they'd be around a corner keeping a close, obvious eye on me."

Nicholas smiled as an admission of guilt. "When did you see 'em," he asked.

"Before I even arrived at Miguel Alma's store," Victor stated.

Nicholas huffed with a sly smile, "Rookies."

Victor again inspected the scene before asking Nicholas, "So, what did Cain do?"

"Bartender and other witnesses say Cain got into a discussion on race politics with the victim, Kevin Frey," Nicholas briefed as he looked over his shoulder at the ambulance. "He's the guy being hauled away in a body bag. There was another gentleman named Steven Brown, somehow he was shot with his own gun. People say he took a shot at Cain, but the bullet deflected back and hit him." He shook his head and looked back at Victor. "But, that was after the events with Mr. Frey. It was in defense."

"So what happened between Frey and Cain," Victor inquired.

"Well, Cain conceded as a gentleman, shook Mr. Frey's hand, and then the guy flipped out," Nicholas explained. "Mr. Frey cut his throat with a broken bottle."

"Jesus," Victor exhaled. "What about the woman being arrested?"

"No one understands that," Nicholas said watching the squad car haul the woman away. "Her name is Alyson Bernardi," he continued. "Bartender says she was flirting with Cain, but Cain refused her advances. When she called him gay, he grabbed her arm and then she started crying. Moments after she started yelling that she was a pimp and a pawn in a bigger pimp's game. She became violent and had to be restrained." He handed the package and the rose over to Victor. "Cain insisted you get these." Victor took the items. He inspected them with a contorted expression. He looked at Nicholas, confused. Nicholas just raised his shoulders. Victor returned the rose. Nicholas laughed. "Thank you. You really shouldn't have."

"Funny," Victor tore into the small cardboard box. He opened the end of it and slowly poured the contents into his hands. There was an architectural compass, a measuring square, and a peg in the shape of the letter G most likely taken from a child's learning toy. Victor looked up at Nicholas.

Again Nicholas raised his shoulders. "I got nothing," the Director admitted.

"Compass, square, and the letter G," Victor wondered aloud.

"Sesame Street?" Nicholas joked.

Victor inspected the objects more closely. He contemplated for a split second before he came up with a suggestion, "Freemasonry. Freemasons."

"Compass and square, G in the middle," Nicholas added it up.

Victor held the objects, balancing them as if weighing them. He was contemplating again. "Is Cain any form of conspiracy theorist? Does he think Freemasons control the world, or something along those lines?"

Nicholas held up the rose. "Remember, we still have this as a clue. How does a rose connect with freemasonry? The Rose Society? There's no such thing."

Victor disagreed. "There's the Rosicrucians. The Rosy-Cross. I still can't make anything of all this."

More vehicles started to arrive at the scene. "Hold your thoughts," said Nicholas lifting a finger and turning his head over his shoulder.

Victor watched the local police quiet the situation. News vans, representing different news affiliates, suddenly pulled up. Victor inspected the news channel insignias on each van. "It's gonna be a field day," he said.

"It'll be what we want it to be," Nicholas responded. "All the patrons have been coached. There was a bar fight, someone was fatally stabbed. The woman was arrested for it. She's crazy now anyway. So, it's simple. We keep the case covered, the news get their story."

"What about the guy with the gun wound," Victor asked.

"What guy?" Nicholas replied, deadpan. Victor understood. Nicholas watched the news vans spill out reporters and cameramen. Nicholas continued to observe the news people. He signaled to Harrison and his crew to watch the scene closely. The men jumped from the van and made their way over to the news scene. Nicholas faced Victor again. "The bartender mentioned that Cain wanted to shake the President's hand. Things are about to get serious."

Victor shook his head, disagreeing. "I don't think so. I actually believe Cain's efforts with the gangs are sincere and not completely self-motivated."

"What," Nicholas yelled in protest.

Victor explained, "Something is leading me to believe that whatever Cain is trying to pull off, the truce between the gangs is an incentive just incase he's killed in the process. I think he wants to leave behind a legacy. I believe Cain wants peace in the streets."

"Then what is his objective," Nicholas demanded to know as if Victor had an answer. "He's leaving a trail of chaos and dead people in his wake."

"I didn't say he wasn't dangerous in his pursuit," Victor assured his Director. He shook his head and lifted his shoulders. "It's just that Cain is looking for something bigger."

Nicholas' face contorted. "Bigger? That would be the biggest thing to aim for. The President. Cain's a militant. His power reaches a black President in charge of the world's greatest army and country."

"I feel as if this is different," Victor replied, addressing more so the voice in his head rather than his Director. "Cain's not just some militant, you know that."

"Look," Nicholas said in a rough voice. "Your investigation today showed that Cain is behind the Gatos and Atherini truce. The rapper Black Mouth is A.J. Dyack's son. Cain is forming an army using these two gangs."

Victor shook his head. "Again, I have to disagree, Nick. Besides, that negates the scenario you just posed about taking control of the President." He looked at his Director. "Plus, those two gangs are a group of scared kids, not an army. Cain's too smart to use them as an army, they'd be wiped out in minutes going up against our Government's army." Victor shook a stern finger. "No. It's not that. Cain is searching for his equal. Someone, or something, with a super power."

"Our country is a Super Power," Nicholas insisted.

Victor quickly disagreed. "No. America's power is built on materialistic things. It's based in the physical. No. Cain is looking for something on *his* supernatural level. That's what my gut is telling me."

"I can't go with your feelings and hunches," Nicholas said, slightly apologetic. "Not when the nation's security is at stake."

"I understand," Victor felt the need to add. "But, you did bring me on this case because of how I can calculate movement. When it comes to Cain, you need all the help you can get."

"Correct," Nicholas exhaled. "I don't disagree with that, but you need to understand this," Nicholas said authoritatively. "You are under my command. I'll allow you to follow your hunches until I believe you're in as much danger as the potential scenario I just spoke of."

There was a sensation on Victor's back. His spine seemed to vibrate. "Yes sir," Victor said.

Nicholas handed him the rose. "Take this, go get some sleep." He slapped him on the shoulder. "We'll clean up the mess here. Report to the underground tomorrow, noon. I want you well rested."

"Yes sir," Victor repeated.

"We have some clues," Nicholas declared. "Freemasonry and a rose." He winked at Victor. "I know you can crack the case."

Victor nodded. He walked back to his car, entered, and then drove away. He repeated the clues to himself on the drive home. Freemasonry. Rose. Mason. Rose. He admired Cain's gameplay.

Christian Lyons flirted with sleep. He was drugged with exhaustion and slowly sunk deeper into a state of rest. He reached out with his arm to place across his fiancée but found the space next to him empty. Christian's heart rushed, his fiancée's absence pulled him completely from slumber's reach. He was suddenly awake, wide-awake. He jumped from his bed and journeyed downstairs, calling for his fiancée. There was no way she could have left in the middle of the night without explanation.

Christian found the front door slightly opened. In his peripheral, down the hall, the kitchen light was on. Christian decided to explore the open door. He approached it cautiously, looking through the opening. He saw his fiancée sitting on the porch, trembling as if cold. Christian walked outside. The night was warm and clear. "Mason," Christian called out to the black woman. He sat down next to his fiancée and asked, "Honey, are you okay?"

"I'm fine," Mason answered. "I'm just wondering what we're going to do."

The two of them gazed up at the stars. Christian felt a little relieved that his fiancée's worries were just based on their wedding, at least, he hoped. "We'll be fine, especially in six months as Husband and Wife," he told her.

Mason dropped her head. "That man today," she said, her voice low.

Christian reacted immediately, becoming angry. "I didn't like that guy. I was doing my best to forget that asshole."

Mason rocked back and forth. "I don't like…"

"I didn't like him either," Christian said, not really hearing Mason's words. "He was creepy."

"I don't like…" her voice went low and then came back. "…touched me."

Christian turned his head, angry at his fiancée's words. He put his hands on her shoulders and said, "He touched you funny, Mason?" The woman's trembling increased. She shifted from Christian's embrace. "Mason, are you okay?"

Mason looked at her fiancé. The images of her two previous lives scratched her vision. Mason saw Christian and his friends raping her. The scenes were quick, spliced, but the emotions carried just the same as when Cain held her hand. She looked away immediately and started to breathe heavy. Christian became frustrated with Mason's behavior.

"Mason, what is wrong with you?"

Mason shook her head and repeated, "I don't like…" her voice again trailed away, coming back with the words, "…touched me."

Christian grabbed Mason's left arm and squeezed tightly. He shook her and asked, "God-damnit," he yelled, alerting and awaking neighbors. "How did that sonava bitch touch you, Mason? Answer me!" Lights from surrounding houses turned on, dogs started to bark.

Mason's right hand dropped under her leg and picked up the kitchen knife. She lifted it and jammed the tip into Christian's side. "I don't like how *you* touched me," she yelled.

Christian let her go and backed up. His side throbbed with pain. Mason went for another attack, but an immovable force stayed her hand. She looked up. There was Cain. Her arm was in his grip. Cain carried no emotion in his face. He was ready to speak to Mason. He was set to tell her to relax and then calm her emotion with his power. But, his presence alone did just that. Mason dropped the knife. She started to cry and then wrapped her arms around Cain.

Christian regained his stance, stepping back while holding his wound. The pain subsided as his anger grew, watching his fiancée lock her arms around Cain. Christian jumped at Cain who lifted his hand and stopped Christian in mid-stride. Cain lifted Christian's body with the same invisible energy and then tossed him through the opened door.

From the shadows came a neighbor, robed and blinking the sleep from his eyes. "Buddy, what the hell do you think you're doing?" The man's wife started to plea behind him to get away. "Honey, just call the police," he said over his shoulder. He pointed to Cain. "And, you…stay where you are. You're under arrest." The man squinted. "Mason, are you okay?"

Cain put his arms around Mason. His eyes looked beyond the man approaching him. They were focused on where the man called over his shoulder to his wife. "He's right, Carla," Cain addressed the man's wife by her first name. "Call the police. And, add an ambulance to the list." Cain held Mason tight, and with her in his arms, he disappeared.

Day Three

Victor's cell phone rattled. It was early in the morning. He walked from the bathroom, wiping the rest of the toothpaste from his mouth. He threw the towel into the sink, and then picked up the phone from his bed. He flipped the cell phone open and read Nicholas' name on the display. Victor pressed a button to take the call.

"Whaddya got," Victor asked. "I thought I had 'til noon."

"We took care of another problem last night," Nicholas notified.

"Cain related?" asked Victor.

"It happened in your area," Nicholas informed. "A kid matching Cain's description took a guy's fiancée. She ran off with him." Victor wondered what the words chosen for Cain's description were. *Young* and *black*? He listened closer to Nicholas' breakdown. "The guy's name is Christian Lyons. He was taken to the hospital after being stabbed by his fiancée. She just flipped out, according to Mr. Lyons. Further, he's white, she's black."

"So, how's this Cain related," asked Victor a little perturbed. "Just because it's race related?"

"Get this," stated Nicholas. "His fiancée's name is *Mason Rose.*"

Victor's eyes went to his desk. There was the compass, the square, the G-peg, and the rose laying atop it. *Sonava bitch*, he cursed. "Is her fiancé okay?"

"He's okay," Nicholas told him. "Though, he's still in the hospital for some work." Victor could hear Nicholas sigh. "Well, we know what the clues mean."

"I don't think Cain gave us the clues to figure anything out," said Victor. "Cain's in the taunting phase. He's laughing right now."

"Get here," Nicholas ordered. "We'll decide what to do."

"Yes sir," addressed Victor. He flipped his cell phone shut. He dropped the phone on the bed and resumed getting ready. He traded his nightclothes for a work suit, his holster strapped around his shirt, gun tucked inside. He scooped up his phone and exited the master bedroom while putting on his suit jacket. He walked down the stairs, through the hall, and into the kitchen. He gathered his wallet and keys from the counter and entered the garage. He opened the car door, slipped in and pressed the remote for the garage door to rise. He turned on his car, waiting for the garage door to lift.

Suddenly, Victor's spine shivered. In one swift motion, Victor removed the gun from his holster, opened the door, and aimed the weapon toward the young black man standing on the other side of the garage door. It was Cain. "Don't move," Victor screamed. "I'll kill ya!"

Cain disobeyed by taking several steps toward Victor. "At last," Cain sneered. He twiddled his fingers at his hips like a gunmen of the Old West. "Here, Victor. Here is where we step closer to our fates intersecting and dangerously coliding."

"I'll decide it," screamed Victor. "You're under arrest. I'm taking you in."

"Really," Cain chuckled as he lifted an eyebrow. "And, where will you put me? Perhaps they'll be ten guards outside my cell, leaving me eight to knock unconscious."

Victor cocked his gun. "Then I'll put you in a pine box," he promised.

Cain put out his hand. The expression on his face was desperate. "Don't you see that I offer insight? In your haste to find me, you have missed—"

"I've missed nothing," Victor yelled. "I've seen a trail of blood."

Cain retracted his hand. "Blood?" He balled his hand into a fist. "I brought peace to a gang war, which will decrease murder and drugs. I brought a father and son back together. I mended the relationship between husband and wife, Latinos and blacks. I've done more in one day than has ever been accomplished in recent history."

"You kidnapped a man's fiancée," Victor spat. "You made another man take his own life, and drove a woman insane. You killed men, back at the facility where you escaped from, that had lives and families."

Cain lifted a finger. "Kidnapping implies taking someone against their will. She left with me by her own choice."

"No, Cain," Victor disagreed. "It was by your *influence*."

Cain huffed. "I showed her truth. The others couldn't handle the insight I offered," he shrugged. "They were each hypocrites. They are much better off."

Victor grit his teeth. "You're lost in a maze of your own moral relativism! I won't applaud your behavior." He stepped closer, gun aimed tight on Cain's chest. "You have opened my eyes, though, Cain. I find no honor in the knowledge you rudely forced on your victims' unwilling minds!"

"An unwilling mind is a stubborn mind," Cain hissed.

"Spoken like a true rapist," Victor retorted. "You're no better than David Reilly."

"Please, are you really going to compare my methods to that monster? Are you actually going to compare my aspects of a warrior to the savagery of beasts?" Cain lifted his hand. "Shall I show you the truth of your circumstances? Shall I show you the truth of whom you serve so unquestionably? A fine, good negro taking orders."

"Is that what this is about," Victor asked. "My hypocrisy as a black man?" He then attempted a joke. "I work for the HNIC, son."

"No," said Cain with a sincere look on his face. "This is about your future as one." Cain turned his back.

"Don't move, Cain," Victor ordered again.

"You won't take me in, Victor," Cain told him.

Victor again promised, "Then I'll kill you."

"Indeed you may." Cain spun around coolly, an arrogant smile painted across his face. "But I doubt you'd do such a thing. If you did, you would fail to discover the final piece to this great puzzle."

"And what is that," Victor asked.

Cain said the answer slowly. Every word was a sentence, all for both Victor's sake, and Cain's melodramatic self-indulgence. "Who. You. Really. Are." Cain started to chuckle. "Haven't you ever heard of the old cliché, '*One must hire a thief in order to catch a thief*?'"

"I've never been a thief, Cain!" Victor shouted.

"And, I have never been an assassin for the Government of the United States," Cain retorted, smile widening as he extended his hand. "So, where do you think our similarities begin?"

Victor's eyes focused on the palm of Cain's hands. He looked back at Cain. "I'm nothing like you!"

Cain squinted. "Really? How do you decode situations so well, Agent Terrence? How is it that you're able to profile so well, or predict, through mathematical precision, the movement of your prey?" Cain walked closer. "Did you check the rearview mirror, or did you just jump out, gun aimed? Did you feel something wrong with the atmosphere, a tingle, or shiver of the spine? That's how it began with me." Cain grit his teeth when he added, "You're older than me, but you're an infant when it comes to your power, which, I'm sure blazes uncontrollably when in the presence of people you don't trust, like your Director." Cain put his hands in his pockets. He stood confidently. "When you figured out my clue to lead you to Miguel Alma, did you dial Director Holt's number, or did you hesitate and close the phone?"

Victor remained still, his gun kept at Cain's chest. The weapon trembled in his hand. He had no words for Cain. The young man in front of him had been playing these types of games for a long time, engaging him would be suicide. Victor tried to block out Cain's words. He also believed Cain was using his power against him to coax him into a trap.

"Do you have nothing to say, Agent Terrence," Cain calmly asked.

"I have this to say to you," Victor yelled. "I hope what you've done, to the lives you've destroyed, weighs heavy on your conscience."

Cain moved quickly! His attack was like a blur. Victor only felt the gun being knocked from his hands. He never saw Cain lunge forward, or swipe his arm. Then Cain appeared, anger burning on his face. His hands gripped Victor's collar and his might slammed the Federal Agent into the rear of his car. The impact caused the car to roll forward, moving against its breaks, and slam through the garage wall.

"Conscience," yelled Cain. He tossed Victor into the wall on the right. He became a blur again, attacking Victor. Cain punched the agent, a solid hit to the jaw. "Don't you dare speak to me about conscience! And, until you gain the insight I have been both blessed and cursed with, don't you ever question my actions!" Cain slammed a fist into Victor's ribs. Another blow crossed Victor's chin.

Victor retaliated with a similar strike, a fist up into Cain's chin. He turned, with a swift rhythm, and slapped Cain across the face. Cain rolled with the hit. Before he could regain stance, Victor's fist crashed straight into his face. Cain smacked against the car. Victor charged Cain like a wild animal. Cain braced himself and reached out with his hands, catching Victor's arms before an attack was made. The two men struggled against each other's force.

"You may pride yourself on loyalty to your agency, but you know nothing of them," Cain barked. He lifted Victor with his power and then tossed him from the garage. Victor's body tumbled onto the driveway. Cain's body was a blur again, and in an instant he was standing over Victor. "You think them noble? Benevolent? Ridiculous! The word 'secret' is part of their title. They hide deep underground." Cain contorted his face, frustrated and disappointed with the man in front of him. "Don't you understand they know exactly what you're becoming? They know what you are? They have studied you the entire time you have been in their company, serving them blindly." Cain was angry. He wanted to kill Victor, but he held back. "For all your power, you are so fucking simple. You will have to conform your ability to them, or be neutralized." Cain balled his fists again. "And, your power will turn against you. The longer you stay in their presence, the more you will start to gain insight to what their objectives are. You will see their origin, their entire purpose, and all they have done. You will go mad trying to walk the line between serving cosmic law, and theirs."

Victor tried to stand. Cain knocked him back down with an invisible force. He kicked the Federal Agent in the side. Cain stepped back, shaking his head. Victor looked up at him. "You just wait, Cain."

"I don't have time," he responded to Victor. "It does not end here." Cain took another step backwards, and then vanished into a cloud.

Victor reached into his pocket and pulled out his phone. He flipped the device open and hit *call back*, accessing Nicholas Holt. "Hello? Victor?" the Director answered.

"He's here," Victor said in an exhausted breath. "Cain. Here. Come…"

Victor dropped his phone and passed out.

When Victor woke up, he was in his family room. He lay across his sofa. Standing over him was Nicholas Holt. Federal Agents swarmed through his house, and also trudging through his lawn looking for evidence of Cain's prior presence. Next to Nicholas was an old man. He had a long hooked nose, thin, graying hair and a lanky physique. On his face was a wide, creepy grin. Victor jumped as he came to. Nicholas put out a hand and told him to relax. Victor sat up on the couch. The two men backed away, giving Victor some room. He checked his watch. It was 2 o'clock. Victor rubbed his head. The man next to Nicholas inspected Victor closely.

His gaze was just as eerie as his smile. Victor felt a little uncomfortable, as if he was naked in the man's presence.

"Victor Terrence," cackled the old man. "You are a long sought soul."

"Nick," Victor said keeping his eyes on the old man. "Who the hell is this?"

"This is Emmett Streamer," Nicholas answered. When he spoke again, it was almost as a whisper. "He deals in the occult." He felt the need to add, "He came to us."

"My role in all this affords me a great level of importance to you," Emmett's eyes focused on Victor. Emmett stared at Victor as if he was a treasure made of pure gold. "And, your role has always been to kill Cain. I know you very well, Victor."

"Great," Victor said rolling his eyes, "Another nutcase."

Emmett addressed, "You may not like me, but we are allies."

Victor stood up. "I can respect that, at least." He fixed his suit. "But any other form of sincerity will come at the simple price of providing answers."

"Look," interrupted Nicholas with a stern voice. "What Mr. Streamer can provide us with are the means to stop Cain." Nicholas put his stern gaze on Emmett. "Those are the only answers you need to provide us with."

Victor sensed something. Nicholas was warning the old man. His stern voice implied that he did not want Mr. Streamer to say anymore regarding Cain's capture than what was needed. Again, Nicholas Holt was securing roadblocks to bar Victor from knowing anymore than he needed to. Victor could sense deceit. He could also sense that the old man wanted to say more; he wanted to go beyond the boundaries that Nicholas was trying to subtly put down. Victor sensed Nicholas' subtle movements. It was in his words, eyes, and tone.

Victor calculated that Nicholas did not want him to know he was truly Cain's equal. Victor had the same power lying dormant inside him, beginning to wake. Victor rationalized that Nicholas was just apprehensive. With the power came the possibility for Victor to lose himself in it, to become just like Cain. Nicholas was not trying to be deceitful as he was trying to keep peace. Victor understood. He wanted to assure Nicholas that he was not like Cain. He was going to use his growing power for a just cause, to serve the agency he was part of. He was not going to be as selfish as Cain.

Victor still had apprehensions of his own.

"I know all about Cain," informed Emmett. "I know what he's after, and where he will go to get it. He wants an object known as Aesop's Diary." Victor noticed Emmett's eyes sway toward Nicholas. The old man wondered if he had said too much. But then, Victor deduced that Emmett had just forgotten an important tidbit. "He believes the President has information on where the book can be located," Emmett added, his eyes going back to Victor.

Victor looked at Nicholas who had a sharp gaze on him. "I told you," said Nicholas.

The two men stared at each other intensely.

"I know where he'll go," said Emmett, breaking the tension. "He looks for a man named Edius Clarke, a Pastor of a local church. We can stop him there."

Victor shifted his eyes to Emmett. "You have a plan?"

Emmett's eerie and devious smile returned. "Indeed."

"We should come with you," said Michael August to Cain.

The other shook his head, disagreeing. "No." Cain then overlooked the Atherini and Gatos soldiers. They partied in the backyard of Leonard Hurtz's mansion in Virginia. Other guests who mingled with the crowd included family members of the inner city gangs, celebrating with their children. "If I fail," continued Cain, putting his eyes back on Michael August and Lorenzo Tejada, "you must keep the streets at peace. If you come, they'll see it as an act of war and bring a heavy fire upon you."

"We'll hold down what we need to hold down," said Lorenzo. "But I agree with Michael, you should have some sort of escorts. Armed."

"I should," said Cain. "But, I won't. This will get far more rough than anything either of you have encountered. Protect the children and the families. Are we clear?"

"Yeah," they said simultaneously, both with reluctance in their voices.

Cain lifted an opened hand. "There's no need to get rough," he joked pointing at the palm of his hand.

Both Michael and Lorenzo laughed. "Nah, nigga," said Lorenzo.

"Good," he shook his head toward the outside party. "Go celebrate."

Lorenzo and Michael walked from the kitchen counter, slid the back door open, and walked to the large outside area holding hundreds of guests. Cain looked up at the ceiling. His eyes were sad. He sighed and made his way through the hall, into the grand entrance, and up the winding stairs. He walked down a long hallway on the top level and came to the eleventh door on the right.

Cain knocked. There was an immediate answer. The voice of Mason Rose gave Cain permission to enter. Cain opened the door and walked into the room. He closed the door behind him and saw Mason sitting on the bed with her legs folded. There was a book in front of her by a poet named Rufus Young. Two other books were stacked next to her. One had the author R. Nicholas. Troy Rowell authored the second book. Mason looked up at Cain and smiled. She then looked concerned as she observed the rare, somber look on Cain's face.

"Do you believe your destiny will elude you," Mason uttered in a voice that matched Cain's expression. "It eluded me for several, brutal lifetimes. I can feel my husband's remorseful spirit as he watched me side with his murderer, enslaver, and my rapist." Anger started to rise in Mason's voice. "I guess it can be said that I suffered from a metaphysical Stockholm Syndrome."

Cain smiled at Mason's choice of words. He walked over to the bed and sat down beside her. Sensing her rising anger, Cain took Mason's hands and soothed her emotions with his power. "He understands, my Queen. We have all suffered the same metaphysical Stockholm Syndrome, as you call it," Cain told her. "And, I'm sorry for what I've put you through."

Cain's apology surprised Mason. "Sorry?" The woman blurted, completely perplexed.

"I did not show you those images of past lives to prove a point, or expose the irony," Cain informed the woman. "I did that because I need the fury locked inside you." He pointed to Mason's heart and added. "And you must not have it here," he moved his finger down and pointed at her solar plexus. "But here. I need it as intent."

"I know, Cain," Mason said with a pretty smile.

"I don't want you to think I'm using you for selfish purposes." He added with a smile, "Though I am."

"I know, Cain," Mason repeated with a little more force, but with the same pretty smile. "I understood your intentions when we met for the second time. I could feel them." Mason stroked Cain's cheek with a single finger. "Have you ever been in love, Cain?"

"Once," Cain said, his heart skipping a beat. He raised an eyebrow and resurrected his arrogant smile. "But then the mirror broke."

Mason burst into laughter. She slapped Cain on the shoulder. "I'm serious."

Cain waited for Mason's laughter to subside before he told her, "She is no longer on this Earth. Her name was Ashaki."

"I'm so sorry, Cain," Mason said remorsefully. She put her hand over his heart.

"Why? I'll see her again," he assured. "Maybe even in this lifetime. I'm still young. I was only nineteen at the time." Cain looked around the room as if the spirit of the woman he spoke of floated through it. "I can feel her much like you can feel your husband."

"Do you think he came back to Earth," Mason asked.

"Possibly," Cain replied quickly. Cain displayed the palm of his hand. "Wherever he is, I'm sure he knows you're in good hands."

Mason reached for Cain's opened palm. She observed the lines in his hands, looking for any signs of an intricate design or pattern that would explain Cain's unique ability. "Where does your power come from?"

"May I go around the world to cross the street, in order to answer the question?" Cain asked.

"Yes, you may," Mason granted politely.

"Well, let me begin with a question or two." He cleared his throat. "Do you know the ancient African word for the phrase *The Throne of God?*" Cain asked. Mason shook her head, no. "It is the same word that was used—through derivatives—to describe *the gods, the head of the royal house, power, wisdom, energy,* and even is the origin for the word *snake.* The word also described *water flowing into soil.* This was in reference to a river, or the energy incased in the spine rising from the tail of the spine, or root, and up to the head, or crown." Mason shook her head again. These clues did nothing for her. But she was intrigued as to where Cain was going with all this.

And then Cain answered.

"It is the word *'nigger'.*" Cain saw the look of surprise flash on Mason's face. He then listed ancient derivatives of this now derogatory term. "*Neggur,* the God. *Neggura,* the Goddess. *Ngr, nagas, nagari, naki, nake, nagi, Ningirus* the god, *N-ger-s* the ancient gods, and much more, including the current terms *king* and *queen.*" Cain huffed. "The uninitiated were not allowed to utter this word in the presence of initiated N-ger-s. How ironic. We still pay attention to these rules." He lifted a finger and a smile. "But what do you think was going through our African minds when came a man whipping, beating, and kidnapping us while screaming this word, which would be the only word understood while being attacked?"

Mason could not help but chuckle at the thought.

Cain smiled. "Perhaps they were thinking: *Why is this man beating me and calling me a god at the exact same time?*" Cain sighed. "And, as the beatings continued, and the word was reduced to a derogatory status, we as a people struck a deal that went like this: *Maybe if we stop acting as gods, this man will stop beating us.*" He leaned close to Mason. "We have kept our end of the bargain, haven't we? Savage as we have become." Cain smiled, arrogant and wide. "Let's say, I woke up one day and decided to re-*nege* on the deal." He kissed Mason's cheek, stood up, and walked toward the door. "Tomorrow, we erase our slave-named signatures, signed on the dotted line."

Day Four

Pastor Edius Clarke was a black, bald, heavyset man. He stood to the applause of his congregation, and stepped to the front of his church. When the congregation quieted down, he said a simple prayer. His audience repeated the prayer in unison. Pastor Clarke then commenced with a sermon about the Curse of Ham. He spoke how it was a long time before black people, engendered through Ham, and cursed as Canaan, were set right by the ways of Christ. Edius preached that it was not until the struggle of slavery, the trial by God, that blacks were lulled from savage, tribal ways, into the light of knowledge, wisdom, and understanding. While Edius Clarke was in mid-sentence, the doors to the congregation blew open. Cain calmly walked inside. Edius jumped back in surprise. The people of the congregation turned their heads, terror and disbelief marked on their faces.

"This is a house of lies," Cain sneered. "This is not my father's house." As he walked down the aisle he turned coolly, walking backwards toward the pulpit. He spread his arms wide and asked, "People, do we still believe in fairytales?" huffed Cain playfully. "How could you be cursed into being black when there was no other man that existed before you?"

"Excuse me, young man," Edius ordered, jabbing his finger at Cain.

Cain kept his back to Edius. "My people, do we not even do the slightest bit of research?" He pleaded. "Do we not understand Ham is symbolic for the element of Earth, its children being mountains, valleys, and beds, cursed to expand, erode, and house all the other elements? Such as Shem, from the ancient word *sem*, meaning *fire*. Noah is an ancient derivative for *water*, rough, drunken tides. And Japheth is not a tribe of whites, but the name of a so-called Greek Titan who was designated to the North, or elevated like the *air*." Cain smiled. "However, as usual, I'm just giving the Cliffsnotes, summarizing. There is so much more to all this. You may wish to indulge yourself in the following literature—"

"Security!" Edius interrupted.

Cain said over his shoulder, "They're sleeping on the job. I'd hire new people." He twirled around and faced Edius. "Perhaps I should enlighten your flock to who you really are, Pastor Clarke." Cain's smile faded. His ears picked up the quickening beat of Edius's heart. "Dismiss the congregation. We have business, you and I."

Edius released the church's congregation. The people filed from the church hurriedly. When there was no one left but Cain, Edius spoke. "What're you here for?" he asked Cain.

"You know where Emmett Streamer is," Cain stated. "I want that knowledge." He opened the palm of his hand. "And it will be extracted by any means." Cain took another step toward the pulpit. The air became heavy, weighing down hard on Cain's shoulders. He could feel a dampening effect through his body.

Cain looked at his hands, his body, and then around the room. He looked up at Edius and grimaced. Edius looked terrified. He turned to run, but Cain was too quick. He lunged at Edius and grabbed the Pastor's collar. Cain shook Edius hard and demanded, "Exactly where in this church is he?" Edius stayed silent. His mouth trembled, his eyes opened wide. Cain felt a presence behind him. He let go of Edius. The Pastor dropped to the floor. Cain stood up straight. "I know you're there, Victor."

"I was told you'd be here," Victor clarified. He walked through the doors, gun aimed at Cain. "But, we both know I would've tracked you down here anyway."

"And, if your superiors told you I was in hell, would you toss yourself into the fire just to please them?" Cain never turned to Victor. He dropped his head and shook it. "They do play with your destiny so well, but they cannot stop fate." Cain slowed his breathing. The weight felt like it was crushing him, but Cain stood strong and tall.

"It's over, Cain," Victor stated. "You're under arrest."

Cain faced Victor. "How long do you think you can keep me locked up?" He said with a soft laugh. "The very object dampening my power can only operate through proper meditation and extreme concentration. Do you think Emmett—" and he yelled the next set of words, "—*who I know is here somewhere*—" he relaxed his voice. "—will dedicate himself fulltime to dampening my powers? He has other plans, Victor. So does the agency he works for. The very agency *you* work for." Cain flapped his lips. "You have been setup, just as you believe *I* have been setup." Cain's arrogant laugh returned as he saw Victor's look of surprise. "Oh, come on. You don't think I knew what to expect when I walked through those doors? I should have gone into acting. Have you learned nothing?" He put his hands in his pockets. "And they call me arrogant."

"You're a villain, Cain," Victor said venomously.

"That will be debated for years to come." Before Cain could smile he felt a searing pain stab his heart, burning him. The pain intensified. Cain bucked and dropped to his knees. A second wave of fire tore through him. He planted his hands on the ground. From the back of the pulpit sauntered Emmett Streamer, the Skeptic Stone in his grip. It looked exactly as its replicated picture in the occult book. However, with its power in use, a strong, blood-red aura glowed around it. The same magical field embraced Emmett's hand.

"Where is your smile now, Cain?" Emmett taunted. "Your feeble skills are no match for the Skeptic Stone's power." The old man concentrated harder. The stone sent another assault through Cain. He screamed and fell completely onto the floor. "Prison has not humbled you at all. You're still arrogant after all this time." He kicked Cain in the ribs. "But you are right about one thing, you are too dangerous to simply keep locked alive." Emmett's eyes went to Victor. "Shoot him, now, while he's powerless."

Victor aimed his gun at Cain. He watched the young, black man struggle as an invisible blanket of energy from the Skeptic Stone wrapped around him. Cain's body contorted, and he screamed. Cain struggled against the stone's effect, but he managed to get to his knees. He puffed out his chest, taunting Victor.

"No," said Victor. "We're taking him in."

"What?" Emmett yelled.

"If he's executed, it won't be here. Not in a church." He looked at the Pastor. "You're relieved, and thank you."

Edius nodded.

"Emmett," called Victor. "Stand him up."

With a concentrated thought, Emmett willed Cain to stand using the power of the stone. Cain's arms remained at his side, bound by an invisible force. Victor holstered his gun and led the way to the outside. They stepped into a bright, clear day. Cain saw on his left, at the far end of the street, an entire brigade of soldiers and vehicles. To his right was a van parked in the middle of the street. Harrison Burke and his team occupied the van. Victor made his way to the vehicle.

Cain did not move.

His immobility caused him pain as he struggled against the will of the Skeptic Stone. "Move," Emmett demanded.

Cain whispered, "*Sun to a shadow. Rose to a thorn.*"[1] he struggled with his words, the power of the stone working against any form of free will. "*Hell...bath no fury...like a woman... scorned!*"

An invisible force knocked the stone from Emmett's grip. The aged man stared in surprise as the unholy object rolled away from him. Cain felt the invisible restraints on him loosen. His power resurrected. Next to Emmett formed the physical body of Mason Rose. Emmett scowled. He went to strike her, but Cain hit him with a telekinetic blast that knocked the old man back into the church.

Mason dived for the stone!

Victor turned, and with amazing speed, tackled the woman. Cain saw the army at the end of the street raise their weapons. He used his power to lift Mason and Victor in the air and toss them inside the church. He used the same power to shut the doors. The brigade of soldiers opened fire on Cain. The black man walked into the middle of the road, bullets bouncing off him by way of an invisible shield. Cain pivoted toward the army and taunted them with a smile and a wave to continue firing.

The army ceased their assault.

The van behind Cain roared to life. Harrison put the car in gear and yelled over his radio, "I have him in my sight!"

The radio cackled back, "Are you crazy? Do not engage!"

Harrison disobeyed the order and drove forward at an alarming speed. Cain kept his back to the oncoming van. He folded his arms and shook his head with a sneer. The van slammed into his back! The vehicle jumped as if running into a well-braced, metal pole. Cain was unmoved by the impact. The van flipped upwards and twirled in the air, the front of the vehicle caved in. It rolled in the air, over Cain's head. It smashed against the ground, scraping and sparking. Cain used his power to throw the vehicle down the road. The van's sparks increased as it headed straight toward the brigade of soldiers, the sparks transforming into flames that engulfed the vehicle like a fiery hand. It crashed against a military vehicle located near the armed troops and exploded.

Several of the soldiers had already scattered before the explosion occurred. Cain watched the soldiers run. He took a step forward to engage them but was suddenly struck by a large object. Cain hit the ground. The heavy, wooden church door covered him. He tossed it off him and got to his feet. Victor stood at the front of the church. The remaining door to the holy sanctuary hung loosely on a hinge. Emmett held Mason in a grapple hold around her neck as he stood behind Victor,

---

[1] Lyrics from the song "Fury" by Prince from the album 3121.

struggling to restrain the woman. Cain lifted his hand to help her. He was going to crush Emmett's neck with a swift, telekinetic blow.

Victor's body became a blur. He collided with Cain, halting the young man's attack on Emmett Streamer, knocking him into the empty lot across the street. Cain hit the ground, rolled, and jumped to his feet. But there was Victor, already there, ready for another attack. He made another violent contact against Cain's body, slamming his shoulder into Cain. Again, Cain soared through the air. His body arced over a building. Victor jumped after him. His leap was a little too high, as he was untrained in these newfound powers. But, he put his legs together and torpedoed down onto Cain's chest while both remained in the air. The impact forced Cain's descent to quicken. Victor vaulted from Cain's torso, flipped backwards, and landed on the sidewalk.

Cain crashed in the middle of the road where there was heavy traffic.

A large truck sped toward Cain as he tried to stand. He looked over and gasped. Before he was crushed, he turned his body into an ethereal state. The truck passed through his ghostly form and continued down the road. When the traffic ceased, Cain returned to his physical state. He rested on one knee, panting, his lip and nose running blood.

"Only you can hurt me, brutha," Cain yelled at Victor. "They're counting on that."

Cain's image blurred as he catapulted himself at Victor. His body impacted hard against the Federal Agent, tossing him into the abandoned building. Cain stood up and balled both his fists. He concentrated and used his power to crumble the foundations of the building, collapsing the structure and burying Victor. Cain jumped back to the open lot, and then started to run across the street toward the church. He saw Emmett toss Mason aside and run down the street toward the Skeptic Stone. Cain increased his speed as Emmett dived for the impious item. Cain ran into the church, wrapped his arms around Mason, and disappeared. Emmett snatched the Skeptic Stone, but was too late. His hunt eluded him.

From across the street, out of the rubble of the abandoned building, walked Victor, dusting himself off while cursing Cain's escape. Both he and Edius joined Emmett's side. "He knows," said Edius to Emmett.

"Knows what?" Emmett asked in an annoyed manner.

"He knows where the diary is," Edius sighed. "Aesop's Diary."

"How," Emmett hissed.

The Pastor admitted guiltily, "He pulled the information from my mind when he grabbed me."

Emmett caressed the Skeptic Stone as he pondered a strategy. "No matter," he brushed aside. "All it means is that he will come to us." The old man peered at Victor. "And, you will kill him then."

"So young with his power, Nicholas," reported Emmett in a low voice, "and he was almost Cain's equal."

Nicholas contemplated Emmett's information, the two of them standing in his underground office. "After Cain is neutralized, keep Victor under control with the stone."

"Yessir," said the old man.

"We can't trust him until we are absolutely sure he won't turn on us," Nicholas rationalized. "Then, we'll make sure he's able to put the Gatos and Atherini back at war with each other."

"And the woman?" Emmett asked. "Mason Rose?"

"We'll lock her up for the murder of her husband," Nicholas stated.

"He's dead?" Emmett questioned.

Nicholas raised an eyebrow. "He will be."

"Is there anything else, sir," asked Emmett.

"Yes," Nicholas said, "Get that fucking diary out of here. Have it sent to the White House and put on one of the bookshelves in any of its rooms."

Emmett smiled at Nicholas' devious plan. "If Cain looks for it there—"

"We'll be able to expose him as a terrorist and national threat," Nicholas finished. "And that's only if he survives his encounter here."

They were inside Nicholas' office, thirty floors below the earth. But atop the building they were underneath, Cain's ethereal form materialized into his physical frame. Earlier, Cain had extracted the information that the object of his desire, Aesop's Diary, was held in the prison he escaped from three days ago. It was buried in the very prison he had been incarcerated in for two years. And so he returned to the sanctuary of his enemies. Cain knew all too well that this was a trap. He perched at the edge of the building, waiting for his time to strike. The moon shined bright. Cain sensed that Victor was nowhere near the premise. They were not prepared to spring their trap. This was ample time for Cain to contemplate his own plan. Cain knew what to expect and what to do.

At the same moment, Nicholas was expressing his concern over Victor's whereabouts. Emmett reported that he disappeared. Victor claimed he needed time alone, to think. This information upset Nicholas. He screamed at Emmett for allowing Victor to leave his presence. Emmett protested that Victor just physically evaporated with his newfound abilities. And because Cain was the intended target, Emmett thought nothing of using the stone's power against Victor. He also figured it would have caused suspicion in Victor if the stone was used against him. Emmett also assured that his extra-perceptive knowledge witnessed Victor killing Cain.

High above them, the elements for Emmett's extra-perceived scenario mixed together to play out. Victor crept up behind Cain, and Cain turned around before Victor's advance became threatening. "We have a bit of a problem," said Cain. "I'm not going to kill you."

"Then I'll have to kill you," Victor decided.

Cain smirked. "I didn't say I wouldn't fight you, Victor." He then became angry. "Or break your legs, your arms, twist your spine. I may not kill you, but I will hurt you beyond reason."

Victor stepped closer. "I don't think so, Cain," he said. "I feel as if I'm your equal now."

Cain laughed at Victor and reminded him, "You're beyond me in age, but you are very much an infant when it comes to your powers."

Victor had been conserving his power, building the energy inside him to slay Cain in a single strike. He knew he was no master of his newfound power as Cain was with his. Victor had to kill Cain as quickly as possible. Cain just had to hurt Victor and avert destiny.

Both black men charged one another. To the average eye, their bodies were a flash. Cain gripped Victor's neck and squeezed. His hold tightened. Cain could feel Victor's windpipe. Perhaps he would carry the deed further and end Victor's life. There would, after all, be another to live out the destiny Victor was chosen for. But, Victor did not simply stand still. He fought back, slamming his fist into Cain's face and knocking him away. Cain rolled backwards, toward the edge of the building. Victor's eyes went wide as he caught his breath. Cain balanced himself on the ledge, and then lunged forward for another strike. Victor timed his swing correctly. His fist rolled across Cain's cheek. He hit Cain in the stomach. Cain doubled over. Victor grabbed the back of Cain's hood and pulled back. Cain looked up at him, a smile on his face.

"Now choose," said Cain. "It's time for you to serve, not me, not an agency, but your destiny and fate. Have a threesome with those bitches."

Victor hit Cain again. The impact tossed Cain from the roof. He dropped to the pavement below. Cain's impact left a ragged impression on the ground. Victor looked over the edge and spied Cain's contorted body. His eyes were closed. Victor jumped over the ledge, gliding down toward Cain's body, defying gravity's pull by slowing his speed toward the pavement. His jacket fluttered as his body magically lowered to the ground. Cain did not stir. Victor knelt down and checked his pulse. He scooped up Cain's body and walked into the building.

The lobby was empty. The building was closed for Sunday. But, the agents who knew the building's true use still had access. Victor accessed the elevator and walked in, Cain still in his arms. The doors closed. Victor breathed heavy, and then he shook his head. He made his choice, the destiny he would serve. He lay Cain's body down and used his card to open the second set of buttons. He pressed the button to lower the elevator and it descended. Victor sat down next to Cain's body. He put his knees up and wrapped his arms around them. He put his head down and waited for the elevator to stop.

The elevator doors opened, and there stood Emmett Streamer on the other side. In his hands were the Skeptic Stone and an ancient book called Aesop's Diary.

Emmett's eyes immediately went to Cain's slumped body, and then moved to see Victor. His eyes went back to Cain. He marveled at the sight of his fallen adversary.

"He's dead, Emmett," said Victor standing up. The old man was still stunned. "Take his body to a cell. I'll ask Nick what should be done with him."

Emmett nodded. "We were just speaking about you," said the old man, his words breaking. He was still in disbelief. Cain was dead. Victor and Emmett switched places. Emmett only took his eyes off of Cain to turn around and watch Victor head toward Nicholas' office. The door closed and Emmett sighed. He never looked at Cain again. As much as he was in awe at Cain's lifeless body, he was just as repulsed by his presence, even if he was dead.

Emmett took a moment to sigh relief.

Cain grinned.

His eyes opened.

He lifted his body, crawling up the wall. He focused his eyes and grin on Emmett Streamer.

The Skeptic Stone started to glow, warning. It rattled and alerted Emmett to Cain's presence. The old man turned quickly, baring his teeth like a wild animal. He growled toward Cain. Emmett lifted the stone and increased its power to keep Cain from attacking. The elevator stopped, the doors opened. Emmett hit the button to hold the elevator from use. He backed out of the elevator slowly. He threw Aesop's Diary in front of Cain to taunt him. "You're so close, Cain."

Cain just continued to grin deviously, despite the stone's power pinning him to the back of the elevator. He started to laugh menacingly as he spoke, "Victor's power may be increasing, but no one can deny the truth." Cain held out the palm of his hand. "I choked him with it."

"Then *I'll* kill you," Emmett yelled.

"I doubt that, Emmett," Cain said confidently.

Emmett increased the power of the stone. "I will choke the life from you, Cain!"

Cain started to slump to his knees. His smile never left, not even his confidence. "I doubt that, Emmett," Cain repeated.

Emmett called over his shoulder, "I need help!" Five guards were alerted. "Your move, Cain."

Cain's knees touched the elevator floor. He spoke, *"Sun to a shadow, rose to a thorn. Hell hath no fury—"*

An invisible hand grabbed Emmett's arm. Pressure increased on his wrist. The same pressure crushed his wrist inward. Emmett dropped the Skeptic Stone, his magical hold on Cain lost. Mason Rose materialized next to Emmett. She held his wrist and then swung Emmett's arm away. Cain blurred past Emmett and Mason, stopping in front of the five soldiers called for assistance, submachine guns aimed directly at Cain.

"I'll kill you all in the same sequence you fire your guns," Cain warned. "Who wants to pull their trigger first?"

The men dropped their weapons and ran.

Cain returned to Emmett. The old man held his wrist while on his knees. Mason was holding the Skeptic Stone. She squeezed the mystical object and shattered it into pieces. Emmett hung his head. He smacked the ground with his good hand.

"I tried to bring balance to this world," Emmett yelled.

Cain lifted his hand. "And, I will succeed where you failed," he told the old man. He twisted his hand around, twiddling his fingers. Emmett's head twisted, and his neck popped. He dropped dead. Cain and Mason walked into the elevator and hit the button to descend. Cain picked up Aesop's Diary and caressed the book. He inspected its leather cover. There was a peculiar symbol painted at its center. Over what appeared to be a black planet, resided a caricature of the sun adorned with a face and a mass of wavy, pointed tendrils. Partially covering the face of the sun was a caricature of a crescent moon, looking like an old man. Floating around this cosmic display were four dark purple planets tattooed with their own symbols in their center. One symbol was of the continent of Africa. A second planet was engraved with a heart and fist. Floating inside a third planet was an African drum. And, barely visible within the fourth and final small planet, was the image of an ancient, black woman—crowned with an Afro.

Cain decoded the symbols and their meaning.

He beamed a humble smile as he exhaled relief.

At the same moment, Victor confronted Nicholas. The Director of the underground facility was sitting at his desk. Victor stood at the front of the desk and knocked on it as Nicholas refused to look him in the eye. "Get up, Nick. We have a problem."

Nicholas stood instantly. "What the hell's wrong?" he asked.

"What's wrong," Victor repeated. "How about the fact that I had a building fall on me and I survived. That's for starters." Victor took a deep breath. "I've seen stones bring a man to his knees, a van explode after hitting a man who was unscathed by the impact, invisible women, and all the elements to this case. What the hell is *wrong*? How about, for starters, you not giving me any clarity on the matter."

Nicholas hesitated to speak. "I'm not authorized to give you those answers yet," he said.

Victor shook his head acceptingly. "I can respect that." He put his hands out. "Maybe, in time." He said.

"Maybe," Nicholas shook Victor's hand.

Immediately, Victor had all the answers. He saw all the lies that made up Nicholas Holt. He was not a physical body. He was an illusion that was formed from lies and light. There was nothing but lies, and the truth was exposed. There was conspiracy and deceit. There was treachery and cover-ups. And even more frightening was that Nicholas was just the first rung on a long ladder. Victor let go of Nicholas. The Director was well aware of what had transpired. He shook his head, disgusted.

"So what are you going to do, Victor?" Nicholas asked. "Are you Cain's substitute?"

The door opened. Cain walked in with his trademark grin. "Nicholas, you offend me." He stood next to Victor. "There is no substitute for me." He reached out with his power and choked Nicholas to death. The Director slumped to the floor. Cain tossed Aesop's Diary on the desk and opened to a blank page. "Now for the answers they could never give you, Victor."

Mason walked into the room.

Cain took a seat in Nicholas' chair. He ignored the body lying next to the desk. Victor sat down and stared at the book. "What's this all about, Cain?"

Cain pointed to the open book. "That is a magical book blessed by ancient priests of Abyssinia. It has the ability to create the reality written inside of it." He then pointed to Victor. "You're the only one who can write in that book, Victor. Fate has chosen you."

"I don't have a pen," Victor said in a low voice as he inspected the blank pages in front of him.

"Just shape your fingers as if you do," Cain instructed. "Then write over the page. The words will appear." Cain sat back in the chair. "There are some rules, however. You cannot write the book out of existence. And, if you negate me, fate will re-birth me. If you negate yourself from this responsibility—"

"Fate will re-birth me," Victor finished.

"You learn quickly." Cain folded his arms. "Hopefully, if you do negate yourself, maybe next time around you won't be as stubborn and reluctant to do your job."

Victor snickered.

Mason stood at the side of the desk. "What do we write, Cain?" Mason asked.

The young man contemplated. "We will be responsible for whatever we write in this book." Cain said. "So, that is a brilliant question. What shall we write, indeed? Let it be creative. We have taken down the factions that have tried to negate our creativity. We are now responsible for what we write."

There they stood. Two black men and one black woman standing inside a room marked one hundred and one. The pages of the book were blank, waiting to be filled. The illusion was now removed. The curtain was drawn back. The wizards had been exposed as small men. Hope bloomed brightly. It was potential creativity waiting to be written, expressed in an empty, magical book.

Fade to Black.